The street was crowded with traffic and people hurrying home after a long day at the office and at first, Honor didn't notice the long black limo parked just along the entrance to her building. At least not until a man in a chauffeur's uniform stepped in front of her. "Ms. St James? Ms. King has sent a car for you."

Honor stopped, glancing at the limo in surprise. The windows were tinted, hiding whoever was inside completely from view. "Oh," she said slightly nonplussed. The pub wasn't very far away and she hadn't expected a lift. "That's very kind of her."

The chauffeur pulled open the door for her and stood there, waiting.

An odd foreboding went through her as she stared into the dark interior of the limo, one that had nothing to do with the cold. As if once she got inside, she'd be taken away s̶̶̶̶̶̶̶

# MINE TO TAKE

**JACKIE ASHENDEN**

St. Martin's Paperbacks

This is a work of fiction. All of the characters, organizations, and events protrayed in this novel are either products of the author's imagination or are used fictitiously.

MINE TO TAKE

Copyright © 2014 by Jackie Ashenden.
Excerpt from *Mine to Keep* copyright © 2014 by Jackie Ashenden.

All rights reserved.

For information address St. Martin's Press, 175 Fifth Avenue, New York, NY 10010.

ISBN: 978-1-250-05176-9

Printed in the United States of America

St. Martin's Paperbacks edition / December 2014

St. Martin's Paperbacks are published by St. Martin's Press, 175 Fifth Avenue, New York, NY 10010.

10  9  8  7  6  5  4  3  2  1

To Paul. Because everything.

# ACKNOWLEDGMENTS

Major thanks go to my awesome agent, Helen Breitwieser, for believing in the Nine Circles and for all her work in getting them where they needed to go.

Also to my amazing editor, Monique Patterson, for loving this book, for her fantastic editorial help in making this book the best it could be, and for her patience as I tried to get cell phone reception in the middle of a farm on the Welsh coast.

To Maisey Yates, best CP in the world, for kicking my butt and telling me I had to write the 'misfit billionaires club idea RIGHT NOW'. Without you this series wouldn't exist.

To my family—my husband and my girls, for putting up with my crazy writer obsessional tendencies.

To the friends who were up at Pataua the summer I was writing the proposal for this series—sorry for not being there guys, but look what happened?

To my cell phone for being indispensable while talking to agents and editors at various different points in England as this book was in the process of being sold.

And lastly, to Paris. Best city in the world to get the news you've waited your whole life for: the sale of your first print book.

# CHAPTER ONE

Gabriel Woolf walked into the quiet of St. Sebastian's, his mother's favorite church, and stopped, stamping the snow from his motorcycle boots. He hadn't been inside the church for over twenty years but he still remembered the smell, of old stone and incense. Candle wax and piety. And guilt. Lots and lots of guilt.

Yet it wasn't guilt that brought him here. It was a promise of the worst kind. The kind you make to someone on their deathbed. His mother's deathbed to be exact. And there was no getting out of a promise like that. No fucking way.

So here he was, the day after her funeral, ready to confess his sins like the good Catholic boy he'd never been.

Luckily it wasn't going to take long. Not because he didn't have any sins to confess, because he did. Hundreds of sins all swimming around inside him, tainting his blood. Tainting him right down to his bones. No, it was because there was only one sin that mattered to his mother. Only one sin that had *ever* been important to her.

Gabriel stared around the interior of the church, trying to spot the confessionals. There wasn't anything special about the place, not even when he'd been a kid coming to Mass with his mother. St. Sebastian's had been a run-down city church trying to do the best for its dirt-poor parishioners and it looked like nothing had changed. It wore neglect like an old suit, frayed at the cuffs, missing some buttons, hems dirty. Just like the rest of his shitty old neighborhood.

Thank God he was long gone out of it.

Eventually he spotted the confessionals down to the side of the altar, near the sacristy. An elderly woman came out, which clearly meant a priest was there doing his duty.

She gave him a glance as she passed, her expression fearful—no prizes for guessing why. He didn't exactly look like a typical believer. And even though his tattoos and scars were hidden by his leather jacket and jeans, his clothes wouldn't hide his identity.

To the world at large he was Gabriel Woolf, construction magnate, but to the people of this neighborhood, he was "Church," president of the Avenging Angels motorcycle club who owned this little patch of New York. He hadn't been president for a good many years, but that didn't matter. People still remembered. People were still afraid. And shit, they had every right to be.

Gabriel ignored the woman. So Church was finally in an actual church. What a fucking joke. The Reverend, his mentor at the motorcycle club and a man fond of biblical aphorisms, though not a believer either, would have laughed himself hoarse.

He made his way down to one of the enclosed confessional boxes and pushed open the door. Man, he remembered waiting outside one of these things for his mom, tracing patterns on the dusty floor with his toes. He'd never managed to work out as a kid why she'd taken so long because she'd been the purest person he knew.

It was only as a teenager he'd understood. Corrine Woolf had always felt dirty.

The space inside the confessional was tiny and as the door shut, a sudden claustrophobic feeling gripped him.

Christ, why was he here again? He didn't believe, not when he'd been a child and not now. His sins were his own, not for God. Not for anyone.

"Promise me, Gabriel," Corrine had begged him in the hospice, thin and wasted from the cancer that was killing her. "You have to promise."

They hadn't gotten on for years, not since he became a club prospect at sixteen and she'd turned to her faith, but she was still his mother, so of course he'd promised. And he was a man who kept his word.

He knelt and tried to remember the right phrase. "Forgive me, Father, for I have sinned. It's been . . ." How long had it been? Better round down. "Twenty years since my last confession."

A silence from behind the grille. Then the priest's voice. "Twenty years? That's a long time, my son. What brings you back to us?" He sounded young. A boy.

Gabriel shut his eyes. Why the hell was he thinking about the priest's age? What did it matter? All that mattered was the promise he'd made to his mother. The only promise to her he'd ever been able to keep.

"I'm not back. I wasn't ever here in the first place. I'm fulfilling a vow. That's all."

"A vow?"

"I have a sin to confess, priest. You wanna hear it or not?"

Another silence, this time an offended one. But something in Gabriel's tone must have alerted the guy to the fact that Gabriel was not to be screwed with because the priest only said, "Tell me then, my son."

*I am not your son. I am the son of a beast.*

"I want to kill my father," Gabriel said.

The priest perhaps had heard this kind of thing before because he didn't sound the least bit surprised. "And will you act on these thoughts?"

"No. I've decided on another plan of action."

"Forgiveness perhaps?"

Forgiveness. Such a weak, paltry thing. His mother had tried that method and look what had happened. Her death at the age of fifty-one. The doctors had said cancer but he knew the truth. It hadn't been cancer that killed her. It had been shame. Guilt. And loss.

The loss of a future she should have had. A future his father had taken from her.

*A future that you took from her.*

Gabriel bared his teeth in a smile that had nothing to do with amusement.

Yeah, he was as bad as the asshole who'd fathered him. *Rotten to the core . . .*

"Not forgiveness," Gabriel said, still smiling. "I've decided on vengeance."

The others were late. Either that or he was early.

Gabriel shifted in the high-backed wing chair he was sitting in, fingers of one hand firmly wrapped around a glass of rare, sixty-year-old Scotch whisky, the fingers of the other jammed in the pocket of his jeans. Just touching the beads of his mother's antique rosary.

After his confession, the priest had given him some crap about Hail Marys and Our Fathers and looking to his conscience, but it wasn't like he'd ever do that shit. His mother had her beliefs and they'd given her comfort but they weren't for him. So why the hell he was still carrying the thing, he didn't know.

*You know.*

Gabriel took a sip of the scotch. One glass alone cost hundreds but he wasn't aware of the taste.

Yeah, he knew why he was carrying the rosary. It was a reminder.

Like the check for a million bucks in his wallet was a reminder.

Like the handgun he'd kept from his MC days in the drawer beside his bed was a reminder.

Shit, his whole life was a reminder.

He put his head back on the chair, took another sip of the scotch. Tried to calm his mind before the others turned up, staring around the room belligerently.

Christ, he hated this place. The Second Circle, New York's most exclusive private members' club, was his friend Alex's baby and one of nine other "Circles" scattered throughout the world. Alex had named them after the club he'd begun with Gabriel and seven other friends one night after too many shots. The Nine Circles, from Dante's *Inferno,* a favorite of Alex's. Appropriate for a group of damaged people who just happened to have a ton of money. People who'd committed so many sins between them, even the devil wouldn't know where to put them.

Over the years the nine had become four and since then, Gabriel had preferred Alex's more informal name for them—the "fucked-up billionaires." Since that's what they all were.

He scowled. Alex had given them their usual private room, the one with its echoes of an English gentlemen's club. It had a high, vaulted ceiling, exposed brick walls, library bookshelves, and high-backed wing chairs. A fire burned in a huge fireplace, warming the room against New York's icy February chill.

But all the fires, library bookshelves, and expensive scotch weren't going to change Gabriel's opinion. He still hated it.

The atmosphere reminded him of everything he despised. The world of the uber-rich, the famous, the entitled. The world of money where anything could be bought, anything sold. Yeah, it could be said that he was part of that world, especially considering that Woolf Construction, the business he owned, was one of the most successful in the States.

But Gabriel didn't consider himself part of it. Like the rest of them in Alex's club, he didn't fit into that particular world, no matter the size of his own personal fortune. A fact he was glad of. Money corrupted and he was living proof.

Losing patience, Gabriel downed the rest of the hideously expensive scotch like it was cheap bourbon and put the glass down on the table beside the chair with a click.

He didn't have time to wait around here for the rest of them. He had things to do. Things such as planning a bit of personal justice.

He was half out of the chair as the door opened and Alex came striding in, a tall, icy-looking blond woman in a black suit trailing behind him. Gabriel eyed the woman. Lovers weren't allowed at club gatherings and Alex knew that. Except the woman didn't look like one of his lovers. Although Alex was partial to blondes, they usually wore a hell of a lot less than the one standing behind him now.

"What's she doing here?" Gabriel demanded. He didn't bother with the, "Hi, how are yous," despite not having seen his closest friend since the last gathering a couple of months ago.

He wasn't one for small talk. That was for people who had nothing of importance to say.

Alex stopped in the middle of the room, one eyebrow raised.

A gambler who'd made every cent of his money from wins at the table and a bit of astute investment, he looked like the kind of rich playboy who'd had one too many shots and done one too many lines of coke. Exactly what he was, in other words. He wore a tuxedo with the jacket slung over one shoulder, white shirt open at the neck, his black hair ruffled as if some woman had run her fingers through it. But his eyes were blue as a gas flame and sharper than a shard of glass. "*She* is my new bodyguard, dammit. Show some respect."

Gabriel didn't bother looking at her. Whatever point Alex was trying to prove—and he was always trying to prove some point—Gabriel couldn't be bothered with it now. Not so soon after his mother's funeral and finally finding out the name of his bastard father. For twenty years his mother had refused to tell him because she hadn't wanted him to go after the prick, so he'd never pressed her.

But now she was dead and everything had changed.

"She has to wait outside," Gabriel said, meeting his friend's gaze. "You know the drill. No lovers. No strangers."

Alex shrugged and tossed his tuxedo jacket over the back of the sofa in front of the fire. "What's up, Gabe? You sound a little pissed about something."

Alex always knew when he had a problem. And he always called Gabriel on it. The bastard.

"Yeah, you could say that." Gabriel pulled the decanter toward him and tipped some more scotch into his tumbler. "My mother died a few days ago."

Silence.

"Shit," Alex murmured. He waited a beat then turned to his bodyguard. "Katya mine, I think the time has come for you to wait outside. Private, fucked-up billionaire business."

"Of course, sir," his bodyguard said expressionlessly, a trace of a Russian accent tingeing her words.

As the door closed behind her, Alex went over to a long, low coffee table that had been set before the fireplace. On the table was a tray of whisky tumblers, along with cigars and some canapés. Alex ignored the food and the cigars, picking up a tumbler instead and coming over to where Gabriel sat. He said nothing, lifting the decanter and pouring himself some scotch. Then he took a sip, stared at Gabriel. "Why didn't you tell me before?"

"Because you didn't need to know." His mother's life was private and so was her death. She'd hated fuss so he'd made sure to keep her funeral short, simple, and sweet.

One of Alex's brows rose. "Is that so? Funny, I thought we were friends. And usually friends tell each other that kind of thing."

Gabriel wasn't going to defend his reasoning. He hadn't before the priest that morning, and he wasn't going to now. "Yeah, well, I fucking didn't."

Alex's sharp blue gaze flickered. "You're pissed off with me?"

"Not with you." It wasn't Alex's fault that the name on that million-dollar check in his wallet would be familiar to his friend. Very familiar. But that didn't make him any less angry about it. A rage that had been eating away at him for all the years since his mother had told him what his father had done. A rage that had no outlet.

Until now.

"So why are you looking at me like I've personally offended you?"

"How's your stepfather these days?"

The other brow rose this time. "My stepfather? What the hell has he got to do with anything? And, more importantly, why do you think I would know?"

A fair point. Alex had no contact with his family, not since he'd left home at sixteen.

For the past nineteen years all his time had been spent flying from one casino to another, chasing the big poker games and the big money.

But the man who'd married his mother had come along after Alex had left.

Still, the anger that burned inside Gabriel's veins demanded release in some form. "You don't have any contact with him you're not telling me about?"

The other man didn't respond immediately, just took a long sip of his scotch, blue eyes unwavering. "No," he said after a moment, "and you know it, too. What the hell is this about?"

The door opened again before Gabriel could answer, admitting a small, fine-boned woman in black jeans, a black Led Zep T-shirt, and cherry-red Doc Marten boots, hair the color of new-fallen snow peeking out from underneath her black beanie.

Eva King, ex-hacker, now owner of one of the largest software companies in the world, in her "incognito gear." Another founding member of Alex's Nine Circles club.

She pulled her beanie off as the door closed behind her, ponytail uncurling down her back in a silvery waterfall, and eyed Gabriel and Alex. "You two look like you're having a special moment. Shall I go out and come back in again?"

"Yeah, do," Alex said. "Gabe was on the verge of telling me something important and you just interrupted."

"It can wait." Gabriel didn't want to talk about it with the others. It only concerned Alex at this point. Besides, he'd waited years for this, another hour or two wouldn't matter.

"Uh-huh." Eva threw the beanie onto the sofa near the fire and went around the side of it to stand in front of the blaze. "Jesus, the weather in New York doesn't get any better, does it? I think I preferred Zac's island."

The last meeting of the club had been a couple of months ago, on the private Caribbean island owned by the fourth member of the group, Zac Rutherford. Certainly there had been sun, and sure, that had been great, but Gabriel wasn't one for lying around on beaches. He preferred doing things. The venue for the next meeting would be his choice and he'd been thinking about getting everyone up to his Colorado lodge for a couple of days skiing or hiking.

Then again, that had been before his mother had died. Before he'd found the check and seen the name on it. The check that had been dated exactly nine months before he was born.

He'd found it in amongst his mother's things. There had been no note with it, nothing to suggest why she'd been sent such a huge amount of money or why she'd never cashed it. Puzzling, considering she'd spent many years as a teenaged solo parent, struggling just to survive.

But Gabriel knew. Despite the lack of any hard evidence, his gut was certain of the truth.

That money was from his father. His not-so-nameless-any-longer father.

Eva looked up from the fire and sent Gabriel a narrow look. "You're broodier than normal, Gabe. Anything up?"

Mercifully, Alex answered for him. "Corrine died a few days ago."

"Oh, hell." Eva's brow wrinkled, smoky-gray eyes concerned. "I'm sorry."

"Don't be," he said gruffly. "The cancer was getting to the torture stage so I'm glad it's over. And glad she doesn't have to deal with it anymore."

"You should have let us—"

"No, I shouldn't." He reached for the decanter again, taking the little scotch that was left. Something had to cool the fire inside him since the first few glasses hadn't done the trick.

Another silence fell and he knew Alex and Eva were exchanging glances. Probably meaningful ones. Well, he didn't care. He wasn't going to talk about it now.

Eva turned away and stuck her hands out to the fire. She

wore black fingerless gloves, her nails tipped with chipped silver nail polish. Alex had wandered over to the sofa, throwing himself down on it, sprawling like a lazy house cat.

"You said something in your e-mail about an investment opportunity, Eva," Alex said, sipping at his scotch. "Care to share?"

"Not yet." She rubbed her hands together. "You'll like it though."

"Why does that sound like a threat?"

"I don't know. Why does it?"

Gabriel watched them bicker from his armchair.

The Nine Circles weren't ones for heart-to-heart chats, but they looked out for each other, watched each other's backs. All of them knew what it was to be a misfit, a loner. To have nothing and no one. No support, no family to call on. No one they trusted.

That's why the original nine had formed their own little family one night after a poker game. Their own support network. Because, God knew, they had no one else. And sometimes, even that wasn't enough.

A couple of minutes later, Zac finally arrived. The fourth member of their club. Ex-SAS, ex-merc, Zac was now the head of a multimillion-dollar security company. And he looked like the consummate CEO.

Especially in the dark suit with his tats covered up by pristine black cotton and charcoal-gray wool. It didn't take much, however, to realize that Zac's exquisitely tailored façade was just that—a thin veneer of civilization over a man with the heart of a predator.

A quality Gabriel always respected since he was mostly predator himself.

"You're late," Eva said to him as Zac shut the door. "Fifteen minutes to be exact."

"Chill, angel," Zac said calmly, his cultured English

accent at odds with the scars on his face and the casual slang terminology. "I always get here eventually. And besides, the snow was a bastard."

Only Zac could call Eva angel. Mainly because he was the only one who could get away with it. He'd been the one to discover her when she'd tried to hack into his company's client database, and he'd been the one to hire her to make sure no one could ever hack into it again.

Eva rolled her eyes. "Okay, whatever."

Gabriel nodded to Zac from his chair but made no effort to move.

"I heard about Corrine," Zac said to him as he shrugged off his overcoat and slung it over a nearby chair. "My condolences."

"Thank you." It didn't surprise Gabriel that Zac already knew. The guy knew lots of things, especially things he wasn't supposed to know.

"How did you find out?" Alex asked from the sofa. He sounded annoyed.

"I read the obituaries. Like anyone else."

Alex sighed. "I don't read the obituaries."

Zac came over to the fire, reached for a tumbler, then looked around for the decanter. "Maybe you should." He frowned in Gabriel's direction. "Have you finished all that bloody scotch, Woolf?"

Gabriel shrugged, unrepentant. "My mother is dead. I think I deserve it, don't you?"

"Guys, please," Eva interrupted, looking impatient. "Could we forget about the booze for a second? We can get some more in a minute. I want to talk about the opportunity I e-mailed you about."

The last shot of whisky had settled comfortably in Gabriel's stomach, making his limbs feel loose. But the anger inside him still boiled away like a saucepan of water on an open fire. Wasn't confessing one's sins supposed to help? At least that's what his mother had always said. But not today it hadn't. If anything, confessing had only made his anger burn hotter.

" 'Vengeance is mine, sayeth the Lord,' " his mother had always told him. "Not ours, Gabriel. Ours is to forgive."

Maybe his mother had forgiven the man who raped her. But Gabriel couldn't and never would.

What had the Reverend said to him once? "Keep it cold, Church. Don't let emotion get in the way of what you have to do." The Reverend had been the old president of the Angels and had known what he was talking about. Emotion clouded your judgment. Made you weak. And he couldn't afford to be weak.

This anger had to be cold. Clean. So he could deliver justice for his mother with a steady hand.

"Honor St. James," Eva was saying. "That's who."

Gabriel blinked as the name permeated suddenly through the whisky haze.

Alex was still sprawled on the sofa but his posture was now not so much lazy cat as a lion about to pounce. "Honor?" His voice was soft and deadly.

Eva, standing with her back to the fire, smiled. "Yeah, Alex. Honor. Your sister."

Everything inside Gabriel paused.

He and Alex had been sixteen, both of them laborers on the same building site. Alex had just left home—or rather deserted it—yet Gabriel still remembered the woman who'd turned up at the site one day looking for her son, a beautiful woman with black hair and Alex's blue eyes. She'd had a serious-looking eight-year-old girl in tow. A girl who'd stared at Gabriel and Alex as they were summoned by the site foreman. Saying nothing. Just staring. Accusing.

Honor.

Alex never spoke of her, just like he never spoke about any of his family.

"What about her?" Gabriel demanded, instinct suddenly gripping him tight. He could feel Zac staring at him from across the room, golden eyes unnervingly direct.

Understandable really, since two days ago Gabriel had asked him to do some digging into a man called Guy Tremain. The name of the man on his mother's check.

Zac's contacts had turned up all kinds of interesting facts.

Such as Guy Tremain's marriage to Alex's mother nineteen years earlier. His role as doting father figure to Alex's sister, Honor. His successful hotel chain. His reputation as a veritable pillar of the community.

All the while no one knew the most important fact of all: that he was a rapist.

Eva gave Gabriel another one of her narrow, suspicious looks. She didn't trust easily and hated men who took advantage of women. "Why are you so interested?"

"Don't be stupid, Eva," Gabriel said shortly. "You know me better than that. I'm not going to screw with her in that way."

"Then what way? You've been zoning out for the past ten minutes and at the mention of her name you're suddenly all ears?"

Alex was shaking his head. "No," he said. "No and no. Keep out of it, Eva."

"Get a grip, Alex," she said. "She's got one of the best investment firms in the city and I'm not going to ignore her just because she's your damn sister. If you've got a problem with her then perhaps you need to work it out? Have you ever thought of that?"

Alex went even more still, if that was possible, and the temperature in the room plunged.

"Eva, that was insensitive," Zac said mildly enough, though the reprimand was unmistakable. "And also Alex's business."

There was never any pressure to speak of the things they didn't want to talk about. "Don't ask, don't tell" was one of their first rules. Every single one of them had wounds that remained hidden. Eva especially, from what he'd heard.

She didn't look at Zac but her intense gray gaze flickered. "When I need a father, Zac, I'll ask for it, okay?"

Zac opened his mouth to say something but Alex held up his hand. "It's fine. I accept your apology, Eva," he said, even though Eva hadn't offered him one, "but for future reference, can we keep my family out of any of these 'great investment' deals?"

"Tell me about the deal," Gabriel said, ignoring the flare of blue as Alex turned to look at him.

Eva lifted her chin. "You didn't answer my question. What's with the sudden interest in Honor?"

He wasn't quite sure yet. All he knew was that she was connected to Guy Tremain. And perhaps that *did* make her a potentially useful tool. Especially since it concerned claiming justice for his mother.

But he wasn't going to tell everyone else that. Even after all these years it was too personal to tell anyone. That he was the walking, talking reminder of his mother's rape. That he'd spent the last nineteen years of his life knowing that whenever his mother looked at him, she didn't see her son but the face of the man who'd raped her.

Oh, she'd told Gabriel it wasn't true. That she couldn't remember who the man had been but Gabriel knew she'd lied. He'd heard her confessions, after all, whispered so that no one else would hear. Confessions of guilt and shame. And fear. Fear when she looked at her own son.

No. They didn't need to know about that.

Gabriel met Eva's gaze. "You said investment opportunity. So? I want to fucking invest."

Eva stared at him for a long moment. Then she looked down at her hands, examining the chipped polish on her nails. "Honor contacted me personally about a large hotel chain she's needing investors for. Apparently the company's been trying to turn some of the hotels into luxury eco-resorts but ran into serious debt. She still thinks the idea has merit and thought I might want to sink some cash into it because they want to use some of Void Angel's smart tech."

Luxury eco-resorts . . . that was familiar somehow but he couldn't quite place it. A Woolf Construction job maybe? His company did quite a bit of hotel building and certainly one of his own personal areas of interest was in green construction—that was where the smart money was these days.

"How interesting," Zac murmured, his voice soft.

Gabriel flicked a glance at the other man and met amber eyes that were staring calmly back. Must have something to do with the information he'd asked Zac to get for him . . .

Ah, yes. That was it. Zac's contact had pulled up a whole lot of financial info about Tremain Hotels, the hotel chain Guy Tremain owned. About how in debt the company was after an attempt to turn a select few of the hotels into a series of luxury eco-resorts.

Looked like Honor was trying to help her stepfather. Which could mean all sorts of opportunities, if so.

"Yes," Gabriel agreed, folding his arms. "Very interesting."

Alex abruptly pushed himself off the sofa in an impatient movement and went over to a phone that sat on one of the side tables. "Could we get more of the Macallan thirty-nine in here please, James," he said shortly into the receiver, then hung up and turned back to the rest of them. "Sorry, Eva. You're going to have to count me out on this one."

"Because it's your sister?"

"Yeah, because it's my sister."

"Why? Afraid she's going to call you out on the last nineteen years of no contact?"

"Eva," Zac said quietly. "Respect the group."

There was a flush in Eva's pale, fine-boned face, the glitter of something like pain in her eyes. Most of the time she was guarded, sarcasm her armor, but there were some things she felt deeply enough about to let that armor drop. Loyalty was one, the importance of family another. Gabriel could understand it. He'd first been fiercely loyal to the only blood relative he had—his mother. And then, when she turned away from him, the Angels, the motorcycle club that had embraced him and their president, the Reverend, the man who'd been a father figure to him.

Oh, yes, he understood the importance of loyalty.

Eva glanced at Zac and something unspoken flashed between them. Then she looked back to the fire. "I'm sorry," she said stiffly. "It's not my business."

Alex let out a short breath. "I may not contact her but that doesn't mean I don't know what's going on in her life. I try and keep tabs on what she's doing."

This was news to Gabriel, and judging by the expressions on the others' faces, news to them as well. Alex made no secret of the fact that he'd cut off all contact with his mother and sister after his father's death. He'd never explained his reasons for doing so and no one had ever asked, but Gabriel had always assumed that no contact meant no contact.

Alex's expression was unreadable. "That was an apology, by the way."

"I got it," Eva replied. "Well, anyway, I guess you're interested, aren't you, Gabe?"

Interested? That went without saying. Already his mind was turning over possibilities, investigating options.

His whole life had been about doing what had to be done. At first it had all been about mere survival. Making sure the life he and his mom had was secure. Then it had been about safeguarding that security any way he could. Protecting his mother, making sure she'd never have to suffer for the fact that she'd chosen to have him.

And now? Now he'd do what had to be done again.

To take down his rapist father. Get a little piece of justice for his mother.

"Yeah," Gabriel said. "I'm interested."

# CHAPTER TWO

Honor pulled the door of her Midtown office shut with a resounding click, prompting a surprised look from Weston, her PA.

"You're going home?" he said, making an exaggerated show of looking at his watch. "Now? But it's only five o'clock."

Honor lifted an eyebrow. "Thanks for the sarcasm, Wes. You know how much I appreciate it."

"Anytime. But seriously. You live at the office."

Tightening the belt of her cashmere trench coat, Honor picked up her briefcase and crossed over to Weston's desk.

The reception area of St. James Investments was empty, most of her clients long gone, but her PA was still doing some last-minute tasks. He was a workaholic just like she was.

"I'm not going home. I've got a meeting." She placed the folder she'd also been carrying on his desk. "Here's the Cornwall account info back again. I'm finished with it."

Weston picked up the folder and filed it away with his usual efficiency. "A meeting? There wasn't one in your schedule."

"No, I know. It's a personal one." Glancing down at the rose-gold Cartier Tank watch Guy had given her for her twenty-first birthday, Honor checked the time.

She had to be at O'Rourke's, an Irish pub a couple of blocks from her office, in about twenty minutes, to meet with Eva King, the media-shy CEO of Void Angel, one of the country's largest and fastest growing technology companies, and she did not want to be late. Especially since they were going to be talking investments.

The pub was a strange place to meet for a technology CEO but really, what did that matter? She hoped the meeting—which she'd only received a text about that afternoon, necessitating a rescheduling of a number of other meetings—was going to yield some results. Eva had been cagey when Honor had put forward the details of Guy's hotel project and Honor supposed she couldn't blame her. Putting money into a failing business was always going to be risky.

Then again, Eva's company had a reputation for taking risks, as well as constantly being on the lookout for new opportunities, which was why Honor had approached her in the first place.

"Oh?" Weston looked interested. "Sounds intriguing."

Honor just gave him a smile as she turned toward the elevators. "Not really. Need-to-know basis only, Wes dear, and you don't need to know." Finding investors for Tremain Hotels was her baby and with the way it was currently going—badly—it wasn't anything she wanted to crow about.

Besides, Wes didn't need to know that if she couldn't find the money to get Tremain out of debt, he'd be out of a job.

And so would she.

"Spoilsport." Wes pulled a face. "Oh well, have fun."

Honor's smile remained in place until the elevator doors shut. Then it vanished because, really, she had nothing to smile about. Not when she thought of the amount of her own money she'd invested in Tremain. Money she'd put in against her better judgment, purely to help Guy save his company. Money she'd lose if Tremain went down the drain.

As the elevator descended, her phone rang. She checked the screen. Guy, again.

"Hey," she said, answering it. "And no. No news yet." She debated whether or not to tell him about her meeting with Eva, but decided not to. No point in getting his hopes up when she didn't have any concrete answers for him.

"Well, you be sure to let me know as soon as you get any bites." Her stepfather's voice was level but she could hear the undercurrent of worry in it.

"Don't worry, I will. Look, I've had some interest already. Now it's just a matter of reeling them in."

"Who?"

"I can't say just yet. I'll give you an update tonight though, okay?"

Guy sighed. "Yes, all right. Your mother and I are at a gallery opening now but I'll have my phone on me. Call me as soon as you know."

After he'd hung up, Honor leaned back against the railing that ran around the interior of the elevator and shut her eyes.

She'd used every contact she had in an effort to get more backers for Tremain but every single one of them had refused, using words and phrases like "recession" and "economic climate."

God. She'd promised Guy she'd help him save the chain. Promised she'd fix his debts. Because that's what she did—she fixed things. Always had.

*But what if you can't fix this?*

No. That wasn't an option. Guy was the closest thing to a father she had, certainly a hell of a lot better than the bastard who'd been her biological father, and he believed in her. Believed she had the ability to get him out of the financial hole he'd managed to get himself into.

She couldn't let him down. She just couldn't. Not with her own financial security and reputation riding on it as well.

Honor opened her eyes as the doors to the elevator opened, clenched her hand tighter on the handle of her briefcase, and strode out through the foyer.

Eva King was her last hope and by God, she'd get the woman, her technology, and most importantly, her money on board if it was the last thing she did.

Going out through the building's entrance, Honor shivered as the hard winter cold slid icy hands up her legs, the pavement slippery and wet beneath the heels of her black Louboutins.

She drew her coat tighter around her, but even the expensive wool didn't seem to have any effect against the biting cold.

The street was crowded with traffic and people hurrying home after a long day at the office and at first, Honor didn't notice the long black limo parked just along the entrance to her building. At least not until a man in a chauffer's uniform stepped in front of her. "Ms. St. James? Ms. King has sent a car for you."

Honor stopped, glancing at the limo in surprise. The windows were tinted, hiding whoever was inside completely from view. "Oh," she said slightly nonplussed. The pub wasn't very far away and she hadn't expected a lift. "That's very kind of her."

The chauffer pulled open the door for her and stood there, waiting.

An odd foreboding went through her as she stared into the dark interior of the limo, one that had nothing to do with the cold. As if once she got inside, she'd be taken away somewhere against her will, never to return.

*Are you crazy? It's just a car.*

Irritated with herself, Honor shrugged off the feeling. Yes, that's exactly what it was. Just a car to take her to a meeting. A thoughtful gesture by the Void Angel CEO. No big deal.

Smiling at the chauffeur, she got in, the warm interior of the limo a delicious contrast to the icy evening air.

But it wasn't until she'd sat down on the plush leather seat that she realized she wasn't alone.

And it wasn't Eva King in the car with her.

A man sat on the opposite seat, long legs outstretched, arms folded. He wore a pair of faded blue jeans, worn at the knees, a black T-shirt, and a battered black leather jacket.

A workingman's outfit, completely at odds with the obvious luxury of the car.

But the male wearing it was not in any way an average workingman.

He was tall, his head almost brushing the car's ceiling, his legs taking up most of the room in the space between them. Powerful, too. She could tell by the breadth of his shoulders and the way his leather jacket pulled tightly across them, and the cotton of his T-shirt stretched over the contours of his chest. There was something rough about him, something brutal. An aura of menace that, along with his appearance, should have been intimidating.

But Honor wasn't intimidated. She knew him.

He was Gabriel Woolf, infamous owner of Woolf Construction, one of the biggest and most successful private construction companies in the country.

Yet that wasn't the only reason she knew him, why every time he appeared in the media she'd stop whatever she was doing and watch. She knew him because he'd been the teenage boy standing next to her brother nineteen years ago. The day her mother had finally tracked Alex down and dragged Honor along to convince him to come home. The last time she'd ever seen the big brother she'd once adored with every breath in her body.

She'd never, ever forgotten.

Catapulted suddenly back into the past, Honor completely forgot about the meeting she was supposed to go to, about where Eva King was and why Gabriel Woolf was here instead.

"Where's my brother?" she demanded before she could stop herself. "Where's Alex?"

Gabriel's eyes were very dark, in stark contrast to the deep, tawny gold of his hair. There was a brutal beauty to his features. God, she still remembered his face from all those years ago—even then he'd seemed hard. And when she'd looked into his eyes, all she'd seen was anger. It prowled around inside him like a caged animal. Back then it had frightened her.

Now she could sense it still, colder, hungrier, but this time it didn't scare her because he wasn't the only one who was angry.

He didn't move. Just stared at her. "Nice to see you too, Miss St. James." His voice was deep, lazy. A deceptive voice, the note of sensuality of it, the thread of heat, completely at odds with the cold look in his eyes. "It's been a while."

Honor folded her hands on top of the briefcase in her lap. "Nineteen years to be exact and you didn't answer my question."

"You want to talk about your brother now?"

"Knowing he's okay would be something."

He studied her with an oddly detached kind of focus, as if he were looking at the results of an experiment he'd just conducted. It made her uncomfortable. "Yes, he's okay."

If okay could be applied to a lifestyle as dissolute as

Alex's was reputed to be. "Where is he?" she demanded again.

"What makes you think I know?"

"You're his friend, aren't you?"

"And you're assuming that why?"

Because once, nineteen years ago . . .

*That doesn't mean they're still friends now. Also, do you really care that much about Alex?*

He'd left her. Left her and her mother alone after Daniel St. James's suicide, and hadn't contacted them. Not once. So no, she didn't care.

With an effort, Honor made herself relax. "I'm probably assuming a great many things, actually. Sorry, I don't usually make demands of strangers in cars."

"Not so much a stranger since you know who I am already."

"Yes, well. You're pretty recognizable." Honor lifted one hand and leaned across the space between them, holding it out. "Nice to meet you once again, Mr. Woolf."

For a second Gabriel stared at her hand held out like an olive branch as if he didn't quite trust it. Then slowly he unfolded his arms and enclosed her hand in one of his. "Likewise, Miss St. James."

Her breath caught as a wave of heat washed over her skin at his touch, her heart suddenly racing. She had to fight to keep the reaction from showing in her face.

Damn, was that what she thought it was? It had been a while since she'd felt anything like sexual attraction to a man, so she couldn't be sure.

Honor pulled her hand away, trying not to make her shock too obvious. "And that's as good a question as any to start with. I thought I was supposed to be meeting with Eva King."

Gabriel leaned back against the seat, folding his arms again. "You were. I'm a friend of Eva's. She passed on a few details regarding your quest for investors and I decided I was interested."

Not expecting it, Honor blinked. "You're interested in Tremain Hotels?"

"Yeah, I am."

"But . . . why?"

His dark eyes were watchful as if he was gauging her reaction. "I'm in the construction business, Miss St. James. And green construction is the way of the future. It's where the money's at. Of course I'm interested."

For a minute Honor didn't quite know what to say. She'd been expecting to meet Eva, not the man she'd forever associate with Alex's disappearance from her life. But this was a good thing, wasn't it? If he was as interested as he claimed, then having a company like Woolf Construction as a backer could only be an asset.

And perhaps she might be able to get a bit more information about Alex from him, too. Not because she wanted to make contact—no, he'd burned that particular bridge a long time ago—but something she could take back to her mother, who'd found his abandonment particularly hard to take.

"You look surprised," Gabriel said.

"Of course I'm surprised. I wasn't expecting you."

"You'll get over it."

Honor shifted in her seat. "What about Eva then?"

"Don't worry about her. She'll be involved with the tech side of things. But I'm going to be handling everything else."

There was something about the way he said it, so arrogant—so confident—that instantly got her back up. Annoyed and trying not to show it since he was a potential client after all, Honor folded her hands back on her briefcase again. "I see. So, I take it we're not going to be meeting in the pub then?"

His eyes had taken on a strange glitter. "That wasn't Eva's plan. That was mine, but right now I've changed my mind."

Honor found herself gripping her briefcase tightly, a strange little twist of fear curling in her stomach. "Oh?"

"Yes. I think we need a little bit more in the way of privacy."

"Mr. Woolf—"

Abruptly he sat forward, a sharp movement that made her heart beat fast. "Are you afraid of me, Miss St. James?" The words were soft, but there was an underlying roughness to them that Honor found almost menacing.

Her fingers felt cold against the warm leather of her briefcase, the edges sharp, digging into her knuckles.

Gabriel Woolf. What did she know about him? The rough-edged CEO of Woolf Construction. The man she'd watched over the years—not with any conscious intent, but she'd been aware of him nonetheless. Was he a man to be afraid of?

Oh, there'd been rumors about him, about how he'd gotten the money to start his company so young, especially when he'd grown up on the streets. Rumors that he'd been a drug dealer at some point, with gang links. It was a well-known fact that he'd been the president of an outlaw motorcycle club, a fact the media loved to play up. But he'd never had any charges brought against him, nor did he ever answer questions on the subject.

Yet even without those rumors, he was rather frightening. Tall, clearly muscular, and exuding such a sense of cold, powerful, tightly leashed anger, he was like a coiled spring. Or a loaded gun ready to go off at the slightest touch. So yes, maybe she was afraid of him. And, for some reason, also fascinated by him.

"No," Honor said. "I'm not afraid of you." She'd learned a thing or two when it came to dealing with powerful men, the kind of men rife in the world of high finance. One was to never admit to fear.

Gabriel's dark eyes didn't leave her face. "You're in a strange car with a strange man going fuck knows where and you're not afraid?"

Was he trying to intimidate her? Put her off? He was out of luck in that case. Because the second lesson she'd learned was to never back down.

"No," she repeated. "Should I be?"

She was lying. He could see it in her stillness. In the flicker of her blue eyes as they regarded him from underneath straight, glossy, black bangs.

Her face was pointed with a sweet little bow of a mouth, long thick eyelashes, and a straight nose. Her fine-grained skin pale and soft.

She looked high-class. Sophisticated in a fancy coat and shoes with distinctive red soles. He knew shoes like that— he'd bought numerous pairs for lovers before.

Expensive. Just like her. She had that perfectly presented, smooth look to her that only the priciest kind of woman had.

The kind of woman that a man with a past like his wasn't ever supposed to touch.

"Yeah, you should be afraid," Gabriel said. And he meant it. He was hard. Ruthless. Had done some bad stuff to get where he was today and regretted none of it. The only rule he had—and one he never broke—was to never harm a woman. In fact, when he'd been president of the Angels, he'd become the go-to guy for women having trouble with their boyfriend, or husband, or who'd been menaced by some stranger. Go to Church, they said. He'll sort it out.

And he had. He'd taken pleasure from it. And if some guys had gotten hurt it was their own fault. Of course, a psychiatrist would have had a field day with that. Would have said he saw his father in each abuser.

The psychiatrist would have been right.

Then again, a little fear never hurt. It was healthy. Guaranteed respect. And sent her fair warning not to screw with him.

Honor raised an eyebrow—a mannerism that was startlingly reminiscent of Alex. "And why is that?"

"Because I'm not a nice man, sweetheart."

"Sweetheart? Oh, please."

He almost smiled at the look on her face. "Honor, then."

"That would be preferable."

"Good to see you, Honor." He didn't offer his hand again. He could still feel the warmth of her palm against his from their previous touch. A subtle heat that rested on his skin like a ray of sun. Dangerous. But useful.

Sure, he'd never hurt a woman but he had no problem with using her if it was necessary.

"Nice to see you again, too," Honor replied with stiff courtesy. She didn't say his name and he suspected that was deliberate.

Again he had to resist the urge to smile. Had she felt this electricity between them, too? And was she discomforted by it?

He watched her shift around on the seat, her knuckles white where they clutched the handle of her black leather briefcase. Oh yeah, she was.

"So where are we going if we're not going to the pub? Or do you have a lair you're dragging me off to?" she asked, again with the raised eyebrow and a certain dry humor. Nervous and trying not to show it, he guessed. Easy enough to tell by the way she was clutching that briefcase.

"I have a private club I'm a member of," he replied. "I thought we'd go there to discuss your proposal."

He wasn't much for fancy restaurants or exclusive bars. That was Alex's territory, not his. But Honor St. James didn't belong in a place like O'Rourke's. With her brother's coloring, black hair, and blue eyes, she had a delicate, catlike beauty that drew the eye. Drew attention.

And he didn't want attention. He preferred to get on with the job, not create a fuss.

"Okay." She patted the top of the briefcase. "I brought along some information you might—"

"I've got the information already," he interrupted. After the meeting with the others two nights ago, he'd got his research team to look into Tremain Hotels, turning up everything they could find.

The chain was, indeed, seriously in debt, which was excellent news from his perspective. And also the basis for the plan he'd been turning over in his head for the past couple of days now. A fairly simple plan when all was said and done—sink money into Tremain. Buy as much stock as he could. Make sure he had the controlling shares. Then maybe he'd bankrupt it. Or maybe he'd keep the lot and make Tremain Hotels part of his own empire.

Whatever he'd do, one thing was certain. He'd take something of his father's and make it his. And he'd make sure Tremain knew who it was who'd made him pay. And why.

"You have?" Honor blinked. "Oh, right. Of course you have. And I guess you've read over the various reports that I sent to Eva?"

"Yes. But I'm not discussing that now. We'll have plenty of time after we reach the club."

She opened her mouth. Shut it again. "Perhaps we can talk about my brother then."

He hadn't quite decided how he'd tackle her questions, because obviously she would have them. Alex had just shrugged his shoulders when Gabriel had asked him about it. "Tell her or don't tell her," he'd said. "I don't give a shit."

"I'm still his friend," Gabriel said, deciding. "If that's what you want to know."

Her eyes were dark, like Indian sapphires, the expression in them unreadable. "So you see him then? Regularly?"

"Semi-regularly, yes."

"Does he know . . ." She stopped, looked down at her hands. "Does he know you're meeting me?"

"Yeah, he does."

"I see. I don't suppose . . ." She trailed off again. "No, don't answer that question."

"Did he want me to pass a message on to you?" Gabriel finished for her. "No, he didn't." Brutally honest perhaps, but it was better to know these things straight up.

Honor's posture stiffened a little but her expression remained neutral. So she had armor. He supposed a woman like her must need it, working as she did in such a male-dominated industry. "Well," she said, a thin film of ice coating her words, "I didn't expect him to. Not after nineteen years of silence." Her blue eyes were very direct. "I don't suppose you had anything to do with that, did you?"

"No. That was all Alex's decision."

"Ah, okay, then." She looked down at her hands again. "That answers pretty much all my questions in that case." The cold had bled out of her tone, leaving behind it a hint of pain.

Gabriel studied her. He'd never judged his friend for leaving his mother and sister after his father's death. Mainly because he'd known a man driven by demons when he saw one and Alex seemed driven by the entire population of hell. So when Alex had told him he'd left home and wouldn't go back, Gabriel had accepted it. Who was he to judge anyway? After the things he'd done? If Alex needed to leave to survive whatever was eating him up inside, then Gabriel had no problem with that.

Yet looking at Honor now, hearing the echoes of an old pain in her voice, he couldn't help wondering at his friend's continued refusal to make contact.

*It's not your business. And you can't afford to get involved.*

No. He couldn't. The only thing that mattered was taking down Tremain. Honor's stepfather. That was the extent of it.

He had to stay on target and that meant finding out more about her relationship with the guy. About why she was trying to save his company. Look for any weaknesses that could be exploited.

The car began to slow, coming to a halt outside the Second Circle Club.

Honor stared out the window, her eyes widening a little. She glanced at him, then back at the elegant old building outside. "Here?"

He rather enjoyed her look of disbelief. Part of him would always get a kick out of shocking people who judged him on his past and the streets he'd come from.

"Yeah, here. Pretty good for a working stiff like me, don't you think?"

Her blue eyes flicked back to him. "You? A working stiff? I think you haven't been a working stiff for a long time, Mr. Woolf."

"Gabriel."

"When I'm ready, Mr. Woolf. When I'm ready."

A small thrill of unwelcome anticipation went through him at her resistance. Smooth, sophisticated women had never been his thing. He preferred earthier women. Women with no hang-ups, who could look after themselves and didn't mind if things got a bit rough. Who had no expectations of anything more than a couple of nights of good, dirty fun.

Not women like Honor St. James, in other words.

Yet there were sparks in those blue eyes of hers. Sparks that promised a man a challenge. A good fight. And if there was one thing he enjoyed, it was a good fight.

Still, he needed to play it cool here because there were too many variables he didn't know about. Before he made any move he had to do some more research. Into Tremain. Into Honor. Into the relationship between them and whether he could exploit that as well as this investment opportunity.

Guy Tremain had to pay for what he did. For what he had taken.

And the only one who could make him pay was Gabriel.

Honor didn't know much about the Second Circle other than it was one of New York's most exclusive private members' clubs and getting your name on the list was supposed to be next to impossible. Well, that and the fact that her brother owned it. Not that that meant a damn thing to her.

She was surprised Gabriel Woolf was a member though. He didn't look like the type who'd value such exclusivity. In fact, he was renowned as much for his down-to-earth business approach as he was for the fact that he never wore suits. She'd often heard the media make a big deal about how he was still a regular Joe—apart from the rumors about his past, of course—but looking at him now, Honor couldn't understand how on earth they could have assumed that because he didn't look like any working-man she knew.

She watched him as they entered the club, nodding a

wordless greeting to the doorman, striding past the concierge in the foyer who murmured something about a table being ready for them in the restaurant.

A rough, brutal kind of power clung to him. An uncivilized, bad-boy charisma only enhanced by the jeans, T-shirt, and leather jacket he wore. Honor found it mesmerizing. The way he moved, with such innate confidence, as if the world was his to bend to his command and if it didn't, then he'd make it. Perhaps with a baseball bat.

There were a lot of confident men in the financial sector. Men in expertly tailored suits with clean-cut college good looks and the arrogance to match. But in comparison to Gabriel they suddenly all seemed like little boys playing at being men. Playing at being dangerous.

Because this guy was the real deal. And why she should like that, she had no idea.

What she did know was that letting her fledgling fascination with him show would be a mistake.

*"I'm not a nice man, sweetheart . . ."*

No, she suspected he wasn't. But part of her dearly wanted to find out just how bad he really was.

Gabriel showed her into the restaurant and she had to fight not to stare. The place was beautiful. High ornate ceilings with chandeliers that glittered like ice crystals, low booth seats upholstered in red velvet, and circular tables of dark wood surrounded by red velvet armchairs. Some of the tables had curtains and here and there were groups of people she recognized. Politicians for the most part, but she also spotted a couple of well-known actors and their entourages, a singer with a group of admirers.

It was just the kind of place she would have loved to have been a member of simply because of the luxury factor. Nice things were Honor's guilty pleasure. The one weakness she allowed herself, harmless and easily controllable. Designer labels and quality fabric, velvet pillows on her bed and expensive French Champagne in her fridge.

It was kind of shallow, she knew that, but still, she liked knowing that everything she had was hers, that it had been paid for with her own money and could never be taken away from her. Unlike all the things the debt collectors had repossessed when she'd been a kid, when her father's gambling debts had come to light.

Gabriel gestured to a table set in a secluded part of the restaurant, the lighting low and intimate, giving the illusion of privacy. A waiter hovered, indicating that he'd take her coat. Honor took it off and handed it to him but kept hold of her briefcase, sliding into the booth, the red velvet smooth against the backs of her legs.

She tensed when Gabriel, instead of sitting in the armchair opposite her, slid in beside her. He wasn't sitting particularly close and yet, Honor found herself aware of the distance between her body and his all the same.

An awareness she didn't particularly want.

Annoyed with herself, she put her briefcase down on the seat between them, demarcating a clear line. "So, Mr. Woolf," she began. And no, she wouldn't give him his first name just yet. Withholding it had clearly irritated him and she had the feeling she'd need the advantage when it came to cutting a deal. "I take it you're genuinely interested in investing in Tremain Hotels?"

He leaned back against the red velvet of the booth, the battered leather of his jacket creaking as he folded his arms. "What's your connection?"

"Excuse me?"

"I've read some of the info you gave Eva. Tremain Hotels isn't a client of your firm and you don't have a stake in it. Their debts are also massive. Letting it go under would probably be the best thing and yet you're not. Why?"

There was no point in hiding her connection. It was

easy enough to find out anyway. "Guy Tremain is my stepfather. He's poured a lot of his heart and soul into the eco-resort idea, and I think the returns on it could be good. Especially given the interest in eco-tourism these days."

Gabriel's dark eyes on her were sharp, focused. "But it's not just about the returns, is it?"

A vague sense of threat gripped her. She didn't want to reveal her stake in it just yet. It would give him a potential weakness to exploit and, of course, he would take advantage of it. He was that type of man. Careful not to let her unease show, Honor gave him a cool smile. "Please, Mr. Woolf, I'm in finance. Returns are everything."

He stared at her for a long minute until the waiter came with the drinks list and diverted his attention.

Honor allowed herself a small, quiet breath. She didn't know why he unnerved her quite so much. But something about the look in his eyes made her feel as if he'd stripped away her armor. Turning her back into that eight-year-old girl, holding her mother's hand and staring at her brother as they'd confronted him all those years ago. The brother who'd once been the golden boy of the family, the brother she'd once adored and who'd left her without even a good-bye.

She still remembered the fact that Alex hadn't looked at her. Not once. But Gabriel had. Stared at her with that same detached ferocity as he was right now. Back then she'd hated him, deciding with the logic of a child that he was the one to blame for taking her brother away.

Hated him and yet feared his cold, dark stare at the same time.

All these years later, she still felt the echoes of those same emotions, still felt the anger, the hate, and the fear.

*You can't let it affect the deal. You know you can't.*

No, she couldn't. She had to approach this the way she

approached every problem. Keep cool and calm and logical. This had nothing to do with the past. This was all about the future. Her future and Guy's. Anything else was unimportant.

The waiter handed Honor the wine list and she ordered something, she didn't remember what, her attention consumed by the man sitting next to her. The way the muted light of the restaurant turned his hair a deep, rich gold and gave his eyes the dark, depthless quality of a quiet lake at midnight. Softened the raw beauty of his face, making him seem approachable. Less dangerous. Almost normal.

After the waiter had gone, he said, "You're pretty clever, little girl. But you don't fool me."

No, he wasn't approachable. Or less dangerous. And she must be sure never to make the mistake of thinking he was.

There was a cut crystal water tumbler on the table in front of her so she picked it up, using the movement to cover her deepening unease. "What are you talking about?"

"It's not the returns. You're doing it for him, aren't you?"

Something in his posture, in the way he was looking at her, made her feel exposed. Leaning on one elbow, she turned fully to face him. "He's my stepfather. I'll leave you to draw your own conclusions."

"Trying to rescue him from his own bad debts?"

"I'm trying to help him, yes."

"Uh-huh." Leaning his head back against the red velvet of the booth, Gabriel shot her a look from beneath surprisingly long, dark lashes. "Why don't you tell me about it, baby? In the interest of full disclosure."

Honor's jaw tightened at the underlying note of command in his voice. And the patronizing pseudo-endearments. Little girl. Baby. What the hell was that all about? Putting her in her place or something? She wanted to tell him where he could stick it but of course, if she wanted to make sure Tremain Hotels remained viable, she had to keep Gabriel as a potential investor happy. She had to keep her personal emotions out of it.

"He's new to the eco-tourism market," she said crisply, annoyed that she had to explain. It made her aware of the fact that she'd invested quite a bit of her own money in something she wouldn't have touched with a ten-foot pole in the normal scheme of things. "There were a few errors in his research."

"Must have been some pretty major errors given the debt."

"Forgive me for asking, Mr. Woolf, but how does this concern you?"

"I'm looking at investing a fair amount of money into his business. His failing business. I'd say that concerns me quite a bit."

Of course it did. And she was being overly defensive. Mostly because the whole thing worried her, too.

At that point the waiter arrived, bringing Gabriel's beer and the glass of red wine she'd apparently ordered. Another chance to take a much needed breath.

"Dinner?" Gabriel asked her as the waiter brandished a menu.

But she wasn't feeling very hungry or keen on spending more hours than were strictly necessary in Gabriel Woolf's disturbing presence.

"No, thank you," she said. "I have a few things to do tonight."

*Since when did you let a man get to you like this?*

Honor sipped at her wine as Gabriel waved the waiter away, uncomfortable with the thought. Never, that was the answer. Oh, there had been plenty of men over the course of her professional life who'd thought she was an easy target. They saw someone young, feminine, and thought they could take advantage. She'd proved them wrong, of course. She'd had to.

Without respect she was nothing.

But Gabriel Woolf wasn't like any of them and she wasn't quite sure how to deal with him.

"You want to save him? Your stepfather, I mean."

Honor met Gabriel's dark gaze. "Yes," she said flatly. The confession revealed another weakness but she knew dissembling wouldn't work with this man.

"Why?"

"That *definitely* isn't your business."

"If you want me to give you money, little girl, then it most certainly is my fucking business."

"Stop calling me that. I'm not a little girl."

"Aren't you?" The look in his eyes was steady. As if he could see right down to her soul. "A little girl trying to save her daddy. Yeah, that's what you are. And what do you think he'll give you in return? A car? A house? A sparkly new dress?"

The aura of danger coming off him had become even more intense though he hadn't moved. Not even to pick up his beer.

"I'm not sure what you find so offensive about it." She put her hands in her lap so he wouldn't see them shake. "But my motives should have nothing whatsoever to do with your decision regarding investing in Tremain Hotels."

"Then perhaps I won't invest after all." He reached out, picking up his beer. Taking a leisurely sip. "Perhaps I've found something better to do with my money."

Oh, crap. If she wasn't careful, this opportunity might slip away and then she'd be left with nothing. Then Guy would be left with his business folding and her mother once more neck-deep in debt along with her husband.

Along with herself. Wouldn't that be a great reputation breaker? The hot-shot investor who bankrupted herself because of a bad business deal. An emotional investment.

"Fine," she said. "Guy Tremain was more of a father to me than my real father ever was. And now that he's counting on me to help him get this off the ground, I'm not going to fail him. Does that clear things up a little for you?"

Gabriel took another sip of his beer and put the glass down, leaning back against the red velvet of the seat. "In that case, count me in."

# CHAPTER THREE

Gabriel approached the door to Alex's penthouse suite at the Second Circle and stopped. His friend's Russian bodyguard was standing in front of it looking tall, impassive, and quite lethal in her black suit, her blond hair tied back in a severe ponytail.

"I'm sorry, sir. You can't go in. He's busy," she said before he could speak.

"Busy? With what?"

The Russian woman's startling green eyes didn't even flicker. "With whom."

Christ. So Alex had some bimbo he'd picked up from somewhere in there, did he? Well, too bad. Gabriel didn't have the patience for it today. There were questions he needed answers to and he needed them now.

After his meeting with Honor the night before, it had become imperative to find out more about the relationship between her and her stepfather. If Honor was one of the man's weaknesses—and given her defensiveness toward the guy, he suspected she was—then he had to know about it.

Alex had been very clear the night of the group's meeting that he'd been keeping an eye on her, and if that was the case then he'd have information that Gabriel could use. Investing in Tremain Hotels was one thing, but that was just money. Honor wasn't though. Honor was personal. And he wanted to make it personal.

"Is that right?" Gabriel said. "Well, I don't care who he's got in there. I need to talk to him."

The bodyguard didn't move, standing in front of the doorway, impassive as a plank of wood. "I'm sorry, sir," she said again. "My orders are to let no one in."

"I'm not no one, sweetheart."

She opened her mouth, probably to reiterate her orders yet again, but at that point the door opened and a woman—a rather famous actress if he was correct—came out. She smiled at him as she put on her other stiletto, shaking back a tumble of blond hair. "Later, Alex, darling," she called through the open doorway behind her and sauntered off down the hallway.

"You can go in now," the bodyguard said expression-lessly.

"No fucking kidding," Gabriel muttered and stepped through the doorway, shutting the door behind him.

The Second Circle's hotel rooms were available for any of its members to stay in—all except the penthouse suite, which Alex had claimed for himself. The place was vast, all floor-to-ceiling windows and exposed brick walls, polished wooden floors and antique furniture upholstered in sumptuous fabrics. All very expensive. All very Alex.

"Oh, it's you," his friend commented, coming out from the bedroom, a sheet tied around his waist and trailing on the floor. He leaned against the door frame between the bedroom and lounge, running a hand through his black hair. "What's up?"

Gabriel walked over to one of the rich, purple velvet-covered sofas, and sat down, elbows on his knees. "Tell me what you know about Honor."

Instantly the expression on Alex's face became guarded. "What?"

"Oh, don't give me that crap, man. You know I met with her last night about this hotel business. Aren't you even curious to know how that went?"

Alex folded his arms. "No."

"Bullshit."

"I'm not." His friend shifted against the door frame. "Look, what exactly do you want to know about her? I'm going to Vegas tomorrow and I've got a shitload of stuff to handle before I go."

"So you do keep an eye on her then?"

Alex's blue gaze didn't waver. "Yes. I meant what I said when I told the group I did."

"Then what's her relationship to Guy Tremain?"

All at once the look on Alex's face hardened fractionally. "You've got a thing about him, haven't you? What's the deal, Gabe?"

"Nothing I want to tell anyone about." He wasn't going to go into confessing his plans. He'd already done so with the priest, that should be enough. The whole situation was too personal. Too private. Touched on too many painful things.

"Not even me? Your oldest friend?" Alex raised an eyebrow, a mannerism so like his sister that Gabriel had an almost uncomfortable flashback to Honor sitting beside him the night before. All polished sophistication and dry, sarcastic humor.

"Fuck no," Gabriel said bluntly.

"Then why should I tell you about Honor and Tremain?"

Slowly Gabriel sat back on the sofa, staring at the other man. "Sounds like you're a bit concerned about her."

Alex didn't move but his posture became tense. "She's my sister."

"A sister you haven't bothered to talk to for years."

"Oh, Christ, not you as well. I get enough of that crap from Eva."

Gabriel lifted a shoulder. "Hey, you have your reasons for not talking, I got mine, we're all good. I'm just pointing out that it's a little rich for you to get all protective of her now."

The other man didn't say anything for a moment. Then he let out a long breath. "Okay, well, I don't know a lot. They're close, that much I do know. Apparently Tremain sees her as a daughter."

*"Guy Tremain was more a father to me than my real father ever was . . ."*

Gabriel turned over Honor's words from the night before in his head. So the feeling was mutual. Interesting. Very interesting indeed. Because he could use that.

His mother had just been minding her own business, trying to earn money by cleaning hotel rooms to save up for a decent education. Until she'd been raped in one of those hotel rooms. Tremain Hotels to be exact. By Guy Tremain himself.

Ruining that business, ruining the man, would be poetic justice.

"Yeah, that makes sense," he said aloud. "That's the impression I got from her last night."

Alex didn't respond but some emotion Gabriel couldn't read flickered in his eyes. Perhaps he missed her?

"She asked after you," Gabriel said. "She asked me where you were."

The other man looked away. Then he turned and stalked back into the bedroom.

Gabriel let out a breath. Okay, so Alex may not want to know these things, but Gabriel figured some part of him was hungry for news nevertheless. The mere fact he still kept tabs on his sister after all these years spoke volumes.

Pushing himself off the couch, Gabriel went over to

the bedroom doorway and leaned against it. Alex had pulled on a pair of jeans and was reaching for a T-shirt.

"Don't tell me anything else," his friend said shortly. "I don't want to know."

"Yeah, you do."

"No, I don't." Alex jerked the T-shirt down then turned to face Gabriel. "I lost the right to know nineteen years ago."

"So why bother keeping an eye on her?"

"Because I didn't trust Tremain."

The news sent a small, cold shock down Gabriel's spine. He felt himself tense. Honor was small, a delicately built woman. Like his mother had been. Jesus. "Why?"

Alex met his gaze. "I don't trust anyone. Not even you, brother."

"Good plan." Gabriel tried to relax, let the tension out. "I wouldn't either." Surely Honor wouldn't have responded so defensively to his criticism of Tremain if something sketchy had gone on? Her response had been genuine, he was sure of it.

After a moment, Alex said, "So you're going to invest in this hotel thing then?"

"Yeah. Seems legit. I got my finance and legal teams onto it this morning so we'll see what happens."

Alex put his hands in his pockets and looked down at the floor. "She . . . seemed well to you?"

Well? Interesting word to use for Honor St. James. He could think of other words though. Beautiful. Sexy. Intriguing. Challenging.

"She did," Gabriel said, keeping those to himself since brothers didn't need to know them.

Alex looked up. "And did she seem happy?"

"I thought you didn't want to know."

The other man looked away again. "Yeah, you're right, I don't. Now, where the hell is my phone?"

* * *

Honor celebrated the deal with Gabriel Woolf by taking her stepfather out for lunch at Leonard's, one of the more exclusive restaurants near her office. Guy's response the night before to the good news had been oddly muted. Especially when she'd mentioned that Gabriel Woolf was going to be one of the investors. But she'd hoped that when she had a chance to speak with him face-to-face about it, he'd understand what a good deal this was going to be.

That Gabriel Woolf's money would enable them to dodge an extremely large and lethal bullet.

Unfortunately it appeared that understanding was not forthcoming.

Guy's long, blunt fingers toyed with the napkin across his knee, a slight frown on his handsome face. He was in his sixties, a tall, powerfully built man with a penchant for expensive suits and handmade shoes, and ridiculously vain about his gold hair. Which Honor suspected he dyed to stop the creep of gray.

"I'm not sure about Woolf," he said, pushing away the salad he'd only half-eaten.

Honor tried to find some patience, but it was difficult. She'd thought Guy would be pleased—no, she'd thought he'd be ecstatic—to finally get the backing he needed to save his hotel chain.

"What's the problem with him?" Honor asked. "You can't argue with his money."

Guy raised a hand to his perfectly coiffed hair, touched it lightly. "I'm not sure I want a man like him associated with Tremain Hotels."

"Why? Because of those ridiculous drug dealer rumors?"

"They're not exactly rumors. He was definitely involved with some outlaw motorcycle gang and you know what kinds of things those sorts of people are involved in."

She suspected she did. Gabriel Woolf did have the look of a man who would do whatever was necessary to get what he wanted. A man who probably *had* done whatever was necessary. It intrigued her.

*You're also attracted to him.*

Well, yes. She was. But he was a potential client and she made a point not to go there. It was bad business. Besides, even if he hadn't been a client, she didn't have time for a lover these days, not when her company consumed most of her life.

"Well, okay, so he was involved with some kind of biker gang," she said. "But that was years ago. He's a fairly respectable businessman now."

Guy smoothed the napkin out with small, precise movements of his fingers. "Forgive me, Honor, but you have no idea what he's like now."

"Neither do you."

"Au contraire. I spent a good part of this morning investigating Woolf Construction and not all of it is good."

Honor raised an eyebrow. "Such as?"

"A number of things. Which I'm not going to go into now but suffice it to say I have my doubts. Significant doubts."

"Things, Dad? Seriously?"

"Honor, please." He picked up the napkin from his knee and put it on the table. "Gabriel Woolf is not someone I want associated with the chain. I want you to find another investor."

A burst of irritation went through her. "There are no other investors. That's the problem. No one wants to touch Tremain."

"What about Void Angel? You mentioned Eva King was interested?"

Yes, she was. But Gabriel had told her, at the end of

their meeting the night before, that Eva would put forward money only if Gabriel did. Honor had received an e-mail confirming it from Eva herself.

"Eva's conditional on Gabriel. If you don't want him, you'll lose her, too."

Her stepfather, who never swore, cursed under his breath and looked away over the crowded restaurant.

What on earth was his problem? What did he know about Woolf that she didn't?

"What's going on?" Honor asked. "I thought you'd be pleased about this."

His attention flicked back to her. Then he reached over and patted her hand where it lay on the table next to her wineglass. "I appreciate the work you put into this, dear, I really do. Never doubt that."

"I can hear the 'but.' "

His gaze became oddly focused. "Are you sure you can't find any other investors?"

"Uh, no. I've been working on this for months, you know that. No one wants to take on a failing hotel chain in this economic climate."

Guy looked pained. "Honor, please."

"I'm sorry, but 'failing' is the only word for it." She placed her other hand on the table and looked at him. She didn't know what his issue with Gabriel Woolf was but he had to put it aside. Because it wasn't just him who would lose if Tremain went down the drain. There was her mother, too and God knew, she had already been involved in the spiral of bankruptcy and debt with one man. She surely didn't need to go through it again with another.

Anyway, that wasn't even considering all the money Honor had invested in it herself.

She'd even told herself that there was a chance for some good returns. But that had always been predicated on whether or not she'd be able to get other investors to come to the party. And if she couldn't?

*No more Louboutins for you . . .*

No, dammit, it wasn't about all the pretty things she'd no longer have the money for. It was her reputation as well. She was known as one of the top investors in the city, so how would it look if she made a bad investment herself? Not good, obviously.

Honor gritted her teeth. "You don't have a lot of choice, Dad. You either take on Gabriel Woolf or you file for bankruptcy. Those are your only two options."

Guy let out a breath and picked up his wineglass. He, too had a taste for the finer things in life. Especially wine. Taking a sip, he frowned at her over the rim of his glass. "There have to be others," he said, as if expecting her to magically produce them.

"There aren't. Believe me." Trying for calm, she went on, "Think of my mother. She barely survived my dad and his debts. Going through the same thing with you would be a killer."

It was true. Elizabeth St. James had been a beautiful trophy wife whose whole world had been her children and the charitable work she'd spent most of her time on. And when Honor's father had died leaving her saddled with the gambling debt no one had known anything about, she'd fallen apart, leaving an eight-year-old Honor to fend for herself.

If Elizabeth hadn't met Guy, Honor shuddered to think what would have happened.

The look in her stepfather's eyes changed. Became softer. "Yes, that's true. And then there's the money you've invested, too, dear girl. Don't think I've forgotten about that."

Honor wanted to wave that away but couldn't bring herself to do so. Money was important. People liked to think it wasn't, that it couldn't buy you happiness but those people didn't know what it was like not to have it. To have everything taken away, leaving you with nothing. She still remembered the debt collectors. The look of shock on her mother's face as one of them had wrenched the diamond tennis bracelet off her wrist. The lack of understanding in her expression. How could they owe money? Her husband was an eminent lawyer, earning six figures.

But of course, as they'd found out, that wasn't all he was.

"Well, yes," Honor said. "There's that, too. But it's your company. You have final say."

Slowly Guy eased back in his chair. "What was he like?"

"Who?"

"Gabriel Woolf."

That didn't take much thought. "Smart. Sharp." *Sexy.* "Dangerous."

Guy's expression darkened. "So you know what I mean?"

"Yes, okay, I do. But regardless of what he was like, it's his money that counts."

"I suppose so."

At that moment, Honor's phone began to ring. She glanced down at the screen and felt a small shiver go down her spine as she saw the number. Gabriel.

"It's him," she said. "So is that going to be a yes?"

Her stepfather was scowling at the phone.

"Dad?"

"Yes," he said at last. "Since we have no choice."

A certain amount of relief poured through her, though she didn't let it show. "Great," she breathed. Then picking up the phone, she hit the answer button. "Hello, Mr. Woolf."

"You've got me on your phone already? I'm flattered."

The roughness of his deep voice made something clench hard in her stomach.

She tried to ignore the feeling. "Don't be. I have all my business contacts programmed into my phone. So you'll be pleased to know my stepfather has okayed Woolf Construction as an investment partner."

"Not that he had any other choice, am I right?"

"Oh, we had choices. Your offer was merely the best."

"But you're pleased, aren't you, little girl?"

"Am I?"

There was a small pause. "Oh, come on. Surely you didn't think I wouldn't find out about your own investment in Tremain?"

Irritation crept under her skin like a burr. Dammit. She hadn't been ready for him to find that out just yet. "Since it wasn't a secret, no, I didn't think that," she said coolly, aware of Guy's gaze on her from across the table.

"So you do have something to lose if this doesn't pan out."

"We all have things to lose, Mr. Woolf."

"Very cryptic, sweetheart. I think I'm going to enjoy finding out what those things of yours are."

"What do you mean?"

"I have a condition before I invest a dime in Tremain."

Honor went still, conscious of her heartbeat accelerating. A condition from Gabriel Woolf? She had a feeling that whatever it was, it wouldn't be good. "What is it?" she asked with as much of her earlier cool as she could muster. "And if this is a thinly disguised pickup line, you can think again."

A soft, surprisingly seductive laugh came through the phone. "Oh, baby, none of my pickup lines are ever gonna be thinly disguised, believe me. If I want you, you'll know all about it straight up."

She didn't know why that comment should make her

feel breathless, set her heartbeat racing. Because though he was a very attractive man—yes, he was, she could admit that to herself—he wasn't a man she would ever want. She preferred men with more sophistication, who were far more civilized than he was.

"Tell me." She hoped she sounded poised and calm.

"If I'm investing in Tremain Hotels, then I'm going to want to see what I'm getting for my investment."

"Well, certainly I can organize a visit to—"

"I haven't finished," he interrupted mildly. "I don't want a visit. I want a personal tour."

Honor flicked a glance at Guy. Her stepfather looked back. A cold expression had settled into the lines of his face. It made him look like a stranger. "What do you mean by personal tour?"

"What do you think I mean? I want to be shown around one of the hotels personally. By you."

A weird shock went through her. "Me? Why me?"

"You're a fellow investor, aren't you? Plus, I've heard of your reputation. I'm sure you wouldn't invest in a bad bet, just like I'm sure if anyone knows all there is to know about the company it'll be you."

She found she was gripping the phone hard. "There are many better people who could show you around, Mr. Woolf. I can even get—"

"I don't want anyone else, Honor. I want you."

She opened her mouth to voice an instinctive denial. Then stopped herself. What was the big deal? Why was she protesting? His request was reasonable and hell, even if it wasn't, if he'd made it a condition of his investment, then she had no choice but to agree to it. Just like her stepfather had no choice.

Guy's pale blue gaze was intent. "What is he saying to you?" he demanded. It was obvious that even though he couldn't hear what Gabriel was saying, he didn't like it one bit.

Honor took a little breath.

"Am I interrupting something?" Gabriel asked.

"I'm not sure you'd care if you were or not." Honor held up a finger to Guy and mouthed, *"Give me a minute."*

Guy frowned.

"No, you're right. I damn well wouldn't. So, what do you say?"

Still taken off guard, Honor murmured, "I . . . I'm not sure I have the time. I'll have to check my schedule."

"I want an answer now."

"Why?"

"Because I'm fucking impatient." He said the word with a certain amount of relish, as if he wanted to shock her.

It didn't. "You've said that word before," she said mildly. "It doesn't offend me, you know."

Again that laugh. "I guess that means I'll have to find something else then." And it didn't sound so much like a threat as a promise. "So, are you going to make the time for me, sweetheart? Or are we going to continue arguing about it?"

A personal tour. What did it matter? She could do that, couldn't she? "No," she replied, in a voice that wasn't entirely level. "I'm sure I have some time in my schedule for you."

"Good. Make it a week." Then he hung up.

# CHAPTER FOUR

"I don't like it." Eva sat back on the leather seat, arms crossed, shoulders hunched, glaring at Gabriel.

They were in her limo again, mainly because she was uncomfortable around large groups of men, and the building site Gabriel was currently working on was certainly full of men. He'd offered to meet her in the club but she'd refused, saying she was out and about anyway and was impatient to hear about how things had gone with Honor.

Zac was with her, as he often was, a large, calm, silent presence sitting in the seat beside her.

"I know you don't like it," Gabriel said, his hand resting on the hard hat he had on one knee. "But you agreed to let me handle this, Eva. You can't back out now."

Eva scowled at him. "I shouldn't have said yes."

"Why? What's the problem now?"

"You're taking advantage of her. I just know it. Why else would you have told her that Void Angel wouldn't invest if she didn't agree to you?"

Yeah, he was taking advantage. But he didn't have time for other people's scruples. Sometimes you had to do bad shit for the overall good. Like the way he'd let himself be used as a drug mule when he'd been a kid so he could earn some cash. Money so he and his mother could survive. Like when, years later, he'd become part of the club who used to make those drug runs, working his way up the hierarchy with ruthless determination until he was in a position to kick the drug-dealing scum out of his neighborhood. The brothers hadn't liked it, but by that stage he'd earned enough fear and respect that no one challenged him.

There were other ways to earn money, after all.

"Collateral damage, Eva," he said shortly. "Civilian casualties happen in war, right Zac?"

The other man gave him a level stare. "Not when they concern Eva they don't."

Zac had always been protective of her. Overprotective as far as Gabriel was concerned. Eva could look after herself, something she'd consistently proven in the five years since she'd joined their little group.

Then again, she had quite definite opinions when it came to protecting women. Gabriel had his suspicions as to why—he knew for a fact she had an entire Void Angel research team dedicated to hunting down and stopping the white-slave trade. Perhaps if she knew what he was doing, she'd agree with him.

Then again, it wasn't anything to do with her.

Eva flicked Zac an irritated glance. "Oh, for Christ's sake, don't be an asshole. You said you were here to talk about the deal, not be my guard dog."

Zac's calm demeanor didn't change in the slightest. "I'll do what I need to do, angel. Whether you like it or not."

Eva opened her mouth, probably to deny this, but then Zac added mildly, "I have to say though, I'm rather keen to find out just what war Gabriel thinks he's fighting."

"None of your fucking business," Gabriel growled, annoyed. "Honor isn't my main area of interest anyway so calm the hell down."

Eva gave him a narrow look. "Not your main area of interest? Then what—"

"Tremain," Zac interrupted softly. "It's Tremain you're after."

Gabriel said nothing. He just looked at the other two sitting opposite him, keeping his face expressionless, letting them draw whatever conclusions they wanted.

"Ah," Eva said at last. "Okay then." There was recognition in her gray eyes. Like she knew exactly where he was and what he was doing. "Don't ask, don't tell?"

One of the club's rules. They only shared what they wanted to share. No one pushed for more.

Gabriel inclined his head in an almost imperceptible nod. Maybe that would keep Eva off his back about Honor. Not that the tech CEO had anything to worry about on that score.

*Are you sure about that?*

He had a sudden flashback to Honor's smoky voice during their phone call earlier that day. *"I have heard that word before. It doesn't offend me you know . . ."* A flame of pure heat licked up inside him. He did love a challenge and Honor's words had been all challenge, making him want to find out exactly what would shock her. Mess with all her smooth, perfectly put-together sophistication. Maybe that made him a cliché but who the hell cared?

It's the devil, his mother would have told him. The devil tempting you to come out and play.

Problem was he'd played with the devil before. And liked it.

"Okay," Eva said after a long moment. "We're still good. But if I hear you're screwing with her—and don't think I don't know it's a double entendre—then I'm pulling Void Angel from the deal."

Gabriel met her gaze. There was clear, cold certainty in her smoky gray eyes but he caught a glimpse of burning anger beneath that ice. Eva had had some bad shit in her life, just as they all did, and it had left its mark.

"I don't hurt women, Eva," he said, wanting to acknowledge that anger because hell, he knew all about anger.

She looked away, down at her hands, which were folded neatly in her lap. "Yeah, fine."

A tense, uncomfortable silence fell.

"Angel, we have another meeting . . ." Zac's voice was smooth, gently reminding. Moving the conversation on.

Gabriel gave the other man a smile, one that didn't have anything to do with amusement. "The information about Tremain doesn't leave the group. This is mine. Understand?"

Zac's long mouth curved, amber gaze steady, not in the least bit perturbed by the underlying tone of threat in Gabriel's voice. "First rule of fucked-up billionaires club is you don't talk about fucked-up billionaires club. You don't need to remind me."

Gabriel gave a hoarse laugh, gripping his hard hat in one hand. "And you can never be too paranoid, Zac."

"Amen to that," Eva muttered. "Now get out of the car, Gabe. I've got shit to do."

"Oh, God, Vi, you're not meditating again, are you?"

The woman sitting cross-legged on Honor's battered red velvet couch opened one eye. "I was trying to. Guess I'm not anymore."

Honor walked into the lounge area of her expensive Upper West Side apartment and sat down in one of the armchairs opposite the couch, kicking off her red leather Jimmy Choos and dumping her purse beside them.

Violet Fitzgerald, rebellious heiress, Honor's best friend since school, and currently crashing on her couch since arriving back from Paris a week ago, watched her with assessing blue-green eyes. The way she was sitting, along with her blond dreadlocks and dripping silver jewelry, made her look like an idealistic hippie back-packer in the process of touring around India, "finding herself."

"What?" Honor resisted the urge to rub her eyes, tired-ness creeping into her bones. She hadn't realized until now how much the stress of having to deal with Guy and the whole debt problem had affected her. And it wasn't over yet. She still had this week with Gabriel Woolf to con-template. A whole damn week. She had no idea how she was going to fit that into her schedule but she was going to have to somehow.

"You look tired," Violet said, settling into the red cushions. "Tough day at the office?"

They really were nothing alike. Violet was all arty and free-spirited, rejecting her old-money New York family and their expectations at the first opportunity. Jetting off to Europe without giving a crap about her responsibilities. Not that Honor could blame her. The Fitzgeralds *were* a family who placed great stock in doing what was right and proper. They still believed in marriage as the perfect career move for their only daughter, for God's sake. No wonder Violet had always chafed against the restrictions they put on her.

Unlike Honor, of course. Who'd stuck by her own family. Who took her responsibilities seriously and was still, after all these years, trying to fix what had been broken by her father when he'd taken his own life.

"I am tired," Honor said. "And yes, tough day at the office."

Violet smoothed the silk of the wraparound Indian-print skirt she wore, silver bracelets clicking together as she did so. "You work too hard, hon, that's your problem. You did at school and you're still doing it."

"When you own your own business, you have to work hard."

But Violet wasn't fooled. "It's all this stuff with Guy, isn't it?"

Honor sighed and crossed her stocking-clad feet at the ankles. "Yes. I finally got a backer for Tremain Hotels but . . ." She stopped. This should be a good feeling, shouldn't it? So why did she suddenly feel so unsure?

"But what?"

It had been a long time since she'd confided in another person. Keeping up a calm and in-control front was vital to the success of her business, and she'd found keeping her worries and insecurities to herself was a good way of achieving that. Plus, before Guy had come along, her mother had tended to go to pieces at the drop of a hat, so Honor had had to stay strong for her sake.

But keeping up that front was exhausting, and despite the years that had passed with Violet in Europe, the two of them were still best friends.

"The backer is Gabriel Woolf."

Violet raised a pale, pierced eyebrow. "The construction dude?"

"Yes, the construction dude."

Her friend's eyebrow rose a little higher. "The hot construction dude?"

Honor opened her mouth then closed it. Anything she said now would only incriminate her. "If you mean the owner of Woolf Construction, then yes."

"But that's great, isn't it? You were worried you weren't going to come up with an investor."

"It is great. It really is."

"Then why are you scowling?"

Honor tried to unknit her brow. "He . . . had a few conditions."

"Uh-huh. And these conditions are . . . ? Come on, hon, I know you like to cultivate reserve but it's me here, okay? Didn't I tell you all about that French guy on the metro?"

Oh, yes, Violet had. Violet had told her *all* about it and even now, Honor wanted to flush with embarrassment at her friend's full and frank description of her one-night encounter. On a subway. Some things should never be spoken about, even between friends.

"This hasn't got anything to do with you and that French man," Honor said primly, pulling at the hem of her black pencil skirt. "Guy wasn't happy about Mr. Woolf coming on board but—"

"Hey, hey, whoa there." Violet held up a hand, bracelets making a silvery tinkling sound. "*Mr.* Woolf?"

This time Honor did flush. "I call all my clients by their title."

"Bullshit you do. Yesterday you were talking about George this and Eva that."

"Eva told me she didn't have a title."

"And George?"

Damn. There was a persistent crease right down near the hem of her skirt. She really needed to talk to the dry cleaner about that. "Is an old friend."

"He is not." Violet folded her arms. "This Woolf guy is getting to you, isn't he?"

Honor took a breath. She honestly didn't know why she didn't want to acknowledge Gabriel Woolf's effect on her. Maybe it was because admitting it felt like the start of a very slippery slope, one she couldn't afford to fall down. But then, Violet *was* a friend. Someone she trusted.

"Yes, okay, so he is," she said reluctantly.

Violet, bless her, didn't make any pleased noises or look satisfied. She only frowned instead. "Not good, I take it?"

"No. Not really. Because . . ." She hesitated. "He's dangerous, Vi. He . . . unsettles me. And you know if there was anyone else I could get, I'd get them in a heartbeat. But there isn't. There's only him."

Her friend nodded, chewing on her lip. "Dangerous? How?"

"You must have heard the rumors about him."

"Hey, I've been in Europe for five years. And I'm sorry, but I didn't take my subscription to *People* magazine with me."

"Okay, okay. There are rumors about how he got his start with his company. Drugs and gangs and such."

Violet rolled her eyes. "Hate to break it to you, hon, but show me the billionaire who hasn't been involved with something sketchy."

Unfortunately this was true. As she had good reason to know firsthand. "So that's not the reason he's dangerous, I admit."

Her friend's turquoise eyes gleamed. "You want him, right?"

"I didn't . . . I mean, I'm not—"

"I may not have heard rumors, but I've certainly seen pictures of him. He's hot. Why wouldn't you want him? Shit, I'd jump his bones in a second."

Honor could feel another blush creeping up on her. This was stupid. She wasn't a teenager anymore. With an effort, she stopped fiddling with her skirt and leaned back in her chair. Made herself meet her friend's interested gaze. "It's business. Strictly business."

"Bah, business. You always were such a rule follower." Violet shook her head, long golden dreads falling over her shoulders. "So what about these conditions then? They're making you antsy, I can tell."

A rule follower. Yes, she was at that. But there was nothing wrong with following the rules. As long as you were the one who got to make them. "I have to give him a personal tour of one of Guy's hotels. For a whole damn week!"

A smile curled one end of Violet's mouth. "Hon, I think he might like you."

Heat settled right down low in Honor's gut. Unexpected and unwanted. She shifted, hoping to get rid of it. "I don't care what he thinks of me." *Liar.* "I don't have the time for this stupid tour." An edge of temper had crept into her voice but she didn't bother to hide it. In fact, it felt good to let a bit of her irritation at the arrogance of Gabriel Woolf out.

Violet fell back against the couch cushions, arms still folded. Grinning, damn her. "Oh, no, no, no. It's not that you don't have time for it. You don't want to go because he makes you hot."

Honor gritted her teeth silently. "Maybe I'm attracted to him. But's that got nothing to do with anything. I still don't have the time to take a week away from work."

Violet made a skeptical-sounding noise. "Uh-huh. Why don't you say no then?"

"I can't. If I don't do what he wants then he's pulling his money. Eva King of Void Angel is going to invest, too, but she won't without Woolf. So if I don't organize this tour, I'll lose both our investors."

"Hmm, sounds like a case of rock versus hard place." Violet waggled her eyebrows suggestively. "Hard places can be nice, you know."

"Does it always have to be about sex with you?"

"Are you kidding?" Her friend's eyes opened wide in mock surprise. "What else makes the world go around? And don't tell me money 'cause then I'd have to kill you."

Honor sighed. "This isn't funny, Vi."

The amused look faded from Violet's face. "Okay, I hear you. Are you worried about him? I mean, seriously. If you think he's going to do skanky things—"

"No," Honor interrupted with absolute certainty. Because she didn't get that kind of vibe from Gabriel at all. It was more . . . *You don't trust yourself around him.* No. Hell, where had that thought come from? Because it wasn't that either. Definitely not. "I'm pretty sure he's not that kind of dangerous. It's more that I don't want to make any mistakes around him. Guy's hotel chain is at stake here. His whole livelihood. I can't afford to do anything stupid."

"As if that'll happen. I don't think you've ever done anything like that in your entire life."

For some reason that did not feel like a compliment. "Thanks for the confidence. I think."

"But really, what would stupid entail anyway?"

"Well . . . you know . . ."

"What? Falling into bed with the hot construction CEO?"

"Vi, please."

"Yeah, yeah, I know you're embarrassed." Violet unfolded her arms and leaned forward again, elbows on her knees. "You're adorable when you're being prudish."

"I'm not being prudish. You can't tell me falling into bed with him would be the world's most fantastic idea."

"Ah, so you *do* want to fall into bed with him then."

Honor eyed her. "I didn't say that."

"You don't have to. Your skin has a wide and varied vocabulary."

"I can't, Vi. It's business. It's too important for ridiculous things like sex to get in the way."

"Sex is not in any way ridiculous. At least not when it's good." Slowly, Violet straightened. "I know this is a very personal question but—"

"No, please don't."

Violet ignored her. "When *was* the last time you got laid?"

"Oh please, we're not having that discussion, are we?"

"Why not? It's a vital question."

"For you maybe. I don't suppose you had any brain waves about dinner?"

"I made a casserole and don't change the subject."

Honor blinked. She wasn't the world's best cook and last time she'd heard, neither was Violet. "You made dinner?"

"I learned a few things in Paris," Violet said with a knowing look. "And not all of them were about giving head."

"Vi, for God's sake."

"What?" With a sudden, lithe movement, her friend uncoiled from the couch in a tinkling of bracelets and a swish of silk skirts. "You need a glass of wine. Or twenty. Just wait here, I'll get you one."

Honor put her hand over her eyes. No, she didn't need a glass of wine. What she needed was a good shrink to tell her exactly why she found Gabriel Woolf so damn disconcerting. And fascinating.

A thread of sandalwood perfume drifted near. Honor took her hand away to find her friend standing beside her chair looking concerned.

"Hey," Violet said. "You're really worried about this, aren't you?"

Honor let out a breath. Because the little issue of Gabriel Woolf and her attraction to him wasn't the only problem. There was something else that had been sitting on the edge of her consciousness, just biding its time. Waiting for her to remember.

The apartment's thick curtains hid the night glitter of the city outside but it couldn't keep out the sounds of traffic or the distant blare of sirens. A busy, noisy life going on outside the quiet of the room.

"It's not just about Gabriel Woolf," Honor said at last. "There's also Alex."

"Alex?" Shock passed over Violet's delicate features. "But how?"

"The two of them were friends, remember? Woolf told me he's still in touch with him."

"Jesus."

"Yes. It's going to make for an interesting week." Understatement of the year. Probably of the whole damn century.

Violet frowned down at her. "This could be good, Honor," she said after a moment. "You wanted to know what happened to Alex, right? Now's your chance."

"Actually I don't know if I want to. He left without a word and . . ." She stopped abruptly, the old anger a small hot ball in the center of her chest. No, she wouldn't let herself feel it. She wouldn't expend any more emotion on the brother who had abandoned her and her mother. She downright refused to.

Violet was silent and Honor didn't feel the need to offer any further explanations. Her friend knew the deal anyway, had been the ear Honor had poured out all her teenage angst to back when they were still at school together.

"What about your mom?" Violet said at last. "I would think she'd want to know."

The exhaustion crept deeper into Honor's bones. Of course her mother would want to know. Alex's disappearance had just about killed her. "I guess I *really* have no choice but to go now."

Violet moved, her fingers brushing reassuringly over Honor's where they rested on the arm of her chair. "Don't worry, hon. You can handle this Gabriel guy. You'll be fine. Now, how about you kick back while I go pour you a wine?"

Honor only nodded. And hoped like hell that her friend was right.

\* \* \*

The arrangements took Honor nearly a week. Weston did something miraculous and somehow managed to clear her schedule, though it meant working a few twelve-hour days in order to get through the work she already had on her plate so that it wouldn't back up into unmanageable proportions while she was away. Then she had to organize things with Guy and one of his hotels.

The chain stretched around the globe, but only two had been fully remodeled into Guy's idea of a luxury eco-hotel, one in Mexico and one in Vermont. Although the idea of Mexican heat appealed to her—especially given the winter New York was currently experiencing—Vermont was closer. Plus Mexico felt too much like a vacation, and this was definitely not going to be a vacation. This was purely business. She was going to have to bring some work with her since Gabriel had insisted on a week, but she really didn't mind that. Anything to keep her mind on the job and not on the fascinating Mr. Woolf.

She decided not to give Gabriel the choice of which hotel, sending him the details of the Vermont property in a terse and to-the-point e-mail. She hoped he'd respond in a like fashion but—predictably—he didn't.

A whole minute after pressing send her phone rang.

"Mr. Woolf," she said, not even bothering to check her caller ID. "You have an issue with the details I sent you?"

"You got a problem with Mexico?"

Honor swiveled her chair around to look out of the windows of her office, staring sightlessly across Midtown New York as Gabriel's rough, heated voice brushed over her like velvet.

In a building across the street, a man was making himself coffee. Honor concentrated on him, watching him through the windows so she didn't feel the strange restlessness that gathered inside her as Gabriel spoke.

"Mexico can't accommodate us," she lied. "Vermont is closer."

"Pity. I would have liked to see you in a bikini."

The man was pouring cream into his cup. Stirring. "I don't have a bikini," Honor replied. "Besides, a bikini is hardly appropriate work wear. This is business, Mr. Woolf. In case you'd forgotten."

"Oh, I hadn't, little girl. When it comes to business, I never forget."

"Can we do without the patronizing endearments, please?"

"I was going tell you that I'd stop it with the 'little girl' if you stop it with the 'Mr. Woolf.' But I've decided I like the 'Mr. Woolf.' So I tell you what, you pick one endearment and I'll leave it at that."

The man across the street was now ladling in some sugar. It appeared he liked his coffee very sweet. Honor took a slow, silent breath. Arguing about names was ridiculous. Pointless. Yet she couldn't seem to stop herself. She knew it was a game he was playing with her, a manipulation, and though every part of her told her it was a bad idea, she couldn't seem to resist playing it, too.

"I've changed my mind," she said. "How about I stop calling you 'Mr. Woolf' and you can be 'little boy' instead?"

He laughed, a soft, liquid sound that made her toes want to curl inside her expensive stilettos. "You want to play my game? Is that how this week is going to go? Because I gotta tell you, I'm not at all unhappy about that."

"I don't play games, Mr. Woolf. I do business."

"I'm sure you do. In which case if it's business you're after, you'd better stop flirting with me."

No, she would not react. She would not let him get under her skin. "Time is money, and this conversation has already taken up more of both than I would like. Is there anything more you'd like to talk to me about?"

"No, I think we're done. The Vermont place looks good." The heat had vanished from his voice, leaving it rough and cold. "I'll get a chopper to take us."

"Thank you but I can make my own way." Honor made sure her tone was the very essence of politeness. There was no way she was going to be reliant on him for her transportation to and from the hotel. Something told her she'd need to be able to get away in a hurry if she had to.

"Yeah, okay," he said.

Honor blinked, nonplussed by his capitulation. "Fine. That's settled then."

"You sound surprised. Did you want me to insist?"

"No, of course not."

"You could ride with me instead." There was the barest hint of amusement in his voice.

"Ride? On what?" She didn't even know why she was asking since she already knew she didn't want to "ride" with him.

"My bike. I've got plenty of room for you on the back." Again with the amusement that got under her skin like a burr under a blanket.

"Thank you, but I believe I'll drive."

"Of course you will. In that case I'll see you up there, sweetheart." He didn't wait for a response, hanging up almost immediately, leaving Honor feeling vaguely frustrated and annoyed.

*Of course you will.* The arrogance implicit in that small sentence. As if he knew her. Knew everything about her.

The kitchen across the street was empty, the man making his coffee long gone. But this time Honor didn't notice.

If Gabriel Woolf wanted to play head games with her, then dammit she'd play them.

But if he thought he was going to win, then he was in for a nasty surprise.

# CHAPTER FIVE

At the top of the hill Gabriel pulled the Norton up on the side of the icy road and checked his GPS. Not far to go now. The hotel should be just up ahead and around the corner. Kicking down the stand of the bike, he raised the visor of his helmet to take a good look at the surrounding view. Mountains and forest heavily covered with snow, an icy lake to his left. The snow lent a muffled, dense quality to the silence around him that reminded him of his lodge in the Rockies. A peace that he'd never found inside a church, much to his mother's disappointment.

But it had always been that way with him. Once, a teacher at school had shown him a book about nature and there had been pictures of mountains, forests, and lakes. Places the noise and the dirt and the squalor of the city hadn't touched. Afterward he used to dream about going to such places because he imagined them to be cleaner, purer than the shitty tenement he lived in with his mother. Quieter, too. More peaceful.

Dreams about going and living in a cabin in the woods, by a lake. Where he'd fish for his mom and they'd be happy.

Fuck, what an innocent he'd been back then.

Gabriel sat back on the bike, inhaled, then let it out, his breath clouding in the cold air. Alex had his clubs and the women he lost himself inside of. Zac had his Caribbean island. And Eva . . . well, who knew what Eva had since she never revealed anything about herself. But this was his. The forest. The silence. A break from the anger that seemed to devour him whole whenever he was in the city.

The ride from New York had taken him over five hours, but he hadn't minded. Speed and the wilderness and silence in his head. Sometimes that was all he needed.

At that moment his phone buzzed in the pocket of his motorcycle leathers. Briefly, he debated not answering it since when he was away, he was damn well away, but then again, it could be Honor.

Dragging the phone out, Gabriel glanced down at the screen. But it wasn't from Honor. It was from Alex.

*You want to go out tonight? Second Circle. 9 p.m.*

Gabriel hadn't told his friend about this week he'd planned with Honor. He hadn't told anyone except a few of his people, and as far as they were concerned, he was in an important meeting for a week and wasn't to be disturbed. No one needed to know what he was doing or what his plans were.

He stared at Alex's message. The guy clearly kept tabs on his sister but did he know Honor wouldn't be around this week either? Would he put two and two together? He might, considering Gabriel had already made it known he was interested in Honor's investor quest.

Perhaps a different kind of man might have felt guilty about using his best friend's little sister in such a way. But guilt was the one emotion Gabriel never let himself feel. Not when his mother had had enough for both of them.

Besides, it wasn't as if he had anything to feel guilty about. He had his rule. He wouldn't harm her. What he wanted was information and he'd use whatever he could to get it. Even the attraction that burned between them. Christ, he'd be stupid not to.

*No,* Gabriel texted Alex back at last. *I'm out of state this week. Catch you when I get back.*

There was a moment's pause, then a reply pinged back. *All the more chicks for me then.*

Gabriel snorted and stuck his phone in his pocket. Then he kicked the bike's stand up, opened the throttle, and pulled out onto the road.

Ten minutes later he turned onto a long driveway that led through densely packed, snow-clad trees. Eventually it opened out onto a wide sweep past an elegant wood-and-stone building—the main lodge.

Gabriel cast a professional eye over it as he pulled up and parked his bike, approving the simplicity of the architecture. The building wasn't fussy, with clean lines, a steeply pitched roof, and wide eaves. It had clearly been built to a high-spec and from what he could see, the workmanship was solid. There was nothing cheap or shoddy about this place. Tremain had obviously spent, and spent big on it.

A valet ran out as he got off the bike but Gabriel warned the guy off with a look. No one touched the Norton, let alone drove it. Grabbing his only piece of luggage, a battered leather kit bag, Gabriel slung it over his shoulder and headed for the entrance, pulling off his helmet as he went.

The interior of the hotel was all dark wood, thick carpet, and subtle lighting, giving it an air of quiet, discreet luxury. As he approached the reception desk, the concierge, a precisely coiffed blond woman, looked up and gave him a welcoming smile. "Ah, Mr. Woolf. Good afternoon. We've been expecting you. Are you ready to check in?"

Gabriel didn't bother with pointless niceties. "Is Ms. St. James here yet?" he asked brusquely.

The woman's smile didn't falter, which was kudos to her professionalism. "Not as of yet. She did say she'd be here about four, which is any moment now."

That was good. If she wasn't here yet, he had a chance to check on the accommodations she'd arranged for them. Because he was betting she'd placed herself a long way from where he was, and that just wasn't going to happen. He wanted them to be close together. Mainly so he could unsettle her, get under her skin, because people who were unsettled often let slip things they didn't mean to say.

"What rooms have you got us in?" he asked, leaning an elbow on the desk.

The woman's gaze flickered over him in a way he'd long come to recognize. Helpless interest. Lucky for her, she wasn't his kind of prey.

"Ah . . . Ms. St. James has organized one of the cottages by the lake for you and a room in the main lodge for herself."

Of course she had. "Change it," Gabriel ordered. "Ms. St. James will be in the cottage with me."

The only surprise the receptionist betrayed was a slight tightening of the mouth. Good. Perhaps she'd be allowed to keep her job when Gabriel became owner.

"Certainly I can do that," the woman said. "But perhaps I should check—"

"I think you'll find Ms. St. James will be perfectly happy with the arrangement." He let his mouth curve, giving the woman a meaningful look.

She picked up on his meaning right away, at least judging from the flush that crept over her face. "Oh, I see."

"I'm sure you do."

"I'll change the arrangements immediately, Mr. Woolf."

He let his smile linger. "Excellent decision."

"What's an excellent decision?"

Gabriel didn't move for a second, keeping his back to the hotel's entrance, anticipation curling tight in his gut. So Honor had arrived. What perfect timing.

Slowly, he turned around.

Honor stood in the middle of the foyer, small, fine-boned, and immaculate in a tailored black trench coat belted tightly around her narrow waist. In one hand was the handle of a little wheeled suitcase, following behind her like a dog on a leash, while the other held her cell phone. The cold had brought a flush to her cheeks, making her blue eyes seem even bluer. She tucked away her cell into the purse she wore over one shoulder and raised an eyebrow at him in that way he remembered from their meeting at the club. Imperious and slightly mocking.

He leaned back against the reception desk on his elbows, taking in the sight of her and not bothering to hide it. Shit, he couldn't deny there was chemistry between them. Intense chemistry.

How long since he'd experienced attraction like this? A long time. Maybe never . . .

"Were you trying to tease me, baby?" he drawled.

A wary look flickered in her eyes. "Tease you?"

"Yeah. With the sleeping arrangements." He gave her a slow smile. "You had us in separate rooms."

The flush in her cheeks deepened. She glanced at the receptionist briefly before looking back at him, and he could see she was already assessing the situation, trying to figure out what was going on. After a moment she said, "I thought you would prefer it." Her expression gave absolutely nothing away

Goddamn but she was good.

"After one little argument?" He shook his head. "Sweetheart, no. What I prefer is you in my bed."

Her jaw tightened, her gaze flicking to the receptionist again, gauging the woman's reaction a moment before coming back to him. "I see." Her voice was rock-steady and still as cool as the fall of snow. "Well, by all means, change it if you like."

So. No protest. No argument. She wasn't going to give him any of the expected reactions, was she? Interest curled like a hook, digging into him. Fuck, that was good. No, that was fantastic. Because he didn't want this to be easy. Things were always so much sweeter when you had to fight for them. He should know. He'd fought like a bastard for everything he had.

"Oh, don't worry. I already have. You and I will be in the cottage near the lake."

Honor smiled and it wasn't the smile of a lover. It was sharp as an icicle and just as cold. "That's wonderful." Her attention turned to the receptionist and her smile became much warmer. "Thanks, Heather. Hope it wasn't a bother to change."

"Not at all, Miss St. James. Shall I get Sam to bring your bags down?"

"That would be great." Honor's gaze caught his and she raised that eyebrow again. "Coming, Mr. Woolf?" The delicate sarcasm that edged his name was a challenge of the subtlest kind. And Christ, if she thought it would go over his head, she was dead wrong.

She had no idea who she was taking on, she really didn't. And if he had any decency at all, he would stop right now and leave her alone.

But he wasn't going to stop. Because the fact was he had no decency. None at all. Decency was one luxury he'd never been able to afford.

Honor waited until Sam had delivered their bags into the wide, open living area of the cottage. Then, as the door closed behind him, she turned back to the man whose overwhelming presence made the spacious room feel like a tiny closet.

He stood over by the huge picture window that looked out toward the lake, the backdrop of the icy expanse of water and the surrounding snowcapped mountains behind him, and for a second she didn't know what was more impressive, him or the view. Dressed in black motorcycle leathers, a white T-shirt stretched over his powerful chest, he looked big and mean and downright intimidating. Which should have warned her off. Yet somehow, she found that just as compelling and magnetic as she had the night they'd met.

*This is a job, remember? You have to keep things professional.*

Yes, this was business, wasn't it? Then again, there was no business-related reason she could think of as to why he'd changed their accommodations or made it look like they were sleeping together.

No, the only reason she could think of was that he'd done it to screw with her, get some kind of reaction. To up the game he was playing.

Fine. She'd come prepared. He could up whatever the hell he wanted, she could handle it. She hadn't gotten where she was today by being a pushover.

Honor folded her arms, betraying none of the anger she felt. "So, I assume I'll take the second bedroom?"

He studied her for a long moment. "You're not going to mention the fact I just blatantly changed your booking?"

"No. Did you want me to?"

A smile curved his sensual mouth. "Oh, very good," he murmured approvingly. "You're learning. And I suppose you're not going to let on how angry you are about the fact I let the receptionist believe we're lovers either?"

"I'm not angry. I don't care what the receptionist believes."

His dark eyes swept over her. "Bullshit. You're angry, sweetheart, but you're trying very hard not to show it."

Honor kept her expression absolutely neutral, determined not to let anything slip. She lifted one shoulder in a casual shrug. "Does this really matter? Look, if you want us to share the cottage then fine. It's no skin off my nose."

"Uh-huh." He was still a second, watching her. Then he shrugged off his leather jacket in a smooth movement and tossed it carelessly down on the couch. With a slow, easy stride, he crossed the room toward her and in spite of herself, Honor's breath caught, a surge of adrenaline rushing through her. Her body wanted her to run but she held her ground. Flight had always been more Alex's style than hers; she was fight all the way.

Gabriel stopped inches away, looking down at her. There was something disturbingly perceptive in his gaze that made her feel like he'd peeled her open, laying bare all her fears and desires. Her darkest secrets. She forced herself to look back, meet him stare for stare.

"You're not going to give me a thing, are you?" he murmured, his dark, husky voice making the words sound intimate. Sensual. "Do you have any idea how much of a challenge that is to a man like me?"

Her heart began to race, but she'd had a lot of practice at staying cool under pressure. "I'm not here to challenge you, Mr. Woolf." Thank God her voice was steady as a rock. "I'm here to discuss this investment and that's all."

"Bullshit you're not here to challenge me." The light was behind his tall figure, gilding the blond spikes of his hair and shadowing his face, making his eyes seem even darker. "Standing there all cool, calm, and collected in that tight little trench coat. Acting like I don't affect you in any way. What's that if not a challenge?"

Dammit. There was no escaping her physical reaction to his nearness, her heart racing faster, an ache gathering tightly down low inside her. She could feel his warmth and he smelled of leather, a rich, spicy scent that made her think of what it would be like to ride with him on the back of that massive black motorcycle she'd seen parked outside the front of the hotel. Her thighs spread on either side of his, her arms around his lean waist, pressed up against his back, leaving everything behind. Her mother, her stepfather, her business . . .

*No. Don't go there. Don't even think it.*

God, no. Not when she kept the weakness deep inside herself. The wild, irresponsible part of her that loved a challenge, a game, an adrenaline rush. It was a vulnerability she and Alex had inherited from their father and she knew where it ultimately led: to destruction. She indulged it every so often with a little harmless credit-card abuse at her favorite shops, but that was it.

Control. That was the key. It had kept her away from the abyss for years. She could not afford to let it slip now.

"You don't affect me." She kept her arms tightly folded and her voice cool and steady. Telling him. Telling herself. "Which is why I don't give a damn where I sleep. But all that aside, haven't we got more important things to do than trade double-entendres?"

His laugh, a soft, lazy sound, felt like the brush of velvet over her skin. "Don't worry. We have plenty of time for all those important things. I'm not interested in talking business right at the moment."

"So what are you interested in talking about then?"

He tilted his head to the side, his gaze following down the line of her body and back up again, making it very,

very clear what he was interested in. "I would very much like to talk about when we start fucking."

The word was a harsh, sharp jolt. But there was also a brutal eroticism to it that touched something raw inside her. That wild part . . .

Honor took a small, silent breath to steady herself. "Charming, as ever, Mr. Woolf. I'm flattered, obviously. But you should know that sex isn't part of my negotiating method." She managed a patient smile. "Besides, I never mix business with pleasure."

The expression on his face didn't change. "That's a shame. And ordinarily, I'd leave it at that. But in this case, you're ignoring one very important variable."

"I am? Well, don't keep me in suspense, please."

Without any hurry at all, Gabriel reached out and deftly pulled open the belt that held her trench coat closed. Then he settled his large, shockingly warm hands on her hips and tugged her right up against him.

He did it so slowly. She had plenty of time to get away. And afterward, she couldn't understand why she hadn't. Why she hadn't stepped back, told him not to touch her ever again. But she didn't. Her arms unfolded and she just stood there, her mind utterly blank as her body settled against his, as the heat of him burned like a furnace through the layers of leather and wool and silk. Burned until she was sure she could feel it against her bare skin.

"Sexual chemistry," he said. "That's the variable you're forgetting, Honor."

She didn't move. To be honest, she couldn't move. Even thinking was difficult right now. She didn't know where to put her hands so she kept them by her side, trying to keep her fingers relaxed and loose. But it was difficult with his body right . . . *there. Oh yes, right there . . .*

"What about it?" she asked, struggling and failing to stop the huskiness from creeping into her voice. To stop herself from melting against the hard expanse of his chest.

His fingers flexed on her hips, squeezing gently, and her breathing almost stopped. God, she wasn't that hard up that his slightest touch could steal everything from her, was she?

"Sweetheart, if you have to ask me that question," his voice was soft, rough, and hypnotic, "then you've never felt it before."

She could feel his hips against hers, the ridge of his cock pressing between her thighs. Large and hard, just like the rest of him. She found herself looking up into his eyes. They were black as night, a velvet kind of darkness that would wrap her up and drown her in sensuality. In heat . . .

*He'd be rough. Would probably hold her down. And he'd fuck her, make her take him and she'd love it. The ultimate rush . . .*

He gave another one of those husky laughs. "Looks to me like we've got an interesting week ahead of us, hmm?" Then before she was ready—way, way before—he let her go, stepping back and turning toward the door to the bedroom. "Think about the answer to my question, Honor," he said casually as he went ahead and pulled it open. "I want the answer as soon as I've finished my shower."

She couldn't think. Her brain felt fuzzy, the blood hammering in her veins. How on earth had that happened? "What?" Her voice sounded all thin and breathy. Dammit. "What question?"

"I thought I was clear. But if you need me to repeat it, I will."

It was a struggle but she managed to pull herself together enough to say, "Oh, you mean the question about us fucking?" She was pleased with herself as to how casually she said the word, since she almost never cursed.

"I can tell you the answer right now. Never, Mr. Woolf. You and I will never start fucking."

Gabriel's smile was that of a predator. "Keep telling yourself that. But you and I both know I could have had you over the arm of that couch not five seconds ago. And you wouldn't have stopped me."

She had no answer to that. Because she suspected the bastard was right, she wouldn't have. Which was a warning sign. If he could overwhelm her control as easily as that then she needed to be doubly on her guard. Her body might crave him, but that didn't mean she had to give it what it wanted. That was how addiction began.

Honor lifted her chin and gave him back the cool stare she'd patented years ago. "Would you have even asked?"

She thought she saw something that was less than his usual arrogant assurance flicker in his eyes. Something that was almost like . . . unease. "I always ask," he said flatly. "Always." Then he turned and went into the bedroom, pulling the door shut after him.

Honor stared. And for some strange reason, it felt like she'd won.

Gabriel sat in the guest library of the hotel later that evening and stared at the screen of his laptop. He was supposed to be checking e-mails, but for some reason he couldn't seem to concentrate. His fingers tightened around the crystal tumbler of single malt he'd brought in with him and he raised it, swallowing a mouthful. The alcohol burned, joining the other fire already burning in his gut, making it impossible to concentrate.

He shifted in the old leather armchair, grimacing. Trying to get the hard-on in his jeans to lay the hell down and leave him alone.

He hadn't had it so bad in years. Honor St. James and her sexy little body. He hadn't been wrong about their sexual chemistry, and yeah, he'd lost his head a bit, wanting a reaction from her, some kind of fucking acknowledgement instead of that cool stare she kept giving him. He, whose self-control was always ironclad.

Christ, he was an idiot. Sure, he'd known there was attraction there, but he hadn't realized until he'd touched her how strong it actually was. She'd felt . . . so good against him. Her warmth and softness at odds with her cool, calm exterior. Then she'd looked up at him, her blue eyes gone dark and deep. Smoky with desire. And he'd felt something inside him shudder and wake up.

A beast he kept chained and locked away.

*"Would you even have asked?"*

Abruptly Gabriel closed the laptop, dumped it onto the table beside him and drained the scotch in his tumbler. Then he pushed himself out of his chair and began to pace around the room, propelled by a strange kind of restlessness he didn't have a name for.

The hotel library was the same as most he'd been in, lots of tall bookshelves and wood-paneled walls. A huge fireplace with a fire burning bright. A few high-backed chairs and sofas scattered around. A bit like their meeting room at the Second Circle.

There were no other guests around so he gave in to the restlessness, pacing over to the fire then to the bookshelves, to the heavily curtained windows then back to his chair again.

He'd fucked up. Pushed her too hard, been too blunt. Let their attraction get in the way. He wanted information from her and that meant he needed her open and receptive, not offended and pulling away. Even worse that *she* was the one who'd gotten under *his* guard rather than the other way around.

He hadn't liked her dig about him not asking. It made

him uncomfortable, made him aware of his own boundaries and how he was testing them with his plans for her.

Damn woman was too smart and too perceptive for her own good, and it was going to mean he had to get a firm grip on this chemistry. Change his approach. Find a new game plan.

He stopped near the fire as his phone began to ring. Digging it out of his back pocket, he checked the screen. Eva. Interesting.

Hitting the accept button, he answered it. "What's up?"

"You at the hotel?"

"Yeah."

"Does it look promising?"

"Your stock, standard luxury resort so far. I'll know more once I have a chance to look around the property."

"Okay, well, I found something . . . interesting. I'm not sure if it's anything to worry about yet, but I thought you should know."

"What is it?"

"I wanted to see their computer system, check out their level of security, etcetera."

Gabriel knew what was coming. "You hacked in?"

"Their security is shit."

"Uh-huh."

"Good thing they're wanting Void Angel's investment, that's all I can say. Anyway, so I was checking out the reservation system—not just this hotel, but the whole chain— having a look at guest numbers and things, and I noticed that they've had a quite a few cancellations."

"So? That's unusual how?"

"They were all cancellations less than twenty-four hours before the guests were due to arrive."

Gabriel stilled, staring sightlessly at the fire. He knew crime. These days he was all about the straight and narrow, but over the years he'd developed a kind of sixth sense when it came to suspicious activity. And this had suspicious written all over it.

"How many cancellations are we talking about here?"

"For each hotel not more than two or three, but the chain as a whole? Worldwide? Enough that I noticed. I mean, it could be nothing. Bad hotel reviews maybe or just coincidence."

"But you don't think that."

Eva paused. "No, I don't."

"Any ideas about what's going on?"

"A few. I'll keep investigating and see what I can come up with. I'm beginning to think that the financials aren't the only thing sketchy about Tremain Hotels."

Intriguing. Was Tremain up to something other than just bad management? "Let me know if you find anything then."

After he'd ended the call, Gabriel stuck his phone back in his pocket, continuing to stare into the fire for a long moment.

If there was something sketchy about Tremain, then Eva and her hacking skills would track it down. But she wasn't the only one who had resources. He had a valuable source of information all of his own, a source who was, right at that moment, down in the cottage, probably getting ready for bed.

He smiled. Honor St. James might turn out to be even more useful than he'd thought. All he had to do was find the key to unlocking her.

And he would.

He always did.

# CHAPTER SIX

Honor stepped away from Gabriel and Lindsay, the hotel manager, glancing down at her phone to see who'd texted her. Another one from Guy checking up on how things were progressing with Gabriel and whether he'd made an investment decision. That was the third one today.

She frowned. She knew he wasn't happy, but did he really need to keep texting her about it? He wasn't usually this impatient.

The whole morning had been taken up with giving Gabriel his promised tour of the hotel, with Lindsay along to answer questions about the day-to-day management. It had been, quite frankly, exhausting. Gabriel was a man who missed nothing and had a question about everything, from the kind of wood used in the construction, to the energy efficiency of the solar panels on the roof, to the staffing levels of the hotel during the off-peak season.

He was now, as they stood near the boathouse on the icy lakefront, grilling Lindsay on occupancy levels, and it was a relief not to have his fierce attention focused on her for a few moments.

Her breath frosted in the icy air as she quickly texted Guy back a *"no decision made as yet"* response, then pocketed her phone in her coat, glancing over to where Gabriel and Lindsay stood.

He'd left her alone the night before, staying up in the hotel's library to "work." She'd had a room service dinner and then decided on an early night, her heart thumping, all her senses on high alert as she'd undressed for bed. Like he was going to come and batter down her door, throw her on the bed and take her, eat her up like the wolf he was named for.

A totally ridiculous thought and yet she'd lain there in bed, unable to sleep, half terrified, listening to every sound, and the other half of her . . . *wanting him to do exactly that.*

No. No, of course she didn't want him to do that. How stupid to even imagine she would.

And when she'd woken up in the morning, decidedly unravished, she'd been relieved. She'd needed the breathing space and some time to get her head back in order. Time to make sure her armor was firmly in place. Yes, he was a temptation, but now that she knew just how much of one, she'd be on her guard. She wasn't going to be as weak as she had been the day before. She couldn't afford to be.

He was a client. And that was all.

Footsteps sounded and she looked up as Gabriel came toward her, stalking across the snowy ground like a panther, his hands thrust into the pockets of his jeans, heavy black boots making crunching sounds in the snow.

She straightened. Already she could feel herself tensing up in response to his nearness, which was irritating in the extreme. "I hope you left poor Lindsay alive. I don't think he was expecting to be grilled quite so intensely."

Gabriel lifted a shoulder. "He's still breathing. You have a problem with me asking questions?"

"No, but we don't often have investors who want to know every single detail."

"Details are important. Especially where money is concerned. And most especially when it's my money."

"Fair enough. You have more you want to see?"

"Not today." The winter sunlight gilded his hair in stark contrast to the darkness of his eyes as they swept over her, assessing.

"Good," she said, trying to ignore the accelerated beat of her heart. "Then you won't mind if we go inside now. In case you hadn't noticed, it's cold."

He didn't move. "I owe you an apology, Honor."

For a second, she wondered whether or not she'd heard him correctly. "Excuse me?"

"Do you really want me to say it again?"

"Actually, yes. I think you should."

The corner of his long mouth turned up, the hint of a smile softening the brutally handsome cast of his features. "You like to push the boundaries, don't you, sweetheart? I'm apologizing. For my behavior yesterday. I was out of line."

Honor tried not to let her shock show. She didn't think Gabriel Woolf was a man who apologized a lot. Or even at all. "Well, thank you. And yes, you were."

Another opaque sweep of those dark eyes. "Will you let me make it up to you?"

She gave him a wary look, not quite sure how to take this apparently penitent, sincere side of him. "How?"

"I was wondering if you'd like to go for a ride with me. Shake out the cobwebs a little. Leave business behind for an hour or so."

"A ride? On what?"

"What do you think? I have a bike."

"You're kidding."

The opaque look faded, a glint of wickedness in the depths of his eyes that should not have been as seductive as it was. "What's the matter? You don't like my bike?"

It wasn't so much the bike—though riding on the back of that huge black machine seemed a little insane—as the thought of wrapping her arms around him, of her legs on either side of his, that fantasy she'd had in the cottage the day before. Such temptation . . .

"I have no feelings about your bike either way," Honor said, staunchly ignoring the vision in her head. "But it's cold and I don't have the appropriate clothing."

"And if you were to have appropriate clothing?"

"It's a moot point since I don't."

Gabriel glanced through the trees toward the main building of the hotel. "Okay," he said in a neutral voice. "Your loss." Without another word he turned and began striding back along the snowy path to the hotel.

Honor stared after him. What? Gabriel Woolf accepting a refusal? Without even trying to get her to change her mind? Irritated with the strange discomfort that sat in her gut, Honor began walking up the path after his tall figure.

First an apology and then the offer of going out with him. Odd. Didn't seem like his usual modus operandi. Up until now, he'd been blunt to the point of offensiveness about what he wanted and he certainly hadn't liked her refusing him.

A man who got his way. That was Gabriel.

So why had he accepted her refusal without a word? More to the point, why did she care? She didn't want to go for a ride on his big black bike. Not at all.

*Perhaps he didn't really want you to go after all?*

But then why would he have asked in the first place?

Honor frowned and shrugged away the thoughts. God, it seemed way too teenage and desperate to be analyzing his intentions so thoroughly. She was a professional woman in her late twenties with her own business and quite enough other things to worry about without being fixated on a man as dangerous and so obviously wrong for her as Gabriel.

A couple of minutes later, Honor stepped back into the hotel foyer, shivering in delight as the warmth of the central heating chased away the winter chill. Gabriel had vanished, God knows where, but she wasn't about to go after him. Her feet were uncomfortable in the snow boots Lindsay had found for her to borrow on their trek over the hotel's grounds, and all she wanted to do was get the boots off and sit in front of the fire at the cottage.

"Ms. St. James?"

She looked over to see Heather smiling at her and tapping a couple of extremely large bags sitting on the reception desk. "These came for you."

"Really? I'm not expecting anything." Slowly, she walked over to the desk and examined the name on the bags. Hers. Frowning, she pulled open the edge of one and peered inside. Something black and leather was folded up. Her frown deepened. "Where did these come from?"

"A courier brought them in first thing this morning."

There was store branding on the front of the bags but she didn't recognize the name. Weird. She looked in bag number two. More leather and something shiny in dark blue. Reaching into the bag, she slowly withdrew the shiny thing. A motorcycle helmet.

"Oh," she said, understanding beginning to dawn.

"Now you can't say you don't have anything appropriate to wear," said a deep voice from behind her.

God, how did the man manage to move so quietly?

Honor turned and found herself catching her breath yet again.

Gabriel stood behind her, a black motorcycle helmet casually held in one hand. He was wearing his leathers and she still hadn't forgotten how incredibly sexy he looked in them, even though she quite desperately wanted to.

"What are these?" She waved a hand at the bags.

"A couple of things to wear in case you change your mind about a ride."

"But I already told you I'm not going on a ride with you."

"You said you didn't have anything to wear. Now you do."

Honor silently wished him to hell. Sadly, he remained standing there. "I have work to do," she managed, somewhat lamely.

"That's not the best excuse I've ever heard."

"It's not an excuse."

"Isn't it?" He raised one straight dark brow. "There's nothing to be scared of. Just you and me and some fresh air."

She hated the way he kept challenging her as if she was a kid who needed to prove herself. Because she wasn't a kid. She was a grown woman who didn't have to prove anything to anyone.

*But when was the last time a man kept you on your toes like this one?*

She couldn't remember. A long time. Mainly because she preferred easier men.

Against her will, excitement began to kindle in her gut. "Don't be ridiculous," she said in what she hoped was a level tone. "I'm not scared."

Gabriel's mouth curved as he walked over to her, and she couldn't help tensing up as he came close. He slid his arm around her waist in an easy, affectionate movement, urging her up against his big, powerful, leather-clad body. "Baby, I'll keep you safe. You know that." His voice was dark and rough and full of warmth, that smile playing around his mouth.

All for the benefit of the receptionist, naturally. Keeping up the lie he'd perpetrated about them being lovers. It made her want to slap his face and push him away but that would reveal way too much. But deep in his eyes, that challenge glinted. Like he knew how much she hated this and wanted a response from her. As if he relished it.

Adrenaline spiked in her bloodstream, a dangerous rush, and before she quite knew what she was doing, she'd put her hands on his chest and was rising up on her toes, brushing that cruel, smiling mouth with hers. Answering his challenge.

And as soon as she'd done it, she knew it had been a stupid move. Incredibly, ridiculously stupid.

A bolt of something elemental and wild shot straight down her spine. Like summer lightning or the howling force of a hurricane. For a minute she couldn't move, standing there, her hands pressed to his chest, her mouth touching his, turning to stone as the wildness between them began to grow in a chaos of sparks and flashes of electricity.

Then the voice of reason said very clearly in her head, *no*.

Honor drew back, fighting for breath, trying to be calm while everything inside her was still whirling from the tornado that had struck. There was shock on Gabriel's face, and something else, a glimpse of something as desperate and hungry as the chemistry that had ignited between them.

She'd surprised him then.

Satisfaction gripped her and even though she was still trembling inside, she kept a cool smile on her face. "Of course you'll keep me safe, darling," she said, allowing a touch of sarcasm to rest on the endearment. "I suppose I'd better check and see what you got me."

She turned around, not wanting to look at him again quite yet, busying herself with the bags, conscious of the receptionist's fascinated gaze on the pair of them.

*You kissed him, you idiot. He's a potential client and even apart from that, he's far too much for you to handle. What the hell were you thinking?*

She hadn't been thinking, that was the problem. She'd just responded to his unspoken challenge without a thought, wanting to push him harder, revel in the wild surge of excitement at testing him.

Dangerous to indulge that part of her. That sensual weakness. So damn dangerous. Kissing Gabriel Woolf was a slippery slope she could fall down and never stop falling.

Honor forced the fizzing, bubbling excitement away, pulling open one of the bags instead.

There was a movement behind her, Gabriel's leather-clad elbow resting on the reception counter. She kept her attention on the bags, but it was difficult to concentrate when every sense she had seemed attuned to the figure of the man standing next to her.

She drew out a biker jacket. It was surprisingly heavy, the leather padded and soft.

The receptionist made a sighing kind of sound. "Wow. Nice."

It was. Too nice.

Honor folded it up and put it back in the bag. "You shouldn't have," she said to Gabriel. "This is wasted on me."

"Is it?" This time his voice was utterly neutral. Enough to make her glance at him. There was no shock or hunger on his face now, his features expressionless. "I'll send it back then." He turned his head to look at the receptionist. "Heather, could you ring the store these came from, please? Tell them I need to get a refund on—"

"Wait," Honor said, interrupting before she could think straight. "I didn't say I didn't want them." She didn't quite know why she didn't want Gabriel to send them back, especially when she wasn't going to be using them, but . . .

His gaze came back to hers. "If you want them, put them on and meet me out front in five minutes. If you don't, leave them here and I'll send them back." He pushed himself away from the desk with a lazy movement, then turned and walked toward the entrance without another word.

Honor watched him go, her heart thumping. God, what the hell was she doing? Every time he got in her vicinity she felt like she kept making mistakes. Daring him. Kissing him. Fighting him. Allowing herself to get carried away by him when she should be keeping this all about business. All about Guy and Tremain Hotels.

Yet she couldn't deny the excitement and adrenaline still fizzing through her like champagne out of a freshly shaken bottle. Or the way her mouth was still burning from the touch of his.

Matching wits and crossing swords with Gabriel was thrilling in the way discovering a fabulous new project to invest in was thrilling. Or trading the stocks of a particularly volatile company. There had always been a reason she liked the world of high finance and it wasn't only because of her talent with money. She liked the buzz and the challenge of it, too. The adrenaline rush of the gamble . . .

*Of course you do. You're like your father. Like Alex.*

Honor caught her breath. No, she wasn't like them. She was aware of her weakness. She wouldn't give in to it and destroy herself in the process like they had. Her gambles were always calculated, always safe.

The problem was that Gabriel wasn't safe. Not even for a moment.

Making a sudden decision, Honor pulled the bags off the counter and walked down to the cottage with them.

Perhaps this was a bad idea, but maybe the best way to

handle this was to stop fighting him and go with the flow. Take the ride. If she went into this with her eyes open, fully conscious of the dangers, she'd be okay.

A calculated risk. Her favorite kind.

Honor didn't know how he'd managed to find her size but the pants, the jacket, the gloves, and the boots all fit perfectly, even though she found moving in them strange. The leather pants and jacket were tight. It was like being encased in armor, an image that probably wouldn't go amiss when dealing with a man like Gabriel.

Five minutes later, helmet in one hand, she walked back up the path to the front of the hotel. He was still there, crouched beside his big, black Norton, fiddling with something on the wheel.

Honor took a slow, silent breath. "So," she said. "What about this ride then?"

His blond head turned, dark eyes sweeping over her. He didn't move, just stared. Then he rose to his feet in a fluid movement. "Everything fits." It wasn't a question.

Her mouth felt dry. That look he'd given her had contained a certain amount of very obvious heat. "Evidently. How did you know my size?"

"I snuck a look at your clothes." He didn't even have the grace to look ashamed of himself. "Have you tried the helmet?"

"No."

He strode over to her and once again, she couldn't help her reaction, tensing, every single nerve ending alight. How stupid to have kissed him. Now how the hell would she cope with holding on to him on the back of a bike? So much for a calculated risk.

He took her helmet and lifted it up, gently sliding it down over her head. Sound became muffled, her peripheral vision eliminated. All she could see was him in front of her. "That fits, too. What about the gloves?"

Speaking was a touch difficult with a helmet on so she lifted her hands in the padded leather gloves, her fingers warm for the first time that day. He didn't say anything, taking her hands unexpectedly in his and examining the fit. Thank God for the leather protecting her from the touch of his skin because even though she couldn't feel him, she could still hear her heart beating uncomfortably loud in her ears. "Those look fine," he said, dropping her hands. "Come on, I'll help you onto the back."

"I can do it myself," she protested. The last thing she wanted was to be helped onto the bike by him, even with all the leather protecting herself.

"Of course you can," he said. "Be my guest." He stood back with his arms folded, watching as she awkwardly threw her leg over the bike and clambered on. There was distinct amusement in his eyes, which she decided to ignore.

"Okay," she said, a trifle breathless, settling herself on the seat. "Let's go."

He smiled and she felt that electricity between them again, alive and dangerous, crackling like static in the air before a storm. "Okay, sweetheart. Hold on tight." He picked up the helmet that sat on the seat in front of her and put it on. Then he got on the bike.

Honor held her breath. She swore she could feel the heat of him even through two sets of leather. God, perhaps this hadn't been the greatest decision after all.

He turned his head. "Unless you want to come off the back, I suggest holding onto me."

Well, she kind of knew this was expected.

*What are you afraid of? You can handle this.*

Of course she could. It was only temptation and she'd resisted so far.

Honor leaned forward and wrapped her arms around his waist and yes, she *could* feel the heat of him through the leather. The power and the strength of his body like the bike beneath them. A hot engine encased in hard steel.

Gabriel kicked the stand up and started the machine. She could feel the roar of it go through her, keying into the excitement she'd felt the moment before she'd kissed him. The moment before she'd accepted his challenge.

Her arms tightened around his waist and behind her visor, despite herself, Honor grinned.

He didn't give her any warning, just opened the throttle and took off.

He'd never liked riding with other people. Even when he'd been with the club, he wasn't one of the guys who had their old ladies on the back, not that he'd had an old lady anyway, since he preferred being solitary. It was easier as a leader. But he had to admit, there was something about riding along a snowy forest road with Honor St. James holding on tight to him.

She was a small, slight presence behind him but he could feel her. Oh yeah, he could. Her thighs on either side of his, her arms holding him tight, her gloved hands a light pressure against his abdomen.

He was satisfied she was there, that she'd chosen to come with him. He'd wondered at first whether his different approach would work since even with his apology she hadn't seemed all that impressed. But he should have known appealing to the part of her that loved a challenge would be successful.

Though she hid it well, she was a gambler at heart, just like her brother. Thriving on risk, the thrill of the odds, the rush of the win. That kiss she'd given him had been evidence enough of that.

He could still feel that kiss, too, a reverberation that had gone deeper than any kiss had a right to go. He didn't

want to think about that. Or about the way something inside him had answered her—or at least wanted to answer.
This physical attraction between them had to be managed
carefully. Otherwise, it was going to take over and he
couldn't let that happen.

On either side of them snow-laden trees whipped by, the
icy chill of the wind clawing at their clothing. He opened
the throttle, building up a bit of speed, but not too much
since the road was wet. He'd planned on doing a circuit of
the lake, including stopping at a rustic looking store-café
that sold Vermont's famous maple syrup and maple candy.
She might like that, and he could buy her a hot chocolate.
Talk to her about things other than business. Get her off the
defensive for a moment.

Hell, perhaps he could even give her some more information on Alex, though he knew his friend wouldn't want
him to.

*He wouldn't want you being with Honor either and yet
here you are.*

Too bad. Gabriel had a lot of respect for his friend but he
couldn't afford to have any scruples when it came to taking
Tremain down. It was too important. The whole of his
early existence had been bent on clawing himself a life
from the shit hand he'd been dealt, a life for his mother
and himself that meant being safe and having enough
food to eat. And when that had been accomplished, he'd
had to fight to hold onto it, to protect those who mattered
to him. And fought he had. With everything in him.

Twenty minutes later, the trees gave way to a small
lakeside town. The store was on the shore, a rustic wooden
building with a porch out front and a snow-covered sign
indicating its wares. He guided the bike into a parking
space nearby and put the stand down. Honor's grip loos-
ened instantly and fell away, as if she couldn't wait to stop
touching him.

If he hadn't felt the spark between them he may have found that discomforting. But he didn't. He knew why she pulled away and it made him smile behind his visor. A smile he made sure wasn't there as he took his helmet off.

"Why are we stopping?"

Gabriel got off the bike and turned. Honor had taken her helmet off, too, her cheeks flushed pink, her inky hair mussed. She smoothed her hair back into place, looking around her as she did so.

"I thought you might like a break from the wind. Plus the store here does a mean hot chocolate."

Her eyes were very blue in her flushed face, glittering in the snow-bright sun. "How do you know? I hate to say it, but you don't look like a hot chocolate kind of guy."

"I stopped here for one on the way from New York. I happen to like it." Christ, she was lovely, she really was. And she had no idea that the way she sat there on the back of his bike, dressed in tight-fitting black leather, made him hard. Made him want to peel her clothing off and uncover the soft white skin beneath it. "And what kind of guy do you think I am anyway?"

"I think you'd be more at home in a pub with a beer than a rustic store eating maple syrup candy."

"I am that kind of guy. I'm also the kind of guy that wants to buy hot chocolate on a cold winter's day for a lovely lady friend."

Her flush deepened, and he knew that annoyed her because her eyes flickered as she looked away. "I suppose I could have one."

"Sure you could. I hate drinking alone."

"As long as I buy my own."

"You're going to argue over a couple of dollars?"

"I tell you what," Honor said, sliding off the bike with slightly less awkwardness than she had getting on. "You let me buy you a hot chocolate. It's only fair since we're riding your bike. Not to mention the fact that all this gear I'm wearing is yours."

"Okay," he said and watched her face.

Sure enough, surprise flared over it. Clearly she was expecting him to protest. "Oh, well, good. Drinks are on me then."

"As long as you stop calling me 'Mr. Woolf.' Seems stupid, especially after you kissed me."

She looked away down the street, smoothing her hair again, holding her helmet in one hand. "It wasn't a real kiss and you know it."

"Bullshit," he said softly. "You were trying to get back at me and I understand that, but pretend kisses don't usually feel like that one did."

She glanced back at him. "And what did that one feel like?"

He wanted to laugh. Oh, she was good, very good indeed. Pushing the boundaries, confronting him. Giving him back as good as she got. It excited him.

Goddamn, why couldn't he use their chemistry to his advantage? Especially since she'd just handed him the key to her particular lock on a platter: all he had to do was appeal to the gambler in her, the wildness that lurked under the surface of her skin.

He met her gaze and held it. "It's hard to put into words. Perhaps I should just show you instead."

For an instant a blue spark glowed in the depths of her eyes. Then her lashes fell, silky black, hiding her expression. "Oh, I don't think we need to go that far. Come on, let me buy you a nice hot chocolate. If you're very lucky I'll even ask them for extra marshmallows."

He let her buy the drinks, which they took out into the weak winter sunlight and sat on a park bench beside the lake. Snow was heaped in drifts and it wasn't exactly the most comfortable place to be, but there was no wind and it was better than listening to the loud music blaring through the store's speakers.

"So," Honor said, toying with her drink. "Why the bike ride?"

"Because I hate being cooped up for too long. Plus I like the wilderness out here."

"But why invite me? I hate to say it, but I'm not much of a wilderness person."

Gabriel leaned back against the bench, legs outstretched, ankles crossed. "I noticed. If you must know, I thought we got off on the wrong foot initially."

"That was wholly your fault, not mine. You virtually blackmailed me into coming here."

"What do you want? Another apology?"

"Will I get one?"

"Fuck, no. That was entirely business-related and when it comes to business I don't apologize for anything."

She took another sip of her hot chocolate. She'd taken off her gloves, cupping her hands around the paper cup. Her fingers were slender, pale, and beautifully manicured. Just like everything about her.

"So what about it then?" Honor asked. "If you're expecting friendship, you're out of luck."

"I don't expect you to be my friend, but I thought that since we'll be spending a week together we should at least be on speaking terms."

"A week . . . yes. That has me a little puzzled, I have to admit. What are you expecting to have happen?"

Gabriel glanced at her. She'd left a good amount of room between them on the bench, sitting slightly angled toward him, a crease between her brows. What did he expect to happen? Guy Tremain's secrets spilled any way he could get them, that's what.

*And if they're spilled onto your pillow?*

Well, shit. He wouldn't say no to that either.

"I thought I might talk to you about Alex," he said.

She paled, her eyes suddenly huge and dark in her face. And for the first time in years, he felt an odd pang of . . . something in the vicinity of his chest.

"Alex? What—" She broke off and looked away, gripping her cup in her hands. "I'm not sure I want to know."

Christ, whatever that feeling was, he sure as hell didn't like it. Ignoring the sensation, Gabriel said softly, "Are you sure about that?"

Honor didn't reply immediately, her attention turned to the view of the frozen lake. "He left when he was sixteen. Without a word. Just . . . disappeared. Then every so often we'd see him in the media, at some party or casino. We thought eventually he'd get in touch but . . . he didn't." She raised her cup, took another sip. "Alex didn't care. And you know what? I don't think I care about him either."

"When you say we, you mean . . . ?"

"My mother and I."

A silence fell.

Gabriel studied her set face. Pale as the snow around them. "He had his reasons. And you're wrong, he does care."

"Does he? You'll forgive me if I'm cynical about whatever those reasons were."

"He's kept an eye on you for a number of years, Honor. I know that much."

"Oh, has he? So, he knows all about how we lost everything after our father shot himself? How Mom basically lived on antidepressants and vodka when he disappeared?" Her voice was cold. "I had to clean her up every night and put her to bed. Not that we had a bed since most of our belongings were repossessed to pay Dad's gambling debts." She paused. "I was eight."

And Alex had been sixteen. Haunted by whatever had

happened to him in that underground gambling den his father had dragged him into. He'd never spoken of it to Gabriel, but then Gabriel had known the day he'd found Alex bleeding from the mouth and pale on the sidewalk outside the casino that something had gone down. Something bad.

Gabriel had been a fully patched member of the Angels by that stage and had enlisted a doc used by the club to check his friend out. Alex told him that night that he wasn't going home ever again. So he'd come to stay in the shitty run-down apartment Gabriel shared with his mother, never saying a word about his family. In fact it wasn't until the day his mother had turned up with Honor in tow that Gabriel realized he'd even had a sister.

A sister who'd obviously been scarred by what had happened all those years ago.

That strange, slightly painful emotion shifted around in Gabriel's chest. Guilt maybe. Or sympathy. He ignored it, whatever it was. Anger was the only emotion he'd ever been able to deal with.

"So, you had it hard," he said. "You're not the only one."

She flicked him a glance. "Are we talking about Alex still?"

"Not entirely."

The cold look on her face faded, curiosity glinting in her eyes now. Which was excellent. Curiosity would only help him when baiting the hook that would draw her in.

"I expect you had a difficult upbringing, too, didn't you?" she said after a moment. "How exactly did you and Alex meet anyway?"

Difficult question this one, especially as he'd first met Alex at that underground casino. The Lucky Seven, it was called. Patronized almost exclusively by the upper echelons of New York society, there wasn't only gambling that went on behind its secret doors. Drugs, prostitution. Anything that could be bought, the Lucky Seven sold.

And Honor's father had dragged his son into it. How much did Honor know about that? She'd mentioned her father's debts so she obviously knew he'd been a gambler. But did she know Alex used to count cards for him? And if she didn't, was it really his place to tell her?

*That's not what you should be asking yourself.*

No, he shouldn't. Any information he gave her had to be in aid of his greater goal. Tremain. And just like he'd been single-minded and driven in his rise from the streets, he had to be focused about this.

Slowly Gabriel sat forward, his forearms on his knees, holding his cup of cooling chocolate in his hands. "You know your father was a gambler?"

"We figured that one out after the repo men came to take everything away."

"Big debts then?"

"Major ones. According to the coroner, gambling wasn't the only thing he was addicted to. They found traces of cocaine in his system, too. Of course we only found this out after he died." Her voice held a bitter edge. "Dad's last little gift to us. But what's this got to do with Alex?"

Gabriel watched her face. "Alex is a mathematical genius. And a card counter. Your father thought he could help him win."

Shock crept over her finely carved features. "What do you mean, 'help him win'? Did Dad take him to Vegas? But I didn't—"

"Your father didn't play in Vegas," Gabriel interrupted gently. "He played in New York. In my neighborhood."

She blinked. "But . . . I don't understand. Mom said he went to Vegas every second weekend. And the bank—"

"It was an underground casino. The club I used to ride with did security for it."

Her throat moved, her eyes wide, staring at him. "Why are you telling me all this?"

"Because that's how I met Alex. I was a club prospect at the time, hanging around and helping out on the door. Your father sometimes took him inside, sometimes left him out on the sidewalk and I got to talking to him."

Honor didn't say anything for a long moment, looking abruptly away out over the lake. Then with a quick movement, she got to her feet. "I'm cold," she said in a voice devoid of any expression. "I think it's time to go."

Honor couldn't get a breath. She walked back to where Gabriel had left the bike, not caring if he'd followed her, barely even aware of where she was. She needed a minute to get away, get her thoughts together after the bombshell Gabriel had just dropped.

What she knew about her father was that he'd killed himself after his gambling debts had finally caught up with him. Debts he'd incurred from a casino in Vegas that were in all likelihood attempts to finance a burgeoning addiction to cocaine.

An addiction that he'd kept secret, along with those debts, right up until his death.

But it seemed that her father had even more secrets than anyone had guessed. He hadn't been in Vegas after all, but New York. And he'd used Alex to count cards . . .

She'd been eight when her father had died. A shot to the temple from a pistol in his desk. Her mother had found him and the sight of her beloved husband in a pool of blood had sent her straight to the bottle. In the middle of a binge, she'd once told Honor her father had killed himself because Alex had left. A small part of her had always blamed her brother for that and yet it seemed there was more to that story, too.

Daniel St. James had taken his son into an underground casino to count cards. A boy of sixteen. Was that why he'd left?

Shock moved through her in a slow, cold wave, her hands trembling as she fumbled with her gloves.

The circumstances around her father's death and the revelation of his gambling debts had shattered the family. But she'd never dreamed that there would be more.

Secrets. God, how she *hated* secrets.

The crunch of snow beneath heavy boots. "Are you okay?"

She looked up to meet Gabriel's dark eyes, his gaze sharp and focused, making her feel exposed. Vulnerable.

"Yes," she said, nearly dropping one of her gloves. "I'm fine." A total lie.

"No, you're not." He reached out unexpectedly, taking her hands in his. And her breath caught at the touch.

"Don't," she said thickly, trying to pull away.

But he only held her tighter, his large warm hands wrapped around hers. "Your fingers are freezing. Putting them into gloves like that is a mistake. Give them a minute to warm up."

A fizzing, tingling sensation was moving over her skin, up her arm, down through her body. Like she was touching an electric fence. Great, this was all she needed. In addition to the shock, she now had to cope with her physical response to him.

She took a breath, keeping her gaze on his hands holding hers. His fingers were long and blunt, white scars crisscrossing them. There were other scars on the backs of his hands, long cuts and round circles. For some reason, despite the crap he'd just dumped on her, all she could think about were those scars and the faint, tantalizing roughness of his fingers against her skin. The hands of a workingman, not a desk jockey.

He'd had a difficult childhood, too, or so he'd told her. And the "club" must refer to the motorcycle gang he'd been part of. Had he gotten those scars at that time?

*Why the hell are you thinking about him? When he's basically blown apart everything you knew about your family?*

God, she had to handle this, not go to pieces. She wasn't her mother, helpless and weeping on the couch, consoling herself with drink. Nor was she her father, who'd chosen suicide rather than face the reality of his actions.

No, she had to stay in control and think things through logically, like she did at work. More information was clearly needed.

Honor pulled her hands away and he let her go this time. "Tell me what you know about Alex," she said harshly. "All of it."

The look on his face was cool, impersonal and for some reason, that helped. Sympathy would have undone her. "There's not much more to tell. One night I found Alex sitting on the sidewalk outside the casino with blood all over his face. He wouldn't tell me what happened, but he asked if he could come back to my place because he didn't want to go home. So I let him."

"Did he say why? Did he say anything about coming back?"

"No. He never mentioned his family at all."

"What about my father? How did he get involved with this?"

"I don't know. I just saw him go in about once a week and sometimes he'd be there on the weekends, too. Like I said, the club did security and we weren't allowed inside so I don't know what went on."

"But what about the casino?"

"What about it? The Lucky Seven is just about an institution. A place for rich assholes to buy whatever the hell they want, not just for gambling."

"Drugs?"

Gabriel's gaze was steady. "Anything, Honor."

The cold settled down inside her and stayed there. What had been missing from her father's life that he'd put at risk his high-powered job and his family purely to chase a high? Why hadn't he been stronger? Why hadn't he resisted? And why, for the love of all that was holy, had he brought Alex into it?

She didn't remember much about Daniel St. James, only that he'd always seemed to prefer his son to her and that Alex had idolized him. Yet he'd let something happen to Alex at that casino and from what Gabriel had just told her, it had been something awful. Then he'd killed himself.

She looked away, feeling even colder. There would never be any answers to those questions because the only person who could answer them was dead. And as for Alex . . .

"He doesn't want to talk to me, does he?" she asked quietly, staring at the snow.

Gabriel didn't ask who she meant; he knew. "No."

A brief silence fell.

"I'm sorry," Gabriel said at last.

Damn him. She hated how he seemed to be able to read her so easily. "Another apology, Mr. Woolf? What *is* the world coming to?"

"If it's any consolation, I made Alex contact your mom after your father died. To at least let her know he was alive."

"No, that's not any consolation." How could it be when he'd refused to come back even then?

Honor took a deep breath, anger beginning to burn through the shock. An anger she'd thought she'd long put behind her. "I think I've had enough revelations for one day. Can we go now, please?"

As soon as they got back, Gabriel dropped her off near their cottage and went to park the bike. She didn't bother to change, merely slipping out of the jacket once she was inside, then picking up her phone and dialing her mother's cell.

"Darling," Elizabeth St. James said warmly. "How's Vermont?"

"Cold." She hesitated. "Mom, what do you know about Daniel?" He would never be "Dad" to her, not after the way he'd left her.

There was a silence at the other end of the phone.

"What do you mean?" her mother asked eventually.

"I mean the gambling. What do you know about it?"

"Do we have to talk about this now?"

"Please, Mom."

Her mother sighed. "I don't know much of anything. I thought he was having an affair, with all those conference trips to Vegas." Another pause. "What's all this about, Honor? Why are you asking me this now?"

Honor stared out the window at the snow-covered trees and icy lake beyond. Her mother hadn't read the coroner's report and refused to believe her late husband had been taking drugs. But the gambling debts hadn't been so easily dismissed. Had she known he'd been visiting an underground casino rather than going to Vegas? And that he'd taken Alex with him? Good question. Because if Elizabeth didn't know then Honor couldn't tell her. Her mother was a fragile woman, both physically and emotionally, and her husband's death had taken her years and the very finest rehab Guy's money could buy to recover from.

"Oh, I just heard a few things," Honor said carefully. "There were rumors that . . . he wasn't going to Vegas after all, but a casino in New York."

"What?" There was puzzlement in her mother's voice. "No, of course he wasn't in New York. He was in the casinos in Vegas, that's what the bank said."

So, no, her mother didn't know. Honor rubbed her brow tiredly. "Yes, well, that's what I thought," she said.

"Where did you hear these rumors? From whom?" Elizabeth asked.

Oh dammit. She shouldn't have said anything. "They're just rumors, Mom."

"I need to tell Guy." Her mother sounded upset. "I don't want rumors going around about Daniel. This family has been through quite enough as it is."

"Don't worry," Honor said, going into soothing mode. She couldn't face upsetting her today. "Let me deal with it, okay? It'll be fine."

Her mother took an audible breath. "All right then, darling. But do let Guy know if it gets out of hand. You know how lies like that upset me."

But were they lies? She hadn't asked Gabriel whether what he'd told her was true or not, only taken it for granted that it was. Perhaps she needed to demand some proof.

At that moment she heard the cottage door shut and footsteps coming down the hall. A second later, Gabriel appeared, a tall, dark figure in black leather, filling the doorway.

What perfect timing.

"I will," she said into the phone. "I have to go, Mom. Take care, okay?"

Ending the call, she laid the phone down carefully on a nearby side table then turned to face him. He said nothing, hitching his shoulder against the door frame, watching her in that disturbingly perceptive way of his.

"How do I know you're telling the truth about my father?" she asked abruptly, breaking the thick silence.

"Why would I lie?"

"For any number of reasons, I should imagine." She folded her arms. "I wouldn't trust you as far as I could throw you."

"That's your prerogative, I guess. But hey, you don't have to take my word for it. If you want proof why don't you give your brother a call? I've got his number."

"You said he doesn't want to speak to me."

"He doesn't. Good luck with getting him to answer."

The anger simmering in her gut froze solid, her throat closing. Once, years ago, she'd found out Alex's number and given him a call. He'd never answered and never responded to the message she'd left. She hadn't tried again.

Hating the knowing look in Gabriel's eyes, she turned away. He knew she wouldn't call him and she hated that he knew. She wasn't a coward, but the hurt her brother's silence had caused went deep.

*What would knowing the truth change anyway? Whatever happened with Alex and your father, it was a long time ago. You can't fix it now.*

No, she couldn't. Which made it easy to deal with in many ways.

"Thanks, but I'll pass," she said, moderately pleased with how calm her voice sounded. "It doesn't matter anyway since it all happened years ago."

"Are you sure you don't want his number?"

"Quite sure." She found a chilly smile from somewhere. "I've got quite a few work calls to make and e-mails to check, so if you haven't got anything else you need me for this afternoon . . . ?"

Gabriel ignored the question. "You're sure you're

okay? I know all that about your father was a hell of a thing to dump on you."

"Why did you then?"

"You wanted to know how Alex and I met."

"No, talking about Alex, period. You were the one who brought up the subject, not me."

He was still leaning casually against the door frame, but the look on his face was anything but causal. There was a hard, almost calculating glint in his eyes. As if he was debating what to tell her.

"You did it on purpose, didn't you?" she said suddenly, not sure how she knew, only that the glint in his eyes had warned her. "Why? And the ride . . . That wasn't just a 'let's get out into the fresh air' thing, was it?"

He didn't move. "What makes you say that?"

A burst of adrenaline shot through her. He was playing with her. Like he'd done from the beginning, because that's what he was. A game player. "There wasn't any reason for you to bring my brother up. Or tell me about my father, but you did."

"I thought you'd want to know."

"Really, Mr. Woolf? Or was it because you're involving me in another one of your games?"

He raised a brow. "Games?"

"Don't be so disingenuous. It doesn't suit you."

A thick, heavy silence fell.

Gabriel smiled. A slow-burning, wicked smile. "You're a smart woman, Honor St. James. Too smart maybe."

She took a silent breath. "You bastard."

He didn't even have the decency to look ashamed of himself. "You're right, I am a bastard. And you should never make the mistake of thinking otherwise."

"Don't worry, I won't." The low-level anger that had been there ever since he'd told her about Alex and her father began to boil. Yet something else was there, too. That heady, illicit thrill. She'd seen through him and now she was certain the gloves were going to come off. Part of her was . . . excited by the thought. "You must want something from me pretty badly to use information about my brother against me."

"Let's be clear. I didn't use it against you. I mentioned Alex because I thought you needed to know. But sure, the ride itself wasn't purely out of the goodness of my heart."

"Oh?"

"No. I wanted to go riding with you so I could have that fucking hot little body of yours up against mine on the back of the bike."

She swallowed, her mouth suddenly dry.

The look in his eyes glinted. "Don't look so surprised. I've always been up-front about what I wanted from you."

He had. Brutally so, in fact.

*Dangerous. So dangerous.*

Yes, and she should be telling him where to go. Or at least packing everything up and leaving him here. But she couldn't. There was this investment hanging over her head still and besides, leaving would be tantamount to letting him win.

*What happened to going with the flow?*

No, she wasn't supposed to be fighting him, giving in to the burn of excitement that matching wits with him gave her. But then she couldn't allow him to get the upper hand either. Because once he had it, she'd never get it back.

So how to handle him? She could be ruthless when she chose to—hell, you didn't get to have your own investment firm by being a pushover, after all—and no one could ever accuse her of being weak. She couldn't afford to be.

*You know how . . .*

A small electric thrill shot down her spine, mixed with a healthy dose of trepidation. Oh yes, she knew. She'd always sworn to herself she'd never use *that* particular weapon, certainly not when it came to business. And not only that, it would be a temptation that would push her own control to the limit.

Then again, this would be another calculated risk, wouldn't it? If she was aware of the dangers, she could handle it. Handle him.

"Yes," Honor said levelly. "You have. And I suppose I don't need to ask you what that is."

He shifted against the door frame, folding his arms, the glint in his eyes becoming hotter. "No. Though I don't mind saying it again if you need a reminder."

"You want me?"

He didn't look away. "Of course. You."

She didn't want to think about how that made her feel, that he wanted her enough to be a complete bastard about it. That he would use anything he could to have her. "Why? You could have any woman you wanted. You don't need me." She paused. "Oh, I know, it's because I resisted, isn't it?"

"Why wouldn't I want you? You're beautiful. Fucking smart. And we have major chemistry going on. Plus you're one hell of a challenge mentally and that excites me. Why wouldn't I use what I could to get you into my bed?"

*Don't be flattered, for God's sake!*

But it was too late. She was, the warm glow of it sitting in her stomach along with the anger and excitement, that fizzing electricity.

No one had wanted her like that in a very long time . . .

She folded her arms. "If you think I'm going to fall into your arms after that, you've got another think coming."

# CHAPTER SEVEN

Gabriel balled up his napkin and tossed it onto the table. The chair opposite him had remained stubbornly empty the whole evening and he supposed he deserved it.

*No supposing. You did deserve it.*

Irritated, he sat back and took another cursory look around the hotel restaurant. Another example of thought and great workmanship. The place had a quietly luxurious vibe to it, lots of vaulted ceilings and exposed roof beams. A huge brick fireplace with a roaring fire. Tables in alcoves with armchairs for seating and lots of crystal glasses and snow-white tablecloths. During the day there were probably views out across the lake but the outside was now in darkness, the only thing visible was the snow heaped up outside the glass, making the interior feel warm and cozy.

There were a few other guests lingering over their meals but no sign of Honor.

When he'd phoned down to the cottage about dinner, she'd said that she'd possibly join him or possibly wouldn't. But not to expect her.

He'd thought she'd come just to spite him. To show him she wasn't going to let their last interchange get to her. Yet she hadn't turned up.

For some reason that annoyed him. Like she was

backing down or conceding him the challenge. A disappointing thought when so far, she'd proved a fucking fantastic opponent.

Still, maybe this was part of her plan. Getting him to sit here alone through dinner while she stood him up. And yeah, he *did* deserve it.

Reaching out, Gabriel picked up his glass and swallowed the dregs of the beer he'd ordered to go with his steak. Then he set his jaw as he put the glass down, casting another glance at the doorway. Still no Honor.

Shit, he *had* made a mistake in bringing Alex up, but then he hadn't been expecting her to see through him like that so easily. He should have known though. He'd meant every word when he'd told her she was smart, because she was. Very.

Which was going to make her eventual capitulation to him all the sweeter.

How long had it been since he'd played such a complicated, delicate game with a woman? Fucking never and Christ, he was enjoying it more than he'd ever thought possible.

He was quite certain he was going to win their little game, of that he had no doubt. But getting there was the interesting part. After all, an easy victory was no fun for anyone.

A waiter approached the table. "Would you like anything else, Mr. Woolf?"

"Not here," he said shortly. "I'll have a glass of the Macallan seventy-five in the library."

"Certainly."

Gabriel waited another five minutes, then pushed back his chair and made his way out of the restaurant, going down the wide, wood-paneled hallway to the library.

It was late and there were no other guests there. His

scotch was waiting for him like he'd ordered, in a tumbler beside the leather armchair he preferred.

He'd been there most of the last few hours, dealing with some shit about a site down in Florida that was causing him hassles. Then going over some files his research team had sent him about Tremain's financial situation. That had proved interesting reading. The guy's situation was dire, he knew that already, but what he hadn't realized was that someone had already put a fair amount of money into Tremain Hotels. A company called St. James Investments. Honor's company.

She'd already admitted to him that she'd invested in her stepfather's business, but what she hadn't let on was the level of her investment. Which was significant. If Tremain went down there was a good chance St. James would, too.

It was a bad investment, anyone could see that, which meant that Honor had done so out of the goodness of her heart. Risking everything, even her own company, out of . . . what? Duty? Love? What kind of hold did the guy have over her?

Gabriel shut the library door behind him and went over to where he'd left his laptop, flicking the screen up and entering his code to unlock it. The spreadsheet was on-screen, the damning figures all over it. He frowned as a feeling he wasn't used to shifted inside him. The one he'd experienced today by the lake, as he'd told Honor about Alex and seen her face go white. Concern. For her.

Fuck, why? What did he care whether her company went down with Tremain's or not? He wasn't here to save her. He was here for information, nothing more.

He reached down and picked up the tumbler, took a sip of the scotch.

Jesus, he couldn't afford to be worried for her or any

shit like that. Only anger was allowed. That kept him going. That kept him strong.

"I'm sorry," a feminine voice said from behind him. "I missed dinner."

A heavy, hot sensation uncurled inside him, satisfaction and arousal settling in his gut. He paused to push the laptop closed and to put his tumbler back down on the side table. Only then did he turn around.

Honor had shut the door behind her, coming into the room. Disappointingly, she wasn't wearing her motorcycle leathers now but had changed into a tailored, black, silky blouse and one of those pencil skirts she seemed to like so much, this one in dark blue. She wore a pair of delicate sapphire-colored pumps with a spindly heel that made her legs look long.

Beautiful. Sophisticated. And extremely self-possessed. As though the shock of this afternoon had never existed.

Clearly she'd come to make her move.

Anticipation tightened in him. "The steak was good," he said. "Your loss. Did you get room service?"

"Yes. I had . . . extra work things to do that I wasn't expecting."

"No, you didn't." He smiled, letting her know he was as ready for whatever move she'd come here to make as she was. "You were punishing me."

Honor raised a brow. "Was I? That might work if I thought you cared whether I joined you for dinner or not. But you don't."

"Are you kidding? It's always painful when the gorgeous woman you thought would be joining you for dinner stands you up."

Her expression remained neutral, as if the compliment made no difference to her whatsoever. "You don't look like you're in pain."

"I hide it well." He skirted around the side of the chair

and sat down. "So, are you only here to apologize or do you have something else you wanted?"

She came over to the couch and placed her hands on the back of it. "I thought you were the one who wanted something."

"I do. But like I told you, the next move is yours."

"You're not a man who concedes a move, Mr. Woolf."

"Perhaps I felt bad."

"I don't think that's the case."

"Maybe not. But I like a woman who can see through bullshit."

"And I prefer an honest man."

Gabriel leaned back against the chair, studying her. "Do you? Or maybe what you really like is a man who challenges you."

"I'm not sure you're in any position to tell me what kind of men I like."

"You're excited by the thought of having someone to fight. It gives you a rush."

She smiled, long dark lashes veiling her gaze. "I think you're attributing too much to me, I'm afraid. I didn't come here for a fight. I came here to ask you exactly what you need in order to give me your decision about Tremain Hotels."

"A week. That's what I said. I need to examine this place thoroughly and look over the various financials before I make any kind of decision."

"No, you don't. I think you've already decided. I think you made that decision even before you got here."

Smart. Sexy. God . . . He shifted in his chair, watching her. The fire glossed over her inky hair, giving her face a wash of color, reflecting a glow deep in her dark blue eyes.

"So why am I here then?" he asked softly.

She took her hands off the back of the couch and walked around the side of it. "I can only assume you're here for me, though why you should go to all this trouble, I can't imagine."

"You're underselling yourself."

She strolled closer to his chair. "Seems a lot of work to take yourself away from your busy company merely to look over this hotel. In fact, if you wanted to sleep with me, why didn't you hold the investment offer over my head?"

"Ah, but that would be blackmail."

"You don't strike me as the kind of man who would balk at a little blackmail." She reached down and picked up his tumbler full of scotch, took a sip. "Hmm. Macallan?"

"You know your scotch."

"I have expensive tastes."

He let his gaze drift down her body, all her slender curves on show in the beautifully tailored clothing she wore. "Yes, you most certainly do."

"So, why didn't you?"

"Why didn't I what?"

"Blackmail me into bed?"

Gabriel looked up into her face. Color tinged her cheekbones. He could still feel that kiss of hers on his mouth, the touch of her fingers as he'd held her hands in his. "You're assuming that sleeping with you is all I want to do."

A spark of something that looked like surprise glowed briefly in her eyes. "What?"

"If sex was all I'd wanted then yeah, I could have blackmailed you. But I didn't."

"Why not?"

"Because blackmail is like using a hammer to crack an egg. It's clumsy. And while I may be a fucking beast at heart, I'm not a clumsy one."

Her gaze made its way down his body as if she couldn't

help herself, the color in her cheeks deepening. "If you don't want sex then what else do you want?"

"I didn't say I didn't want sex. I said that's not *all* I want."

"Then what?"

He very much wanted to reach out and curl one hand around the back of her thigh, pull her in close to the arm of his chair then slide his palm up over the curve of her butt. But he wasn't going to touch her again. Not like he had in the cottage the day before. No, this time she had to come to him. "Your permission. I want you to want it, sweetheart. I want you to want me. I want you to say 'yes.'"

She gave a short laugh. Then tipping back her head, she drained his glass before setting it back down on the table beside him. "You're going to invest."

"How do you know?"

"Because you're right. I do want you." She took a breath, her eyes glittering in the light. "Tell me what you want from me, Gabriel."

The sound of his name was like an arrow, piercing him straight through. It had never sounded so erotic. Holy fuck, it had been worth all the times she'd called him "Mr. Woolf" just to hear her say it.

His muscles tightened, fighting the urge to get up and grab her, tear the clothes from her, push her up against the wall, and have her sink her sharp, hungry claws into him. The beast, all that black passion, threatening to break free.

But it wouldn't. It just fucking wouldn't. Yes, he wanted her and he wanted her pretty damn badly. Yet he wasn't about to break years of perfect self-control over his urges just because one small, blue-eyed, black-haired woman said his name.

"Are you sure you want to know?" he asked softly.

"I wouldn't be here if I didn't." She paused. "And I'm tired of you holding the reins." She moved, stepping over his outstretched legs, putting her hands on the arms of his chair and leaning forward. Aggressive as hell and fucking sexy. "I want the control back. So how's this for a deal? If you don't invest in Tremain hotels then I *won't* fuck you."

She'd never done this before in her whole life, come on strong to a man who was a virtual stranger to her. It was like having an out-of-body experience. The scotch had gone straight to her head—mainly because she'd also had a glass of wine beforehand for liquid courage—but the thing that was really making her buzz was the adrenaline. A great, surging rush of it, making her say things she never thought she'd say, do things she never thought she'd do.

Gabriel sat in his chair, his big, long body utterly still. The light from the lamp on the table at his side threw the powerful lines of his face into shadow, his eyes so dark she could have sworn they were black. But she could see the heat in them. Feel it radiating from him.

He wasn't in his leathers tonight, wearing faded jeans and a black T-shirt instead, the fabric pulled tight over the incredible muscles of his chest. The simple clothing only emphasized how sexy he was, all muscle and power and heat. Like the motorcycle he rode.

*With an icy heart. Don't forget that.*

Oh, no. She wouldn't. He was a game player, cold and calculating. Using what he could to get what he wanted. But that was fine, she wasn't after anything more.

What she wanted was control over this situation. Over the intense physical feelings that flooded through her whenever he was around. She was sick of him keeping her on the back foot all the time, surprising her, shocking her. It was time to give him a taste of his own medicine. Get back a little bit of the power. And like him, she would use whatever weapon she could.

Tonight her weapon of choice was sex.

It was a potentially dangerous move, but she was strong. As long as she was in control, she'd be able to handle him without losing herself.

"That," Gabriel said softly, "is a very compelling argument."

He didn't smell of warmth and musky leather now. He smelled of winter, pine and fresh snow, the bite of ice at the back of the throat. "I take it you'll be investing then?"

"With an offer like that, how could I refuse?"

"Didn't think you would." Her gaze moved over his body, a rolling kind of heat moving through her veins. He was so not the kind of man she'd ever thought she'd want. Rough and dominant and raw, without an ounce of smoothness or polish in him. So not her type. Yet she wanted him all the same. Because some part of her loved the danger of him. Loved that he had no slick, sophisticated veneer nor felt the need to have one. And appreciated, too, his brutal honesty.

"You asked what I wanted," he said into the thick silence of the room.

She looked into his eyes. "Tell me."

"I want you to lift your skirt. Get in my lap. Fuck me right here. Right now."

The heat in her veins ignited. He didn't move, didn't try to touch her or reach for her. Only pinned her to the spot with those black eyes and his dark voice, the words harsh, blunt, and erotic.

Yes, he was dangerous. Because she wanted to do all those things he'd said. Prove herself to him in some way. Prove that she wasn't afraid, that she would meet any challenge he set.

*Be careful. Don't let the rush go to your head.*

"You don't think I'll do it, do you?" she murmured.

"Perhaps you won't. This is a public area and the door isn't locked."

"Do those things bother you?"

"No. But they bother you, don't they?"

Honor straightened up and still he didn't move, only sat there, watching her. He was hard, she could see the rigid line of his erection through the denim of his jeans. He made no move to hide it and for some reason, she liked that very much indeed. He wanted her and that knowledge gave her power.

*God, are you really going to do this?*

Well, she hadn't come in here to talk, had she? Besides, he didn't think she would. Which meant she had to. Yes, it was probably another mind game he was playing with her, but she had her own she wanted to play. Let him think she would do what he told her to. Let him believe she was at his mercy. It would make it extra sweet when she turned around and showed him exactly who he was dealing with here.

She didn't turn to check the door, moving toward him, sliding her skirt up to her thighs so she could straddle him. It was kind of awkward in a pencil skirt, the fabric stretching tight as she placed one knee down on the chair cushion on either side of him. There wasn't a hell of a lot of room but she managed it, kneeling upright, looking down into his face. The heat of his body was intense, searing the insides of her knees where they touched his thighs. She almost didn't want to sit down, half-afraid she might go up in flames on the spot. But fear wasn't part of this equation so she ignored the feeling, slowly lowering herself so she was sitting in his lap.

He remained motionless as she sat, her hands gripping the back of the chair, and she could feel the vibrating tension in him, his muscles coiled and tight beneath her. The look in his eyes burned, the line of his jaw rigid.

"This," she said, her voice not quite steady, "is how much they bother me."

Another silence fell, so thick and charged she could hardly breathe.

He had his elbows on the arms of the chair, his fingers loosely linked together. His gaze dropped down her body to where her thighs were spread on either side of his. "Are you sure you know what you're doing?"

Now that she was here, the physical reality of him beneath her, no, not really. But it was too late to pull back now, at least not without revealing herself. She'd chosen to do this and she was committed. As long as she remained in control of herself, she'd be okay.

"I'm sure."

Gabriel unlinked his fingers, moving the tips of them to the hem of her skirt, touching lightly. "You'd better. Because if you think I'm going to suddenly turn into some kind of good guy at the last moment, you're going to be disappointed."

"I don't." Her voice sounded thick, not like hers at all.

Painfully slowly, he began to ease her skirt up her thighs. "I meant what I said about what I want, Honor."

She swallowed, her throat dry, her heart hammering in her chest as he raised her skirt higher and higher. "You sound like you're the one having second thoughts," she said, trying to sound cool and knowing she didn't.

"Just making sure you know that you don't have to do this. All you have to do is say the word and I'll stop at any time."

Her skirt was now up around her hips, his attention on where her thighs were spread on either side of his. "I . . . I'm not going to say the word."

"Black lace," he murmured. "My favorite." He ran the tip of one finger up her inner thigh and she shivered, heat washing through her, the heavy, insistent ache settling down between her thighs. He shifted his hands, palms resting hard and hot just above her knees, his thumbs brushing back and forth on the soft skin of her inner thighs.

She couldn't seem to stop shaking, that nagging ache gathering tighter and tighter.

"You know what I think?" Gabriel said softly. "I think you're playing head games with me, baby."

Honor gripped the back of the chair, looking down at him. She felt the same as she had on the back of his bike. Terrified and yet exhilarated, with all that power and contained energy between her thighs. A machine capable of giving intense excitement and yet also the possibility of complete destruction. Except Gabriel wasn't a machine, he was a man. Which somehow made him all the more dangerous.

*Like you didn't know that already.*

She swallowed. "What head games?"

"Being a good girl and doing what I want." His stroking thumbs inched higher, making the breath stutter in her throat. "Do you actually want this or are you doing it to push me? To prove something?"

"D-does it matter?"

"It's not going to change what I do now. Once I decide I'm going to take an offer, I fucking take it." His thumbs moved agonizingly higher, almost grazing the underside of her sex. Almost but not quite. "But when I told you I wanted you to want me, I meant that, too. So if you're doing this purely to get me to invest in Tremain then . . ."

Honor sunk her nails into the fabric of the chair, fighting to breathe through the thick desire that gathered in her throat. She looked into his dark eyes. "Then what?"

His hands stilled, his expression completely unreadable. "Then I might have to stop."

No, he was not going to take the control away from her

like that. She was the one calling the shots here, not him. She reached down, took one of his hands and placed it between her thighs so his palm rested directly over her sex. "Does that feel like I'm only doing it to get you to invest in Tremain?"

Something moved in Gabriel's eyes. Changed. A dark fire burning brighter, hotter. "Say 'yes,' Honor. I want to hear you fucking say it."

The word came out before she could think about it. "Yes . . ."

His fingers flexed, pushing gently against her, sending an electric bolt of sensation directly to her clit, making her draw in a sharp, harsh breath.

"Wet. Hot." His fingers flexed again, his palm pressing down, the heat of it making it difficult to concentrate on anything else. "That's some proof, baby. But tell me, if your stepfather's business wasn't on the line, would you be sitting there, letting me stroke your pussy like this?"

No.

*Yes.*

Honor trembled, desperate for more than the gentle movement of his fingers, wanting to ease the terrible ache inside her. But God, she had to think, had to concentrate. Had she made a mistake here? She'd counted on her control being better than his but that light, tantalizing movement was driving her crazy.

She took a silent, shaking breath. "My stepfather's business is on the line, so I guess you'll never know the answer to that, will you? Now, are you going to do something or are you going to sit there and talk all night long?"

His mouth turned up in a wicked half-smile that made the breath she'd just drawn in vanish again. "Oh, I'm going to do something all right. Keep still. Hold onto the back of the chair. And let me do all the work."

Gabriel didn't wait, hooking the fabric of her panties

to one side, baring her. Then he slid his fingers over her slick folds, stroking gently before easing a finger inside her in a deep, slow glide.

She gave a strangled moan, her eyes closing, a lightning strike of pleasure bursting through her.

"You like that?" His voice was rough and soft, velvet stroked the wrong way. "You're all hot and wet and tight. This is for me, isn't it, baby? All for me? Answer."

She didn't even think about not obeying. "Y-yes. It's for you." She rocked her hips, moving instinctively, gasping as he added another finger, a delicate stretch.

"You've been thinking of me doing this, haven't you? My fingers in your pussy, making you moan. Making you come."

"Yes." The hard leather stitching on the chair back bit into her palm as she tightened her grip, his fingers moving, sliding out of her then in again. Slow. Deep. "God . . . yes . . ."

"Tell me what else you've been thinking about. All your dirty fantasies, I want to hear them."

A voice inside her head whispered a warning, but it was so hard to think clearly, pleasure gathering tighter and tighter as his fingers moved. She couldn't think of the last time she'd had an orgasm that hadn't been entirely self-administered.

*Have you ever had one that wasn't?*

But no, she didn't like to think about that either. Or about the things men had said to her, the nice, intellectual, respectful types she went for who never pushed her or challenged her. Never made her sit in their laps and whispered dirty things into her ears.

"Tell me, baby. You can't come until you tell me."

"You," she said in a voice that she barely recognized as hers. "Screwing me on your bike. I'm in . . . your lap . . . like . . . like this and you're inside me."

Hot darkness glinted in his eyes, the movements of his fingers slowing, maddening her. "That seems . . . tame. I think you can do better than that."

She didn't know where the words came from but they came out all the same. "You're holding my hands behind my b-back. So I can't struggle. I can't . . . fight. I can . . . can only . . ."

"Feel," he finished softly. "Yes, that's what you want, isn't it? To not be in control for once. To not have your head telling you what to do all the time. Only to feel."

Like she was feeling now, the tightness of pleasure, the ache. The restlessness. The burn. *Too much. Too much.*

She tore her gaze away, closed her eyes so she didn't have to see what was in his, the rhythm of his fingers changing, becoming faster, making everything get even tighter, more intense.

"I don't . . ." she panted, "I don't . . . want . . ."

An arm curled around her waist, holding her still, the warmth of his body pressing against her front. His fingers moving, faster, faster. His thumb circling over her clit, sending a streak of white light through her whole body.

She opened her mouth, a strangled sob coming out of it, her body gathering itself into a tight, hard knot.

*Too much. Way too much.*

Yet she couldn't stop it.

Another pass of his thumb and a column of pleasure shot straight up her spine, spreading out through her body. The sob became a cry she couldn't keep inside, more ecstasy ripping through her, the raw energy of it laying waste like a force of nature.

She could feel herself shattering, breaking apart, and the feeling was so terrifying she tried to rip herself free of him but he only held her tighter, like he was holding her together.

Biting down on the sobs, she kept her eyes fiercely shut, riding out the intense aftershocks.

Oh, God, how had that happened? Usually she had to fake it because she could never let herself go enough to come, at least not when she wasn't giving herself pleasure. But not with Gabriel. He'd given her an orgasm so quickly, undermining her control so easily.

*Intense. Powerful. Addicting . . .*

Fear clawed its way inside her. To be so exposed, so vulnerable to a man like him would be a fatal mistake.

Honor waited until she felt his arm loosen around her, until her legs felt less like jelly and more like they could actually carry her. Then she moved, sliding off his lap, pushing down her skirt. Turning and walking toward the door.

"Honor?"

She didn't pause. It wasn't backing down or running away, no, it definitely wasn't. She only needed space, some time to get her armor back in place.

"Where the fuck are you going?"

She pulled open the door and went through it.

# CHAPTER EIGHT

Gabriel was out of the chair and halfway to the door before he caught himself. Because what the hell did he think he was going to do? Chase her down the hallway? Pin her up against the wall and demand an explanation? His cock might have no problems with that, but hell, he did. He didn't run after women.

"Fuck," he bit out under his breath, running a hand through his hair, pacing from the chair to the window and back again.

He was so hard he ached. He couldn't get the feel of her tight, wet pussy around his fingers, the scent of her arousal, and the soft sob she'd made as she'd climaxed out of his head.

She'd been so unbelievably sexy, daring him, challenging him. And just as he'd known it would be, her final capitulation had been so fucking sweet. He hadn't been able to take his eyes off her as he'd touched her, watching the color rise on her face, the blue of her eyes darken, thick black lashes falling on her cheeks.

He wanted her out of that prissy blouse and tight little skirt. He wanted her naked. White skin on white sheets, her legs spread, her back arching as he tasted her. Sobbing in his ear as he pushed inside her. He wanted her surrendering to him, letting go of that precious self-control of hers, giving in to pleasure and to him.

Jesus Christ, he'd thought she was into it. He'd thought she'd wanted it as badly as he did. And yet . . . she'd come apart in his arms then ran as if the hounds of hell were on her tail.

What the fuck was that all about?

He looked toward the open doorway. Had he fucked up yet again? And if so, how? All he'd done was given her an orgasm, a pretty intense one from the sounds she'd made.

He cursed, pacing over to the fireplace, looking moodily down into the leaping flames. Letting her go was what he should be doing because he never chased a woman who didn't want to be chased.

*But you still haven't gotten anything about Tremain from her.*

"Fucking hell," he muttered, shoving his hands into the pockets of his jeans.

He had two choices. Either he went after her to find out what was wrong or he stayed here and gave her some space. Normally, his gut instinct would tell him which choice to make but that gut instinct didn't seem to be working too well around Honor St. James.

*You know what you want to do.*

Gabriel let out a breath. Yeah, shit, he knew. He needed to go after her. See what the problem was. Because if he was the cause, he had to fix it. He wanted more information about Tremain and if he started asking questions, there was no way she'd answer them now.

*Are you sure it's only about Tremain?*

Yeah, well, of course it was. Everything was about Tremain and the justice he was going to mete out in his mother's name. Sure, that little seduction scene had been pleasurable and he couldn't deny he wanted more of that for himself, too. But his focus had to be on his ultimate goal.

Stalking over to the door, he went out and down the hallway to the hotel foyer. Outside it was snowing, the air freezing through his T-shirt but he barely felt it, his boots scuffing through the snow as he walked down to the path to the cottage.

Swiping his card, he pulled open the door, barely pausing to scrape the snow off his boots before striding down the hallway and into the lounge area.

Honor wasn't there.

Cursing, Gabriel turned and went back into the hall, crossing to the bedroom she was using. The door was closed but not locked so he pulled it open and went in.

Honor was standing by the bed, her suitcase open, throwing clothes into it. Her head jerked up as he came in, her eyes huge and dark in her face. Shock crossed her finely carved features before it vanished, leaving behind an expressionless mask.

"What the hell are you doing?" he demanded.

"What does it look like?" she replied calmly. "I'm packing my bag."

Anger sharpened inside him. "You're not leaving."

"The hell I'm not."

"No, you're not. It's late and it's snowing, and the driving conditions are going to be shitty."

Honor tossed a silky white blouse into her case. "Are you seriously telling me what to do?"

He folded his arms. "Yes."

"I see. So are you going to lock me in? Because that's the only way you're going to stop me from leaving."

He didn't understand why he should be so disappointed by the thought, but that didn't stop him from feeling it. "You're not leaving," he said fiercely. "You're running away."

She stilled, holding a skirt in one hand. "I'm *not* running away."

"I give you an orgasm, then you bolt from the room and start packing? Of course you're fucking running away." He held her gaze. "I'd like to know why."

"That's none of your business." She folded the skirt, laying it in her suitcase.

"Bullshit it isn't. Especially since I was the one giving you the orgasm."

"Not everything is about you, Mr. Woolf."

His patience, already at a breaking point, snapped. Shoving himself away from the door, Gabriel stalked into the room. "Oh no, we're not going to go back to that 'Mr. Woolf' shit again." He strode around the bed to where she stood, her expression set in stone, blue eyes glittering. "You called me by my name, climbed in my lap, let me touch you to orgasm, then you ran away like I'd burned you. I want to know the fuck why."

She lifted her chin, shoulders squaring. "What does it matter to you? Or is it a case of blue balls and you're too damn lazy to use your own hand?"

He stared at her, searching her pale face. "Did I hurt you?"

Her jaw tightened. "No."

"Because I don't hurt women, Honor. Yeah, I'm a cold-hearted bastard but I won't hurt a woman on purpose or do something she doesn't want."

"No, you manipulate them instead."

"That goes both ways, little girl. You didn't have to climb into my lap the way you did. No one forced you into it."

"You forced me to come here with you though."

"Did I?"

"Of course you did. Your investment offer was based on me giving you a personal tour of the hotel."

"You didn't have to come."

"I did if I wanted you to invest in Tremain."

"That was your choice."

She turned away, silky black hair falling forward, veiling her expression. "You're a bastard, Gabriel Woolf. A certified, grade-A bastard."

Like he didn't know that already. But this was the first time that hearing it made him feel . . . shitty. As if her opinion mattered to him. A complication he didn't need and couldn't afford. "I never pretended I was anything different," he said. "You knew what you were getting yourself into when you came into the library. I told you. And yet you still got in my lap." He took a step toward her. "If you didn't like the orgasm I gave you, then just say so."

"Oh, if it's your prowess you're worried about then don't. The orgasm was earth-shaking." The edge of sarcasm in her voice was cold and sharp.

"I couldn't give a fuck about my prowess. You're scared and you won't tell me why."

Honor ignored him, reaching for another blouse that was lying on the bed. He grabbed her wrist and pulled her gently around to face him. There was anger in her eyes, color on her cheeks. "Let me go."

"I didn't pick you for a coward, Honor."

A fierce blue flame leapt in her eyes. She stepped right up close to him, inches away. "You want to know why I ran? Because the first orgasm I ever had that wasn't via my vibrator had to come from you."

His breath caught, a bolt of something hot and intense shooting through him in response. A primitive satisfaction he couldn't deny.

She saw it, her lip curling. "And naturally enough now you think you're God."

"No, I think what fucking poor taste in men you must have had up until now."

Her gaze flickered. "Let go of me."

He ignored her. Jesus, he didn't understand it. She was beautiful, intelligent, articulate. Yet she'd never come with a man before. Why not? Had she only chosen losers in bed or were there other reasons? "Why? Why me?"

Her mouth was a hard line. "I have no idea. It should have been with a man I like and respect, not with . . . with someone I don't."

He studied her, looking into her glittering blue eyes. She was a fighter and she'd been battling him since day one, playing his game like a pro. A strong woman who didn't take any crap. A woman who liked to be in control. "It's because I won't do what you say like a good boy, isn't it? You're used to being the one in charge all the time, but you're not with me. And you like it. It turns you on."

"That's ridiculous. Of course I don't like it."

"I felt you come around my fingers, baby. I heard you sob in my ear. You didn't just like it, you loved it."

Her cheeks flushed, her gaze flickering away from his. "Please, I need to go."

Oh, no, she wasn't going anywhere. Gabriel tugged on her wrist, pulling her closer. "That scares you, doesn't it? Not being in control. Not being in charge."

"I don't know what you're talking about."

"Yes, you do." He took her other wrist in a gentle grip, then, before she could move, held them both behind her back, forcing her body against his. Her breath hissed in her throat, her blue eyes gone dark. She smelled of flowers, of musk. An arousing, sensual scent that made him ache. "No wonder you've never had a decent orgasm. You haven't met a man strong enough to give you what you want. A chance to let your guard down."

She didn't fight him but her body was stiff with tension. "Th-that's not true."

"No wonder you prefer your vibrator. You get to control all of the action, how deep, how hard. You never have to give yourself up to anyone. Never have to trust." It was wrong of him to do this, strip her of her protection. Expose her, make her vulnerable. But he wouldn't stop. To get the information he wanted, he had to get closer to her. "You like me holding you like this, don't you?"

"No." She didn't struggle, didn't move. "I hate it."

"You're such a liar. You love it because you don't have any control. Because I'm in charge now, not you."

She said nothing, turned her head away. The blue silk of her blouse pulled tight across her breasts as she breathed, the warmth of her body seeping through him. Christ, with her resting against him he'd gone from being cold to blazing like a furnace.

"You're always the one in charge," he went on softly. "Making the decisions, taking action. You can never let yourself go, not even for an instant. Always cool, always calm. Always strong."

Her throat moved, her breathing quickening. "There's nothing wrong with that."

"No, except that I think you don't want to be. You tell yourself you're fine with the way things are, but secretly, you want just one moment where you don't have to be strong. Where you don't have to be cool or calm. Where you can let go."

Her lashes lay on her cheeks, like splashes of black ink. She was still but he could feel the tremble in her body. "That's not true."

"It is true. You told me your fantasy, remember? You want to feel but it scares the shit out of you. And that's why you're leaving."

She was silent but he could see the pulse at the base of her throat racing. Hear the ragged sounds of her breathing.

*This is a mistake. You want this too much. Want her too much.*

The warning was inconvenient, so he ignored it. There was nothing wrong with wanting her. It was passing lust, that was all. He was still in control and that's all that mattered.

"You don't understand," she said, her voice hoarse. "I can't afford to let go. I can't afford to feel."

"Why the fuck not?"

Finally she looked up at him, her eyes dark. "Because I want to too badly."

"You're right. I don't understand."

"It's a weakness. My father ruined himself chasing a good feeling and from what I've seen, Alex is already halfway down that path. Addiction can be hereditary, so what chance have I got? Especially when you make me feel far too good, Gabriel."

There was a painful honesty in her eyes that he wasn't expecting, a momentary vulnerability that hurt for some reason. "It's just sex, Honor. It's not a drug. One night won't make any difference. And besides . . ." He didn't know how or why, but the truth came out of him before he was even aware of it. "You're not alone. Sometimes just feeling is what I want, too."

Her eyes widened, searching his face as if looking for something she'd lost. "You do?"

Fuck, why had he said that? Revealing parts of himself was not in any way part of his plan. Which meant he had to end this conversation before he lost it and gave away anything more.

Gabriel bent his head and covered her mouth with his.

She stiffened for an instant, her arms pulling against his wrists. Then she made a helpless sound in the back of her throat and all her tension melted away, her body going soft against him. Her mouth opened, letting him in, and he tasted heat and the smoky sweetness of the scotch. Christ, she was delicious. She went straight to his head.

He kissed her deeper, exploring her mouth as he gripped her wrists harder, bending her body into a perfect arch against him. Her breasts pressed to his chest, her hips to his, the hard ridge of his cock against the soft warmth between her thighs.

She shuddered, kissing him back, just as hot, just as hungry as he was. The desire that had been simmering inside him ignited into life again, a sharp, intense ache.

He lifted his mouth, looked down into her flushed face, her mouth full and red from his kiss. There was something defiant in her eyes. Something that called to the hunter inside him, that twisted the hunger tighter.

"We made a deal, Honor St. James," he said roughly. "It's too late to pull out now. You had a fantasy remember? It's too cold for the bike, but we can make that fantasy come true right here, right now."

Honor was so aroused she couldn't breathe. And it shouldn't work that way. She shouldn't be so completely turned on by a man holding her wrists behind her back, the length of his powerful body up against hers.

Not just any man. Gabriel.

Her mouth burned from his kiss. Everywhere burned. Like the mere touch of him scalded her and now she was desperate for relief.

She looked up into his eyes and felt stripped bare. Like he saw everything, knew everything. She didn't know how he'd managed to guess those things about her, how he knew exactly what scared her, or even why she'd told him about her fears. But no matter how afraid she was, she wanted to believe he was right. That it was only sex. That one night wouldn't hurt. Because she did want to let go. Wanted, for a moment, not to have to be in control. To not care. To embrace the rush and the sheer intensity of physical pleasure.

But she didn't know how. The thought of letting go terrified her. Because what if it was good? What if she wanted it again? And again, and again, and again? What if she couldn't get enough of him? Of this?

Yet that fantasy of him inside her, holding her hands so she couldn't fight or move thrilled her down to her bones.

She would have no choice but to accept whatever he wanted to give her. No option but to let go.

He shifted his hips against hers, the hard ridge of his cock pressing against her, making her want to rock against it, get the friction she craved. "Tell me more of your fantasy. About me fucking you with your hands behind your back."

She swallowed, afraid to give in. "N-no."

"Do it."

"No." She arched against him, the hard press of his zipper between her legs sending small, sharp electric shocks through her.

He bent his head, his mouth brushing her jawline, then lower, against the side of her neck. Then he bit her.

She gasped, the sensation streaking down her spine, pleasure mixed with a dart of pain that had her trembling. "Oh . . . God . . ."

"The words, baby," he said softly, his breath against her skin. "Or you don't get to have it."

He held her so tightly and there was no escape. No choice now but to give in.

She closed her eyes. "P-please. I want . . . you to hold my hands behind my back and . . . f-fuck me."

His grip on her shifted, her wrists crossed and held in the small of her back by one strong hand. Then she felt his free hand slide under her skirt, his fingers cupping the back of her thigh, sliding upward.

She trembled, shutting her eyes tighter, the breath catching in her throat. His hand slid up to the curve of her butt and stopped, long fingers moving between her thighs.

Oh . . . Holy God . . .

He gently brushed over the lacy fabric of her panties. "You're wet. You want this so badly, don't you?"

Honor shuddered in his hold, unable to stop the soft gasp that escaped her.

Another tantalizing brush of his fingertips. "Tell me. Or it doesn't happen."

"Y-yes . . . please . . ."

"Please who?"

"G-Gabriel. Please, Gabriel."

"Good girl. Now stand just like that. Don't move."

She kept her eyes closed, standing there motionless as he released her, unable to stop shaking, her hands behind her back.

*You should have left while you'd had the chance.*

Maybe she should have. But she hadn't. And now it was too late. She couldn't have walked away from this if she'd tried.

His hands slid up her thighs, underneath her skirt. Fingers hooking into the waistband of her panties, jerking hard, the sound of fabric tearing. She inhaled sharply, some deep part of her, the wild part, thrilled by the roughness of the motion, the pull and release as the lace fell away from her.

Then his hands on her thighs again, urging her forward. She didn't want to look, happy with the darkness. It was easier to concentrate on sensation. She went where those hands put her but when they pushed her skirt up, she trembled. Bare from the waist down and now, he could see her.

She screwed her eyes shut even tighter, trying to calm her breathing and failing.

"Pretty," he murmured, his voice soft and dark, fingers stroking through the curls between her thighs. "You look as good as you feel."

Honor shivered. The blackness behind her eyes was threaded through with spikes of white light, spiraling behind her lids as he touched her. Small bolts of lightning.

"Come here." He pulled her forward and she realized he was sitting on the edge of the bed, making her straddle him. Once she was sitting, facing him, he gripped her wrists and held them behind her back again.

She swallowed, listening. Was he breathing as fast as she was? Was he shaking like she was?

*Does that matter to you?*

Yes, it did. The grip on her wrists released and she opened her eyes, looked down.

Gabriel was in the process of leaning back, undoing his jeans, his gaze on her. And the look in his eyes . . .

The air between them caught fire. Igniting in a sheet of flame, the heat burning the air from her lungs.

He said nothing as he pulled his jeans open, as he reached for the foil packet beside him on the bed. He freed his cock, ripping the packet open and sheathing himself. His movements were slow, controlled, his gaze never leaving hers.

She couldn't temper her breathing, the heat of his body like a furnace beneath her open, exposed flesh. The muscles of her thighs locked. This was too much.

Instinct had her rising as he straightened, his hand reaching behind her to grip her crossed wrists in a tight hold, preventing her from getting away. Those dark eyes were inches from her own, his mouth within kissing distance. "Don't be scared," he whispered roughly. "I won't hurt you."

But it wasn't hurt she was afraid of. It was the fierce,

uncontrollable pleasure she knew he'd give her that she wasn't sure she could handle. Not again.

He seemed to understand though. "It'll be okay. I've got you."

And he kept his gaze on hers as she felt one hand on her hip, guiding, positioning her.

Then his fingers spread her open and he was pushing her down onto him. Sensitive flesh stretched and she cried out, trembling all over, pleasure catching in her throat.

*Too much. Too much.*

Yet his hand around her wrists was a shackle and she couldn't escape from the sensation. Couldn't run. Could only sit there and take it as he moved deeper inside her, fire in the shadowy gaze that pinned her to the spot, which made it so she couldn't move. Couldn't breathe.

"Gabriel . . ." Her voice was a hoarse whisper. "God . . ."

"Keep still." The words were a ragged threat that didn't even sound like him. There was a fierce expression on his face, a muscle ticking in his jaw. His fingers around her wrists were like iron and he was breathing fast, his powerful chest heaving.

She wasn't the only one feeling the intensity of this. He did, too.

For some reason that made it better. Made it easier to cope with.

Honor sucked in a breath, the fear beginning to fade. She wanted to move, anything to ease the ache. "Please . . . let me . . ."

Gabriel bit off a low curse, the hand on her hip gripping her tight. Then at last he let her move, his hand guiding her, his hips thrusting up as she rose and fell on him. The slow glide of him inside her was so intense she had to close her eyes again, biting her lip to stop the moan that crowded her throat.

Her thighs shook. Her whole body trembled. She

couldn't take this. She was going to drown, lose herself in the sharp, vicious pleasure that flooded every part of her. She strained against his hands, arching her body in a reflexive need to get away, reduce the intensity somehow. Escape. Because she just couldn't handle it.

But Gabriel stilled all of a sudden, deep inside her. Then her wrists were free. She blinked, opening her eyes in time to see him grip the sides of her blouse and pull them apart with a sharp jerk. Honor gasped as fabric ripped, buttons flying. He pushed the ruined material off her shoulders, pulling it down her arms.

"W-what are you doing?" she asked shakily.

He didn't answer but then he didn't have to. As he tied the blouse around her wrists, binding them behind her back, she couldn't stop the groan that broke from her. Although he hadn't tied it too tight, it was firm enough she couldn't get free.

He leaned back a little, his intense black gaze drinking her in. Then he gripped her bra and tore that in half, too.

This time she didn't make a sound, shivering as the cool air whispered over her hot skin, raising goose bumps.

Gabriel leaned back on the bed, looking at her. "Fuck . . . yes . . ." There was so much hunger in his expression, a raw possessiveness that should have made her angry. Because she wasn't anyone's to own.

Until now. He wasn't looking at her and thinking money, that was for damn sure. He was looking at her like he wanted to devour her. She'd never imagined how erotic that would be. Never even thought she'd like it. With her hands tied behind her back, naked to his gaze, there was no way she could control this situation. No way to stop him from taking what he wanted. No way to take charge.

There was freedom in that she'd only dreamed of.

The hand on her hip keeping her steady slid higher,

cupping one breast. The heat of his palm scalded her and she moaned as he circled her aching nipple with his thumb, brushing back and forth. At the same time he began to move again, the slow thrust of his hips making her thoughts break apart and scatter under the sheer weight of the pleasure.

"I'm going to make you scream, baby," he said in a low, rough voice. "I'm going to make you scream yourself hoarse." Then he pinched her nipple, hard enough for the pleasure to have a rough edge of pain.

God, why did she like that? She couldn't keep the cry inside her. A wordless sound of desperation.

He began to move faster and the world fell away, narrowed, becoming only the push of his cock inside her, the heat of his body beneath her, the clever fingers on her breast, and the slow, relentless build of an ecstasy that wouldn't be denied.

Honor began to shake, caught on the cusp of something immense. Something vast. Pleasure a living flame inside her clawing to get out. She shut her eyes, panting, sobs crowding in her throat. This couldn't be happening, not so soon. Not again.

"I can't . . ." she said raggedly, hardly even aware she was speaking. "I can't . . ."

"Don't fight it," he said, dark and soft. "Let go." And he shifted, an arm sliding around her waist, the heat of his body pressing hard against her front. Then his hand slid between them, down between her thighs to where they were joined. And he brushed one finger over her clit, so lightly. But it was enough.

Honor stopped fighting. Let go as lightning bolted up her spine and she screamed as a column of fire exploded in her head. Behind her eyes. Flooding her body with pleasure so intense she didn't think she'd survive it.

Gabriel's arms tightened around her and she pressed

her forehead into his shoulder, sobbing as sensation tore
her apart.

Some time passed and the intensity began to fade.

Then he said, "My turn."

His arms tightened further, turning her on her back
onto the white sheets of the bed, still inside her. Then he
slid a hand behind her knee, lifting her leg up high, over
one powerful shoulder, tilting her hips so he could get even
deeper.

She panted, moving restlessly, the heavy laxness of the
first orgasm beginning to fade, tension gathering in the
pit of her stomach. Oh, Jesus, please don't say he was going
to break her. Not again.

"Say my name," he ordered, one arm wrapped around
her leg. "Say it."

"G-Gabriel . . ."

He drew his hips back. "Again."

"Gabriel . . ." The name ended on a cry as he thrust
back in, hard. "Oh . . . please . . . I can't . . . not again . . ."

"You can. You will." He began to move, a relentless,
driving rhythm, the tension in her stomach becoming an
ache, a need, pulling tighter, another climax beginning to
dig sharp claws in her.

Honor gasped, twisting beneath him, but there was no
escaping it. No escaping him. The orgasm crashed over her
like a building falling, leaving her gasping and shivering
as he drove into her, his arm wrapped around her thigh,
his hand on her hip, holding her still.

Then abruptly he growled deep in his throat, his hips
giving one last, convulsive thrust, and his big body shuddered, the growl becoming a rough, hoarse cry.

She couldn't move, didn't even have the energy to speak.
She could only lie there, panting, with her eyes shut, staring at the bright spots behind her lids, feeling him shake
as the release caught him as well.

God in heaven. He'd destroyed her. Utterly wrecked her and left her in pieces. How the hell could she ever recover from this? Would she even want to?

She felt him move, withdrawing from her. Then he reached beneath her, releasing the fabric tying her wrists. Her hands tingled as he drew them from behind her back, gently chafing her wrists.

She opened her eyes, found her vision blurry with tears.

"Wait there," Gabriel murmured. "I won't be long." He left the bed, disappearing into the bathroom en suite.

Honor drew the sheet over herself, shaking and unable to stop.

Sex wasn't supposed to be this way. At least it had never been that way for her. No, she'd never come with any of her lovers but it had been nice. Pleasant. Vaguely pleasurable but ultimately forgettable. Not . . . intense. Passionate. *Soul-destroying. Addicting . . .*

She turned her hot face into the cool pillow. No . . . she had to pull herself together. No falling apart. So she'd let go. Given up control. And yes, it had been incredible. But all that feeling didn't make it mean anything. She wouldn't let it.

It *was* only sex. The intensity was only because he'd given her three orgasms in a row and she wasn't used to it. Not because it felt like he'd ripped away her control, leaving her aching, raw, and vulnerable. *And wanting more . . .*

The bed dipped, Gabriel returning, and she wanted to get away from him all of a sudden. Be alone to recover, build herself back up again. But before she could move, his arms came around her, drawing her in close, and as the heat of his body surrounded her, she realized he must have taken his clothes off—all she felt was hot, bare skin against hers.

"Oh, no," she said, half-desperately, "I can't—"

"Relax, sweetheart." His deep voice was in her ear, full of rough heat. "I think you've had enough for tonight." He ran a hand down her side in a gentle motion, then back up again. A light, undemanding, soothing touch. And despite herself she felt the tension in her begin to lessen.

*Get up. Go. Get away while you can.*

The warning rang loud in her head but she felt strangely reluctant to move. Warmth had begun to uncurl through her body, the raw feeling fading. Gabriel's hand stroked up and down her side, his body like a fire at her back.

She'd never much liked sleeping with another person. Having the bed all to yourself was infinitely preferable to sharing space with someone else. God, sometimes even being held left her feeling constrained and suffocated. Stiff and tense.

But she realized she didn't feel any of those things now. She felt only . . . warm. Loose. A deep sense of relaxation seeping through her.

"Gabriel," she said thickly. "I think we need to—"

"Not now," he interrupted. "I think now we need to sleep."

Honor sighed. She should argue, she really should. Or at least insist he get up and go to his own room. Except she didn't want to. She didn't even want to move.

So all she said was, "Okay."

And five minutes later, she was asleep.

# CHAPTER NINE

Gabriel woke to find the room flooded with the kind of cold, bright light that always came with early morning on snowy days. He wasn't alone, he knew that immediately because he could feel warmth nestled against his side, the scent of flowers and musk surrounding him.

A woman. Honor.

He turned his head and there she was, lying curled against him, her hair spread over the white pillow in a glossy black spill, her eyes shut, still fast asleep. Peaceful. So different from the flushed, panting woman he'd held in his arms. The one who'd screamed as he'd brought her to a second climax. Who'd sobbed as he'd given her a third.

Christ, it had been good. He'd made her lose control in his arms more than once, which was extremely satisfying and all according to plan. Except he couldn't allow himself to get too carried away. He had to maintain his distance, keep himself separate and unengaged.

Nothing could be allowed to get in the way of his anger, and most certainly not lust. He'd never had any problems keeping his distance before, he shouldn't be having any problems now.

He let out a breath. What he should be doing is getting up and going to the hotel gym, indulging in his usual early morning workout. Yet he found himself strangely reluctant to move.

It had been a while since he'd woken up with a woman. While his mother had been sick he hadn't had the time or the energy to waste on sex. It had only ever been a release valve anyway. All he'd ever needed was anger.

He turned on his side, looking down at her.

She was motionless in sleep, her breathing even and deep, her lashes lying thick on her flushed cheeks. Her skin was fine and pale, and he remembered how it had felt under his fingers the night before. Soft. Smooth. Warm.

He let his gaze travel over the curve of her shoulder to the flare of her hips, then to the gentle swell of her thighs. She was lovely, delicate. Not the kind of woman he usually had in his bed. Yes, she had that perfectly put together, expensive look to her. And yet, there was a strength and depth to her other sophisticated women lacked. Behind that cool, calm front lay fire. Passion. A passion that apparently she'd never let out with anyone else.

Her lashes fluttered then they lifted, the deep blue of her eyes looking up into his. And for a second he couldn't remember where he was or what he was doing, something painful constricting in his chest. Then she blinked, her face flushing, and the painful sensation was gone.

"How long have you been staring at me?" she asked.

"A minute or so," he replied with absolute truth.

"Why?"

"Because you're beautiful." And that, too, was the truth.

"Oh." Her gaze flickered away.

"I've been trying to decide whether or not to go have a workout or wake you up and make you scream again."

The color in her cheeks deepened. "Why me? Isn't it your turn to scream?"

He smiled, genuinely amused. "Baby, you're certainly welcome to try."

Her deep blue gaze came to his. "Are you serious?"

Ah, of course. Now he'd become a challenge. He found the thought made him even harder than he was already. "If you think you can do it, why not?"

The look on her face turned to one full of intent, her gaze sweeping down his body. She reached out, placed her palm on his chest over the cross he'd had tattooed there when his mother had reluctantly told him who he was. Where he'd come from. And why she was sometimes afraid of him.

He still remembered the cold pain of the tattoo. Like ice. A welcome respite to the anger that had burned in his heart after his mother had revealed what his father had done to her. Shattering his boyhood dreams of having a proper dad he could look up to.

The anger had cooled now, become sharp, an anger he'd honed over the years into a vicious edge.

But the warmth of her hand heated his skin, chasing away the ice. It made him shiver and he almost wanted to take her hand away. Cold was so much easier to bear than heat. Yet he didn't. Because now her hand was moving down, over his abdomen, farther down, her fingers finding his cock, stroking him.

His muscles tightened, the sweet ache intensifying as she took his dick in her palm, gripping him. "I think I get to call the shots now," she said softly, tightening her hold.

A thread of unease wound through him and he couldn't figure out why. He liked to be in charge during sex because it gave him control, helped him to maintain distance. But plenty of women over the years had jerked or sucked him off and he'd never once lost it with any of them. One blue-eyed, black-haired woman wasn't going to break the habit of a lifetime. Was she?

"Okay," he said. "For now."

Her fingers tightened. "Lie on your back."

Hell, he'd do that. If it kept her hand right where it was. He rolled over. Honor pulled back the sheet and shifted, kneeling between his thighs, her hand still gripping his cock firmly. The sight of her hand wrapped around him shook him on a level he hadn't realized he possessed.

The unease deepened.

She bent her head, the silky ends of her hair brushing his abs, sending chills racing through his body. Then she swirled her tongue around the head of his cock, licking him delicately, like he was her favorite ice cream.

Pleasure uncoiled, stroking over nerve endings that he'd thought deadened long ago. He'd always found physical pleasure a faint, dulled thing but this . . . This wasn't dull. It was sharp, hot. Last night he'd managed to handle it by staying in control of her, but this time, there was no such distraction.

She was making it all about him.

As the realization hit, Honor's mouth opened, almost swallowing him whole. The sensation of slick heat was astonishing. "Jesus . . ." He found his fingers were gripping the mattress, holding onto it as her hand tightened. As she increased suction.

Pressure began to build.

Fuck. He couldn't seem to tear his eyes from where she knelt, the sight of his cock disappearing into her mouth so erotic it left him breathless. She hadn't done this before, or at least not very often, he could tell, and yet somehow that only made it hotter.

Then she looked up at him as she sucked him, blue eyes deep and wide. And with her other hand she touched him, running her fingers up his leg, over his abs, his chest, and back down again. A light, tantalizing touch that shouldn't have been as fucking erotic as it was.

*You don't deserve this. You've never deserved it. Not after all the things you've done . . .*

Darkness lurked just at the edge of his vision, an old pain slicing deep.

Gabriel groaned and reached for her, twining his fingers in her hair. This was wrong. He'd made a mistake. He had to control this somehow. He tried to tug her head up but she shook his fingers away. "Do that again and I'll stop," she said thickly, her breath washing over his aching cock. Then her mouth covered him again and she made a hungry sound at the back of her throat, her movements becoming faster.

Something tight began to crack inside him.

He tried to fight back, gain some semblance of control but there was nothing to hold onto. Nothing except her.

Gabriel arched back on the bed, his hips thrusting into her mouth, his fingers buried in the softness of her hair as the pressure built to intolerable levels.

"Fuck," he groaned. "Honor . . ."

Then it smashed apart and he broke with it, his ragged cry of release echoing through the room.

He released his hold on her hair, just lying there for long minutes, staring blankly at the ceiling, his mind utterly empty of thought. He could feel her fingers tracing lazy circles on his stomach, her body shifting as she sat up. "I think I'll take that as a scream," she said, sounding pleased with herself. "Which means I win." She leaned over him, frowning as she touched the back of his hand where it rested on his chest. "Where did these scars come from?"

He tried to swallow, his mouth dry. "Knife cuts. I did a lot of fighting."

Her fingers drifted lower, moving to the tattoos over his abdomen, the words he'd put there when he was eighteen. The last time he'd demanded his mother tell him the name of his father and she'd refused.

" 'I will repay,' " Honor said softly, her fingers tracing the letters. "That's from the Bible."

His skin felt tight, like something was pressing down on him, squeezing all the air from his lungs. It had been years since he'd felt like this. Years since he'd felt anything at all except anger. Yet she'd broken through his guard, cracked the ice he'd surrounded himself with. Made him feel something else . . .

What was it the Reverend had told him? *"Hold onto your anger, Church. But make it cold. That way it lasts. You gotta have something to drive you and stone-cold anger is the best fuel there is."*

Fuck, he needed to breathe. Get out.

Before he could even think straight, he'd brushed away her hands, slipping off the bed, bending to pick up his clothes.

"Gabriel?" she asked softly.

Fighting for breath, he began to dress in sharp, jerky movements. "I'm going for a ride," he managed to force out.

"What? Now?"

He pulled on his T-shirt. "Yeah, now."

"But . . . Did I do something?" An edge of hurt had crept into her voice. "Say something?"

He couldn't look at her. He had to get out. Into the air, where it was cold and clean and sharp. Where the ice would freeze out the heat she'd made him feel.

Where he'd reclaim his fucking detachment.

"Gabriel," Honor said. "What's wrong?"

But he ignored her. Without a word, he turned on his heel and strode from the room.

"What's happening, Honor?" Guy's cool voice held an edge to it. "I thought I would have heard by now."

Honor turned from the windows and walked back across the room, her heels sinking soundlessly into the thick carpet.

"It's okay, Dad," she said soothingly. "Woolf is going to come to the party."

There was a silence down at the other end of the phone. "Are you sure?"

"Yes." Gabriel had promised her and she was going to hold him to that promise, come hell or high water. "End of this week, we'll have the money." At least, she hoped so.

Another silence. Which wasn't what Honor had been expecting. "Dad?"

"Yes, I'm here." Her stepfather sounded less than excited. He wasn't a demonstrative man but she'd expected more than this.

"This is good news, honestly."

"Of course. Yes. And I'm . . . relieved, obviously."

"Really? You don't sound it."

There was a noise in the background, a car's engine. "Look, I'm going to have to go. When are you back in New York?"

She looked down at her watch. "Tonight probably." At least she would once she'd finished packing.

"Tonight? Your mother said you were there for the week?"

Honor glanced at her mostly packed case. "I was, but . . . there was a work emergency. I'm needed back sooner than I thought."

"Well, get in touch when you get back, okay? We need to discuss this."

Honor frowned. Hadn't they had enough conversations about this already? Still, maybe it was better not to press it now. Face-to-face was better anyway.

"Sure," she said.

"Oh and Honor?"

"Yes?"

"Best not bring Alex up to your mother again. You know how upset she gets."

Honor opened her mouth to protest, then shut it. There wasn't anything to say. Guy tended to get protective when her mother was upset. "Yes, well. I'm sorry about that."

"Something to bear in mind for next time, hmm?"

They spoke for another couple of minutes then Honor ended the call. If she wanted to be back in New York by that evening she had to get on the road before it got too late.

Walking into the bedroom, she took a last look through the drawers and bathroom before going over to the chair where she'd put her case, flipping it shut and clicking down the clasps.

She tried not to look at the tangle of sheets on the bed. Or think about what had happened in that bed.

*The hard warmth of his skin as she'd traced the Gothic lettering of the tattoo on his stomach, the shift of muscles beneath her hand, the musky taste of him in her mouth, the sound of his ragged cry as she'd made him come . . .*

Honor shivered. She'd felt so good making him shake like that. Making him cry her name. She'd only gone down once on a man before and it hadn't been the most pleasant of experiences. But doing that to Gabriel had been . . . intensely powerful and more arousing than she'd ever thought possible. She'd felt so pleased with herself afterward.

Until he'd got up and walked out. And she still didn't know why. Whether she'd given him the world's worst blow job or whether it was something else. He certainly hadn't liked her mentioning the words of his tattoo, that was for sure, so possibly it had something to do with that.

She set her jaw, lifting the case off the chair and putting it on the floor.

A moot point now anyway since she wasn't going to be

waiting around until he decided to show his face. She'd spent the morning hoping he'd come back but he hadn't.

Which was fine. They weren't in a relationship and he didn't owe her any kind of explanation, even if she'd wanted one. And she didn't. What she wanted was to get back home, get back to work. Get back to her life where she was the one in control. Basically anywhere where he wasn't because it was better to be away from temptation than keep trying to prove herself against it.

Trying and failing.

Turning on her heel, Honor towed her wheeled case out into the hallway just as the front door of the cottage opened and Gabriel came in, bringing in a whirl of snow and cold air.

She stopped dead.

He was in his bike leathers, snow dusting his shoulders and glittering in his blond hair. And the cold that came in with him wasn't only from the outside world. There was no warmth in the brown eyes that met hers, none of the heat that had been there last night. Only a detached, flat darkness that chilled her down to the bone.

He flicked a glance down at her case. "You're going?"

Honor braced herself for an argument. "Yes. I know you wanted a week, but I'm not sure staying longer is going to be in our best interests."

"Fine. Leave the bill with me. I'm going to be leaving today myself."

So, no argument then. Why was that so inexplicably disappointing?

"I can settle my own bill, thank you," she said coolly, ignoring the feeling. "I trust our agreement with regard to the investment is still good?"

The look on his face was absolutely unreadable. "Yes. You'll get your money."

"Great. Well, I'm sorry I can't stay but . . ."

"As you say, it's not in our best interests."

"No. And I have quite a lot of work stacking up back in New York." She gripped the handle of the suitcase tightly as tension charged the air between them. "Well, good-bye then, Gabriel. And thank you."

"For what?"

"For considering Tremain as an investment." And because he was just so damn impassive and she wanted some kind of reaction from him, she arched an eyebrow and added, "What else could there be?"

Something flickered in the darkness of his eyes. Then it was gone. "Nothing. I'll see you again in New York to finalize the details." He reached for the cottage door and opened it for her. "Drive safe."

She wanted to say something else. Something about the night before. Something about this morning. But she didn't know what and he gave her no clues. It was like he was a stranger.

*He's always been a stranger, you fool.*

Of course he was, and yes, she was a fool for feeling so disappointed. The night before should have satisfied her craving for him and she definitely shouldn't want more. It was over. Done with.

She would move on and so would he, strangers still.

Honor gave him a polite smile.

And walked through the door and out into the snow.

# CHAPTER TEN

The morning after Gabriel returned from Vermont, he walked into his office on the fortieth floor of Woolf Tower to find someone already sitting in the big leather chair behind his desk.

A small, fine-boned woman dressed in black stovepipe jeans, an Iron Maiden T-shirt, and a battered, black leather jacket. She wore black platform boots with big silver buckles, currently positioned on top of the heavy oak desk he hardly ever used. Her pale hair was tucked beneath the black beanie she favored, her charcoal-gray eyes made to seem even darker by thick black eyeliner and mascara.

"Hello, Gabe," she said flatly.

In no mood for games, Gabriel slammed shut his office door. "How the hell did you get in here?"

"She's a hacker, she can get in anywhere." Zac's cultured tones came from behind him and when Gabriel turned, he saw the other man leaning up against the wall, his arms folded.

"For fuck's sake," he said, not bothering to hide his annoyance. "Haven't you two ever heard of the word 'private'?"

"Your secretary was obstructive." Eva leaned back and put her hands behind her head. "And I couldn't be bothered waiting."

Gabriel stalked over to the desk and stood in front of it, staring at the woman sitting in his chair, who stared back unflinchingly. Her flat look reminded him strangely of Honor, which he really didn't need right now.

"You couldn't have called me?" he asked.

"No. I don't trust the phone."

A fairly typical Eva response. There weren't many things Eva did trust, Zac the exception. "How did you know I'd be back today?"

"Zac tracked your bike."

"Zac *what*?"

"Relax, Gabe." Zac strolled over to the desk from his place by the door, apparently unconcerned he'd been found out and that Gabriel was pissed as fuck about it. "We did it via your phone. Eva wanted to get in touch with you urgently and we needed to know where you were. Saved us a trip to Vermont at least."

Gabriel stared at him. "There's a line, Zac. And you just fucking crossed it."

The other man's amber eyes didn't so much as blink. "This is important. You'll want to hear what Eva has to say."

Jesus, he had to calm the fuck down. He'd thought that long, cold ride back from Vermont would have gotten his head back on straight, put things into proper perspective again. He assumed it had since he hadn't thought about Honor once until just now.

But Eva and Zac getting amongst his shit wouldn't normally have made him feel so on edge. Yeah, he'd be pissed but it was their usual crap and most of the time he went with it.

Yet not today.

*It's her. You know it's her.*

Gabriel ignored the thought, and flicked his gaze back

toward Eva. "Did you find something about the Tremain reservations then?"

"Yeah, I did." She took her feet off his desk and leaned forward. "There's a pattern. For each of his hotels, just about every day, there'll be a certain number of less-than-twenty-four-hour cancellations. Sometimes more, sometimes less, but there's always at least one or two, never zero. I looked into the names of the people making the reservations and canceling them. Some of the names are fake and lead to dead cell phone numbers or defunct e-mail addresses. Some of them are people who had no idea they were even making reservations, let alone canceling them."

This news did not surprise him in the slightest. The moment Eva had mentioned there was something suspicious with Tremain Hotels' reservations, he'd known it was sketchy. And he knew exactly why, too. Hell, he was intimately acquainted with the business since he'd once been involved with it years ago.

"Money laundering," he said. "It's got to be. The money is paid to the hotel and because the reservation is canceled less than twenty-four hours from the reservation time, the hotel gets to keep the money."

"Yeah," Eva said. "That was my thought, too. Because there're lots of microtransactions, they can slip easily under the radar. I mean, they're not much taken in isolation, but when you put them all together, over a worldwide hotel chain, every day? It adds up."

"Hmm." Zac leaned against Gabriel's desk. "Seems our Mr. Tremain isn't quite the upstanding businessman he appears to be. Which makes it interesting that now his company is going down the tubes."

Gabriel stared at him. "You think they're connected?"

The other man lifted a shoulder. "Seems like a strange

coincidence if not. The real question is why he's doing it now."

"Jesus," Eva muttered. "So you think he's bankrupting his business on purpose?"

"Could be," Gabriel said slowly, thinking it over. "Maybe he wants out. Or maybe we're not the only ones to catch the cancellations and he has to cover his tracks. Either way, winding it up could seem too purposeful. Like he had something to hide. But pretending to be careless when it comes to business is better. Or better yet, blaming the failure on lack of good advice even more so."

Eva sat back in Gabriel's heavy black executive chair, frowning. "We can't jump to conclusions just yet. We need to look into this more closely. Find out who the hell's making these reservations and why. Where that money's coming from."

It was a good plan, but Gabriel's gut instinct was already telling him Tremain was guilty. That there was something big behind the man's failing company. And if it was true, if he was purposefully bankrupting himself, it was going to make Woolf Construction's unexpected investment probably the worst thing to happen to the guy.

The thought was satisfying. Yet it wasn't exactly what Gabriel had in mind when it came to his plans for exacting justice. He wanted to be the one who ruined him. He didn't want Tremain ruining himself. And there was another variable he'd been trying not to think about for the past day or so.

Honor. She'd also invested money in Tremain Hotels. And quite a lot of money at that. If Tremain failed, then so would she.

He didn't like the feeling that sat in his gut at that thought. Didn't like *any* of the feelings she seemed to arouse in him. Fucking hell, he hadn't succeeded in his goal of getting information on Tremain out of her in Vermont. And he hadn't because he couldn't seem to think clearly when she was around. He'd had to let her go when she'd wanted to in order to give himself some time to get a bit of fucking perspective.

So she'd sucked cock like a dream. That shouldn't have made him lose it the way he had. Shouldn't have made him walk out just to get away from her. And yet, he'd done both.

It couldn't happen again. He was going to have to go after her, inform her of her stepfather's dealings, but this time, he'd know what to expect. And this time he'd be better at making sure she didn't get under his guard like she had before.

"It might be worth examining those financials again," Zac commented. "See if there's anything dodgy with them."

Gabriel frowned. "Good point. I had a look over them a day or so ago. He's spending shitloads up front, buying quality materials, and using the best of the best to do the work, so that would explain some of his current financial problems, plus he's had a few investors pull out. I'm sure we can find out whether they did so deliberately or whether they were frightened off."

Eva leaned her elbows on the desk, her pale brows descending. "Do you think Honor knows anything about this? She's invested quite a bit of money in Tremain herself."

Gabriel cursed silently in his head. He didn't want to talk about Honor with either Eva or Zac. "She didn't mention it to me." He looked at Zac and changed the subject. "You have any contacts you can use to look into this stuff?"

"I have a few."

"Use them then. If you turn up anything, let me know. I'll deal with Honor." He was conscious of Eva's gaze on

him, but he ignored that. "Now, if you don't have anything better to do, you can both fuck off. I'd like my office back."

Eva pushed back the chair and got to her feet. "I've
got a bad feeling about this, Gabe," she said, her usual,
guarded façade dropping for a moment. "Tremain's covering up something and I don't think it's going to be good.
I want to be involved, especially if Honor's business is on
the line. She shouldn't have to suffer for anything he's
done."

"So what do you want to do? Let the police deal with
it?"

Instantly she scowled. "Fuck no. I wouldn't trust them
as far as I could throw them. This has to be dealt with
by us."

"Agreed. But don't forget, Tremain is mine. Whatever
shit he's gotten himself into, I'm going to be the one who
deals with him directly. Okay?"

Eva threw up her hands. "Hey, you'll get no argument
from me. He's all yours."

After the two of them had gone, Gabriel leaned against
his desk and ran a hand through his hair, unsettled.

Eva's question had him thinking. Did Honor know
anything about what Tremain was doing? Sure, she'd invested her own money but that might have been all part of
the plan. He didn't think she'd be the type to get involved
in something like this, but then again, you never knew.
People did all kinds of shit. After all, it wasn't as if her
family were beacons of honesty.

The thought that Honor may not be all she seemed disturbed him.

Abruptly he pushed himself away from the desk and
walked out of the office.

"Mr. Woolf?" his secretary said. "Your nine fifteen is
here."

"Reschedule it," he snapped on the way to the elevator. "I'll be out for the rest of the morning."

Half an hour later, he stepped into the cold, damp space of St. Sebastian's, still not quite sure what had drawn him here. Only that he needed the icy cold of the church to quiet the restlessness inside him.

A few people were sitting in the pews, their heads bowed. They didn't turn as he entered, too engrossed in their own prayers or problems.

Gabriel slipped into the back pew and sat down, leaned back against the hard wood, and closed his eyes. He could still feel her fingers on his skin, the curious tone in her voice as she repeated the words he'd had tattooed onto his stomach. His vow.

I will repay.

*"Keep it cold, boy," the Reverend had told him. "And don't get distracted. Don't get sidetracked. Not by money or pussy or anything else. If you want to take him down, deliver justice, you have to have a plan. A goal. Keep a clear fucking head. Understand me?"*

He'd understood. Even at eighteen, his heart full of rage at the injustice of his life, he'd known. His anger would destroy him, eat him alive if he didn't direct it. And it might have if he hadn't had the Reverend to set him on the path of cold, clear justice.

The old president was dead now, killed in a gun battle with a rival gang a couple of years after Gabriel had become one of the Angels' most feared enforcers. But he'd never forgotten. Then he'd become the president, keeping the old man's last words close.

*"Revenge is for pussies," the Reverend had said. "Justice is for men."*

Gabriel had earned justice for the Reverend's death eight years later, as club president himself. Driving out the rival MC from their neighborhood through a combination

# CHAPTER ELEVEN

Violet leaned forward and put her elbows on the table, blond dreads falling over her shoulders. "So, dude. Tell me everything."

As soon as Honor had arrived back in New York, Violet had wanted gossip. She had cornered Honor in the kitchen and made her swear to a lunch date to hear all the Gabriel Woolf news.

Honor hadn't been able to think of a decent excuse to get out of it and had decided that perhaps sharing a bit of it wouldn't be so bad. Maybe it would even normalize the whole experience, put it into perspective. A girly chat and a giggle would make it seem not quite so . . . intense. So she'd joined Violet for lunch at a deli they both liked not far from Honor's office.

"Not much to tell really," Honor said calmly, sipping on the latte she'd ordered.

"Bull. Shit." Violet leaned farther forward. "You didn't come back early because nothing happened." She frowned, brushing back a dreadlock threatening to trail into the sugar bowl. "Or *is* that why you came back early?"

"No, not exactly."

Violet abruptly straightened. "You slept with him, didn't you? I can tell. You've got that 'I've just been fucked by an amazing man' look about you."

Much to her irritation, Honor felt her cheeks heat. "Yes, okay. We did sleep together."

"Ha! I knew it." Violet looked triumphant. "It blew your socks off, huh?"

"It was . . . pretty good, yes."

"Riiiight." The other woman picked up the ginger tea she'd been sipping, silver bracelets chiming as they slid down her wrist. "And do I get details?"

"No, you do not."

"Spoilsport. Will I get to meet him? And, more importantly, am I going to need to buy earplugs?"

Honor put down her cup. "No and no," she said firmly. "First of all, you're only crashing on my couch for a limited time and secondly, Gabriel and I were a one-night thing."

"Aww. Really?"

"The only thing we have in common is chemistry, and that's not a good basis for a relationship."

Violet's blue eyes went wide. "Jesus. A relationship? Who said anything about a relationship? If the sex is hot what more excuse do you need?"

"It's not that simple."

"It isn't? What's simpler than meaningless sex?"

Honor looked down at her cup, a tight feeling beginning to form in the center of her chest. "That's just the thing. I don't think I can do meaningless sex. I never have."

Violet frowned. "Hey, are you upset about it?"

No, of course she wasn't. She and Gabriel hadn't forged any bonds. They'd been strangers when they met and they were still strangers now. Nothing had changed.

So there shouldn't be any reason for the tight feeling in her chest whenever she thought of him. Whenever she remembered the cold look in his eyes as he said good-bye. As if he hadn't held her in his arms. Never called her name, his hands buried in her hair.

It was a crack in her armor she really didn't need, and if she told herself she didn't feel it enough times, maybe she wouldn't.

"No," she said, trying to believe the truth of it. "I'm not upset. I just need more than a physical connection."

"Yeah, well, I get that. I mean, I don't really since relationships . . . eww." Violet gave a delicate shudder. "But, well, have you considered one with him?"

Cold dark eyes. Game player. Able to turn on the heat and yet switch it off so easily. Impossible to read. Who demanded control and her surrender.

No, she couldn't have a relationship with a man like that, no matter how exciting he was. No matter how much she'd liked his brand of brutal honesty, or the way he challenged her. In fact all of those reasons were exactly *why* she couldn't go there with him.

Gabriel Woolf was intense, intoxicating. Addictive. A drug she could get hooked on so very easily. A drug that would, in the end, destroy her.

"Definitely not," Honor said. "No, the sex was great but that's it."

"You don't sound convinced."

"I am, honestly."

"Hmm. So what about Alex then? Did you get anywhere with that?"

Honor took a silent breath. Did she really want to tell Vi what Gabriel had revealed? Then again, she couldn't talk to her mother and she had to talk to someone. It was too big a secret to bear all by herself. "Yes, I heard about Alex."

"Oh, something tells me this isn't good." Violet put her cup down. "What is it?"

"Our father . . . was involved in underground gambling in New York. Apparently he used to take Alex along with him to count cards." Honor finally looked up and met her friend's shocked gaze. "Gabriel told me that's how they met. He was with that motorcycle club and they used to do security for the casino."

"Oh my God, really?" Violet blinked. "But I thought your dad went to Vegas?"

Honor shook her head. "The casino was right here." She let out a breath. "I think something . . . bad must have happened there."

"But what? And why?"

"I don't know. But Alex left home really suddenly and without an explanation. We never heard from him again, not even when Daniel died. Which is another thing." She'd only been eight when her father shot himself. But she still remembered the look on her mother's face as they'd brought her out of her classroom at school that day. The look of a woman whose life had shattered. "He . . . well, you know he killed himself. Everyone assumed it was because of the debts, but what if it wasn't? What if it had something to do with Alex leaving?"

Violet's forehead creased. "Such as?"

Honor pushed her latte away, suddenly not feeling like coffee. "I don't know. That's the problem. I don't know anything."

"Gabriel must, though. Didn't you ask him about it?"

"He mentioned that Alex had something bad happen to him at this casino, but he didn't know what because Alex wouldn't tell him."

"Honor . . ."

"And that's the other thing Gabriel told me. Alex has been keeping an eye on Mom and me. Which means all this time, he knew. About our father's death. About Mom's depression. He knew and he didn't lift a damn finger to help. Okay, so something bad happened to him, but what was so bad that he could leave us like that? For nineteen years? He doesn't care, Vi. So why should I care about him?"

Violet picked up her teaspoon and pointed it at her. "You want to know, Honor. Don't lie. And even if you don't, your mom would."

"Gabriel told me Alex doesn't want to talk to me, so that's a moot point. Anyway, I can't bring him up with Mom. It upsets her too much. God, she still thinks Daniel was in Vegas all those weekends. I can't imagine what she'd do if she found out the truth."

"Then perhaps she doesn't need to know. But even if he doesn't want to talk to you, I still think you should try getting in touch with him."

Honor bit her lip. Damn, her friend had a point. Was it only resentment at Alex that was holding her back? Or was it something else? Fear maybe, of what she'd find out?

Her phone, sitting on the table beside her latte, began to vibrate. She looked down and felt everything inside her tighten. Gabriel.

For a second she debated not answering it. *Coward.* Yeah, that was a little too teenage for her. Mentally bracing herself, she picked up the phone and pushed the answer button.

"Hello, Gabriel." God, she hoped she didn't sound as breathless as she feared she did. "This is an unexpected pleasure."

"I need to talk to you," he said without preamble, the dark, rough note in his voice reminding her far too much of things she didn't want to be reminded of.

Across the table from her, Vi's eyes had gone wide.

"A 'hello' back is generally the accepted way to greet people you want something from," she said, determined to remain calm. "As you probably remember, I don't respond well to demands."

"Bullshit you don't. There were some demands you responded very well to. Or have you forgotten?"

Honor looked down at the table. "Actually, I think you're the one who doesn't remember."

To her surprise there was a silence at the other end of the phone. As if she'd scored a hit. "We can talk about that, too, if you want. But this is urgent. It's about my investment in Tremain."

Foreboding gripped her. "What about it? Please don't tell me you're pulling out, because—"

"We need to talk, Honor. The sooner the better."

"We can talk now."

"I'm not doing this over the phone. Do you have some time this afternoon? I'll come to your office."

There was a hard note in his voice, not that lazy tone he used when he was playing with her. Which meant he was serious. Hell, she so did not want to see him, but if this was about his investment then she was going to have to, wasn't she?

She swallowed. "I have a meeting this afternoon."

"Change it."

"I can't. This particular client is flying in from London and I won't be able to get hold of them to reschedule. But . . . I have some time tomorrow. Probably not till later in the day—"

"I'll pick you up outside your office at five p.m."

"But I didn't—"

"Be there, Honor." He ended the call abruptly, leaving her staring at her phone in a combination of shock and annoyance.

Violet leaned on one elbow. "Soooo, are you going to tell me what that was all about? I gather it was Tall, Rough, and Sexy?"

"He wants to talk with me about the Tremain investment."

"Just business then?"

"From the sounds of it." Worry settled in her gut. Whatever he wanted to see her about, it couldn't be good.

Yet despite her anxiety, something else fizzled in her veins. Something she didn't want to acknowledge. Excitement. *Hunger* . . .

Honor pushed the feelings away. "So, dessert?"

"You know," Violet said casually. "You could also ask him about Alex."

God, she so did not want to add Alex into the mix. "No, I don't think so."

"Hey, it's just an idea. I mean, you don't have to get in touch with him or anything. You only have to ask a few questions. And then you'd know, right?"

Honor frowned. "You're kind of annoying, Vi."

"I know it's low of me but still. You'll never know the truth if you don't take this opportunity. Who knows what happened to Alex? And if it's bad, if he had good reason to leave, then wouldn't you want to know?"

It was true. Dammit.

Honor sighed. "You're a pain in the butt."

"So I've heard. Does that mean I still get to share your chocolate cake?"

Gabriel checked his watch. Five minutes after five and Honor hadn't come out of her office. Traffic was as thick as the snow and it was going to take a while to get home as it was. Then again, he wasn't in a rush.

He sat back on the soft leather of the limo seats. "Another five minutes, Smith, and I'll go get her."

"Are you sure, Mr. Woolf? I can easily—"

"No. I'll do it." He didn't want anyone else's input tonight. Because he was going to confront Honor St. James once and for all. Get the truth from her one way or another.

*Be cold. Don't get distracted by softer emotions. Think only of justice.*

From inside the pocket of his jacket, his phone chimed. He took it out and checked the screen. A text from Alex. Why the fuck did his friend always send him texts just as he was about to meet Honor? It was like he had a sixth sense or something.

*You're back early I hear. Vermont too cold for you?*

He was going to have to tell his friend about the things Zac had discovered at some point. He had a feeling Alex would want to know. Then again, maybe some of those things Alex *did* already know.

Quickly, he texted his friend back.

*Business back in NY. BTW, we're going to need to get another Circles club meeting happening.*

A small pause and then Alex's response came back.

*Oh? This is early. Months early.*

Gabriel took another glance out the window. Still no Honor. He returned his attention to his phone.

*I have info we need to discuss. This Saturday.*

Alex responded:

*I'll have to reschedule things but okay. Usual room.*

"Here she comes, Mr. Woolf."

Gabriel looked up as Smith was in the process of getting out of the car. Outside on the sidewalk he saw Honor come out of her building, a familiar black trench coat belted tightly around her slender waist. Like the day he'd met her, she was in one of her tight little skirts, those expensive red-soled shoes on her feet, black boots that hugged her calves this time.

*Her leg propped against his shoulder, his arm wrapped around her thigh. Inside her as she arched her back, letting him slide even deeper . . .*

Jesus Christ, not now. He had to maintain his distance, not think about sex.

Gabriel pushed the memory away as the limo door opened, icy air and snow swirling inside, and then there she was. Sliding onto the seat opposite him, her delicate face flushed with cold, making her eyes glow midnight blue.

*One look into those eyes and he'd forgotten where he was. So much heat. Warming him up from the inside. Burning away the cold . . .*

"Hello, Gabriel," she said.

He almost shook his head to clear the memories, catching himself at the last second. Christ, he had to get a grip.

Leaning back in his seat, he said. "You like to keep me waiting, don't you, little girl?"

"I had a few things to finish up. You had something to say about the Tremain investment. Please don't tell me you're pulling out, because I thought we had a deal."

"It's not as simple as that."

Her gaze met his. "Then what is it?"

The expression on her face gave nothing away. God, she was good at hiding her emotions and her thoughts. But then, he was good at that, too.

"How well do you know your stepfather?"

She blinked, obviously taken aback by the question. "What do you mean?"

"I found things while I was looking over the Tremain financial reports. Irregularities."

"Irregularities?"

This time he was sure he caught a glimpse of uncertainty in her eyes. Perhaps she didn't know anything. Maybe this was news to her. Either that or she was a very good actress indeed. "Lots of reservation cancellations at the less-than-twenty-four-hour mark. You understand what that means, don't you?"

"That the hotel keeps the deposit paid. But that's not unusual, is it?"

"It is if the deposits have been paid by people who don't exist."

Honor stared at him. "I don't understand. What do you mean people who don't exist?"

"I mean that the people who made those reservations aren't actual people."

"Who are they then?"

There was genuine puzzlement on her face. At least, he thought it was genuine. "I had a contact of mine follow the money trail. It leads to places you don't want to know about." He held her gaze, leaning forward, his forearms on his knees. "It looks like your stepfather is running a money-laundering scam through his hotels. You wouldn't happen to know anything about that, would you, sweetheart?"

She'd gone pale. "No," she said in a shaken voice. "No, that's not true."

"It is. I've seen the evidence. And that's not all. There's a reason Tremain Hotels is failing. It looks like he's deliberately running it into the ground."

Honor's throat moved, her eyes wide and dark in her pale face. She shook her head. "No, I don't believe it. He . . . he wouldn't do that."

There was nothing forced in the look of shock on her face, which meant it was probably genuine. She clearly hadn't known about this. A thread of relief wound through him, which didn't make any kind of sense because surely he didn't care whether she was in on it or not. Nevertheless, he was glad she wasn't.

"You didn't know?" he asked, to be sure.

"No," she snapped. "This is the first I've heard of it. Which makes me wonder why the hell I should believe you."

"Because I've got all the fucking evidence on a memory stick in a safe in my apartment."

"In a safe?"

"The information is commercially sensitive." Not to mention volatile. Because it didn't only involve Tremain. It involved Daniel St. James as well.

But she kept shaking her head, glossy black hair brushing her shoulders. "No. You're wrong. You're completely and utterly wrong. Why would he do that? He has no reason to."

"He's getting money from somewhere, Honor. And he has to get rid of it on the sly, that's why he's laundering it."

She went very still, her gaze pinning him to the spot. "I want proof."

Slowly, Gabriel sat back. "I told you, it's back at my apartment. We can go—"

"No." The look in Honor's eyes blazed. "I'm not going anywhere with you until I see hard evidence for these . . . baseless accusations."

Of course she wouldn't. But he really didn't want to show her the evidence now. At least not in a car on the side of the road. The information he'd uncovered was going to hurt her, and that unfamiliar kernel of concern that he only seemed to feel for her didn't want to see her in pain. She needed to be somewhere private. Somewhere protected.

Yet it was obvious she wasn't even going to listen until he'd given her reason to believe him.

Reluctantly, Gabriel reached into the pocket of his jacket, brought out his phone, and began scrolling through his e-mails until he'd found the one Zac had forwarded him. All the important financial information was on the memory stick, but he had a couple of incriminating e-mails that Zac had managed to find. Tremain warning someone that the cancellations had come to the notice of hotel staff and were being monitored. That they needed to let a couple of days pass without a cancellation in order to allay suspicion.

He opened the e-mail and handed the phone to Honor without a word.

She took it, sitting back against the seat, looking down at the screen, the black wings of her hair framing her face. Her finger trembled as she touched the screen, scrolling down as she read, and the concern inside him tightened. He felt the oddest urge to gather her into his arms. Hold her. Comfort her somehow.

An irrational thought. He didn't give comfort. Sure, he'd always protected people who needed protection, defended those he considered his. When he'd ridden with the club, the cops in his neighborhood had deemed him a vigilante and he'd never been unhappy with the label.

But wanting to hold someone? Comfort them? That meant he had to care, and he couldn't afford that distraction.

Jesus, he was getting soft. The Reverend would be turning in his grave.

"I . . . don't believe this," Honor said after a long moment. "How do you know any of this is true?"

"I trust my contacts. And believe me, I know a scam when I see one."

She was silent, staring down at the phone, at the evidence sitting there in electronic black-and-white. Then abruptly she handed it back to him. "Thank you for this," she said tonelessly. "You'll forgive me if I don't stay. I have things I need to sort out." Gripping her purse, she leaned forward to open the door.

Oh no, she wasn't going anywhere. Not when he hadn't finished.

Gabriel pressed a button near his seat and the doors locked with a click.

Honor looked sharply at him. "What are you doing?"

He couldn't let her leave. He had more to tell her, plus he needed to make doubly sure she wasn't involved in this, that she wasn't going to go running off to Tremain to warn him. And also he *still* hadn't got the information out of her.

*It's not the information. She's upset and you don't like that.*

Ignoring the voice in his head, Gabriel leaned forward and took Honor's hands in his. Her fingers were cold like they'd been by the lake in Vermont, so he rubbed them gently with his thumbs.

"Stop," she said thickly. "What are you doing?" There was tension in her fingers, in her arms. "Let me go, Gabriel."

"We need to discuss this properly."

"The person I need to discuss this with is Dad."

"You're going to tell him he's been found out? No, I don't fucking think so." He stroked his thumbs up and down her chilly hands, smoothing her skin, keeping his gaze firmly on hers. "Besides, there's more I have to tell you."

She stared at him, her face so white it was the color of the fresh snow on the sidewalk outside. "What more?"

Shit, he didn't want to tell her. But she had to know. When Zac had traced back the money, he'd found out something else. Honor's father didn't just have a drug problem and gambling addiction. He had a whole other life.

"My contact followed the money trail back and discovered where it was coming from. Who's paying him." She'd gone very still. Silent. "The money's coming from a casino. The Lucky Seven casino."

"But isn't that the one my father . . . ?" She stopped dead.

"Yes." Gabriel tightened his fingers around hers. "Honor,

your father wasn't a patron. He owned the whole fucking casino. He ran it."

She said nothing, staring at him, her hands motionless in his. Then something in her face shut down, shock fading from it, becoming utterly expressionless.

She withdrew her hands from his, sitting back in her seat, smoothing her skirt down and collecting her purse again. "You said you had more evidence on your computer at home? Show me. Now."


Honor barely took in Gabriel's Tribeca apartment when they finally arrived. Shock was still coursing through her system, the world around her dim and unfocused.

She turned as Gabriel came in behind her.

"Your evidence," she said flatly. "I want to see it."

He gave her an unreadable look. "Sure. Give me a minute to get the memory stick and I'll bring up the files on the computer."

Down one end of the open-plan room stood a massive, rustic-looking dining table made out of some kind of dark wood. A sleek silver laptop was open on it.

Gabriel left the room for a minute, coming back with something in his hand. He moved toward the table and bent over the computer, pushing the memory stick into the drive then tapping a few of the keys. Honor followed him, the cold shock that had gripped her in the car slowly spreading through her body. All except her hands. They were still burning from where Gabriel's fingers had touched her.

She felt like she had to move slowly, as if the world had suddenly been revealed to be made of glass and it would shatter at the slightest movement. The same way it had after her father's death and the repo men had turned up. Come to take away all her precious things. The possessions she'd always thought were hers and yet turned out not to be after all.

Just like the stepfather she'd always thought to be a good man wasn't.

Just like her father ended up being worse than she'd ever imagined.

*He owned the whole fucking casino. He ran it.*

She didn't want to believe it about Guy. She *couldn't* believe it of her father. How was it possible that an eminent lawyer could own the kind of place Gabriel had told her about? Where anything could be bought and sold?

*No one knew he had a drug problem. No one knew about his debts. Why the hell shouldn't he run the casino as well?*

She could feel a bubble of hysterical laughter pushing against her throat. Her father and stepfather had been old college friends and now, apparently, they were also criminals. What were the damn chances?

Honor swallowed down the hysteria as Gabriel stood back, letting her see the screen. Part of her didn't want to look but she made herself, looking down at the series of files he'd brought up. E-mails. Accounts. Financial records.

The cold inside her froze into a hard lump of ice.

It was true. All of it was true. Guy was laundering money through his hotels. Money that appeared to have come from a legitimate Vegas casino, but in actual fact had come from . . . She scrolled through another file with a shaking finger . . . a company called Seven to One Holdings. A shell company that according to yet more e-mails was a front for the Lucky Seven casino.

"What about my father?" she asked in a voice that didn't sound like hers. "Where's your evidence he owned that place?"

"Here." Gabriel leaned past her, closed down one file, and opened another. "His ties to the casino have been extremely well hidden but my contact managed to turn up this. His name is on the building title."

She stared at the screen, at what looked like a scanned-in version of a hardcopy property title. And sure enough, there was Daniel St. James's flamboyant signature at the bottom. "But just because he owned—"

Gabriel calmly opened up another file. "Records of deliveries of various different things. Alcohol. Food. A liquor license. Your father has signed off on all of them. On the surface it looks like a bar going on there, but it's not."

Honor couldn't take her eyes off the numbers on the screen. Off Daniel's incriminating signature. "Didn't your club used to do security?"

"Yeah, we did."

She looked at him. "And you didn't know this already?"

"Like I told you, we weren't allowed inside. We weren't important enough to meet with the head guy."

"So this is news to you, too?" That bubble of hysteria was threatening to burst. "What about Alex? Did he know?"

"I don't know. But we did some more digging," Gabriel went on relentlessly. "Turns out the casino was losing money under your father's management. We found records that suggest he was using his own money to pay it back, hence his supposed 'gambling' debts. It was all covered up, of course."

Honor swallowed. "By whom?"

Gabriel stood beside her, his tall figure absolutely still. "Tremain."

Of course. It even made a weird kind of sense.

"What's their connection?" Gabriel continued quietly,

a thin thread of ice running through his voice. "Tremain and your father. Because it's too much of a coincidence that they're complete fucking strangers."

She sucked in a breath, the feeling that the world was slowly breaking apart around her intensifying. "They went to college together. They were friends."

"You didn't think to tell me this earlier?"

"I didn't think it was relevant." The hysteria expanded, threatening to spill out. "We should contact the police," she said, needing to say something. Anything.

"No." The word was final, no room for argument. "No police."

She turned sharply. "But this is illegal. I can't—"

"You're an investor in Tremain's company, Honor. You'll be implicated. There'll be police coming into your office. Seizing your computers. Looking through your files. Do you really want that kind of shit?"

"I have nothing to hide."

"Are you sure?" The look in his eyes was suddenly frightening. "You're not going to go straight to Tremain and tell him what we've found?"

The shock redoubled, a thick coating of ice slowly crawling over her skin. "You really think I'm involved?"

Gabriel's expression was implacable. "You're loyal. I think you'd protect him no matter what. Like you said, he's more of a father to you than your real one ever was."

She took a step toward him, shock beginning to turn into anger. "I would *never* do that. If he broke the law, he has to answer for it. But he was a good man, Gabriel. He helped Mom after my dad died. He got her better, able to cope again. And he was good to me, too. God, he even tried to talk me out of investing in Tremain." She faltered. "He said it was his mess and he'd handle it. But I . . . didn't listen. I went ahead anyway because he hated asking for help."

The hard look on Gabriel's face eased a fraction. "This isn't your fault. You invested in good faith."

"That doesn't change the fact that I put money into his company. And now Dad's going to bankrupt himself and me in the process." She swallowed. "I still don't even know why."

A silence fell, heavy and thick.

Honor turned. "I should go. No, I'm not going to warn him but I need to see him at least . . ."

"No. You don't know what he'll do if he thinks you know about all this."

She glanced up at him. "He wouldn't hurt me. I'm like a daughter to him."

"People do all kinds of shit you think they won't do, Honor. Especially if they're threatened. Believe me, I know." His eyes glittered, the darkness in them suddenly deeper and more infinite than she'd ever imagined.

Of course he'd know. If the rumors about him were true, he'd probably been an even bigger criminal than Guy was.

*Than your father was?*

Honor looked away, nausea clenching hard inside her. Secrets and more secrets. "I should see my mother," she said. "I should ask her about Daniel . . ." She stopped because no, she couldn't see her mother. What would she say? Did her mother know? God, maybe her mother was even involved, too . . .

Honor raised a hand to her forehead and closed her eyes, feeling even sicker.

She'd thought this was over. That after her father's death there wouldn't be any more shocks. And there hadn't been until this. Until Gabriel had come into her life and broken it all apart, spinning it into chaos.

"Honor," he said softly, as if knowing the thought the moment she had it.

She dropped her hand, opened her eyes. "I need to go." She didn't know quite where to go but she had to do something to regain control of her own damn life.

He turned, his big body squarely in front of her. "You should stay. I know this is a hell of a shock, but we have to discuss where we go from here."

"Later. I can't . . . I can't deal with this right now. Okay?" She stepped to the side, only to have him step with her, blocking her exit.

Blinking, she looked up at him. The darkness in his eyes burned all the way through her. Right down into her soul. Fear tightened in her gut, the same kind of fear she'd experienced back in Vermont whenever he'd gotten close. Along with the sharp excitement that always came with it.

"You're not leaving," he said quietly. "Not until you tell me all you know about Tremain and your father."

"I told you. They were friends."

"I want more."

Her mouth dried. "You can't stop me from leaving."

"Can't I?"

"Unless there's another handy button you can press to lock the door from here, then no, you can't."

"I don't need to lock the door." He didn't move, didn't come any closer and yet still it felt as if he was looming over her, overwhelming her. "Because you're not going anywhere."

Anger shot down her spine. He was the one who'd shattered her life. Who'd brought Alex back. Who'd revealed her father's secrets. Who'd exposed the man she'd come to love like a father. Whose very presence cracked the armor she needed to wear in order to feel like she had control over her life.

She'd been right to be wary of him. He was chaos. Everything she didn't need in her life. And she didn't want anything more to do with him.

She stepped to the side again and he blocked her. Breathing fast, she feinted to the other side but he seemed to know exactly what she was doing because her side step only brought her up hard against his chest.

Honor gasped as his arm wrapped around her waist, holding her there. Her heart thudding, she snapped her head up, looking into his face. There was no mercy at all there. No softness. His expression was unyielding, his eyes almost black. "Like I said, you're staying here."

She wouldn't demean herself with a struggle, especially since any kind of movement only made her even more achingly conscious of the leashed power in his big, muscular body. Of the heat pressed against her. The sheer force of nature that was their chemistry. She didn't want anything to spark that particular conflagration, not now.

"So, what?" she snapped. "You're going to bring out the spotlight and start water boarding me?"

"You don't want to know what I could do to get you to talk."

She gritted her teeth. "Look, if you're wanting to know about Guy's business activities, I don't know any more than you do."

"It's not just his business activities. I want to know about his private life, too."

"Why? What use is that kind of information to you?"

"Anything you can tell me will be useful." There was a savage-looking glint in his eyes. "I was looking to invest in good faith, Honor. And if there's one thing I can't stand, it's people thinking they can fuck with me and my money."

For a second, anger was stamped all over his brutally handsome features. A hot, molten kind of rage that, for some reason didn't frighten her the way it should have. Mainly because she got the feeling that he didn't often show genuine emotion. The only other time she'd seen anything like it had been when she'd taken him in her mouth. She'd caught a glimpse of it then, too, a flash of the real man behind his cold, hard exterior.

Desire began to tighten inside her along with a kind of panic. God, why was she feeling this now? After everything he'd told her? She was supposed to be getting away from him, not wanting to get closer.

"Let me go, you bastard," she said, her breathing coming faster, harder. "I don't have to tell you a thing."

His other hand slid along her jaw, behind her ear, his fingers curling in her hair, forcing her head back. "Why are you protecting him?" His voice was a soft kind of growl that sent whispers of heat over her skin. "You said you wouldn't."

"He's my stepfather," she gasped. "He's not a bad man and I won't do anything that will see him hurt."

"No matter if he takes you down with him?"

Honor closed her eyes. She didn't want to look at him. Didn't want to see the truth she knew she was going to have to face sometime. That Guy wasn't the man she thought he was and hadn't been for a long time. That he and her father had knowingly led a secret criminal life. A life that had also somehow destroyed Alex.

Too many links. Too many coincidences. Too many secrets.

"Please," she whispered hoarsely. "Let me go."

He didn't move. Didn't speak. Then the hand in her hair and the arm around her waist tightened almost imperceptibly. And his mouth covered hers.

Deep down, she'd been expecting it, a part of her longing for it. Craving it. In fact, it seemed to be the most natural end to their meeting. Heat to combat the icy grip of shock. God, one of the most intriguing aspects about Gabriel

Woolf was that on the surface he could be so cold, like ice. Like granite. Yet, under that, he was a furnace hot enough to melt metal.

Certainly enough to melt her. Burn her to ashes.

*Are you crazy? You can't do this with him again.*

Yes, she could. And she would. He was a drug she couldn't refuse, an addiction she couldn't resist. And right now, still reeling from everything he'd told her, all she wanted to do was get high. On him.

So she didn't fight. She opened her mouth under his instead and let his kiss take her. Fill her up with desire and hunger. Replace all the shock and the questions with pleasure, with sensation. Anything so she didn't have to think, if only for a moment.

He made a deep, hungry noise in the back of his throat, thrilling her right down to the bone. His fingers curled painfully tight in her hair, pulling her head back even farther, the kiss becoming deeper. Harder. Consuming her.

She dropped her purse and pressed her palms against the wall of his chest, loving the feel of hard, hot muscle beneath the cotton of his T-shirt.

He broke away all of a sudden, his eyes glittering, a stripe of color on his cheekbones. "What are you—" she began, only to have her question cut off as he took her hands and held them behind her back, locking his fingers around her wrists. Then he forced her against him again, gripping her chin in his free hand and taking her mouth in another annihilating, savage kiss.

Somehow it felt different from what had happened between them in Vermont. He'd been slow then. Almost methodical. But he wasn't either of those things now. She could taste desperation in his kiss. Hunger. A wild edge that had her own desire stretched to the limits of control.

Gabriel backed her up to the dining table and before she knew quite what had happened, he'd lifted her on top of it, pushing her back. She sucked in a ragged breath as he slid her skirt up her thighs, then tugged hard on the sides of her panties. The lace that held them together was only a thin thread and it snapped easily. His gaze was riveted to the view between her legs and he didn't look away as he tossed her underwear to the floor. As he spread her thighs wide.

Honor trembled, her hands on the hard wood of the table, pushing herself up so she could see. The sight of him looking down at her, an unbearably hungry expression on his face, was so erotic she could hardly breathe.

At her movement he glanced up, fire in his eyes. "You want to watch me eating you out, baby?"

Heat coiled at the base of her spine. Why did she like the dirty things he said to her? Why did she like his roughness? His dominance? The way he took her control and broke it to pieces in front of her?

*You know why. Because you like letting go.*

"Y-yes," she stammered hoarsely.

"Stay like that then," he ordered. "Take your eyes off me and I'll stop."

So she watched him, her heartbeat echoing loudly in her ears as he leaned down, his big hands holding her legs spread wide, his palms hot on her skin. He licked her, running his tongue up the center of her sex, drawing a gasp from her as fire streaked over her nerve endings. Then he did it again, another long, slow lick that had her shaking, a cry building in her throat. "You taste good," he growled, holding her down harder. "Are you watching? Because I'm fucking hungry."

The muscles in her thighs began to burn and she began to shake as he lowered his head again. The cry escaped as his mouth covered her, his tongue pushing inside her.

She couldn't tear her gaze away from the sight of his blond head between her thighs, of his large, strong hands on her pale skin. Gripping her tightly. Holding her. The eroticism of it made her pant.

How easily he could hold her down, her strength no match for his. How fragile and vulnerable he made her feel next to his height and power. The brutal, dominant masculinity of him. Something about that excited her beyond words. Back in Vermont, it had felt threatening to have her veneer of control stripped away from her. But she didn't feel threatened now. Now, she wanted the escape it gave her. A small taste of a freedom she'd never be able to take for herself.

It made her want to test him. Push against him. See what would happen.

As the pleasure gathered into a tight hard knot, she tried to close her legs, but he wouldn't let her. Keeping them spread wide, he tasted her, exploring the folds of her sex with a precision and skill that had her soft moans beginning to change into a scream.

Her head fell back, her eyes closing. "Gabriel . . . Gabriel, please . . ."

But the mouth between her legs moved away.

Honor's eyes snapped open, her whole body drawn to the edge of breaking point. "No," she panted hoarsely. "No, don't—"

"You looked away." He'd pushed himself back but the look in his dark eyes was still hungry, still feral. "Bad girl."

A wave of heat swamped her. "B-but I . . . b-but . . ."

"Don't worry, I'll give you what you want but it'll be on my terms. When I say. When you can prove to me how obedient you are."

Obedience, yes, that's what she wanted. She didn't want to make decisions now. She wanted to be told what to do, so she didn't have to think. "W-what do you want me to do?"

"Just lie there and watch for now. Because in a minute or two you won't be able to."

He stepped back from the table and in one smooth, fluid movement, he took his T-shirt off over his head, biceps flexing, exposing tanned skin and hard cut muscle. God, he was beautiful. She'd seen him naked before, in Vermont, but hadn't had a chance to fully appreciate the sheer beauty of him till now. Broad shoulders, lean hips. An intricate Celtic cross tattooed over his heart. The one that had intrigued her back at the hotel. And the other one . . .

Her gaze dropped to his fingers as they undid the buttons of his jeans, slowly revealing the Gothic characters of the words tattooed on his abdomen just beneath the waistband of his jeans. *I will repay* . . . Vengeance. But for what? And what did it mean to this man? This dangerous, beautiful, mysterious man . . .

Gabriel pushed his jeans down, taking his boxers with them so that a second later he stood naked in front of her. And all thought left her head entirely. Because why bother thinking when this sight was in front of her? Muscled and lean and hard. So damn hard.

She ached. Everywhere. Her thighs, her sex, her nipples. She wanted to be naked like him, wrapping her legs around his waist and taking the heat of him inside her. Taking the release she craved like air. But no, she couldn't. He'd told her to lie there and watch and that's what she had to do. Otherwise she wouldn't get what she so badly wanted.

Honor took a ragged breath as he tore open a condom packet he'd taken from the pocket of his jeans, watching as he gripped his cock and sheathed himself. Her anticipation began to build, her breathing coming faster.

Gabriel came over to the table. "Obedient. That's what I like to see. But the time for watching is over now, baby."

His hands settled on her hips and without any warning, he flipped her over onto her stomach, pulling her back so her toes only barely touched the ground, her hips resting on the edge of the table. "Hands behind you."

She did as she was told, turning her head to the side, her cheek pressed to the hard wood of the table, feeling his fingers close around her crossed wrists. Her legs were shaking as she tried to get her balance on the floor with her toes, desperate to brace herself. This was going to rip her apart, she knew it, and she wanted it. But she had to find some way of grounding herself so she didn't get lost in the flood.

Honor took a breath, the heat of his bare skin burning against the backs of her thighs. Then she gave a hoarse cry as he began to push inside her, feeling herself stretch around him, the pressure so intense she shuddered, pulling against his restraint, wanting her hands free to ease it, relieve it somehow.

But he didn't let her go, his fingers locked tight around her wrists, intensifying the feeling of being bound and somehow increasing the pleasure at the same time.

"Gabriel." His name was halfway between a plea and a sob. "It's too much. I need . . ."

He didn't reply. Only continued to hold her wrists as his other hand slid beneath her hips, lifting her so her feet were no longer on the floor, the push of him inside her even deeper.

She gave a low, ragged cry, because there was nothing to hold onto. Nothing to brace herself against. She couldn't move, not even to pull away. Completely and utterly at his mercy. She began to tremble. "I can't do this," she whispered hoarsely. "I can't . . ."

Heat against her back, his voice low and rough near her ear. "You can, baby. I know you can."

"I can't."

"You handled it back in Vermont. You can do it now."

Her skin felt too tight, like she was bursting out of it. "I don't . . ."

"You're hot and tight and wet for me. I can feel it. You want to come. You want to come so badly."

Another wave of heat went through her. She did and yet she didn't think she could deal with the intensity of this. With the feeling of helplessness, of pleasure. Of total surrender to him.

*You want to surrender to him. You want him to make you. So you can be free of control. So you can let go.*

"Give it to me, Honor." His voice was full of darkness and heat. "Give it to me now." And he drew back, sliding out of her, then in again, a deep, slow thrust. And again. And again, until she'd forgotten why she couldn't handle it. Forgotten everything except the ecstasy that was breaking her. Cracking her wide open.

He began to move faster, his arm around her hips, his hand on her wrists, holding her tight, giving her no choice but to take whatever he chose to give her.

And she couldn't say the words to make him stop. Something inside her wouldn't let her. Instead she gave a hoarse moan and closed her eyes, surrendering completely.

The climax, when it finally exploded inside her, left her sobbing against the table, tears on her cheeks. She felt him move harder and deeper, his breathing becoming harsh and ragged. Then abruptly he let her wrists go, his arms sweeping beneath her, gathering her against him as he gave one last hard, convulsive thrust and called her name in a raw voice, holding her tight as his own release hit.

Honor kept her eyes closed as he shuddered against her, as the post-orgasm aftershocks moved through her body like little flashes of static electricity.

This had probably been a huge mistake. Yet she couldn't bring herself to care.

The world she'd known for the past fifteen years had shattered and if the only thing she could take from it was the wild, heady pleasure of being in Gabriel's arms, then hell, that's what she'd take.

# CHAPTER TWELVE

Gabriel slapped a hand on the table beside Honor, bracing himself as the after effects of the orgasm ricocheted through him. He was shaking.

Holy fuck. What the hell was wrong with him?

He stared down at her. She lay facedown on the table, her skirt bunched around her waist, revealing the smooth, white skin of her perfect ass. Her head was turned to the side, an inky black veil of hair hiding her face. She didn't move and shit, he didn't think he could either. He was still inside her and the feel of her body clasping him tightly was threatening to make him hard all over again.

How had it happened? He'd wanted to stop her from leaving so he could get that fucking information about Tremain.

Except she'd wanted to protect her stepfather. Which had made him so angry. What had that prick done to deserve her loyalty? Especially when she was faced with the evidence that the man hadn't been who she'd thought. He'd wanted to tell her then, all about his mother. About what that bastard had done to her.

But he hadn't. She'd been soft and warm in his arms, shock and betrayal written all over her face. Because Jesus, she hadn't only been let down by the man she thought of as a father, but she'd also found out her actual father's secrets went deeper than anyone had ever guessed. He'd wanted to give her something then. Something to take away her anguish. And the only thing he could think of to give had been pleasure.

Except he'd forgotten what she did to him. Forgotten how the taste of her, the sound of her crying his name, got under his guard. Totally screwed with his detachment.

How intoxicating it was to have her surrendering her control to him. Fuck, he'd felt like God himself when all the tension had gone out of her and she'd given herself up to him.

Trusting him.

A cold hand squeezed around his chest. Shit, he couldn't breathe.

She couldn't trust him. She couldn't.

Gabriel withdrew and shoved himself away from her. He walked quickly into the hallway and went into the bathroom, dealing with the condom before going to the sink and turning on the faucet. He splashed some water onto his face, his hands still shaking.

This was insane. Okay, so there was something about Honor that really got to him. That made him want to take her rough and hard, imprint himself on her in some way. Rip away that controlled exterior and force her to acknowledge him.

He didn't know why he needed that from her. It didn't make any sense. She was just a woman and he'd had women before. Many women.

*But not like this. Not with their hands behind their backs and their feet off the ground.*

Shit. Screwing her was not supposed to be the goal here. Information was. Which made him escaping into the bathroom ridiculous, especially after making such a big deal about her staying.

Gabriel dried his face off with a towel then strode back

into the lounge area, hoping like fuck his badly timed exit hadn't resulted in Honor leaving. But no, she was still there, leaning against the table, smoothing down her skirt.

As he came in she looked up, and apart from the streaks of mascara on her cheeks, she looked as cool and untouchable as ever.

"What? Worried I might leave?" she said, an acid bite to her words.

"Don't think I haven't forgotten about Tremain," he said. Or the connection between him and Honor's father. A connection he hadn't known about until now.

"I haven't, don't worry." As if unable to help herself, her gaze dipped down his body, color rising to her cheeks, and once again he felt his cock getting hard. Wanting her.

*Why bother fighting it? Why can't you get the information you need and have her, too? Especially if she's into it . . .*

Yeah, she had been into it. She'd obeyed his rules, laying there as he'd instructed. Then she'd put her hands behind her back when he'd asked and although she'd told him she couldn't handle it, she hadn't said stop. She'd only screamed as her orgasm had taken her, her body griping him tight like she'd never let him go.

The way she had back in Vermont.

A burning excitement he'd never consciously let himself feel before began to spread throughout his body.

Honor stared at him as if sensing it, the smoothing movements she was making to her skirt becoming slower. "What?" she said huskily. "Why are you looking at me like that?"

He stalked toward her. "I think you know why."

The table was at her back; she had nowhere to go. Her chin lifted, her shoulders squared. Her gaze flickered though, and it wasn't fear he saw there but excitement.

Yes, she wanted this, too. Wanted this release as badly as he did.

And just like him, she was afraid to want it.

Well, maybe he'd make the decision for both of them. Maybe it was time not to be afraid any longer.

He backed her up against the table, putting his hands on the edge on both sides of her, caging her in. "Why do you think I'm looking at you like that? Because there's another reason I don't want you to go."

Her throat moved, a convulsive swallow, and he couldn't help himself. He reached up and put his fingers around her neck, his palm resting against the base of her throat. He heard the sharp breath she took, saw the way her pupils dilated, felt her pulse race against his palm. "I don't think . . ."

"You want this, Honor. I know you do. And so do I." He stroked the side of her neck with his thumb, her skin soft, smooth, and delicate beneath his touch. "There's nothing to be afraid of. Only pleasure. So why not let yourself have it?"

Thick black lashes descended, veiling her gaze for a heartbeat. Then they rose again, her eyes dark and deep as a midnight sky. "You're wrong," she said softly. "I'm not afraid. Not anymore." And this time it was she who kissed him, rising onto her toes to press her mouth to his, her palms flat against his bare chest, driving the breath from his lungs.

He let her kiss him, tasting the sweetness of her, gripping her throat so she knew he was there, that he was still in charge. Because he had to be. If he wanted to indulge himself with her, he had to have the reins tightly in his grasp.

Her hands slid up over his chest, around his neck as the kiss deepened, her body arching against his. She wasn't holding back now and he could taste it. God, the way she'd surrendered to him on the table had been . . . fucking mind-blowing.

He wanted more.

Gabriel kept one hand on her throat while he ran the other up the back of her thigh beneath her skirt and up farther over her bare butt. "This skirt," he murmured against her mouth. "I want it off. The blouse, too." Then he released her and stepped back. "Take it off while I watch."

She'd gone pink but she didn't hesitate or look away as she undid her blouse and took it off, dropping it over one of the dining chairs. Or as she undid her bra, the black lace falling away to reveal the smooth, alabaster skin of her breasts, her nipples pink and hard.

"Slower," he ordered softly, unable to take his eyes off her because Jesus Christ, she was beautiful.

She obeyed, undoing the button then the zipper of her skirt in a slow, sensual movement, the black wool easing down her hips and thighs. Pushing it off, she stepped out of the fabric, then bent to undo the zippers on her calf-length black boots.

"Leave those on," he said. "Naked with only the boots is sexy as fuck."

Honor straightened, blue eyes meeting his, excitement and desire clear in her gaze. A warm, pink flush washed over her skin as he stepped closer to her, giving her beautiful body a slow, heated once-over.

God, he wanted to do bad things to her. Make her sob. Scream his name. Shake apart at the seams. Strip her down to nothing but sensation. Raw, animal feeling. Affect her the way she affected him.

Gabriel bent and picked his T-shirt up off the floor, folded it into a strip, then held it between his fists so she could see. He didn't say anything. She'd know what it meant.

Her eyes widened but there wasn't a trace of fear there, only a flare of something hot. She took a couple of steps toward him but didn't wait for him to put it on her, taking it from his hands herself and placing the cotton over her eyes, blindfolding herself. Then she turned around, holding it on so he could tie it for her.

The simple gesture made his breath catch for reasons he didn't fully understand. Frowning, he tried to ignore the sensation, tying the fabric into a firm knot at the back of her head. She stood motionless, her hands resting on the table in front of her for balance.

She was blind now.

He pulled her back against him, the soft heat of her pressing against his rapidly hardening cock. With her sight gone, her focus would be on nothing but sensation. Sensation he was going to give her.

"Put your arms around my neck," he said in her ear, his hands resting lightly on her hips.

She did so, her arms coming up and back around his neck, her body arching in a graceful bow. He let his hands slide up her abdomen, feeling the delicate musculature of her torso and then the gentle weight of her breasts as he cupped them in his palms. Her nipples were hard and she trembled as he pinched them gently, making her gasp.

She was small, fragile. And yet . . . There was such strength to her. A stubborn will he both admired and found intensely irritating in equal measure. And doing this to her, having this effect on her, made him feel good in a way that had nothing to do with money or power.

He didn't know why that was but he got off on it in a major way.

Sliding one hand down over her stomach, he let his fingers push through the black curls between her thighs, pinching her nipple hard as he brushed his finger over her clit. She moaned, arching into his hand, and he could feel her wetness on his fingers. Evidence of how much she wanted him.

Fuck, that made him feel good. That beautiful, sophisticated, and smart Honor wanted him. Even though he was stained and broken and tainted underneath.

Gabriel turned his head into the black silk of her hair. "Why do you let me do this to you?" He didn't even know why he asked her, why he wanted to know. But it felt important to understand. "Why do you trust me?"

A tremor went through her. "Because . . . no one's ever given to me what you have."

"I haven't given anything to you. Not a fucking thing."

"That's not true. You give me pleasure."

He gave a hoarse laugh. "You can get that from any guy."

"No, I can't. You're the only one who's ever managed to get me out of my head. Who's ever made me feel." She took a ragged-sounding breath. "You're the first man who even paid attention enough to . . . push me. To help me figure out what I want. When I'm with you I feel like I'm the center of the world. And . . . no one's ever made me feel that before. So, that's why I trust you."

His chest felt tight, a raw feeling he didn't want sitting right in the center. "You shouldn't. I wasn't lying when I said I wasn't a good man."

"That's the other reason. You've never lied to me. You've always been honest about yourself. And I like that, too."

The tight sensation became painful. Yeah, he'd never lied to her, but he hadn't been honest either. And now that felt wrong. Now that made him feel . . . guilty.

Jesus, what a time for his conscience—which he'd thought dead long ago—to wake up. Like fucking Lazarus.

He shut his eyes, pushed two fingers into her, feeling her pussy stretch around him, hot and wet and tight. She writhed, gasping. He pinched her nipple again, hard. A punishment for trusting him when she shouldn't. A punishment for making him feel like he should be equal to that trust. For making him *want* to be equal to it when he knew he couldn't. Not when he'd been using her to get to her stepfather.

"You shouldn't trust me," he whispered into her ear as he thrust his fingers into her again. "Remember that."

Her only reply was a moan, the curve of her butt pressing against his groin, driving his own desire higher.

God, he needed to stop thinking about all this shit. Especially when she was in his arms, shaking and moaning. The feel of her pussy around his fingers. He wanted a taste of the kind of freedom she was experiencing now. Freedom from his fucking anger. To be aware of nothing but pleasure. No holding back.

He withdrew his hand, picked her up in his arms and carried her upstairs and into his bedroom, putting her down onto the bed. She angled her head toward him as he looked down at her.

"Can I take the blindfold off?"

"No."

He crossed to his closet and pulled it open, finding what he wanted from the tie rack then coming back over to the bed. "Put your hands out."

"To tie up? Again?"

"You don't want it?"

"I didn't say that. But . . . maybe the question should be why do you?"

He scowled. "I don't need it."

Again that angling of her head. "Don't you?"

Uncomfortable awareness shifted inside him. Of her fingers on his stomach that morning in Vermont. A gentle touch that had made him feel . . . suffocated.

*You don't want her to touch you like that.*

He stared at the length of silk in his hands. No, he didn't.

Because he wasn't worthy of that kind of gentleness. He'd done bad things. There were deaths on his hands. Each one had been absolutely necessary in order to protect the people in his neighborhood. But he was a sinner. Destined for hell sure as fuck. And she was another sin to add to the list.

Then again, she'd given him her trust downstairs on that table, so perhaps it was time he gave her a little piece of his.

Gabriel let the tie drop onto the floor. "No ties then. But keep the blindfold." He could bear the brush of her hands, but he didn't want to look into her eyes as well. "Lie back."

A smile turned her mouth and that too made something painful catch inside him. Jesus, this woman was fucking trouble and part of him wanted to turn her over like he had before, so he couldn't see her face. Couldn't see that smile. Yet part of him didn't. He wanted to see her come apart and scream his name.

Honor did as she was told. Lying there naked and blindfolded should have made her seem helpless. But bizarrely, he felt like he was the one who was vulnerable. Like she had the power over him and not the other way around.

And the worst part was that it was too late to stop or walk away. He wanted her too much.

Gabriel reached into the drawer of the nightstand and found himself a condom packet. Protected himself quickly. Then he got onto the bed, pushing apart her thighs. She was so wet and hot when he eased inside of her that he had to stop and take a breath, the pulse pounding in his head.

She groaned, arching her back. "Gabriel . . ."

He would never get enough of hearing her say his name, all hoarse and ragged and desperate. He leaned forward, shifting his hips, thrusting deeper, watching, fascinated as pleasure unfurled over her face. Wanting to give her more of it, wanting to see her break.

*You don't have to give her this.*

No, he didn't. But he wanted to. Like he had downstairs, he wanted to give her pleasure, and not for any reason other than because she'd been hurt and he wanted to make it better.

But he couldn't have those kinds of thoughts. He wasn't allowed to care.

Gabriel shut the thoughts down. And when her hands slid up his arms, gripping his shoulders, he closed his eyes and increased the rhythm, deep and hard until he felt her convulse around him, her pussy clamping down hard on his cock, her cry of release in his ears. Then he let himself go and found his own little piece of freedom.

Honor woke up and blinked at the ceiling, wondering where on earth she was. Because she wasn't in her own apartment, with the big velvet comforter she liked to curl up underneath.

This room had a high ceiling with dark, wooden, exposed beams. Big curving windows with plain, heavy, white curtains that made the daylight glow behind them. The walls were mostly unpainted brick except for one which was mirrored and obviously a walk-in closet.

In the mirror she could see herself lying in a massive, heavy, wooden bed, in a tangle of white sheets. Apart from the nightstands on either side of the bed, it was the only furniture in the room.

A clean, bare, minimalist kind of room. Like a monk's cell.

Except the man who slept here was no monk.

Pushing herself up in bed, Honor ran a hand through her hair. Perhaps she should feel worse about it than she did, because obviously spending the night with Gabriel had not been the best idea she'd ever had. Especially after all the shocks of the previous day. Which—sadly—she hadn't forgotten about either.

But she couldn't bring herself to feel bad about it. In fact, all things considered, she felt surprisingly . . . good. Like something binding her had been cut away. A very odd thing to think when she'd spent part of the previous night blindfolded.

A reflexive shiver went through her as she remembered. Gabriel's hands, his mouth, touching her, tasting her. There wasn't one inch of skin he hadn't kissed or licked. Or bitten. And she'd just lain there and taken it. All of it.

She covered her face with her hands for a moment, a blush washing over her skin at the memories. Embarrassed and thrilled and shocked at herself all at the same time.

It had been amazing. An awakening in every sense of the word because unlike in Vermont, she'd finally let herself surrender to the sensations, given herself permission to enjoy it. Revel in it.

*You can't. You know where that leads.*

Honor ignored the insidious thought. Last night, she'd chosen to embrace the passion and, God help her, she wanted that passion again.

Right after she'd had coffee though.

Sighing, Honor dropped her hands and slid out of the bed. There was a bathroom en suite near the closet and she padded in there, naked. The white-tiled shower was huge, the water hot, the pressure amazing, and she wanted to stand underneath it all day. But eventually caffeine cravings kicked in with a vengeance and she had to get out, wrapping herself in one of the big white towels on a heated rail. As she did so she caught a glimpse of herself in the mirror. There were bruises on her neck, breasts, and thighs. Red marks around her wrists. Oh hell, had he put those there?

The thought was dirty and erotic and wrong and she couldn't stop looking at the marks. Liking that they were there. Reminders of him.

Had she given him any in return? She hoped so. And if not, perhaps she could give him a few today.

Pleased with the thought, she came back out into the bedroom, taking a quick look around for something to wear since her clothes were still downstairs near the dining table. There wasn't anything except for his black T-shirt, the one she'd used as a blindfold the night before, now crumpled in a heap near one of the nightstands.

She bent and picked it up, shaking it out. Then she put it over her head and pulled it down. The cotton was soft and smelled of him, and even that had the power to make her nipples harden.

Damn, she was a lost cause.

She went to the doorway—which had no actual door—and out into a long, light hallway of exposed brick and skylights. There was a wide set of stairs at the end of it that led down into the open-plan lounge area she remembered from the day before.

Vaulted ceilings and crescent windows. More exposed brick and polished floors in a dark, pitted kind of wood. There wasn't much in the way of furniture. A massive black sectional sofa, that rustic dining table where she'd lost her mind, a couple of other armchairs covered in worn, faded brown leather. There were no bookcases. No family photos. No knickknacks. Everything was as clean and spare as his bedroom.

Noises were coming from down one end of the huge space, where a wall bisected the area. She went toward it, past the dining table to what turned out to be another open doorway, and peered around the corner.

A kitchen lay behind it, sleek and industrial with lots of stainless steel. Gabriel stood at one of the benches with his back to her, cutting something up on a board.

Her mouth dried. He wore nothing but a pair of his usual jeans, worn low on his hips, the muscular, powerful lines of his back exposed. As was his tattoo, the one she'd only caught glimpses of the night before.

An angel with a flaming sword held aloft, wings outstretched, covered most of the upper part of his back, the words "Avenging Angels" scrolling beneath it. The motorcycle club he used to be a part of.

*You shouldn't trust me . . .*

Honor swallowed. Too late for that now. She did trust him. Trusted him enough to let him blindfold her, tie her up. Do all those things to her. Give her what no one else ever had.

Freedom from control. From responsibility.

*You could get used to that. You could get addicted . . .*

"Are you going to come in or are you going to just stand there?" Gabriel said, not turning or pausing in what he was doing.

Honor shook away the snide voice in her head. "How did you know I was here?"

"I heard you."

"Oh."

"Come in. There's coffee on the stove and I'm making breakfast."

Honor moved over to the big stainless steel stove with an espresso maker on it, still steaming.

"Cups are in the cupboard above." Still he didn't turn around.

She found a cup and poured herself some coffee, adding some cream from the fridge. Holding the mug carefully in her hands, she turned and came over to the bench he was standing at, put her coffee down, and leaned a hip against it. He was cutting up mushrooms, his movements clean and precise, the knife held with almost professional confidence in his big hand.

"So, not only do you blindfold women, you cook them breakfast as well? I'm impressed."

He flicked her a glance, brief and hot as he noted what she was wearing. "I like the T-shirt. It suits you. Keep it on."

She smiled. "Since my clothes aren't around anywhere, I'll have to."

"I had them taken to be dry-cleaned." He looked back down at what he was doing. "They'll come back in a couple of hours."

"Oh . . ." Honor stared at him, nonplussed. "Thank you. That's . . . thoughtful."

"I also called your office. Told them you had an all-day meeting with me and wouldn't be in."

Oh, hell. Work. She'd totally forgotten.

Honor turned, her back against the bench, picking up her cup and taking a sip. The coffee was hot and strong, setting up a glow deep inside her. "Thank you for that, too, in that case. But I don't think we'll need all day."

"We will," he said with such certainty she felt almost duty bound to protest.

"Telling you about Dad, Guy, won't take all day."

"I'm not planning on hearing about him all day. There are a few other things I'd like to do, too."

The glow inside became not so much about the hit of caffeine as of something far more primal. "You're assuming I'm going to agree to those things," she said, trying to sound calm. "Just because I was happy to stay last night doesn't mean I want anything more."

Gabriel finished cutting the mushrooms and put his knife down, looking at her. "I'm not offering you heroin, Honor. Only sex. Or do you genuinely not want to spend the day in my bed?"

She looked away, her heart thudding fast all of a sudden. So, he'd remembered what she'd told him back in Vermont.

"You were honest last night. Be honest now."

"I told you," she said. "You make me feel too good. And I don't . . . want to want you like this."

"But you do."

Honor took a silent breath and met his gaze. ""Yes," she said, unable to lie, "I do."

There was no satisfaction on his face at that, only a look in his dark eyes she couldn't interpret. "Good," he said. "Then that's settled."

It wasn't, but she couldn't find the will to protest. She was halfway down that slope already. Might as well fall all the way.

Picking up the board he'd been cutting on, Gabriel turned and went to the stove, sweeping the mushrooms into a frying pan sitting on top of it. They began to sizzle. "Tell me about your father and Tremain," he said, his gaze on the frying pan. "Tell me everything."

Honor stared at his broad, powerful back. At the tattoo on it. Avenging Angels. Another shiver went through her. "You . . . won't hurt him, will you?" She hated the uncertainty in her voice but although she knew he wouldn't hurt her, she had no such reassurance about her stepfather. "I mean, I know you probably wouldn't but—"

"Don't make any assumptions about me, Honor," he said, his voice flat. "Not when you don't have any idea about the things I've done."

She clutched her mug. The hot ceramic burned her fingers but she held it tightly anyway. "And what have you done?"

"You don't want to know."

"Maybe I do. I know the rumors about the drugs. About—"

"The rumors are true."

Despite the heat of the coffee mug and the warmth of the central heating, a spike of ice went through her. Because it wasn't only the rumors of drug selling she'd heard about. There had been murder, too. Reprisals ordered. People killed. God, had he . . . ?

She didn't want to ask, wasn't sure she wanted to know.

*You knew he wasn't a good guy. He told you. A man like him, with his background, is never going to be pure as the driven snow.*

But she wasn't a coward. And she didn't want more secrets coming out of the woodwork. So she made herself ask, "Even the ones about how you had people murdered?"

Gabriel shifted, muscles rippling over his naked back, somehow making the angel's sword look even more menacing. "I was called Church in the MC. Not because I was good, but because I used to go to St. Sebastian's a lot to meet my mom. There was a pimp who used to hang out around there, abusing his girls. Hurting them." His voice deepened, became cold. "Men like that don't deserve mercy and God's justice didn't extend that far. So, first chance I got, I took that motherfucker out. I was sixteen." He paused and she couldn't help shivering. "Those guys weren't people, Honor. They were animals. Drug dealers and pimps, hurting my neighborhood. It was my duty to protect my patch and I did. Besides, they knew what they were getting into when they tried to take a cut of the Angels' territory. They went into it with their eyes wide open, so don't make the mistake of thinking they were innocents."

There was detachment in his voice but underneath, she could hear a note of something else, something he hadn't quite managed to hide. Anger.

She shouldn't be relieved to hear that. Murder was murder however you looked at it. And yet . . . Did it make it better that he'd done it protecting people? That the people who'd died were criminals?

She took another sip of her coffee, her hands shaking a little. "Did you . . . always do it yourself?"

He didn't say anything for a long moment. "Yes. I wouldn't get someone else to do something I didn't have the balls for. But it wasn't murder, it was an execution."

"Gabriel," she said hoarsely. "That's—"

"Semantics. They killed my people. They hurt them. It was justice."

The silence in the kitchen was thick with tension, the sizzle of the cooking food a strange, domestic counterpoint.

Honor gripped her mug like it was a life preserver. She didn't know what to say, ice moving slowly down her spine.

"I don't regret what I did," he said after a pause. "And I don't expect forgiveness for it. I did what I had to do to protect people the only way I knew how. What I regret is that I even had to do it in the first place." A note of weariness had crept into his cold, dark voice. A bleakness that made her eyes prick with strange tears. "I was seven when I was first given a package by one of the men in the club to take to some guy on a corner," he went on. "I got money for it, a lot of money. My mother found it hard holding down a job so I kept doing it. Who would say no to that much money? It wasn't until I was ten that I figured out what was in those packages. I kept doing it though because we needed to eat." He raised the spatula he was holding, moved the food around in the frying pan. "The old man who gave me the packages, he looked out for me. Taught me things. I didn't have a dad so he was kind of like one to me." Gabriel paused. "And when I was old enough, he asked if I wanted to be part of his club. I said yes. He was the president, you see."

Honor blinked hard, not wanting to say anything, not wanting to even breathe in case he stopped speaking.

"The Angels were my family," Gabriel went on. "They had my back. They weren't good guys, but they had a code I respected. And then shit started to go down, a rival club encroaching on our territory. Our president, that old guy I met, was killed. And I decided I wanted the job because there were certain things in our neighborhood I didn't like. Drugs for a start. Prostitution. So I made sure I got it. And then I made sure our neighborhood was clean."

Another silence fell.

She stared at him, cooking her breakfast and telling her of his hard, violent start in life. The things he'd done . . . "You didn't think about . . . I don't know . . . getting rid of the gangs?"

"That would have left a power vacuum and some other fuckers would have taken over."

"The police—"

"They didn't give a shit. There was only me."

Him and his strength. A protectiveness twisted by the life he'd been born into. She looked away, her throat thick with a grief she knew she shouldn't be feeling. "What about getting out somehow? Finding a different life for yourself?"

"I did. Eventually. There was shit I had to do that I couldn't as part of the MC. So Alex and I went in together to buy that first piece of real estate. I renovated it. Sold it. Everything went from there."

Honor swallowed. "Why are you telling me all this?"

"So you know. So you never go thinking I'm something I'm not. I'm not your friend, Honor, and I'm not a man you want to stick close to. Don't let a couple of orgasms blind you."

She put her mug down, folded her arms across her

chest and the knot of emotion sitting in the middle of it. "You seem very anxious for me to know the worst about you. Why is that?"

He didn't answer, turning off the gas burner and putting the food onto a plate. "Go sit at the table. Breakfast's ready."

# CHAPTER THIRTEEN

They ate in silence. But that was okay. He was sick of hearing himself talk anyway.

He'd been quite deliberate, telling her everything. Making sure she had no illusions about him. Maybe it was because of the way she'd trusted him the night before, or maybe it was because he'd never explicitly told anyone about his past and wanted someone to know. But for whatever reason, it was done now and there was no taking it back.

If he'd been a better man, he would have gone on and told her that he was using her for his own ends. But he didn't, because he wasn't a better man. He never would be.

Pushing away his plate, he sat back in his seat and watched her as she daintily ate her bacon, cutting it up into tiny little pieces and using her fork to eat each piece like a real lady.

A real lady he'd had sobbing in his arms the night before as he'd screwed her senseless.

Desire flared inside him and he let it burn, the perversity of having this delicate, sophisticated woman in bed with a beast like him an incredible turn-on. That he was going to get information out of her after telling her all the bad things he'd done, then take her to bed and make her scream again, only made it more erotic.

Yeah, he was a sick fuck but at least he owned it.

Honor met his gaze as she took another bite of her bacon. The look in her eyes was guarded, her expression neutral. He had no idea what she thought about the things he'd told her, and he told himself he didn't care.

*Liar. You do.*

That was the thing. He couldn't afford to.

"I suppose it's my turn now, isn't it?" she said after a moment.

"All that shit wasn't a transaction, little girl. You're going to tell me about your stepfather whether or not I tell you about my past."

She speared another bacon piece. "All right. What do you want to know?"

"How did your mother meet him?"

"He was a friend of my father's. Like I told you yesterday, they were at college together. After Daniel's death, he . . . helped Mom. She suffered from depression for a few years, drank a bit. Guy got her out of it."

Gabriel watched her, the flickering in her eyes, the tightness around her mouth. "What makes you think he's such a goddamn good man?"

She looked away from him, down to her plate. "I spent those years having to look after my own mother. I was eight, nine. And it was hard. Guy came in and made it all better. Looked after Mom. Looked after me, too. He was there for all my school performances, all my award ceremonies. He was there the way Daniel wasn't. That's why I call him 'Dad.' Because he was more my father than Daniel ever was."

The information didn't sit well with Gabriel. The guy was a fucking rapist so either he hid his evil well or . . . what? His own mother hadn't even counted because she was only a hotel maid? That he'd looked after Honor and her mother while he and Corrine . . .

*Oh sure, he cared. Don't forget that goddamned check.*

Hush money. That his mother hadn't even cashed.

"So apart from his wonderful role-model qualities and his apparently shitty business sense, what else do you know? Did he have any other friends? Colleagues?"

"I'm not sure what else to tell you. No, I don't know anything about his colleagues. I know he was friends with a few other people from college, again, friends of Daniel's, too. They used to have get-togethers sometimes at home. Mom would play hostess." Her brow creased. "If you're wanting any information about why he's doing this with Tremain Hotels, I don't know. He has no enemies. I can't imagine what kind of thing you think I can tell you."

Frustration burned. It wasn't enough. She'd been a child when he'd come into her life and what she knew of him would be colored by a child's memories. But there was that connection with her father . . .

"That money came from the same casino your father ran," he said. "They were friends. He's involved somehow."

Honor glanced away. "I . . . don't want to believe it. Guy was as shocked as anyone about Daniel's debts. He wouldn't . . ." She stopped. "He didn't know. He didn't."

"And yet he was there for your mother. Just waiting to pick up the pieces."

Pain flashed through her blue eyes and behind it, a defensive anger. "Why are you so determined to believe there's something bad behind this?"

"People don't launder money for fucking fun, sweetheart. And they don't run businesses purposefully into the ground. It's not going to be good whatever it is."

"But you think he had something to do with Daniel's death. Isn't that what you're trying to say?"

"I'm not saying that. Yet the links are there." And they were missing something, he was sure of it. "It's too much of a coincidence that Tremain is receiving money from the casino your father used to own."

She'd gone pale again. "He's a good man. He is."

No, he wasn't. He was a rapist. And the life Gabriel had was the life that Tremain had given him. But if Tremain was running his own company into the ground, then the revenge Gabriel had planned—no, the *justice* he wanted—would all come to nothing.

He ignored the strange reluctance to push her that had come out of nowhere. "What happened to your father's debts? How were they paid?"

She looked back down at her plate. "Our belongings were repossessed. My mother's jewelry, family heirlooms. She had to sell the house. It was . . . awful."

It must have been, from the expression on her face. Yet she was damn lucky she even had belongings to repossess. He should have felt righteous anger at the poor-little-rich-girl sound in her voice but somehow, he didn't. He only felt . . . sorry for her.

Irritated, Gabriel ignored that feeling, too. "Did the money from that pay them all off?"

"No. We had a shortfall. And that was when Guy stepped in, because he was Daniel's friend. He helped Mom pay off the rest of the debts."

Gabriel went still. "*He* paid them?"

"Yes. The Tremains are from old money and they have a lot of it. Guy was very generous."

That was the link right there, the link he'd been looking for. For some reason Tremain, who was laundering money for the casino, had also paid off his old friend's debts to that very same casino. Then married his widow. That could *not* be a coincidence.

The crease between Honor's brows deepened. "What are you thinking?"

That strange reluctance sunk its claws into him. This

was not the news she wanted to hear. Her world had already been turned upside down and his suspicions weren't going to make it any easier—if they happened to be true, of course. But he had a horrible feeling they were.

"I'm thinking Tremain married your mother for reasons other than love."

Her mouth opened in shock, all the remaining color leaving her face. "What are you suggesting?"

"That perhaps he married your mother to hide the evidence of the casino's debts. Perhaps even that he was paid to do so."

Honor stood up, the chair scraping harshly on the wooden floor as she shoved it back. "No," she said, her voice hoarse. "No. That's ridiculous. He married Mom because he loved her."

Christ, there it was again. That need to go to her and take her in his arms, comfort her the way he'd wanted to the night before. But again he ignored it.

Whatever Tremain's real reasons, Honor had to come to terms with the fact that the father figure she loved was not the man she thought he was. And never had been. He couldn't help her with that, she needed to deal with it herself.

"I didn't say anything about love. The fact remains that he has connections to that casino. It's too much of a coincidence that he suddenly appears after your father's death, paying off his debts and marrying his widow."

"He was Daniel's friend! He was helping his family out!"

"He's laundering money for the same casino that your father managed. You can't tell me that's not suspicious."

Honor picked up her plate. "I don't want to hear any more, please. I can't . . . I just can't . . ." She stopped and turned abruptly toward the kitchen area, disappearing through the doorway.

Fuck. It.

Gabriel leaned back in his chair and ran a distracted hand through his hair. This was not what he wanted. Yes, he needed to know more about these connections with Tremain and the casino but he also wanted . . . Honor. He'd gotten information, it was true, but he didn't like pushing her. Didn't like making her feel bad. Especially when he wanted her for the whole damn day in his bed. Except after this he was betting that sex wasn't uppermost in her mind.

Shoving his chair back he got up and went to the kitchen doorway.

She had the dishwasher open, bending over it to put her plate in. The T-shirt rode up her thigh, barely covering her butt. His T-shirt. Jesus. That fact should not be making him hard and yet it did.

Honor straightened, shut the dishwasher, and met his gaze. "I need to go," she said flatly. "I need some time to get my head around Guy and what he's doing with the company, let alone having to handle the kind of accusations you're making."

He didn't want her to go. He wanted her to stay here with him.

Gabriel moved away from the doorway, stalking over to where she stood. He put his hands on her hips and backed her up against the counter, holding her there. She tipped her head back, looking up at him, her arms crossed defensively over her breasts. The look in her eyes was guarded but he could see something else beneath it. Pain. Shock.

"If you're planning on confronting Tremain, like I said, you've got another think coming."

"I have to—"

"No, you don't."

"Gabriel, please."

"No." He tightened his hold, not only to prevent her from moving. The sweet smell of her was beginning to cloud his own senses and right at this moment, he couldn't think of anything he'd rather do than pick her up and put her on the counter, bury himself inside her.

She looked away from him, as if she knew exactly what he was thinking. Hell, she could probably feel the fucking hard-on in his jeans. "I'm not going to warn him or anything," she said thickly. "I just . . ."

"Need to get away from me," he finished. It wasn't a question, he knew. Because he was the one who'd shattered her world and when she wanted to protect herself, she withdrew.

She didn't answer but her throat moved as she swallowed, thick black lashes veiling her gaze.

"Fuck that," he said. "Getting away from me isn't what you need."

"Of course," she responded, her voice edged with sarcasm. "And I suppose you're going to inform me exactly what it is I need? Since I don't understand my own feelings."

Gabriel cupped her face between his palms, turning her to face him.

She tried to pull away but he didn't let her, tipping her head back so their eyes met. "Don't," she said thickly, her lashes falling as if trying to hide from him.

But he saw the sheen in her blue gaze anyway. Fuck, she was crying.

He didn't understand comfort. Didn't understand how to make someone feel better because no one had done that for him. The only thing he remembered from childhood was the kisses his mother used to give him when he'd hurt himself. Kisses that had stopped the moment he'd gotten old enough for her to see another man in his face. The man who'd raped her. He'd been ten.

After that there had been no more kisses. No more hugs. His mother had tried not to touch him at all. Only given him lectures on how important it was to be good. Obey his teachers. Obey God. Because the devil knew the evil in men's hearts and could use it for his own ends.

Shit, the devil had already used him.

"You're crying." He brushed a thumb over her cheek, feeling the wetness against his skin. "For him?"

She didn't speak for a long moment. "I loved him," she said eventually. "I mean, I still do. He's . . . my father. But if all of this is true? It means everything is a lie. Every single thing. And I thought . . . I thought all the lies were finally over."

There was pressure inside him, tension pulling tight. He didn't know quite what he was doing, but like he had last night, he'd taken something from her. Something that had been precious. Which meant he had to give something back.

An eye for an eye. At least that was what the Reverend had always taught him.

"I'm sorry, sweetheart." And he was sorry. Sorry that she was hurt. Because he was starting to realize that seeing her in pain made something inside him hurt, too.

"You don't need to apologize. It's not your fault. And I shouldn't be blaming you for it."

He stroked her cheek again then let his thumb move to her mouth, slowly tracing the line of her lower lip. She shivered.

No, shit, he didn't know how to give her comfort. But there was always pleasure. He knew how to give her that. Perhaps it would be enough.

Gabriel bent his head and covered her mouth with his.

She stiffened but he didn't let her go. Gently he pressed against her lower lip with his thumb, opening her mouth, letting him inside. Honor made a soft sound. Then the stiffness gradually left her body and she leaned into him, her hands on his chest, her mouth opening under his, kissing him back.

Desire began to rise, hungry and dark, but he held it back because the kiss was sweet. Sweeter than any other kiss he'd had before and for some reason, he wanted to hold onto that.

Eventually though, sweet wasn't enough.

He lifted his head. "We don't have to think about this now. What I want is you in my bed, like I said."

She was flushed, her breathing fast. "Okay. But afterward . . . I need some space, Gabriel. Some time to sort things out about Dad. A few days at least."

*That's a good idea. She's getting to you and you know it.*

The thought was uncomfortable, but this time he couldn't deny the truth of it. She *was* getting to him. Here he was, kissing her sweetly for fuck's sake, because he didn't like the fact that she was hurting. Which hadn't been part of his plan at all.

So maybe some distance would be good. For both of them.

"Okay," he said. "A few days." Then he gripped her chin in his hand, tilted her head back, and kissed her again.

And this time he didn't stop.

Honor let herself into the town house where her mother lived with Guy. It wasn't far from Central Park, an expensive, elegant neighborhood. Very much her mother's kind of thing.

She stood for a moment in the quiet hallway, letting the icy chill from the winter outside dissipate as heat seeped into her. Her mother liked to be warm and usually had the central heating turned up way too high. Pleasant for the first five minutes and then it got kind of uncomfortable.

Once her feet had unfrozen themselves, she stripped off her coat and gloves, holding them over her arm as she went down the hallway to the front lounge area, putting her head around the door.

Her mother, dressed in her usual string of pearls and designer dress, probably Chanel, was sitting on the sofa with Mary, her housekeeper, going over the pages of a magazine Mary was holding.

Honor didn't say anything for a second, just looked at her mother, grief lying heavy at the back of her throat.

Elizabeth was a porcelain doll of a woman, always beautifully dressed and made up. Her hair was still black— Honor knew she kept dyeing it religiously to keep the gray away. The lines of age and grief around her eyes and mouth showed, but even those weren't as deep as they should have been. Botox was her mother's best friend, since Elizabeth's vanity stopped short of surgery.

But her mother's youthful appearance couldn't hide the air of fragility that surrounded her. A fragility that went deep.

Honor swallowed. What the hell was she doing here? What did she hope to achieve?

She'd promised Gabriel she wouldn't see Guy, at least not yet, not until they had some concrete evidence, yet Honor hadn't been able to stay away.

She'd wanted to see her mother. Not to tell her about everything Gabriel had discovered, but mainly to determine whether her marriage to Guy had been a lie. That relationship had been a constant for the last fifteen years of her life, given her a safe and stable home after the chaos surrounding her father's death. And to discover even that had been a falsehood . . .

That her father had been covering up a double life as a casino boss had hurt, yet given the secrets he'd hidden from his family, perhaps it wasn't so surprising. But the thought her stepfather had lied both to her and to her mother, for years, was devastating. What if Guy had never loved her mother at all? What if he'd been paid to make it look like he did?

*What if he never loved you either? Just like Daniel didn't.*

Honor didn't want to think about that. It was too raw. Too personal. She was here for her mother and that was it.

"Hi, Mom," she said.

Elizabeth looked up, her face breaking into a smile. "Honor, darling!" She got up from the sofa in a graceful movement, coming over to her daughter and enveloping her in a Chanel No. 5–scented hug. "This is a surprise!"

"I'm sorry, I hope you don't mind me coming over without calling first. It was a spur-of-the-moment thing."

"No, of course I don't. Mary, would you mind getting us some coffee? We can go over the menus this afternoon."

The housekeeper smiled. "No, of course not. Here, Miss St. James, let me take those." She took Honor's outerwear and went bustling off to deal with them.

"Come sit." Elizabeth took Honor's hand and led her over to the sofa, sitting down with her. "How was Vermont?"

Was there any point talking about Gabriel?

*No. That's one relationship you definitely don't want Guy knowing about.*

Honor didn't like the automatic thought, as if Guy were guilty already. But then, maybe it was better for her mother not to know. Because, God, she really didn't know herself what was going on there either.

She'd woken up that morning alone, Gabriel apparently having left for work. There had been a note in the kitchen near the coffeepot telling her he'd be in touch but that was it. No mention of what was going on between them and what it meant.

Maybe it didn't mean anything. Maybe a couple of nights of hot sex was all it was.

*Just as well . . .*

"Vermont was beautiful," Honor said, ignoring the sharp disappointment that twisted inside her at the thought. "Lots of snow."

"Perfect," her mother said, smiling. "Guy and I need to take a trip there sometime. Especially during fall when the leaves are turning."

Here it was. Her cue. "You should. It's very pretty. Speaking of Guy, how are you two?"

Elizabeth glanced at her in surprise. "Us? We're fine, darling, why do you ask?"

"Oh, no particular reason. I just . . . wonder sometimes."

"Well, don't." Her mother patted her hand. "Guy and I are fine. Everything's okay."

But everything wasn't okay. Nothing would ever be okay again.

The pressure of all the secrets pressed in on her and there was a moment where she couldn't breathe. "Mom," she began.

From out in the hall came the sound of the front door opening and closing. Then a familiar voice calling, "Lizzie?"

Her mother's face lit up. "In here, darling!"

And if Honor hadn't been able to breathe before, she certainly couldn't now, especially when Guy's tall figure suddenly appeared in the doorway.

He smiled when he saw her. "Honor, how nice to see you. And great timing. I've been meaning to call you."

*Smile, you idiot. Otherwise, he's going to know something's wrong.*

From somewhere, Honor found a smile and stuck it on, her face feeling stiff. "Oh, yes, I've been . . . busy for the past couple of days."

He came into the room, bending to kiss his wife and Honor knew a hug was going to be expected. She made herself get up and give him a brief, unsubstantial embrace before sitting back down again. "So, to what do we owe the pleasure of this visit?" he said. "Playing hooky from work, like me?"

"Oh, no, Wes is holding down the fort for me this morning. I wanted to see Mom, say hi."

He sat down in the armchair opposite them. "Well, it's nice to see you. Darling," he said to his wife, "I need to talk to Honor about some business stuff. Would you mind giving us a few minutes?"

"Business," Elizabeth said with some exasperation. "That's all you seem to want to talk about these days." Nevertheless, she got up, smoothing down her dress. "Well, I'll go and see if Mary needs a hand. You two get the boring stuff over and done with so we can talk about more interesting things when I get back."

Honor swallowed, nervous tension gathering inside her as her mother left the room. She knew Guy hadn't told his wife about Tremain Hotels failing because he hadn't wanted her to worry—at least that's what he'd told Honor. And the fact that he wanted Elizabeth to leave the room meant he wanted to talk about that now. God, she wasn't quite ready for that yet.

As the door shut behind his wife, Guy leaned forward, the smile fading from his eyes, the look on his face serious. "I know I should have organized a proper meeting with you," he said levelly, "but while I've got you here, we may as well discuss Tremain Hotels."

Honor didn't let any of her nerves show. "The investment? Woolf Construction is—"

"Actually, it's Woolf Construction I wanted to talk about."

Oh, God. Honor didn't move, kept her expression entirely neutral. "Oh?"

Guy laced his fingers together. "I know you worked hard to get Woolf on board and I appreciate it, Honor, I really do. But . . ." He hesitated. "I'm afraid I'm going to have to refuse his money."

The nervous tension sitting in her gut wound tighter. She allowed herself a frown. "Dad, you know that's a—"

"A bad decision? I realize it's not in our best interests, no. But I'm afraid I'm going to have to put my foot down. The man is little more than a criminal and I don't want him associated with my hotel chain."

"I'm not sure I'll be able to find another investor. I had a lot of trouble even getting him."

"Yes, I understand that." He gave her a smile that only wound her tighter. "You put a lot of time and effort into saving Tremain and for that I'm grateful. But it's time for me to deal with this mess myself. Okay? I'll find another investor."

Something broke inside her. Because there could be only one reason he wanted to handle it himself: he didn't want Gabriel's money to save the company. He didn't want to save the company at all. He wanted it to go down.

It was all true.

An expression of concern creased his forehead, his blue eyes searching her face. "I'm sorry, dear girl. I didn't mean to upset you but—"

"It's okay," she said, pleased with herself that she sounded together and only vaguely worried. "But you know that's the very opposite of what I'd advise."

He smiled at her again, slightly wistful. "Yes, I know."

"What if you don't save it? You've got my money invested, too, don't forget that."

His gaze flickered. "I haven't forgotten, believe me. And don't worry, I'll make sure you get every cent back."

Interesting that he didn't say "the company will be safe." Because her getting her money back and his company not going bankrupt weren't quite the same thing.

"You have a plan?" she asked, fighting the nausea inside her. Might as well get the info while she could.

"I do." He put his hands on the arms of his chair and levered himself out. "But I'm going to keep that to myself at the moment. Suffice it to say, I think it'll work. Now, I wonder where your mother's got to?"

# CHAPTER FOURTEEN

Gabriel pulled open the door of the Nine Circles club's meeting room to find Eva already there. For once she was alone, Zac nowhere in sight.

"Where's the guard dog?" he asked, shutting the door behind him.

Eva was standing in front of the fire, holding her hands out to it. She felt the cold quite acutely and liked to be as close to any heat source as she could get. "I presume you mean Zac. I have no fucking idea. We're not joined at the hip."

Gabriel came over to the couch in front of the fire, leaning his elbows on the back of it. "You must have had the amputation recently then."

Eva glanced at him over her shoulder. "Jesus, did you actually crack a joke, Gabe?"

"No. Whatever gave you that idea?"

Her gray eyes narrowed. "You're not seething as per usual. What's wrong?"

Good question, though perhaps "wrong" was not quite how he'd phrase it. Honor had given him a call that afternoon to say she wanted to see him tonight and the thought of seeing her had made him feel . . . less pissed off than normal. That should have been a warning sign, especially considering how much his anger meant to him.

Except that he'd elected to ignore the warning. He could do this. He could have both. Her and the justice he meant to deliver. After all, why not? She needed someone after that ordered little world of hers had been blown apart, and he wanted to be that someone. He wanted her, too. Wanted warmth and softness in his life. He couldn't forget her fierce loyalty to her stepfather. It made him wonder what it would be like to have someone fight for him like that. To believe there was good in him no matter what.

*Fucking idiot. There is no good in you.*

He dismissed that thought. He had more important things to think about now. "Perhaps I'm just having a good day," he said aloud.

"You never have good days." Eva's sharp gaze scanned his face. "Hmm, in fact you're not only not seething, you're looking damn smug. Have you got more information you haven't shared yet?"

Gabriel straightened. "We need to wait until the others are here."

He didn't want to have to talk about this twice, particularly to Alex. There were questions he had to ask and who knew what memories it would bring up? Alex could be unpredictable at the best of times and this . . . well, shit, maybe he knew about his father already. But possibly not about Tremain. Still, one thing was for sure: the guy wasn't going to like it.

Eva pulled a face and went to sit in the armchair by the fire, drawing her legs up and under her like a cat. As per normal, there was food set out on the table in front of the fire, a decanter of scotch and some wine. She hadn't touched the food or the alcohol. A teacup and saucer were on a little side table next to her chair, the liquid inside it steaming gently. Probably her usual cup of lemon-and-ginger herbal tea.

Eva had never been one for alcohol.

Abruptly the door behind him opened and Zac came in, brushing the snow off his black overcoat. His amber gaze settled on Eva first—as if checking to make sure she was there—then shifted to Gabriel. "I have something you might be interested in," he said, not even bothering with a greeting.

Gabriel stiffened. "What?"

"Ah. So the others aren't yet aware?"

"What the hell are you talking about?"

Zac didn't look particularly perturbed, shrugging off his overcoat and tossing it carelessly over the back of the couch. He moved around the side of it and sat down, putting the briefcase he'd been holding on the table, disturbing some of the plates of food.

"Christ," Eva muttered from her place in the chair, "Gabriel was right. You're just like a damn dog, shaking your fur and getting into the food."

Zac's expression didn't so much as flicker. "And you like it that way, angel. Don't tell me you don't."

Gabriel skirted around the couch. "What the fuck, Zac?"

The other man opened the briefcase, extracted some papers, and handed them to him without a word. Gabriel looked down. They were financial statements concerning Daniel St. James. Honor's father. They detailed large sums of money paid into his account after his death from a company called Mainline Holdings Limited.

"Mainline Holdings is a shell company," Zac said calmly. "And I'm sure you can guess who's behind that."

Oh yeah, he could. Because he'd gotten his people to investigate into Tremain's financial situation and they'd come up with the same thing. Gabriel looked at him. "How the fuck did you know?" Honor hadn't told anyone else but him that Tremain had paid St. James's debts. And this information hadn't been in the files Zac had sent him earlier.

Zac leaned back against the couch, still calm. His tie was perfectly centered, the red edge of one of his tattoos peeking over the collar of his pristine white business shirt. "I found a few inconsistencies in the data I sent you so I did a bit more research and found these transactions. They were remarkably well hidden. I also noticed that you had your people do some digging. They're clumsy, Gabriel. Very clumsy. You should come to me when you need stuff like this."

Jesus. Time to do another overhaul of his systems security. "Or you could just mind your own fucking business."

The other man only smiled. "Where's the fun in that?"

"Zac?" Eva demanded, her voice low and dangerous. "What haven't you been telling me?"

At that moment the door opened again and it was Alex, late as usual.

He was in a black suit, his matte black tie loose, black shirt open at the collar. His hair was untidy, like someone had run her fingers through it, his blue eyes brilliant as sapphires. "Sorry, I'm late," he said, clearly not sorry at all. "Maya was insatiable. Jesus, is there scotch left or have you drank it all again, Gabriel?"

No, he didn't want to discuss this with Alex. But he was going to have to. Taking a step over to the table, he pulled the top off the whisky decanter and poured a measure out. Then he held the crystal tumbler out toward his friend.

Alex came over and took the glass, his gaze turning sharp. "Oh dear," he said. "You look serious. At least more serious than normal. Which is a bad fucking sign, I guess."

"I suggest you drink that," Gabriel said curtly. "All of it."

Alex's posture didn't change but the look in his eyes cut like razors. "I see. Well, never let it be said that I refused a drink." He downed the scotch in one go and poured himself another. "Tell me." The casual note in his voice had gone now; it was low and flat and dangerous.

Gabriel held out the financial statements. "Look at these."

The other man took them and looked down. He was silent a moment as he scanned the pages. Then he glanced back up at Gabriel. "What the fuck is this?"

"Evidence that your father's so-called gambling debts were paid by Guy Tremain."

Alex didn't move a muscle, his eyes glittering. "And?"

"Who is currently laundering money for the Lucky Seven casino."

"You found this out how?"

Gabriel hesitated. Fuck it, might as well say. "Honor told me Tremain paid the debts."

"Honor?" Eva sounded puzzled. "Why the hell would she tell you that?"

"Because I found out about a reservation scam he was running and I wanted to get more information about him. She was the logical person to ask."

Alex downed the second glass of scotch, then, quite casually, tossed the tumbler into the fireplace where it smashed in a spray of glass and glitter of flames. "Money laundering," he said, his voice deceptively mild. "And everyone seems to know about it except me."

Shit. He should have told his friend earlier. Given him a heads-up at least. But he hadn't.

*You didn't want to. Didn't want to bring that night up for him again.*

Yeah, that was the truth. He still remembered Alex stumbling out of the casino, the shirt he was wearing torn and his mouth bleeding. But that wasn't the worst part.

The worst part was the look in his friend's eyes. Like something in him had died.

That wasn't the look that was there now, though. Anger made his midnight gaze burn bright blue.

"Yet you know something else we don't," Gabriel went on, knowing he had to continue. "Your father wasn't gambling at that casino. He fucking owned it, didn't he?"

Alex's expression didn't change. "Yes. He did."

A strange anger surged through him. One he had no right to feel and yet did all the same. "Jesus Christ, Alex. Why didn't you tell me?"

"Why the hell should I? It's none of your goddamn business."

"The fuck it is. Especially when Honor's involved."

"Oh?" Alex took a step toward him. "And how is Honor involved exactly?"

The other two didn't say a word. They knew. This was Gabriel's job. "I've been investigating Tremain, you know that. And I found out someone was making fake reservations and cancelling them. The money trail leads back to him. So I went to Honor and—"

"*You* brought her into it?" The look in Alex's eyes blazed.

"Yes," Gabriel said flatly. "She's got a lot of fucking money invested in a company he's running into the ground. Deliberately. If he goes down, so does she."

A muscle ticked in Alex's jaw. "That should have been my job, not yours."

"Really? When you've been doing such a great job of it so far?"

His friend's eyes widened, as if he'd taken a blow. "What the ever-loving fuck? You know why I haven't—"

"Yeah, I know why. But you can't come over all big brother now when you've been avoiding her for nineteen fucking years." Protective anger rose. All he could see was the pain in Honor's eyes as she'd told him about how her life had been after Alex had gone. After the brother who was supposed to keep her safe had disappeared, leaving her alone.

His friend was staring at him, blue eyes studying him with a terrifyingly sharp intelligence. And something flared in Alex's gaze. Knowledge.

"You prick," Alex said hoarsely.

Gabriel knew the blow was coming and he didn't avoid it. Standing there motionless as Alex raised his fist and smashed it into the side of his face. Pain exploded like a star with his cheekbone at the center, radiating outward. But he'd experienced worse pain before and didn't make a sound or flinch. Hell, he probably deserved it after all.

"What the hell, Alex?" Eva was saying.

Alex had drawn his hand back again, only to have Zac's fingers wrap around his wrist, preventing him from landing another blow.

"Gentlemen, please." Zac's cultured English voice cut through the tension, polite yet deadly. "This isn't going to make the meeting go any faster and it's already become pretty fucking interminable." The steel in the guy's tone was enough to remind everyone that he could kill them all without even breaking a sweat.

Alex jerked his wrist from Zac's restraining hold, then turned away sharply. He bent down to the table again, poured himself another tumbler full of scotch, then flung himself down into an armchair.

Gabriel's cheekbone throbbed but he didn't touch it.

"Jesus," Eva said with some disgust. "You're screwing her, aren't you, Gabriel?"

"That's none of your fucking business," he replied curtly. "And apart from any of that, it's not relevant."

"The hell it isn't," Eva snapped. "You were supposed to be helping her out not—"

"Shut up, Eva," Alex interrupted harshly. "Gabriel's right, it's got nothing to do with you."

"Hey, you're the one who punched him in the face. I don't think you're happy with—"

"Angel and Alex," Zac cut in, his voice quiet. "We can deal with this later. Right now, the important thing is what's happening with this casino. Which seems to be at the center of all the problems."

Eva made a disgusted noise, but she didn't say anything more. Alex only took another sip of his drink.

Gabriel didn't look at either of them. He knew already they thought he was scum and fuck, they were right. She was far too good for him.

"Do go on, Gabriel." Alex's voice dripped with sarcasm. "What other little gems have you got for us today?"

"You saw. Those financial statements. Tremain paid off your father's debts and then he married your mother. That is not a coincidence."

A thick, heavy silence filled the room.

Eventually Alex said, "Does Honor know about . . . our dad? And Tremain?"

"Yes. I told her."

"Is she okay? What did she say?"

"She was . . ." *Shocked, Hurt. Shattered.* "She doesn't know anything more."

"You have suspicions though," Zac commented.

The fire was warm against his back, but for some reason he felt cold. Alex wasn't going to forgive him in a hurry, he knew that for a fact. And he didn't like it. The other man had been his friend for years—possibly the only true friend he had—and now . . .

*You fucked up. This wasn't supposed to happen.*

More collateral damage he'd have to bear. Because nothing was more important than justice. Nothing.

"Yeah, I have suspicions," he said. "I think whoever

runs the casino paid Tremain to cover up St. James's debts and his involvement. I also think they paid him to marry the guy's wife."

"Why would they want to do that?" Eva picked up her cup, taking a sip of her tea. "Seems a little strange."

"Not if they wanted to hide their existence," Alex said coldly. The mask of careless amusement he so often wore had vanished, leaving in its place a man as sharp as a steel blade. "Not if they wanted to direct attention away from what they're doing. Paying his debts may make people look askance, but if he married my mother? That's more understandable. After all, the things we do for love." He gave a bitter laugh. "I knew there was something about that prick. I knew it."

"I thought you didn't know him?" Zac asked idly.

"He used to visit a lot. Part of the 'Seven Devils' as Dad used to call it."

Something echoed in Gabriel's memory. "Seven Devils?"

"That was Dad's stupid name for his group of old college buddies. A few of them are dead now but Tremain is obviously still around." His friend's gaze came to rest on him. "What?"

Gabriel met it. "The casino's name. Lucky Seven."

Alex's blue gaze darkened. He looked away, his jaw tight. "I never saw Tremain there," he said flatly. "I never saw any of Dad's other college buddies there either."

"That doesn't mean there isn't a connection." He hadn't bothered with the scotch before but Christ, he could do with one now. And yet the thought of alcohol wasn't quite it. He wanted something else, something warmer, softer . . .

*Honor. You want Honor.*

No. Not want. Need.

Fuck. The thought was disturbing on so many levels he shoved it ruthlessly from his head, stalking over to the table and splashing some scotch into a tumbler for himself.

"Don't smash that one," Zac said mildly. "I need something to drink out of."

"Hmm. Doesn't mean there *is* a connection either." Eva was nibbling on one finger as she held her cup of tea in the other hand. "What do you think, Alex? Is it likely this casino is run by your father's buddies?"

Alex's jaw hardened, darkness moving behind his eyes. "Like I said, I never saw any of them there. And apart from that, the only other evidence is a similarity of names. The others . . . Shit, they're just a bunch of rich assholes who talk about their golf handicaps all day. Can't see any of them running underground casinos on the side."

"But it's not just an underground casino, is it?" Zac leaned forward and helped himself to an olive from the bowl on the table. "There's far more than a bit of illegal gambling going on there. Several of my sources are saying that at least half of the drugs currently supplying New York's richest come from this place, plus there's a high-class call-girl operation going on as well." He paused. "We need more information. There's too much we don't know."

Alex flicked a glance at him. "What the hell has it got to do with you?"

Gabriel took a sip of the scotch, the alcohol burning a hot line down his throat. But it didn't seem to burn away the strange ache inside him. An ache that had nothing to with his cheek. "Shouldn't it have something to do with him?" he said curtly. "Aren't we supposed to watch each other's backs? Wasn't that the whole point of this fucking club in the first place?"

His friend didn't say anything for a long moment. Then he drained his glass and pushed himself to his feet. "You want to take this on? Then take it. But count me out. Count me out for the whole fucking thing." He stalked to the door, pulled it open, and without another word, went out, slamming it behind him.

Another silence fell, no less tense.

Gabriel didn't look at either Zac or Eva. "You want to say I told you so? Then go ahead." He stared into his glass. "I should have told him earlier."

"Shagging his sister might also not have helped matters," Zac said.

"Don't you talk about Honor," Gabriel growled. "She's mine to deal with."

"Oh, sure, lucky her." Eva's tone was acid. "And how exactly are you going to 'deal' with her?"

"I told you I wouldn't hurt her and I won't." His fingers tightened around his glass. A lie. Because he would hurt her, he was starting to see that now. When this was over, he would be just another man who'd lied to her.

"Yeah, but does she know that?"

"Let's keep this on the casino," Zac murmured. "I'll see what I can dig up about the shell company fronting it. Probably won't be much since I haven't been able to find anything so far. But it might be an idea to get the names and details of St. James's Seven Devils from someone."

"I'll do it." Eva put her cup back down on the table beside her. "If I can't get it out of Alex, I'll see if I can find it somewhere else."

"I could ask Honor," Gabriel offered.

"No, thank you." She gave him a disgusted look. "I'm sure you've already used her enough as it is."

"Angel, please. That isn't helping."

Eva extended a finger in Zac's direction but either he didn't see it or he chose to ignore it, because instead he looked at Gabriel. "This casino is obviously still in operation, yes?"

"I haven't checked it, but it seems so. At least money is still coming through Tremain's accounts."

"You know where it is?"

"Yeah." The other man was clearly thinking what Gabriel was. "Seems like it might be somewhere I need to visit." That was the most logical step.

"You won't be able to just waltz in there," Zac said. "You'll have to get an invite. Do you still have connections to the club you can use?"

"I left that life a long time ago, but yeah, I might. It'll take some time though. It's been a few years."

Zac put a hand in his jacket and withdrew his phone, typed something into it. "You can leave it with me if you like. I've got some contacts who may be able to arrange something quickly."

"You're not worried it might seem a little . . . suspicious being seen there?" Eva sat back in her chair, crossing her arms. "It's not like you haven't got a public profile."

Gabriel finished his scotch and put the empty glass back down on the table. "I've never been on the right side of the law, Eva. I don't think the casino will find my appearance too surprising. Especially not if I'm bringing a shitload of money to gamble with me."

She frowned. "I'm still not quite sure what you're hoping to find."

"Think of it as a reconnaissance mission. We still don't really know what we're dealing with here until one of us goes and checks it out, right?"

"Yeah. I guess. What about Tremain and his company? I take it you won't be investing now?"

"I got a formal email from him yesterday. He's refused my investment offer."

Her gaze was perceptive, knowing. "What are you going to do now?"

Good question. He was going to have to consider what his next step would be. If ruining the man's business wouldn't hurt him then he'd have to find something that would. But that was his to deal with. And maybe a visit to the casino would give him some clues.

He smiled. "I'll figure it out."

But first, he wanted to get home. Because for the first time in years, he had something to look forward to.

Honor.

Honor came out of her office building to find a car waiting at the curb, Gabriel's driver standing next to it.

God, he'd sent her a car. Not unexpected considering the sometimes oddly considerate gestures he indulged in, but right now, after the decision she'd made, it was unwelcome.

She halted as the driver approached her. "Miss St. James? Mr. Woolf has instructed me to drive you to his home for your meeting."

His home. Ah. That hadn't been where she'd initially suggested they meet. She'd named a bar near Central Park but obviously Gabriel had other ideas.

He thought she was coming back to pick up where they'd left off two days ago.

Unfortunately for him, she wasn't.

With bankruptcy staring her in the face should Guy's company go down, and the added burden of all the damn secrets she'd just found out, her life was starting to spin out of control and she hated the feeling. Which meant that the very last thing she needed was the kind of temptation Gabriel Woolf offered.

She wanted him. Craved the heat of his touch and the mental challenge of his personality. He was intense, fascinating, complex, and all she wanted was to take what he had to give. Use it to escape her life for a little while. But now, more than ever, she had to be strong and resist. Because he was one habit she could not afford to acquire.

"I'm sorry," Honor said. "I wasn't aware the meeting venue had changed."

"Mr. Woolf isn't able to go out this evening. So rather than reschedule, he thought it would be better if you came to him."

Honor took a silent breath. She could, of course, refuse the invite, call Gabriel up and tell him over the phone. Perhaps that would be safer. Yet it also seemed cowardly, and she definitely wasn't that.

She gave the man a tight smile. "I suppose you'd better take me to see him then."

The car was empty when she got in, allowing her a bit of time to relax against the soft leather of the seats and let the warmth of the heating seep through the cold that had taken up residence inside her.

Getting out her phone, she texted Violet to tell her where she was and that she'd be home late. Then, fifteen minutes later, as the car drew up outside Gabriel's place, she smoothed her hair, touched up her lipstick, and took a deep breath, her armor firmly in place.

She would say what she needed to say and then she'd leave.

*Crap. All he needs to do is touch you and you're lost.*

Then she'd better not let him touch her, had she?

The front door opened silently before she had to knock and there he was, in the doorway. In his usual uniform of jeans and T-shirt, a white one this time. He was barefoot and there was a darkening bruise on his cheekbone.

Strange how her heart contracted at the sight of the injury. As if seeing him hurt made her hurt, too. "Oh, no. What happened to your face?" she asked as he held the door open. "Are you okay?"

His dark eyes ran over her with the familiar intensity that always made the breath stop in her throat. "Come in, it's cold."

She stepped into the hallway and he closed the door behind her. "Gabriel, what—"

The rest of her question was cut off as his hands gripped her hips and she was pressed up against the front door, his mouth finding hers, effectively ending any further conversation.

It happened so fast that all she could do was stand there, shocked into immobility by the heat and strength surrounding her. By the hungry mouth on hers, demanding, taking. His familiar scent of leather and spice surrounded her, and she could taste the smoky edge of scotch in his kiss.

Her briefcase and purse dropped to the ground, her fingers suddenly nerveless.

God, what was happening? She was supposed to be telling him this was over. That she wasn't doing this again with him. That she needed some distance, some space. And yet . . .

Helpless desire clenched tightly inside her. It had only been two days and already she felt like she was starving and he was the only food she could eat that would satisfy her.

*You should get out now. While you can.*

Gabriel's hands slid down her hips to the hem of her skirt, pulling it up with a hard jerk. She gave an involuntary gasp against his mouth, bracing her palms on the hot wall of his chest. He shifted, breaking off the kiss and tilting his head, his breath harsh in her ear as he closed his teeth on the side of her neck, biting her hard.

An electric bolt of pleasure shot up her spine, the tiniest edge of pain making it that much more intense.

*Get out. Now.*

His hand slid up her thigh, over her butt, squeezing her. Then his fingers slipped between her legs, sliding under the plain cotton panties she wore, finding her clit with unerring accuracy, stroking with ruthless intent.

Pleasure began to climb, desperate hunger becoming fierce so quickly she could hardly breathe. It was almost frightening how fast she was there, on the edge of orgasm within a minute of stepping into his hallway. Almost terrifying when she'd been so certain she'd never do this again.

She began to tremble because he knew exactly how to touch her. How hard and where. And when his mouth covered hers again, demanding, ruthless, she knew she couldn't do anything else but give in to it.

There was no more space to leave. No moment to take a step back and get herself out of there.

*You could say no if you truly wanted to. But you don't want to.*

Honor shut her eyes, shaking against the door as Gabriel's fingers stroked her, winding everything so tight she knew she was going to come the second he entered her.

No, she didn't want to leave. Didn't want to push him away. She was so tired of fighting, of resisting his pull. And maybe it was too late anyway. Perhaps she was already hooked on the wildness and the heat, the uncertainty and the chaos of him. The passion. The freedom.

Which meant the only thing to do now was to embrace the addiction.

He shifted his grip on her, pulling something out of the back pocket of his jeans. A condom. Which meant he'd clearly planned on this happening between them.

"Gabriel . . ." she said hoarsely, not quite sure what she was going to say but feeling she had to say something.

He didn't respond, pulling open his jeans and shoving

them down on his hips, freeing his cock. Then he sheathed himself and as he did so, she realized his hand was shaking.

Shaking? She looked up into his face. Something burned in his eyes, something she didn't recognize. Something desperate.

"Gabriel," she said again, softer this time. A whisper.

He said nothing. Instead he put her arms over her head, one strong hand holding both her wrists, pinning her to the door. Then he slid his free hand behind her knee, lifting her leg up and around his waist.

Honor took a ragged breath, her hips tilting, the press of his erection against her aching flesh almost too much to bear. He released her leg, then he was pushing into her, a deep, hard thrust that shoved her over the edge of climax, making her cry out as it tore through her.

He didn't stop, didn't pause. He kept moving, a relentless, driving motion that had pleasure beginning to wind tight for a second time.

Honor squeezed her eyes shut again and closed her mouth against the moans that crowded in her throat.

"Scream," Gabriel demanded harshly in her ear. "I want you to scream."

Oh no, if she embraced this then she was going to embrace all of it. She was going to push him. Deny him. Test him. So he would take the control from her. Leaving her with nothing but absolute freedom.

She shook her head, a sharp refusal.

His grip on her wrists changed and she felt him pull one of her hands down and push it between them. She fought him because she wanted to, because it was exciting, but she was no match for his strength. She jerked as he brought her fingers down to where they were joined, making her feel it. The push of his cock inside her, the slick flesh of her sex stretching around him.

"Scream." His voice was ragged. "Touch yourself and scream for me, sweetheart." He shifted her hand higher, so her fingers brushed her clit, his hand covering hers, guiding her movements on her own flesh, relentless as a piercing kind of pleasure flooded through her.

There was no escaping it. No escaping him.

Honor embraced the chaos, a scream tearing from her throat, the thrust of him inside her and the feel of her fingers on her clit deepening the pleasure into ecstasy, a tidal wave she had no hope of stopping or holding back. And she let it. Surrendered to it.

Let it wash her away and all her futile plans with it.

She was barely aware of his own hoarse cry following hers. Barely aware of anything but the aftershocks pulsing through her. He didn't move either, holding her against the door, the heat of his body and the feel of his arms around her all that was keeping her upright.

Silence fell, broken only by their gradually slowing breathing, and it became almost peaceful. Restful. Like she could stay here in his arms, take some comfort from his heat and his strength, and it would be okay. It wouldn't be a failure of nerve on her part.

Eventually though, Gabriel moved and she felt him withdraw from her, unable to stifle the soft moan of protest it brought from her.

Still, he didn't speak. Only looked down at her for a long minute, the expression on his face completely enigmatic. Then he pushed himself away from her and, without a word, walked down the hallway toward the lounge area.

Honor stared after him, still too shaken to move. What the hell?

After a long minute she stepped away from the door, smoothing down her skirt and trying to get herself back in order again. Then she picked up her purse and briefcase and followed him into the lounge.

It was empty.

She dumped her belongings down near the sectional sofa. Her legs felt shaky, her heart going too fast. And she was . . . angry. No, not just angry, she was pissed.

Stalking into the kitchen, she found Gabriel standing at the counter with his back to her, his hands braced on the edge of it, his head bent. Utterly still, tension in every line of his big body. As if he was in pain.

She had a sudden flashback to Vermont. When she'd gone down on him and he'd gotten up and left. Without a word. Like he had just now. As if . . . what they'd done had been too much for him.

Honor blinked, her heartbeat still way too fast for comfort, the sharp edges of her anger softening.

He hadn't waited. Just pulled her inside and pushed her up against the door. His hand had been shaking as he'd put on the condom and he'd tasted of desperation . . .

Had that been her? Had she done that to him?

Suddenly she had to know.

She crossed the space between them, coming over to where he stood, putting a hand in the center of his back. "What's going on, Gabriel?" There was coiled tension beneath her palm, his muscles taut.

He didn't move. "I'm sorry. I shouldn't have done that." There was a harsh note in his voice as if the apology had been forced out.

Damn. It probably had.

"Then why did you?"

Slowly he straightened, keeping his back to her. "I . . . wanted you. And I . . . couldn't wait."

Honor drew in a slow, silent breath. She should stop touching him. She should turn around and walk away like she'd planned. And yet she couldn't bring herself to move. "You have to know that when I came here, I wasn't planning on . . . that," she said softly. "I was going to say what

I had to say then I was going to walk out. And not see you again."

His head bent and he ran a hand through his hair. "Fuck." Abruptly he turned around, and the expression on his bruised face made her ache. There was something lost in it. Like a man finding himself in an unfamiliar country and without a map or landmarks. Or a compass to help him find his direction.

"I would have stopped if you'd said the word. You have to know that." His dark eyes searched her face. "Did you . . . want me to stop?"

She couldn't lie. "No. I should have said something but . . . I didn't. I wanted you, too."

His hand dropped and dark, gold-streaked lashes veiled his gaze. "You should go, Honor. You should do what you planned to do. Turn around and walk away."

Her heart contracted. She folded her arms across the ache. "Why?"

His lashes lifted and this time the lost expression had vanished, nothing but blackness in his eyes. "Because I'm not the man for you. I will hurt you."

*Too late. Too damn late.*

She swallowed. "You wouldn't let me walk away, not if you didn't want me to."

The intensity of his gaze held her fast. "You have a one-minute window. Starting from now."

*You should do what he said. Now.*

But she knew she wasn't going to. She'd already made the decision back there in the hallway. How could she leave anyway? When there was a man behind that blackness. A man who was lost. A man who wanted her so badly he couldn't wait and then had to walk away because what they did together broke him apart. Made his hands shake.

She could not leave that man alone.

All her life she'd wanted to fix things for people. Help

them. Her mother. Guy. Violet. Even Alex. And here was another person who needed her. The man behind Gabriel's dark eyes. The man he tried to hide.

"I'm not going anywhere," Honor said softly. "So, if you want me to leave, you're going to have to throw me out yourself."

# CHAPTER FIFTEEN

Christ, he was a stupid bastard. He should be doing exactly what she said. He was as far as it was possible to get from being a saint and yet he'd always had his line in the sand. Hurting women had been that line.

But he was going to cross it if he kept on down the road he was traveling. And the woman he wound up hurting would be Honor.

She stood there with her arms folded, the very epitome of the smart businesswoman in her little pencil skirt, with the chic white blouse and the sexy blue high heels on her feet, same as the deep midnight blue of her eyes that he was starting to see in his dreams at night.

The color that darkened into black when she was aroused. Like they had when he'd had her against the door because he couldn't keep his dick in his pants. Because he'd gotten impatient waiting for her to arrive and fucking lost his head, a part of him hungry for her heat, her softness. The feel of her skin, the tight clasp of her body. Her arms around him.

Hungry for someone who didn't want to punch his face in for a start.

It had been too much. He had no idea why he'd suddenly been so desperate for her. Why his instinct had been to drown himself in her the moment she'd stepped into the hallway. It had only been a couple of days, after all. Yet he'd wanted her so badly he'd been shaking.

He still did. On a level he didn't understand.

And that was the real fucking problem. He was in danger of letting this become too important. In danger of letting *her* become too important. Which couldn't happen.

"Well?" she said into the silence. "Is my minute up yet?"

*You can't let her go. You know you can't.*

He'd thought he could have both his justice and her, and still be detached. Still be focused. But detachment wasn't shoving her up against a doorway and screwing her senseless because he couldn't wait. Or walking away because he couldn't bear how naked he'd felt afterward. How raw.

*Then if you keep her, you'll have to accept what she does to you.*

Yeah, he would have to. And hope whatever this need for her was, it would burn itself out in time. Because there was no fucking way he was letting her go.

"Yes," he said curtly. "It's up."

"Good." She took a step back and slipped off the coat she still had wrapped around her, slung it over one of the kitchen stools. Then she came close to him, reaching up to gently touch the bruise on his cheek. Her fingers were so cool he almost shivered. "Are you going to tell me who gave you this?"

He could lie but what was the point? "Alex."

Her mouth tightened and her hand dropped. "I thought you two were friends."

"We were."

"So what happened?"

"He guessed what you and I are doing."

"What? How the hell could he know?" She began to take a couple of steps back from him but he couldn't help himself. He reached for her, sliding an arm around her waist and bringing her close, her warmth against his body. Jesus, he knew he was supposed to stay cold, but sometimes all he wanted was some heat. A little bit of human warmth because he'd never had it before.

Her eyes widened, but she didn't resist and after a moment, laid her palms against his chest, a gentle pressure.

"I probably should tell you a few things," he said.

"Such as?"

Slowly, he began to undo the little buttons of her blouse, one by one. "Alex and I are part of a very small, select group. Officially we call ourselves the Nine Circles club, but Alex prefers 'the fucked-up billionaires.' Eva King is part of it. And so is another friend of mine, Zac Rutherford."

She said nothing as he pulled open the last button, her blouse falling open to reveal a long strip of pale skin. "We're a kind of family more than a club; we watch out for each other."

"He hit you." Her hand touched his cheek again.

Gabriel brushed her throat then let his fingers trail down, her skin unbearably soft beneath his touch. "He was right to."

She shivered as he stroked the gentle swell of one breast. "No, he wasn't. What we do has got nothing to do with him."

"He feels responsible for you."

"He lost that right years ago." She traced the line of his jaw, brushing his lower lip. He couldn't remember the last time anyone had touched him so gently, so carefully. As if he would break. "I can't think why he still thinks he has it."

No wonder he always felt the need to tie her hands. If she kept touching him like this he probably would break. "He's protective of you."

Her mouth tightened. "I suppose he already knew about Daniel and the casino?"

"Yeah."

"What a surprise. Can we not talk about him right now?"

Understandable. He didn't really want to talk about Alex either. Or think about the disgust in Eva's face. The look of disapproval on Zac's. They hadn't liked it when Honor's name had come up.

*Because they can sense what a prick you are at heart.*

A weird feeling gripped him. Like the ground he walked on was unsteady. The group had been together for years and they fought and bickered and made up like a family. But Alex had never hit him. And Zac and Eva had never looked at him with disgust.

Until now.

He looked down at the line of skin revealed by her open shirt, trying to concentrate on that instead of what had happened with the others. He didn't like the feeling that sat in his gut. Guilt.

Hell. He was turning into his mother.

Gabriel slid a finger under the edge of the white lace of her bra, stroking the silky skin underneath. "Anyway, we help each other out with things occasionally. Eva and Zac have been helping with Tremain. They have . . . particular skills that can be useful from time to time."

Honor's fingers came to rest near the neckline of his T-shirt, her thumb resting on his collarbone. "They know?"

"Yeah. Eva was investigating Tremain anyway, as you know, and she was the one who turned up the problems with the reservation system. She and Zac investigated further and found the money-laundering details."

"I guess . . . Alex knows that, too, then?"

"I thought you didn't want to talk about him?"

"I don't. I just wondered."

"Yeah, he does." The guilt twisted a little tighter. He should have told his friend earlier and not in front of the other two, but he hadn't. And he hadn't missed the flare of pain in Alex's eyes. That place, that casino, had so many memories for both of them and none of them good.

Honor's thumb moved back and forth on his collarbone, the touch oddly soothing. Her gaze was on the movement, dark lashes hiding her expression. She was silent a long moment. Then she said, "I went to see my mother a couple of days ago. I only wanted to . . . see her. She used to suffer from depression and if she ever found out about Dad, I don't know what that would do to her. Anyway, I went to see if she was okay and . . ." She stopped. "Dad was there."

A sudden, intensely protective urge rose up in him. A feeling he hadn't had since he'd been with the Angels and had a whole neighborhood to look out for. This time the feeling was centered entirely on Honor.

Tension flooded through him. "Did he do anything? Did he hurt you? What?"

She shook her head. "He's not that type of man, Gabriel."

"I don't give a fuck what type of man he is. If he hurt you I'll—"

Honor put a finger over his mouth, stopping the words. "He didn't hurt me. And there's no need to get all alpha about it, okay? But he did tell me that he wasn't going to take your money. That he was going to find a new investor." Her finger dropped away. "And that he didn't want me to handle it anymore." Pain moved in the depths of her eyes before her lashes fell again, veiling them. "Which I guess proves that you were right after all. He doesn't want to save his company."

There was an unfamiliar tightness in his chest, the protective urge clawing at him, squeezing him. And he realized he hated that she was in pain, and that he wanted to do something for her.

"Yeah, I got an email from him yesterday refusing my investment." He paused. "Did you mention your own investment to him?"

"He told me not to worry. That I'd get my money back."

"How much will you lose, Honor?"

Her thick, black lashes were still. "Everything. Which makes me a fool, right?"

Gabriel put a finger under her chin and tipped her head back. She looked up at him and this time, the anguish in her eyes wasn't hidden. "No. You love him and wanted to help. He's the one who's a fucking idiot."

"It's not even the fact that I'm going to lose my company that hurts the most. It's the fact that he knows what I put into Tremain, the risk I took on, and he's going to run it into the ground anyway."

"You don't have to lose everything," he said, stroking her chin with his thumb. "Not if you let me help you."

"How?"

"I have money, Honor. You don't need to lose your company if I invest in it."

Something flashed across her face, an expression he couldn't read. He felt her stiffen, her muscles tensing as if to pull away so he shifted his hands, gripping her hips to hold her in place.

"Gabriel," she began. "I don't want—"

"Listen to me." He cut her off. "I'm not giving you the money. It'll be Woolf Construction investing in a very promising up-and-coming financial consultancy. Shit, call it venture capital if you like. I've done that before with other companies. But if it'll stop you from losing everything you've built then why the fuck not?"

She pulled her head away, but remained where she was, resting against him. "St. James is my business. I didn't want anyone else to have a stake in it. Especially not . . ." She stopped.

"Me?" he finished. "You especially don't want me investing, right?"

"I don't know where this is going, Gabriel. You and I, I'm talking about. And I don't like mixing business with my private life."

"You crossed that line a long time ago, little girl. When you invested in Tremain." He knew she wouldn't want to hear that but it had to be said. "And as far as you and I go, my investment in your company is a separate issue from us sleeping together."

She looked up and this time he could see the businesswoman behind her eyes. Cool and calm and in control. "The fact remains that you would still own at least half of my company. So what happens if . . . this all goes bad?"

"You trust me with your body but not your company?"

"I don't want to be dependent on anyone. When Daniel's debts were called in, before Dad came to the rescue, we lost everything. I don't ever want that to happen to me again."

"And yet you invested in Tremain's company. Invested heavily, putting yourself knowingly at risk."

Her gaze flickered. "I had to help fix it."

Of course she would. She was that kind of person. The kind who wanted to help, no matter what it cost her. He'd seen those kinds of people back in his old neighborhood, the priests, the social workers, people who worked for the charities. Running themselves ragged helping. Such self-sacrifice for so little gain.

They hadn't made a difference. The only thing that had was when he'd become president of the club and he'd made change happen himself. With force.

"You're going to lose everything when he goes down anyway, Honor. You know this."

"I can't risk it, Gabriel. I can be in your bed, but that's it. I can't take anything else."

He looked down at her, studying her expression. "Because you want it too much? Is that it?"

Her throat moved as she swallowed. "I already want you more than I should. If you offer me this, I'm going to want more. I might end up wanting . . . everything."

"You're not your father, Honor. You're not Alex. And I'm not a fucking drug. I'm just a guy offering to help you."

The tips of her fingers moved on his chest, back and forth. "Maybe." The word was uncertain. Clearly she didn't believe him.

He put his hands over hers, holding them against his chest. "So that's why you're staying? Because you can't help yourself?" He wasn't going to ask the real question. The one that would betray a vulnerability he didn't want to feel.

Yet she seemed to know anyway. "No," she murmured. "I stayed because I think you need something, Gabriel."

Yeah, he did. But if she thought she could fix him like she wanted to fix the situation with Tremain, she was wrong. He was broken. He'd been born broken.

He shifted his hands, sliding them around her waist to the small of her back, finding the small button on the waistband of her skirt, undoing it. "I know what I need," he said, suddenly sick of talking. Sick of thinking. "I need you. Naked. Right now."

Much later he woke to find a cold moon shining through his bedroom windows, Honor lying curled beside him, naked and warm. He didn't know what had woken him but he knew he wasn't going back to sleep anytime soon.

He got up, pulled on his jeans, and went downstairs. If he couldn't sleep then he could work—he always had shitloads of work.

Pulling up his e-mail he found a message from Zac who'd apparently already gotten him an invite to the casino. He had to admit, the guy was fast.

After sending off a reply, Gabriel pushed his chair back and stalked over to the windows, restless and edgy.

The world outside was cold, snowy, the dark broken up with the sharp edges of neon lights.

What the hell was he going to do about Tremain? If he wasn't careful his plans were going to go to hell in hand-cart. With the bastard running his own company off a cliff, Gabriel had nothing to hurt him with. Unless he could interfere with those plans himself. But then, perhaps he didn't need to. He had all the information he needed to ruin Guy Tremain already.

Evidence of his money-laundering scam. Proof that he'd paid the debts his friend had run up managing what amounted to a sophisticated drug and prostitution ring. Confirmation he'd been paid by the casino involved in that ring. All of that was enough to take to the police if he wanted, or he could use it himself.

Definitely enough to ruin the man's life. He had him by the balls, that was for sure.

*And what are you going to do with her afterward?*

A strange emptiness yawned wide at the thought so he shoved it away.

Fuck, no point in thinking about that yet. Once Tremain's life was ruined, then he'd have time to consider what was next.

Gabriel let out a breath, put his hands in the pockets of his jeans.

*Honor won't like how you got close to her because you wanted information about Tremain.*

Guilt lay heavy inside him. A massive stone he couldn't seem to get rid of or ignore. So many people had lied to Honor, kept things from her. And she was still picking up the pieces. He would be just one more.

He stared at the snowy view outside the windows.

At this rate he'd be making his way to the confessional if he wasn't careful.

Warm arms slid around his waist and he went still, tensing in surprise.

"What are you doing up?" Honor's voice behind him sounded sleepy.

How the hell had she managed to creep up on him like that? Without him hearing? Shit, he'd been too busy staring outside and fucking brooding to hear. "I couldn't sleep."

Her fingers laced on his stomach, the heat of her slender body up against him seductive. A soft touch in the middle of his back. Her mouth in a kiss. "I wondered where you'd gotten to."

There was something . . . good about the feeling of her arms around him. The warm glow of her resting against his back. Almost . . . *comforting?* Christ, that was a thought he did not want to follow. He didn't need comforting. What he needed from her wasn't a hug, that was for damn sure.

Yet he couldn't bring himself to move. Because he liked her arms around him. Liked the soft brush of her mouth against his back. He hadn't been simply held by anyone in a long, long time.

"You should be asleep," he said.

"I know. But I woke up and you were gone."

*Move, you fucking idiot.*

Slowly, reluctantly, he did so, turning around in the circle of her arms. She was wearing the T-shirt he'd taken off earlier that evening, the hem coming to mid-thigh, leaving lots of bare leg on show, the tips of her nipples pressing through the fabric.

She wasn't looking at him but at his chest, her fingers brushing the tattoo of the cross over his heart. "When did you get this?"

He wasn't supposed to be sharing facts about himself with her and yet he found himself answering all the same. "When I was sixteen."

"Why?"

"It was a reminder."

Her fingers lightly traced it, raising a shiver across his skin. "Of what?"

"Of where I came from." From rape. Violence. Fear.

"Why the cross?"

"Mom was Catholic."

"Oh." Her fingers drifted lower to the vow across his abdomen. Tracing the outline of the words. "Explain this then. *Vengeance is mine; I will repay, saith the Lord.* Romans 12:19."

At her touch the muscles of his stomach tightened, more shivers chasing over his skin, his cock hardening. "You know your scripture."

"I went to a Catholic girls' school." Her thumb brushed the Y. "What do you have to repay?"

*You could tell her.*

"Not what. Who."

Honor looked up at him, her eyes dark in the shadowed room. "Who then?"

"My mother was hurt a long time ago. And I promised I would get justice for her. Justice from the man who did that to her."

She didn't say anything, just looked up at him, her gaze disturbingly perceptive. "She was hurt? How?"

"She was raped." It sounded so stark, his mother's secret guilt and shame.

Concern flooded her face. "Oh. How awful. I'm sorry."

"It happened a long time ago." But it had left its mark. Had consumed her. Like the cancer had eventually consumed her.

She placed a hand on his chest, the warmth of her touch spreading out. Dangerous, that warmth. It could melt things. Things that needed to stay hard and cold. Yet he couldn't seem to make himself remove her hand, just like he couldn't seem to make himself stop talking. It was surprisingly easy.

"She was very young. A maid at a hotel. She was raped by the owner while she was cleaning up one of the rooms."

"That's terrible." Her thumb moved on his chest, a stroke over and over. And he was growing to like the way she touched him. Wished she wouldn't stop. "They never caught him?"

"No. But I will."

He saw her throat move, saw worry shift in her eyes as she looked at him. "You know who it is?"

"Yes." *The stepfather you love. I'm going to ruin him.*

More worry, the edge of fear creeping into her gaze. "Gabriel, what are you going to do?"

He put his hand over hers, stilling the movement. "Hurt him."

"Gabe—"

"Not physically. I don't do that anymore. But he will suffer, Honor. I'm going to make sure of that."

Her gaze flickered and he felt her body stiffen against his, as if in preparation to move away. Well, that was probably good. She should understand truly what kind of man he was because she didn't seem to see the truth. But he didn't want to lose the warmth of her yet so he kept his hands where they were, covering hers. Pressing her palms to his chest, the glow of her heat like embers on his skin.

"She lost her job," he went on, unable to stop the flow

of words. "She was left with nothing after it happened. She tried to go to the police, but they weren't interested. She was just another dirt-poor fucking immigrant with nothing and no one. Her attacker was rich and powerful and she couldn't say a word against him that would be believed. Afterward, she couldn't find another job. No one would hire her because he'd bad-mouthed her everywhere. She survived on welfare and the charity from her church, and on that only barely."

"I . . . I'm sorry."

"He has to pay, Honor. And there's no one else who can make sure that happens but me."

She looked away from him, resistance bleeding out of her. But he could see the pulse beating fast at the base of her throat. She was afraid.

*Fucking finally.*

"I told you I wasn't a good man," he said in a low voice. "You should listen." He took his hands away from hers, expecting her to step back.

But she didn't. She kept her palms on his chest, her gaze lowered. "What are you going to do to him?"

"Ruin him. Financially and emotionally so he knows what it's like to have nothing."

She looked up at him at last. "Who is he?"

*Tell her.*

Gabriel looked down into her pale face, into her shadowed blue eyes. "No one you know," he said softly.

He was lying. She didn't know how she knew, but there was something in his face, something in his voice that told her. But she didn't want to think too deeply about it because the implications were too much for her to handle quite yet. Like the fact that if he was lying then the man he was talking about *was* someone she knew . . .

But no, she wasn't going to think about it. Not now.

Not when he'd given her a little piece of himself. That was the most important thing. The most precious.

She looked away from the dark, brutal charisma of his features to the black ink on the hard planes of his abdomen. A promise of personal vengeance.

It made a violent kind of sense. Gabriel Woolf wasn't a man to sit by when others got hurt, she'd learned that about him if nothing else. And even if his version of justice was twisted, she could understand why he might feel that way. Hell, if anything similar had happened to her mother she would feel the same. Except luckily for her and her mother, she'd had Guy, not to mention the fact that she hadn't been born into poverty the way Gabriel had.

*"He will suffer, Honor."*

Presumably the way his mother had suffered. An eye for an eye.

"It's a little bit Old Testament, isn't it?" she said.

"He committed a crime," Gabriel said, his dark voice slightly rough. "He has to pay for it."

"So what does that make you? Judge, jury, and executioner?"

"Yes." He said it without hesitation.

Honor touched the words on his skin again, feeling his muscles tighten under her fingers. This was the thing that was driving him, that lay at the root of his anger. It had to be. "Do you have proof?"

"Of his guilt? Yeah, I've got all the fucking proof I need."

"How does your mother feel about it?"

"My mother is dead," he said flatly.

Honor looked up at him at that. The expression on his face was the one she saw so often. Hard. Cold. But underneath she sensed his anger. Hot. Burning.

"I'm sorry," she said again, a useless, stupid phrase, but it was the only one she had.

"She died a few weeks ago. Cancer."

So recent. God, she hadn't known. "Gabriel, I'm so—"

"No," he cut her off in that same flat tone. The one she was starting to think concealed something more. "Don't say that again. Don't be sorry. Death was a mercy."

"She was in pain?"

Darkness flickered in his eyes. "She was always in fucking pain."

Stillness settled inside her. "You're not talking about the cancer now, are you?"

"Cancer isn't the only thing that hurts."

Beneath her palms she could feel his heartbeat, strong and sure. He was so powerful, this man. On the surface so icy and emotionless, but he wasn't either of those things. There was heat inside him that he only ever let out when he was in bed with her. And in it lived his anger.

"What else hurts?" she asked, moving her fingers over the smooth, tanned skin beneath her hands.

"Guilt." His voice was almost a whisper. "Shame. Fear."

She'd bet everything on the fact that he wasn't talking about his mother now. That he was talking about himself.

There was no sound in the room, the silence broken only by the sirens and horns of the night traffic of the outside world.

Honor slid her hands apart and put her arms around him. Rested her head on the muscled wall of his chest. "Tell me, Gabriel," she murmured.

He waited there, motionless.

Honor shut her eyes. If he pulled away she would understand. It would hurt but she'd understand. Their relationship—or whatever the hell this was—probably didn't allow for confidences, but she had to try. She wanted to try. Everyone needed someone to talk to, even a man like him. *Especially* a man like him.

"She had no one to turn to but that church," he said roughly. "No one else to talk to. And I used to sit outside the confessional when I was a kid and I heard what she said. How ashamed she was. How guilty. She was a single mom as well so she got shit from people about it. She told the priest every day she lived with the evidence of her shame and how she could never get rid of it." He stopped all of a sudden and she could hear how fast his heart was beating. Feel the sudden rush of breath as his chest expanded. Like he was afraid.

But how did that work? What was a man like Gabriel Woolf even afraid of?

Honor didn't speak because if she did, this moment might end and she didn't want it to. She wanted to hear whatever it was he still had to say. So instead she tightened her arms around him. Held him.

"I didn't understand at the time what she was talking about," he went on, his voice hoarse. "But it hurt to hear. I felt . . . responsible."

A lump rose in the back of her throat. "How old were you?"

"Seven, I think. Yeah, must have been."

She could picture it. Seven-year-old Gabriel outside the confessional. Waiting for his mother. Listening in and hearing . . . that. No child should ever have to bear that kind of burden.

"I wanted to help her. Do something to make her not feel so guilty or ashamed. But I didn't know what to do. Because I didn't know why she felt that way."

"What about your father?" Honor asked thickly. "Where was he?"

The big body in her arms stiffened. "He was out of the picture." The finality in Gabriel's voice suggested that not asking any further questions on that particular subject would be a good idea.

She swallowed, her chest tight with sympathy. "So, what happened?"

"We survived on church handouts. And when I was old enough I took the packages from the Angels' club members and I delivered them for cash."

"Because you wanted to protect her," she murmured, understanding. "You wanted to fix it."

There was a silence.

Then Gabriel said, "There are some things you can't fix."

Honor took a silent breath then lifted her head, looking up into his face. "But you're trying to fix it now, aren't you? This vengeance thing is part of that, isn't it?"

There was no expression at all on his features but she could see the burning in his dark eyes. "Yes."

She lifted a hand, touched his cheekbone and the bruise on it. "What are you so angry about, Gabriel?"

"I think that's enough fucking questions for one night, don't you?"

The cold was back. In his voice, in his eyes. Like a mask he wore. It made her hurt for him. Made her ache. Because he was hiding something. The thing he was so angry about. That had driven him to tattoo into his skin the reminders and vows. The shame and the guilt wasn't only his mother's, it was his, too. And she wanted to know why.

Her hand drifted down to the waistband of his jeans, undid the button. Slid her hand inside his boxers to where he was already hard and hot and heavy.

His breath hissed as she wrapped her fingers around him. "I don't think you want to play that game with me now, sweetheart," he said roughly.

"Why not?" Her hand tightened. God, she loved the feel of him. Warm silk over steel.

"Because you won't get any answers from me that way."

"This vengeance you want," she said, ignoring him. "Has it got something to do with the casino?"

"It might."

She met his gaze, brushed her thumb over the head of his cock, felt him shudder. "What aren't you telling me?"

He stared back. "You don't want to know."

And that wasn't a lie. This time he was telling the truth.

God, she was so close to understanding him. Like he was a locked door and she could see the key right there in front of her. But the look on his face told her she did not want to know what lay behind that door. Did not want to know what would happen if she unlocked him.

But ever since her father died, she'd hated secrets. Hated the power they had. Hated how her world always felt fragile. Like glass and anything could shatter it. Anything at all.

Such as this man. He could shatter not only her world but her along with it.

If she let him. If she gave him that power.

*What do you mean "if"? You've already given him that power.*

Yeah, she had. Which meant she had nothing left to lose.

Honor ran her thumb over him again, watching as the fire in his eyes burned higher. "Actually," she said. "I think that this time I do."

# CHAPTER SIXTEEN

It wasn't going to happen. She might want to know, but that didn't mean he had to tell her. And he wasn't going to. Not yet.

*You want to tell her. You want to tell her everything.*

Christ, she had her hand around his cock and he was hard and aching for her. And it wasn't only sexual. Oh, sure, there was that, but also another kind of ache. One that went deeper than sex. An ache he didn't even realized he could feel and yet, one that felt like it had been there for a long time.

Like he wanted more. Her fierce loyalty. Her understanding. Her care. But he couldn't have any of those things, could he? Not when he was tainted.

What would happen if he told her what he was? Would she look at him the way his mother had looked at him? When she thought he didn't notice. Her eyes full of fear and other things, complicated things that he, as a child, didn't recognize.

He knew that part of her had wanted to get rid of him. That she wished he'd never been born. But she'd kept him because abortion was a sin. He was her cross to bear and bear it she would, a burden he could feel the weight of on his own soul as well as hers.

That weight had crushed his mother. It wouldn't crush

him. But he wouldn't let another have it either. Especially not Honor, with her own burdens to bear.

"No," he said. "This is one secret you're not going to find out."

*But she'll know. Eventually.*

He'd never thought too deeply about how she might feel, finding out that her stepfather was a rapist. Because he hadn't cared how that might affect her. His mother and the shitty life she'd had had been the only things that mattered.

But now it was different. Now, even though he didn't want to, he realized he cared. He didn't want her to find out. Didn't want her to have this final betrayal. Didn't want to utterly destroy her image of the man she loved like a father.

Perhaps she wouldn't have to. Perhaps he could keep it from her. He'd never intended for the knowledge to become public because there had never been any definitive proof. He'd only intended to confront Tremain with what he'd done, fling the knowledge in his face as he pulled the man's company down around his ears.

"I could get it from you," she murmured, her hand squeezing him tighter, the low ache of desire beginning to bite.

He could end this. Take her mouth and render her mindless with pleasure. Make her forget everything but the touch of his hands. But for the first time it felt wrong to use that against her. Almost as if what was between them was too important to be used as a weapon like that.

*Why the fuck are you thinking shit like this? You weren't supposed to get involved.*

Gabriel reached down, pulled her hand away. "Go back to bed, Honor."

She stared at him. Silent. Then she stepped back and he thought that for once, she was going to do what he told her to. But instead she reached for the hem of her T-shirt and pulled it up and over her head.

Moonlight and neon painted her bare skin. Silver and gold and blue and red.

And even though he'd spent all night exploring that beautiful body of hers, his breath still caught at the sight of her, his cock pressing painfully against the zipper of his jeans.

He took an unthinking step toward her but she held out a hand, her chin lifting, the look in her eyes determined. "Oh no, you're not touching me. Not yet. Not until you tell me what I want to know."

"What do you want to know?"

"Everything, Gabriel. I'm sick of secrets and I'm sick of lies. I told you I'd end up wanting everything and that includes whatever it is you're hiding."

"And how, exactly, do you think you're going to achieve that?"

She tilted her head, her eyes dark, studying him. "I thought I might use . . . this . . ." She straightened, ran her palms down her sides, arching her back. The move was provocative, sensual. Sexual. And it made the ache in his cock worse.

Jesus. He wasn't prepared to use their chemistry this time but apparently she was. The irony of the reversal wasn't lost on him. "Don't," he said, unable to keep the harsh edge from his voice. "Don't use sex to get what you want. That's not you, Honor."

She raised a brow. "Why shouldn't I? Especially when you were the one who started it. Playing your dominance games with me. Why can't I do the same thing now?" Her gaze was unflinching. "If I have to fight dirty I will." She paused, licked her lips. "But I guess if that's too much for you then by all means, go back to bed yourself."

"You don't want to play this with me," he said roughly. "You'll lose."

"Oh, will I?" Slowly she lifted her hands, cupped her breasts. "I'm not sure that's true." Her thumbs brushed her nipples and she let out a soft sigh. "You're not the only one with power, Gabriel Woolf. And you're not the only one who knows how to exploit a weakness."

No. Fuck that. He didn't want to play these games with her. Not here. Not now.

He didn't say anything, beginning to walk toward her instead. This was his show. His game. He was the one in charge. And if she thought she could take the control from him, she had another think coming.

"Stop," Honor said, her voice hard, authoritative. "Touch me and I'll walk out of here right now and I won't come back. Not ever."

Gabriel stopped dead. Bluffing. She had to be bluffing. But her gaze was cool. Like an archer watching an arrow they'd loosed, knowing without a shadow of a doubt it would hit the target.

She wasn't fucking bluffing.

*Ignore her. Let her walk out. Don't let her manipulate you like this.*

He should do all that. Because she was getting to him in a way she wasn't supposed to. A way he'd never intended. But for some reason he stayed where he was. Staring at her.

"What do you want, Honor?" he asked at last.

"Answers. The truth."

"And if I tell you everything?"

She met his gaze. "I will do whatever you want. Anything you want."

"But you already do that. You have to give me something I don't have yet."

She didn't answer that immediately, her gaze roving over his face. Searching. "A friend, Gabriel," she said after a long moment. "You don't have a friend."

Unease turned over inside him. "Bullshit. I have friends."

"What? Those people in your billionaires club? Alex? He punched you in the face and those other two . . . Do they really know you? Do you trust them?"

The unease deepened, a strange sense of loss opening up inside him. An emptiness he hadn't been aware of until now.

*"You gotta lock it down, kid,"* the Reverend had said. *" 'Cause vengeance is a long, costly, lonely fucking business to be in."*

So he'd hardened himself. Locked it down. Closed himself off from everyone and everything. It was easy. Certainly easier and far less painful than giving a shit. Easier than trust.

He didn't need anything but his anger.

"I don't trust anyone," he said. "And no one needs to know me. I don't give a shit about that."

Slowly, she came toward him, the light from the outside moving over her body. Her nipples were hard and he suddenly wanted, more than anything in the world, to push her down onto the floor and bury himself inside her. Cover himself in her warmth, her heat. Her scent. Her taste. Surround himself with her, fill up the empty places inside him. Places he hadn't known existed until now.

"I think you do," Honor said softly. "Everyone needs someone to trust. Someone who knows them and who has their back no matter what. Everyone needs a true friend."

She was close now and everything in him wanted her. But if he touched her she would leave and . . . he didn't want her to.

*Fuck. She's getting to you, you prick. Walk away. Walk away now.*

Gabriel turned. A ride, that's what he needed. His bike and the cold wind and the silence of the forest. The open road. Space to get his head back on straight. Clear his mind. Find the cold heart that he needed.

"I don't need anything," he said. "And you've got nothing I want."

Then he walked away, heading toward the door that led to his underground parking garage where he kept his bike.

The stairwell was unheated and cold but he welcomed the chill, trying to freeze the ache that seemed to linger in his chest, the heat still burning in his groin. Trying to not see the image of Honor, naked, bathed in neon and moonlight, coming toward him, the expression on her face painful in a way he didn't want to admit to.

The garage was unheated, too, the concrete icy under his bare feet. Skirting around the couple of cars he'd bought, and the truck he liked to drive when he was working on site, he went to the back where he kept his motorcycles. He had a large collection, but his favorite had always been the black Norton. British bikes had always appealed to him and this one, a Commando, was the one he preferred out of all of them.

He went to the cupboard off to one side where he kept his bike leathers, pulling it open and putting on his jacket and boots.

"Don't be such a fucking coward." The voice behind him was feminine and full of contempt.

He turned.

Honor was standing near his bike, still absolutely naked.

Jesus fucking Christ, she'd followed him. She must be freezing.

"What the hell are you doing?" he demanded. "Get back upstairs. You'll freeze to death down here."

"No." She remained exactly where she was. "Why should I be the one to leave? I'm not the one running away."

"I'm not—"

"The hell you're not. You won't give me answers and the one thing I offer you, the one thing I know you want, you fling back in my face. Tell yourself all you like you don't need anyone, but we both know that's an excuse. You're scared, Gabriel."

He shut the cupboard, harder than he'd meant to, the sound echoing off the hard concrete of the walls and floor. "You don't know what you're talking about. Now get back upstairs before I carry you up there myself."

Honor folded her arms and he could see the goose bumps on them, the shiver that wracked her as she did so. Her feet were very white. Everything about her, except her hair and her eyes, was very white. "I'm not going anywhere. N-not until I get my answers."

He took a step toward her, only stopping himself from touching her at the last minute. "Get the fuck upstairs before you freeze to death!"

She moved. But it wasn't in the direction of the stairs. Instead, she closed the space between them, sliding her hands beneath his jacket, wrapping her arms around him, pressing her cold skin against him. "Why?" she murmured. "When you can warm me up?"

Gabriel stilled. She'd told him not to touch her and yet she was touching him everywhere, her hands stroking his back beneath his jacket, her warm breath against his bare chest. The press of her naked breasts against him was cold but not for long, her skin beginning to warm up again.

"I can give you what you want," she whispered, her mouth brushing his skin. "I can be your friend. I can be the one you trust. The one you talk to. The one you know will never turn against you. I think you need it, Gabriel. I think you need me."

He shuddered, unable to help it. Unable to stop the rush of desire that flooded through him.

*You have to be cold. Detached.*

But how could he be when she was here warming everything up? Melting everything. He couldn't be. He didn't want to be.

"You can tell me," she whispered against his skin. "You can tell me anything." Her hands moved along his spine. Comforting. "You don't have to carry these things alone."

Fuck the not touching. Fuck the cold. Fuck everything.

Gabriel caught a hand in her hair, tangled his fingers through it, and pulled her head back. Kissed her upturned mouth. Hard. Hungry.

Honor made a sound in her throat. Not protest. She surged up in his arms, kissing him back with her own hunger, her own strength. Her teeth sunk into his lip, nipping him, sending a sharp jolt of pain down his spine. Making him rock hard in seconds flat.

He couldn't wait for this. Not for a bed. Not for anything. But the floor was like ice which left him only one option. He picked her up, carried her over to the Norton. Then he sat on the bike, holding her in his lap, facing him. She had her arms around his neck, still kissing him, a hot, demanding kiss that left him fighting for control.

He put a hand between her spread thighs, all raw heat and wetness, wanting to claim back the control from her. Flicking a thumb over her clit, he slid a finger inside her and she groaned against his mouth, her body trembling. Wrenching her head away, she gasped as he slid in a second finger, her eyes dark. "L-looks like I'll be . . . walking away after this," she panted.

Christ, her no-touching rule. But it was too late for that now. And he could make sure she wouldn't walk.

"You're not going anywhere." He moved his hand, sliding his fingers deeper inside her, his thumb circling the hard bud between her thighs, savagely pleased by the way her body shuddered under his touch.

Her head fell forward, silky hair against his shoulder. "Y-you can't force me, Gabriel. If I stay, it's because I want to."

She was hot now, the feel of her body around his fingers insanely erotic. Force her. God, how had it come to this?

*You should have let her go . . .*

He should have. But he hadn't. And now it was too late. "You're not going," he said hoarsely, slicking his thumb over her clit. "I won't let you."

She shivered, her breathing harsh and fast against his throat. "You don't want me to."

"No." The word escaped him before he could stop it. "No, I don't want you to."

"Then," she said simply, "I won't." And she lifted her head and kissed him. No violence this time. Only softness. Sweetness. Her arms wound around his neck, her hips rocking against his hand. Gentleness and strength. "You make me feel so good." A soft murmur against his mouth. "You make me feel . . . like myself."

He didn't understand why that cracked something in him. Why a few simple words should change things. He fisted a handful of silky black hair, pulled her head away so he could look at her face. Look into her eyes. They were wide and dark, meeting his.

"Why?" he demanded harshly, not even sure what he was asking.

"Because I can be myself around you. Because you're my friend."

"No. I'm not. I'm not anyone's friend." And he twisted his hand, stroking her so she moaned, helpless in his grip.

"I . . . don't care what you say," she said raggedly. "That's my decision, not yours."

Jesus, what could he do to make her change her mind? Make her see him for what he was? Who he was? Because he didn't deserve her friendship. Or her trust. Or her loyalty. Not someone like her.

But he didn't want to hurt her. Which left him with only one option.

The truth.

Slowly Gabriel withdrew his fingers from her.

"No," she said. "Don't stop."

The heat of her seeped into him, the musky scent of her arousal making him so hard he could barely think. But she wanted the truth and so he would give it to her.

"Gabriel—" she began.

"I told you my mother was raped," he interrupted hoarsely. "Well, that wasn't the end of it."

Honor blinked, the flush of desire staining her cheekbones, her eyes still dark. "What?"

"She got pregnant. She had a child."

Her eyes went wide, shock beginning to creep into them.

"She had me."

Honor shivered, the heady pleasure he'd been giving her dissipating, making her aware of the chill of the air around her. Of the icy darkness in his eyes. Pain. Guilt. Shame. He hadn't been talking only of his mother's. He'd been talking about his own.

Words—so useless, meaningless—got stuck in her throat. She didn't know what to say.

He was the child of his mother's rape. What *could* she say to that? There was a legacy there that made her feel cold all over, that made her ache with grief for him.

"So," she said thickly, "this justice you're seeking is from . . ." She couldn't say it.

"Is from my father?" Gabriel said it for her. "Yes."

His father . . .

*"He was the owner of the hotel. No one you know."*

The connection formed, knowledge breaking over her, and she wasn't only cold now. She was frozen right down to the bone. "G-Guy," she whispered, horrified. "Guy is your father?"

He didn't say anything but his hands on her hips tightened, his dark eyes holding hers, the look in them relentless.

"How do you know?" she demanded. "What proof do you have?"

"When my mother died I found a check in her belongings. It was from him. Dated the day she was raped."

"That's the only proof? A check?"

Anger lit in his eyes and this time, there was nothing cold about it. "Why the fuck else would my mother have a check from Guy Tremain? A check dated the day she was raped? It was for a million bucks, Honor. Money that she needed, especially after I was born. But she never fucking cashed it. There's only one reason. It was from the man who hurt her and she didn't want to touch it."

She was so cold now. She couldn't stop trembling. All this time, he'd known. All this time he'd had Guy in his sights and he hadn't told her. That her stepfather was a rapist and he was his son.

No, it couldn't be true. She just couldn't get her head around it. Guy had never been violent. Not toward her and not toward her mother. Not even once. It didn't make any sense.

"You don't believe me," Gabriel said and there were undercurrents in his voice she didn't have a hope of understanding.

"Why should I? You have a check and a supposition. That's all."

His fingers pressed into her hip. Hard. His eyes had gone black, an intense, crushing darkness. "I *know*, Honor. I know it's him."

*I will make him suffer . . .*

"You can't—"

"He took her future away from her. She wanted to be a nurse, did you know that? She wanted to go to college. Get a good job. She came here with so many fucking hopes and he took them all away from her." His voice was low, savage with anger. "The prick *ruined* her life. He destroyed it. *I* destroyed it." He took a harsh breath. "And this is the only way I can fix it."

Her heart raced, adrenaline pumping so hard through her she could barely get her lungs to work. She couldn't seem to stop shaking, the icy chill of the room freezing her. But the look in Gabriel's eyes was hot. A volcanic rage she'd only caught glimpses of. A rage she could feel humming through him like electricity through high-tension wires.

He wanted to fix things. Like she'd spent her life trying to fix things.

Things that couldn't be fixed.

She ached for him. For the pain and the rage that burned in him. For the burden he must be carrying. But . . . this was Guy. And he had no proof.

"I know what you feel you have to do," she said, trying to stop her teeth from chattering. "But you must have proof, Gabriel. You have to be sure."

"I am fucking sure!"

"Guy would never hurt anyone. You have to believe me, he wouldn't. I know him and he hasn't got a violent bone in his body."

Contempt twisted his features. "What the hell would you know? He's been laundering money for God knows how long and no one was any the wiser. He could have raped hundreds of women and you'd never know."

"But there could have been—"

"Mom was raped by the owner of that hotel. She told me. And Tremain was the owner. His name was on the check that he gave her." Rage burned in Gabriel's eyes. "That motherfucker raped her then thought he could buy her off with *money*." The way he said the word made it sound dirty. "Do you know what it's like when your own mother looks at you with fear? Knowing that she doesn't see her child in your face but the man who hurt her? Can you ever possibly know what it's like to understand you're the reason she's in this mess? That you're the reason her life turned to shit? And there's *nothing* you can do about it?"

There was so much fury in his eyes. So much pain. She could see it burning bright beneath the blackness, beneath the cold.

"She couldn't do anything to that bastard," Gabriel said in a savage voice. "But I can. And I will."

She wanted to hold him. Wanted to do something for him. Drain all that pain and fury. But when she lifted her icy hands to his face, he said, "Don't touch me. If you know what's good for you, you'd get as far away from me as you could."

"Gabriel," she began but he put her off the bike. Zipped up his jacket. Put on the helmet that sat on the back and pressed a button on his key ring that opened the doors to the garage. Then he gunned the bike, the garage roaring with the sound of the engine and the screech of tires as he took off into the night.

There was nothing else she could do but turn around and make her way back upstairs.

Shivering, she pulled a woolen throw from the couch and wrapped herself up in it, sitting down in one of the armchairs. The darkness and the silence enveloped her, the warmth of the central heating beginning to take the chill from her skin.

But nothing could take the chill from her heart.

She'd never seen a man so angry. Or in so much pain.

And apparently Guy was the cause. Guy was Gabriel's father, or so he believed.

Guy was a rapist.

Honor bent and pressed the heels of her hands over her eyes.

*"Do you know what it's like when your own mother looks at you with fear?"*

That happened to him. She'd seen her rapist in her son. Oh, God, no wonder he'd said he'd felt responsible for his mother's guilt and shame. In his mind, he was.

A lump rose in Honor's throat. She should do what Gabriel had told her. Leave. Get out while she still could. Go and see Guy. Warn him maybe. Because she couldn't believe he'd done what Gabriel had accused him of. She just . . . couldn't.

But . . . she couldn't leave Gabriel, not when he was hurting like he was.

*You know what this means.*

Of course she did. If she was giving up the man she considered her father for him, it meant she was hooked. And it was too late to protect herself. Too late to save herself. She was in deep and there was no escaping.

Her throat ached. Her chest tightening as the truth of her feelings sank deep inside her. This was the ruin she'd feared because there was no way he felt the same about her. She didn't even know if he was capable of it. Yet she wasn't going to let that minor detail get in the way.

No matter how much he tried to deny it, Gabriel had no one else. Only her.

*"I'm the reason her life turned to shit . . ."*

He blamed himself. It wasn't his fault and yet he took the responsibility for his mother's life all the same. Because that's what he did. He shouldered the burdens that were too heavy for other people. He took the responsibility for things no one else wanted.

Why? Did he think there was no one else to help? Did he think he was alone?

Tears prickled. Because she knew the answer to that already.

"Not anymore, Gabriel," she whispered into the darkness. "You're not alone anymore."

Slowly, she lifted her head and wiped her eyes. Then she pulled the blanket around her even more tightly and sat back in the armchair to wait.

Honor opened her eyes abruptly knowing something had changed.

She was still sitting in the armchair in Gabriel's apartment and it was still dark. But now a tall, powerful figure stood in front of her. Her heart began to thump painfully hard in her chest, even though she knew who it was. There was a chill in the air and she could taste snow at the back of her throat. He'd brought the winter back inside with him.

Good thing she was warm.

He said nothing, and she couldn't tell what he was thinking because the darkness hid his face.

It didn't matter anyway. She was here, that was all that mattered.

Honor threw aside her blanket. And opened her arms.

He didn't move for a long moment and she could hear his breathing, fast, labored. Then, slowly, like a tree falling, he dropped to his knees in front of her and leaned forward, his arms coming around her waist, a vise holding her tight, turning his face against her stomach.

She put her arms around him, folded herself over him. He was so cold and she could feel tremors running through the big body kneeling in front of her.

She said nothing because this went deeper than words. This was where only silence and warmth could help. The physical warmth of another person to remind him he wasn't alone. That he wasn't as isolated as he seemed to think he was.

That she was here for him.

And he took what she offered, his breath hot on the bare skin of her stomach, holding her so tight, the tremors slowly fading. But not the tension. That remained.

Honor ran a hand down his leather-clad back then laid her cheek on his shoulder. He smelled of leather and snow. Cold wind and loneliness. She closed her eyes, letting her body heat into him, melting away that cold and tension.

She didn't know how long he stayed like that, kneeling at her feet, holding onto her so tightly it was like he was afraid she'd disappear. Eventually she felt the muscles of his back flex, his body shifting. She eased away to give him some room.

But he wasn't leaving. His fingers slid around her wrists, holding them tightly down on either side of her thighs. Then he lifted his head slightly, hot breath passing over the sensitive skin of her stomach. "You stayed." His voice was dark, rough, possessive. "That makes you mine."

"Yes." There was no point disagreeing. This was what she'd stayed for. This was what she was giving him. Besides, she'd been his from the moment she'd first laid eyes on him.

His mouth brushed her stomach and it was her turn to shiver, aching physical awareness rushing over her. She was still naked and the arousal of earlier in the evening was still there, pulsing beneath the surface of her skin.

"I want everything," Gabriel murmured, the dark, rough note in his voice making her heart beat faster.

Making the ache inside her more acute. "Give me everything, Honor."

She closed her eyes again. "Yes. It's yours."

The brush of his mouth against her inner thighs, hot kisses that had her catching her breath. Her muscles went tight as his mouth moved higher, between her legs, nuzzling her. She inhaled sharply. Only to have him pull back, releasing her wrists.

"Gabriel . . ."

Carefully, he slid a hand behind her knee and lifted one leg, then the other, over the arms of the chair, spreading her wide. Then he leaned forward, his big, muscular body pinning her, trapping her in the chair.

Not that she cared. She didn't want to move anyway. Her breathing had accelerated and when he bent his head, covering her sex with his mouth, she didn't hold back the sound he brought from her. A choked cry. She put her hands in his hair, curling her fingers tight as he licked her like he had all the time in the world. Long slow licks that had her gasping and arching back.

"Watch," he growled against her skin. "I want you to watch."

She obeyed without thought, looking down, meeting his black eyes. And she kept looking as he lowered his head again, watching his mouth move on her slick flesh, tasting her. It was unbearably erotic seeing her legs spread wide over the arms of the chair, his blond head between them. It was almost too much but she'd promised she'd give him everything. And she would.

His tongue pushed into her, deep and slow and she panted, crying out, her gaze pinned to him and what he was doing to her.

The orgasm gathered tightly inside her, a hard, aching knot of sensation that felt impossible to contain. He didn't wait, giving her another lick that sent her over the edge, shuddering and calling his name as the climax rushed through her.

He didn't give her more than a couple of seconds of respite. Kneeling upright, he grasped her, pulling her off the chair, taking her down to the floor, the silk Persian rug that covered the floorboards soft against her back. Then he shrugged off his jacket, tore open his jeans, found a condom from his back pocket, and protected himself. Settling between her legs, he thrust inside her, a hard, deep movement that had her gasping, her sensitive flesh stretching almost unbearably.

Then he stopped, deep inside her. His arms slid around her and he gathered her close, sitting up so she was in his lap, facing him, his dark eyes mere inches away.

"Gabriel . . ." she murmured, his name like a prayer.

His hands slid up her back, arching her forward so her breasts were thrust high. Then, keeping one arm around her, he stroked her side, cupping one breast, teasing her nipple with his thumb as he began to move again, rocking gently.

"Mine," he whispered, that hand running all over her, stroking, teasing. Light and gentle. "You're all mine. Say it, Honor. Say the words."

"I'm yours," she gasped out, her hands on his shoulders, nails digging in. Giving him exactly what he wanted. What she'd promised him she'd give. "I'm all yours, Gabriel."

"And you're going to stay mine. Aren't you? You're going to stay and never leave."

She gave him the promise without a thought. "N-no . . . never."

His movements began to get faster, harder. The darkness in his eyes became all-encompassing, swallowing everything.

*He'll ruin you. Destroy you.*

The thought flashed bright in her brain then was gone. Perhaps she wanted to be ruined. There were worse ways to go, after all.

His fingers slid into her hair, the strands gripped tight in his fist. Pain prickled over her scalp but she welcomed it. Embraced it. Let herself be overwhelmed totally by it. And when his mouth claimed hers, she opened to him.

She was surrounded by him. His taste, his scent, the heat of him inside her, around her. And she let it happen. Because she'd promised she'd give him everything and she did. No holding back.

She wanted to give him this. It was all she had. Because she didn't think he'd accept anything else.

When the climax came he was kissing her and she screamed against his mouth, pleasure cascading through her, sharp and intense. Bright and powerful.

And then she felt him shudder, too, his breathing harsh and ragged as he turned his face into her neck, his arms like steel around her.

There was no escaping this.

She was his. Irrevocably.

# CHAPTER SEVENTEEN

Honor was trembling in his arms but he wasn't going to let her go. He'd told her everything and she was still here. Which made her his.

*Not quite everything.*

No, not that he'd purposefully gotten close to her because of her relationship to Tremain, but she didn't need to know that. Perhaps she'd never need to know that. But all the rest . . .

She knew now exactly what she was dealing with. The kind of man he was and what he wanted. His justice. And maybe he shouldn't have told her. Maybe in doing so he'd relinquished a little bit of his power, but shit, it was too late now.

He was just so fucking tired of carrying the weight of that burden by himself.

Honor's head had dropped onto his shoulder, the softness of her breathing against his throat. She was curled into him, her arms around him, all softness and warmth and silky pale skin.

Christ, the moment he'd come back from his ride and found her sitting there in the armchair had knocked the breath from his body.

He'd thought she would have left. Fuck, after everything he'd dumped on her, he was sure he'd come back to an empty apartment. But no. She'd been there. Nestled into that armchair, asleep. Waiting for him. And then she'd woken, tossed aside her blanket, and opened her arms.

He'd never had anyone welcome him home like that. Never had anyone take him into their arms and hold him. Saying nothing. Expecting nothing. And in that moment, it had become clear to him exactly what he was going to do.

She was his now and he was going to keep her. He was never going to let her go.

After a long moment, he rose, and holding her in his arms, he carried her upstairs to the bedroom. Laid her in the bed, wrapping the comforter around her to keep her warm.

He went into the bathroom and had a brief shower, getting rid of the last of the icy chill of the snow and the searing cold of the air as he'd ridden through the streets.

He'd been so angry he'd had to get out. He'd had to leave before he did something stupid. Said something stupid, though he'd already said nearly all he could possibly say. He'd tried to find his cold detachment, the icy rage that had gotten him through the long years up until this point. But he hadn't been able to.

And then she'd been there. And opened her arms. And in the warmth of her, he'd found something better than icy rage. A kind of peace.

Gabriel slipped naked into the bed beside her, gathering her in his arms and holding her close, her back to his front, her butt fitting perfectly against his groin.

"What are you going to do?" she asked after a long moment.

He didn't need to ask her what she meant. "I'm going to go to the casino."

"Why? What do you think you're going to find there?"

"Information."

"About what?"

"About why Tremain is laundering money. What the connection is between him and your father. Proof that he married your mother because he was paid to."

"Please don't say you're doing this for me."

"No. You're not the only one who was hurt by what happened there."

"Alex." The name was a soft whisper.

"Yes." Gabriel tightened his arms around her. "I'm not doing this to hurt you, Honor, you have to understand that."

"I do."

There was a small silence.

"What are you going to do with all this information? If you find any?"

He'd told the truth, he didn't want to hurt her. But justice was more important than people's feelings. More important than hers. And his own.

"I'm going to use it against him," he said.

Another silence.

"I'm coming with you," she murmured.

Protectiveness, a harsh, brutal feeling swept through him. "Fuck that. You're not going anywhere near—"

"I think I'm owed it," she interrupted quietly. "Don't you?"

He couldn't think of a protest to that because yeah, she did. Her father had owned that casino, had let it ruin both him and her brother. Had shattered the life she'd known. It was dangerous as hell but yes, she was owed. He, out of all people, understood that.

"All right," he said. "But only on the condition that you follow my orders when we're there. That place isn't safe."

"Yes."

He stared at the mass of silky black hair in front of

him then closed his eyes and inhaled her scent. Something inside him calmed. "You can't tell Tremain. Not about any of this. He's mine to deal with."

She didn't say anything, but he could feel the tension in her body. He knew this was hard for her and a part of him was sorry he'd told her. And not for himself this time, but because it was painful for her.

"Honor," he murmured. "You have to promise me."

"I promise," she said at last.

Gabriel kissed the back of her neck, then her shoulder, feeling her shiver in his arms. He loved how responsive she was. Loved how having her here, in his bed, made something raw and painful inside him hurt less.

He felt her hands settle on his arms where they crossed over her breasts, her thumbs stroking, sending small bolts of electricity right through him.

Desire coiled tightly in his gut. Powerful, insatiable.

But he forced it away. There was no hurry, after all.

She was his now.

Gabriel parked his bike in an alleyway Honor wouldn't have gone into in broad daylight let alone eleven o'clock at night. It was dark and wet, with dirty snow collecting in drifts against the Dumpsters in one corner of the alley. She could hear people shouting not far away, the smashing of glass somewhere else, a man laughing drunkenly closer than she would have liked.

She would have been terrified if not for the man standing with his hands out to her, preparing to help her get off the bike. A little difficult when she was wearing a tight-fitting blue silk sheath dress, her favorite blue Manolos on her feet. She'd hoped they'd get to the casino in one of Gabriel's limos but he'd decided the bike was less conspicuous.

Not that he could be inconspicuous if he tried.

He hadn't made any concessions to the fact that the casino was apparently high-class and demanded a certain dress code. All he'd done was put on black jeans and a casual black shirt, his usual leather jacket over the top. Not that they'd turn him away, she suspected. He looked dark, powerful, and very, very dangerous.

Fear tightened in her stomach. Strange that she should be so afraid for him, for what he might do and the toll it would take on him. Because for all his power, for all the aura of danger about him, he was vulnerable in a way no one else knew about.

But she did.

She'd insisted on coming tonight for a number of reasons. She wanted to see the place her father had owned, of course, but mainly she wanted to find proof that Guy was everything Gabriel had told her he was. And if not . . . then she would have to stop Gabriel from doing whatever it was he was going to do.

She didn't want him to have the ruin of an innocent man on his conscience.

Honor put her hands into his, her fingers cold despite the leather gloves she wore and let him help her off the bike, loving the care with which he handled her. For all his strength, he could be gentle and in the past two days, she'd learned quite a lot about his tenderness.

It was strange how the mere fact of telling him she was his had quieted something hungry in him. She'd found freedom in embracing her need for him, too. In no longer resisting the intense craving for him whenever he was around. Sure, this addiction was going to destroy her in the end, but she'd take it while it lasted.

As she steadied herself on her rather ridiculously high heels, Gabriel pulled something from the pocket of his jacket. A long, black box. "This is for you," he murmured, holding it out.

Honor stared at it, taking it in her hands. "What is it?"

"Open it."

Her heart beating strangely fast, she did so, pressing the little catch that opened the box and lifting the lid. The dim light of the alley made it difficult to see, but then a car passed on the street outside, the headlights shining briefly into the darkness, lighting it up. Making the jewels that lay on the box's white silk interior sparkle.

Honor caught her breath.

It was a necklace, almost a collar. Made of multiple strands of platinum formed in the shape of a climbing briar, with thorns and leaves and flowers. And each flower was a deep, blue sapphire. It was the most exquisitely beautiful thing she'd ever seen.

"What . . . ?"

"It's a gift."

She looked up at him. The car had moved on, casting the place into darkness again, but she could still see the gleam of his eyes and the sensual shape of his mouth, the hard line of his jaw. He didn't look away from her.

"You're mine, Honor. And I wanted to give you something to remind you."

A couple of weeks ago she would have found that statement insulting. But now . . . a part of her loved that she was his. Because hell, she wasn't anyone else's, was she? Not her mother's. Not Guy's. Not her father's. They'd all chosen someone else. Something else.

She hadn't cared. She'd had her business and that had been enough for her.

But that had been before she'd met Gabriel. Before she'd realized she wanted more.

*What more?*

Something caught, painfully tight in her chest. No, more didn't bear thinking about. It really didn't.

Instead she picked up the necklace, watched the light glint off the sapphires. "It's . . . beautiful."

"Here," Gabriel took it from her. "Turn around. I'll put it on for you."

Honor did so, sweeping her hair out of the way. His fingers were warm on her nape as he laid the necklace around her neck. It felt heavy and cold but only for a moment, the heat of her skin warming it up.

"I bought it because you like pretty things," he said quietly as he did up the catch. "So, I thought you might like this."

Her breath caught. She stared at the wall of the alley in front of her, running her fingers over the strands around her neck. "I do like it," she said thickly. "I like it very much."

More warmth at the back of her neck, his mouth as he kissed her. "Are you ready?"

Ah, damn. It was time to go. And she didn't want to all of a sudden.

Didn't want to face whatever they'd find at this casino, proof of Guy's guilt or otherwise. Nor did she want this moment with Gabriel to be lost. This moment where he gave her gifts and kissed the back of her neck like he cared.

But it would be lost. Carried away under the relentless demands of the justice he felt he had to deliver.

Yet what would he say if she asked him not to do this? If she asked him to take her home instead? Make love to her until they'd both forgotten this place even existed? He'd say no, of course. And she couldn't take that right now.

Grief caught in the back of her throat but she forced it away as she turned to face him. "Yes," she said levelly. "I am."

Gabriel's dark eyes swept over her. "They'll probably

know who you are. You have the story we agreed on settled?"

They'd discussed this earlier. The casino might realize who she was, no matter how many years had passed since a St. James had passed through their doors. But if she was seen with Gabriel, making it clear she was with him and that she wanted to see her father's old kingdom, then there shouldn't be a problem. After all, Gabriel Woolf was notorious for not being on the right side of the law. No one would question his sudden arrival, especially with a woman on his arm.

"Yes," she said.

"And if I say it's time to go, then you go. Whether I'm with you or not."

That she hadn't been too happy about. But then if things went bad, she wasn't going to be able to help him anyway. The only thing she could do would be to get out and call the number Gabriel had given her. The number that would get her Zac Rutherford.

"Yes," she said again.

"Good. And if that happens, come back to the bike. Zac will find you."

Honor pulled a face. "Come back here? By myself?"

"You'll be safe. This is my territory, remember? People know who owns this bike and if you're on it, they'll know I own you, too. And no one touches my property without permission."

A little flash of annoyance at his arrogance went through her. "I'm not your property."

He smiled, a savage edge to it that perversely thrilled her. "If I was still president of the Angels, you would be. You'd wear the club colors, with 'Property of Church' on the back so everyone would know you were mine."

"Sounds incredibly chauvinistic." So why did she like the thought of it?

"It's the way it is." His gaze dropped to the necklace he'd bought her. "Tonight though, I'll be happy knowing you're wearing something I bought you."

"I should count myself lucky in that case." She took his hands in hers, rose up on her toes, and kissed him. "But you're cute when you're possessive."

A short laugh broke from him and it was a moment before she realized it was completely genuine.

"Damn," she murmured, smiling. "Did I just make you laugh?"

One corner of his usually stern mouth turned up and her heart broke a little inside her chest. "Don't get used to it." He laced his fingers through hers. "Come on, let's go see what we can find out."

They stepped out of the alley and into the street.

There were people around, pretty damn shady looking people. Loud music blared from speakers at a late-night store across the road; a group of men stood around arguing and drinking from bottles in paper bags, flicking cigarette butts into the dirty snow on the sidewalk. Neon and flickering light from the dingy streetlights shone on the wet pavement.

Honor didn't look around too closely. She felt out of place in her designer dress, with a fortune's worth of sapphires around her neck.

She glanced surreptitiously at Gabriel. He'd come from here. These were his streets. This was where he'd lived, an experience so far removed from hers they may as well have been born on different planets.

So she made herself look. Made herself see the dirty streets, smell the rotting trash that the cold couldn't quite keep at bay. Made herself glance into the eyes of the people they passed. There were no smiles here, only wariness and desperation.

She swallowed, her throat thick and tight.

These were also the streets where her father had been. And Alex.

God . . .

Gabriel crossed the street, approaching the late-night store with the group of men standing around outside it. Trepidation knotted in the pit of her stomach, easing only slightly when Gabriel slid an arm around her waist, pulling her in close as they approached the shop entrance.

The glances of the group were openly lascivious when they touched on her, turning threatening as they turned on Gabriel.

Then someone said, "Holy fuck. It's Church."

A ripple of tension went through the men around the door, several of them backing away.

A massively built man near the door straightened and managed to stand so he was blocking the doorway. "Mr. Woolf," he said in a perfectly level voice. "Nice to see you back in the neighborhood."

"Good to see you, too, Jimmy." Gabriel stared at him. "You doing security here?"

The bouncer dropped his gaze, almost deferential. "Yeah. And I'm gonna have to ask you for an invite. I'm sorry, but everyone has to have one. The lady, too. You understand."

"Sure, I do." Gabriel put his hand in his back pocket and took something out of it.

A pair of black dice, and on each, in the place of the one spot, a red jewel glittered. The invite, presumably.

Jimmy nodded once and stood aside. "Welcome, Mr. Woolf. You may go in."

They walked down the back of what looked like an ordinary corner store with magazine racks, fridges full of drinks, and candy by the register. The door behind the counter opened, revealing a dim hallway. Another man was there and he nodded at them both as they passed, holding open yet another door.

Honor stepped through and blinked.

She was in a windowless room, the walls covered in red velvet, the carpet dark. The lighting was dim but evocative, black leather couches along one wall, red glass candle holders on the table, light flickering. A man in a wrinkled tux sat there, smoking a cigarette, his gaze hooded as he watched them.

Ahead of them was a doorway, a red velvet curtain over it. Near the doorway was an exquisitely carved, black Chinese-style table, a beautiful blond woman in a red gown behind it. She smiled as they approached. "Good evening, Mr. Woolf. Miss St. James. Welcome to the Lucky Seven. Your invites please."

Trepidation knotted tighter in Honor's gut. They knew who she was already.

Gabriel handed over the pair of dice, dropping them into the woman's palm. She studied each die carefully before putting them in a black glass bowl on the table. There was a large quantity of dice in there already.

"We're honored to have you," she said, looking at Gabriel meaningfully. "The VIP room is at your disposal, of course. As this is your first visit, would you care for a tour?"

"No," Gabriel answered shortly. "I'm sure we'll find our way around."

The woman's gaze flickered over Honor and she had the sense she was being cataloged. And priced. "I think you'll enjoy yourselves," the woman said softly. "We cater to everyone. Anything you need, only say the word." She smiled, her mouth full and red, her attention back on Gabriel. "And I do mean anything."

As subtle invitations went it wasn't the subtlest.

But Gabriel was already turning away, his arm around Honor like an iron band, taking a step toward the curtained doorway and pulling back the sweep of red velvet.

Honor caught her breath as a massive basement room was revealed.

Chandeliers hung from the ceiling, glittering like complicated icy stalactites, hanging over the gaming tables and the crowds clustered around them. There was an air of opulence about everything, the red velvet on the walls, the black carpet on the ground, black furniture and flickering candlelight. Waiters in black uniforms moved through the crowds, trays of drinks in their hands. All of them were, without exception, women.

The crowd itself was largely male, all in tuxes. Laughing, drinking. Some smoking. There were some other women here and there, glittering in designer gowns and jewels, and all of them beautiful. They hung off the arms of the men, or leaned seductively over them as they played the tables. Only a few were actually playing themselves.

"God," Honor murmured as they walked down the small staircase to the gaming floor, conscious of the stares as they came down. "This place looks like a high-class brothel."

"It is," Gabriel replied, his gaze cold as it swept over the crowds. "Like I said. You can buy anything you want here. Anything at all."

Honor shivered. What the hell had she gotten herself into? What the hell had Guy gotten himself into? Had he wanted to save her father from this? Or had he helped in his downfall?

*"I'm going to use it against him."*

Gabriel's words replayed themselves in her head. Flat and cold and determined.

She'd promised him she wouldn't tell Guy or warn him

in any way, and she hadn't. But that didn't mean she was going to sit back passively and let him ruin her stepfather. Or himself.

She glanced at him as they moved through the crowd, the look on his face hard. A man so sure of his power on the outside and yet inside . . . He hurt.

Well, she wasn't going to let him have the ruin of an innocent man on his conscience. The things he'd done to survive, she wouldn't wish on anyone, especially the burden of responsibility he'd taken on.

She couldn't let him have this, too. She just couldn't.

His arm around her tightened and she knew they were garnering a lot of stares, most of them acquisitive of her.

"Where to first?" she asked under her breath.

"The bar. Give people a chance to look at us."

Down one end of the huge space was a black marble bar, the wall behind it lit up in red, giving the bottles of liquor on the shelves an eerie red glow. Like blood.

There were a few people standing at the bar or sitting on stools, talking and laughing amongst themselves.

Honor began to notice a few other men in the crowd, all massively built, wearing dark suits and sweeping the crowd with a searching gaze. Security, no doubt.

Gabriel stopped at the bar. He didn't ask her what she wanted, ordering two scotches.

"Thanks," she murmured as the barman pushed over two crystal tumblers. "But not sure I'm up for scotch."

He glanced down at her, dark eyes enigmatic. "You liked it in Vermont, as I recall."

A flush swept through her. Oh yes, she had. She'd knocked back his scotch and climbed into his lap. God, this was not the time to be remembering that.

She picked up her tumbler, lightly knocking it against his. "This better be a single malt then. Cheers."

"*Sláinte*." He watched her as he picked up his own glass, sipping the amber liquid in it.

Honor did the same, the alcohol sitting warmly in her stomach, easing the trepidation in the pit of it. "So, were you one of those guys? Like the one standing near that pillar?"

"What, security? No. Not inside. We weren't allowed inside, remember? The club ran interference in the street. Like the men you saw out front earlier."

"So you've never been in here?"

"No." He looked away from her, out over the crowded gaming tables. "But Zac gave me all the information I need."

A man standing beside Gabriel turned toward them, looking very definitely and very suggestively at her. "She's beautiful," he said as if Honor wasn't even there. "How much?"

"She's not for sale," Gabriel replied before she had a chance to speak, not even bothering to look at the man.

"Aww, come on," the man said, grinning. "Everything's for sale down here. Name your price."

Honor gave him a cool look. " 'She' is also standing right in front of you."

The man laughed. "Honey, I've won big tonight. Give me a blow job and fifty grand is yours."

Gabriel shifted unhurriedly, turning toward the guy. "Didn't you hear the lady? I suggest you fuck off before I take more appropriate steps."

Anger flooded over the man's face. "Hey, buddy, I don't know who you think you are but—"

"I'm Gabriel Woolf and you're getting in my fucking space."

Beneath the cold darkness of his voice, Honor could hear something else running through it. A thread of heat. Of anger.

Unthinking, she put a hand on his arm, not to stop him but just to let him know she was there. That she was okay. Instantly she felt the muscles beneath her hand flex and then, just as suddenly, release.

Whatever the man saw in Gabriel's face was enough to have him back off, muttering.

"It's okay," she murmured. "I can deal with idiots like that. I've dealt with them often enough at work."

"Not while you're with me you don't," he said curtly. "Come on, I think it's time we hit the tables."

He went for the roulette table first, ostensibly looking at the wheel, all the while keeping an eye out over the crowd. There were a few people he recognized, rich businessmen who moved in certain circles, the kind of businessmen who used to look down on him when he'd first gotten into the construction game.

Now they avoided his gaze as if ashamed. As well they might, being here. On another night he might have found that satisfying but not now. There was something of far more importance happening tonight.

Honor stood beside him, the sapphire collar he'd bought for her glittering in the subtle lighting of the casino. She looked fragile, beautiful. A figure made out of porcelain.

Yet he knew she wasn't as fragile as she looked. That there was strength underneath that polished, sophisticated veneer. And passion. And heat.

As the roulette wheel turned and the ball flew around the inside of it, he was suddenly achingly conscious of her beside him. The warmth of her body in her tight, blue dress. The scent of her cutting through the cigar smoke that hung in the air. The sight of her pale throat circled with the jewels he'd given her.

She turned her head, caught him watching her, her lovely mouth curling up in a smile.

He knew the sense of satisfaction that gripped him whenever he looked at her was wrong. But shit, she was his. And he liked knowing that. Liked knowing she knew it, too.

*Fuck, would you get your head back in the game? This isn't the time to be getting distracted.*

He looked away from her, back down to the wheel that was beginning to slow.

No, he couldn't be distracted. He'd come here for information, for proof, and he was going to get it. Of course there was no way the casino would give him anything for free but that was okay. He was prepared to get the information by any means necessary. First, he had to find out who was managing this operation and then he'd get himself some answers.

He could, if he wanted to, advance his plan to publically take Tremain down now. But there were more undercurrents here than he'd realized. More connections to be made. Honor's father. Tremain. The friendship between them. And this casino in the middle of it.

The wheel stopped spinning, a murmur of approval resounding. He'd bet a large sum on number ten and he'd won. He allowed himself a smile as his winnings were pushed across the table to him, sliding an arm around Honor's waist and pulling her close.

"Seen enough?" he murmured in her ear. He didn't want her here. It was far too dangerous and it would only get ever more so once he went to meet with the big boss.

"Are you trying to get rid of me by any chance?" she murmured back, raising an eyebrow.

"You know I didn't want you to come. This isn't the place for you." He bent his head, gave her a very public kiss, unable to resist the urge.

Color stained her cheekbones, her eyes as blue as the

sapphires around her neck. "I think I have more right to be here than you."

"You wanted to see the place. Now you've seen it."

She smiled at him. A smile that didn't reach her eyes. "What are you planning, Gabriel?"

"Didn't we discuss this?" He released her, leaning over the table to gather his winnings. "This is reconnaissance. Information gathering."

"Yes, but you didn't tell me how we were going to go about getting it."

"The operative word here is 'I,' Honor. 'We' are not going to go about getting anything."

A flash of temper sparkled in her gaze. "And once you've gotten whatever information you've managed to find?"

They hadn't spoken about this over the past two days, ignoring the subject as if it didn't exist, slaking their hunger for each other physically instead. Just as well. He knew she didn't believe his accusations about Tremain or agree with his need for justice, and that was too fucking bad.

He had justice to mete out and he would do it, regardless of what she thought.

*What if there's a cost? What if it costs you her?*

There was always a cost with anything. Always. And if the cost was Honor . . .

His throat closed, an ache in his chest. The cost wouldn't be Honor. He'd have both. He'd make sure of it. "Then I'll cross that bridge when I come to it," he said, not wanting to have this discussion with her now. "I think we'll try our hand at blackjack."

She didn't speak as they moved over to the blackjack table, but as he put a hand on the small of her back, he could feel the tension in her spine. "I think we should visit the VIP area," she said quietly. "See if we can't get an idea who the boss of this place is."

He glanced down at her, watching the expression in her eyes as she gave the surrounding gamers another sweeping glance. She was looking for something, like he was.

A sudden suspicion turned over inside him. She'd told him she wanted to see the place where her father had ruined himself, yet he knew that wasn't the whole reason. There were always deeper reasons, other motivations. Always.

"Why are you really here?"

Her gaze met his and if he hadn't known her, he wouldn't have seen the flicker in her eyes. "I told you, I wanted to see where Daniel—"

"That's not the whole reason."

Her mouth tightened. "Proof," she said flatly. "I'm here for proof. For Dad. I don't want to see you hurting an innocent man."

The suspicion in his gut became something else, something sharper. Like pain. Though why it should hurt that she didn't believe him, he had no idea. "He's not worth your care—"

"It's you I care about." She cut him off, anger flickering in her eyes. "You don't want that on your conscience and I don't want that for you either."

He stared at her, shock creeping through him. *"It's you I care about . . ."* Him, she cared about. Even though he knew she must have felt something since she'd stayed after he'd revealed everything to her, the words still resounded inside him like an echo, making him feel like the biggest prick in the world. Because he didn't deserve her care. Not after all he'd done.

His conscience . . . His conscience was tarnished all to shit. What was one more thing to add to the list? Not that Tremain was innocent.

"Forget about my conscience," he said. "That isn't your concern."

But something in her gaze softened, making the awful tightness in his chest get even worse. "Someone has to think about it. Someone has to care about it. Especially if you're not going to." She put a hand on his chest, smoothing the black cotton, her touch leaving a trail of sparks and a sweet kind of pain he tried not to feel "You've taken on too much as it is, Gabriel Woolf. You don't need anything else adding to your burden."

He didn't want to have this conversation now. Not here. Not when he was getting so close to what he wanted. Perhaps it was time for her to leave. Get out so he could do what he had to do. He wanted her safe and he wanted her away so she wouldn't have to see how badly misplaced her care actually was.

He didn't answer her as they stopped at the blackjack table. Only held her close as he played. He didn't much like gambling—that was Alex's thing, not his—but he'd give her another couple of minutes. And then he'd make his move.

As luck would have it, the guy who'd had the temerity to ask her how much earlier was at the table, too, and the prick *still* didn't realize that looking at Honor was going to get him hurt.

Gabriel won again and as he collected his chips, he whispered into Honor's ear, "You need to leave."

She pulled back in surprise, eyes widening. "What? Now?"

He met her gaze, held it. "You promised me you'd leave when I told you to, no questions asked."

"But—"

"Honor. It's time for you to go."

She didn't flinch, staring at him. "What are you going to do?"

He didn't answer, reaching for her, putting his hand in her hair, tipping her head back then covering her mouth in a hard kiss. He could feel the tension in her, her muscles tight with shock. But he wasn't going to relent. She couldn't be here when this went down.

He pulled back. "Go. Or else I'll pick you up and carry you out myself."

Honor's gaze met his for a long, uncountable moment. Then she looked away. "Don't do anything you'll regret. Please."

A part of him wanted to reassure her that he wouldn't. But he couldn't promise that. He would do what he had to do to get what he wanted. Like he always did.

So he said nothing at all, watching her turn from the table and make her way through the crowd to the stairs. As she disappeared through the curtain at the top of the stairs, he took out his phone and texted Zac. His friend would be there to meet her when she came out of the casino and take her home.

He waited another five minutes until Zac's response told him she was safe.

Then he leaned against the table and turned his gaze on the prick who'd been ogling Honor. The guy stared belligerently back, which was just perfect.

"What the fuck are you looking at?" Gabriel demanded in a low, dangerous voice.

The guy lifted a shoulder and turned away, only now sensing that perhaps provoking him wasn't the best idea. Too late.

Gabriel pushed himself away from the table and skirted around it, putting a hand on the man's shoulder and pulling him around. "I asked you a question, buddy."

The man, to his credit, didn't flinch. "What's your problem?"

"You looking at my woman is a problem. You asking her how much is a fucking problem."

"I never meant—"

Gabriel didn't hesitate. He pulled back his fist and punched the guy in the face. A gasp of shock went up around the table, people exclaiming and standing back. The man he'd punched dropped like a sack of potatoes.

Then he waited. Sure enough, a minute later, a voice said, "If you'd like to come with me, Mr. Woolf?"

Gabriel turned to the security guard standing at his back. They wouldn't touch him, of course. Nobody would touch him, not here. "About fucking time," he said.

# CHAPTER EIGHTEEN

Honor stepped out into the dirty streets once again, anger simmering just under her skin. Dear God, she was an idiot. She'd gone in there with nothing, no plan, no way of being able to combat him if he decided he wanted her gone. Well, sure enough he had and where the hell did that leave her?

He was going to do something, she was sure of it. Something bad. But she had no doubt he would have done exactly as he'd promised—picked her up and carried her out—if she'd protested.

Either way she wouldn't be able to stop him.

The men on the pavement outside didn't even look at her. They'd seen her come in with Gabriel which meant she was his, and obviously they didn't want to get on his bad side by giving her grief. She should have found that reassuring but for some reason, now, it only made her angrier.

What the hell was she supposed to do?

"Miss St. James?" A deep, English voice came from her right.

She turned.

A man stood on the pavement, swathed in a black overcoat. A tall, massively built man, possibly even bigger than Gabriel. Coal-black hair and the most startlingly amber eyes she'd ever seen. Like Gabriel, an aura of menace surrounded him even though he was smiling, and there was something watchful in those golden eyes of his, something that made her shiver.

"Who are you?" she demanded, resenting like hell the interference from yet another powerful-looking man. "How do you know my name?"

"I'm Zac Rutherford," the man said, still smiling. "I'm a colleague of Gabriel's." He held out a long-fingered hand covered in a black leather glove. "Pleased to meet you."

Honor glanced down at the proffered hand but didn't take it. "A colleague? One of his billionaire friends?"

Apparently unperturbed by her refusal to shake hands, he put his hand back in the pocket of his coat. "Yes, indeed. As is Eva King—I think you know her? Anyway, Gabriel wanted me to see you got home safely so here I am. I have a car just around the corner."

So Gabriel hadn't wanted her to wait outside. He'd organized for her to be delivered home. Like a package.

"Do you know what he's doing?" she demanded. "Do you know what he's planning?"

If he was surprised by her question, Zac gave no sign. "Information, that's what he wants."

She searched the other man's handsome features, looking for any signs that he might have some inkling as to what Gabriel was doing. There were none. His face was absolutely impassive. "That doesn't answer my question."

"No, I realize that." He gave her a slight smile. "But not all questions need to be answered. Will you come with me? Those pretty shoes of yours are going to get wet if we stay out here much longer."

God, like she cared about her stupid shoes. "No," she said. "I'm not going anywhere."

Zac stepped forward, the smile fading from his face. "Miss St. James," he began.

"Let me deal with this," a lighter voice said. Out of the shadows next to Zac, another, much smaller figure materialized. A woman in black. Black skinny jeans and heavy boots, a black leather jacket, a black woolen beanie covering her hair. She had small, delicate features and wary gray eyes, heavily outlined in black eyeliner.

She seemed quite young yet the look in her eyes was that of a much, much older woman.

"I'm Eva King, Honor," she said. "It's good to meet you at last." Eva didn't hold out her hand, both of them remaining firmly in the pockets of her jacket.

So this was the woman she'd approached initially with her investment queries. And these two were the ones who'd uncovered Guy's supposed money-laundering business.

"You know," Honor said bluntly. "About my stepfather."

"Yes," Eva said. "We do."

"And you know Gabriel is trying to—"

"Take him down? Yes." Eva gave her a flat, rather unnerving stare. "You want to stop him?"

Honor paused, unsure of what to say next. Did they know about Gabriel's rape accusations? She didn't want to tell them herself since that wasn't her secret to give. "Guy Tremain is my stepfather," she said after a moment. "I don't want him hurt. And I don't want . . . I don't want that on Gabriel's conscience either."

Something moved in Zac's amber gaze. "You're worried about Gabriel?"

"Of course I'm worried about Gabriel. He's . . ." She stopped, the weird grief catching in her throat. Because what was he to her? Not a boyfriend, that's for sure. A lover certainly.

*He's more than that . . .*

Yes, he was. But she couldn't think about that now.

"A friend," she finished. Because that's what she'd promised him. "I don't want him to do anything he'll regret later."

Eva tilted her head, a frown creasing her pale forehead. "You've invested a great deal of money in your stepfather's hotel chain. And it looks like he's running his company into the ground on purpose. You're going to lose everything. Aren't you . . . I dunno, pissed about it? Don't you think he should pay?"

The cold had deepened, her breath puffing in a cloud of frosty air as she exhaled. Honor pulled her coat more firmly around her. "Yes. If it's true."

"It's true all right. Gabriel must have shown you the financials."

"He has but . . ." There was one other thing she didn't know. And it didn't look like these two knew either.

Gabriel had told no one but her.

"Might I suggest we go back to the car?" Zac interrupted smoothly. "It's a little chilly to be discussing this here."

Honor shifted on her feet, glancing back at the entrance to the casino. The group clustered around the front of it were still shifting around, talking and smoking. Beer cans littering the ground.

"Fuck," Eva muttered. "You *do* care about him." The other woman said it like it came as a shock.

No, it was more than care. Far more.

Honor turned her back on the casino. "I'll come back to the car. But we're not leaving here until he comes out of that place. Understand?"

Gabriel followed the security guard off the gambling floor and out into a small, dimly lit narrow corridor. At one end was a door. The guard knocked once and it opened, leading out into an opulent office. More red velvet on the walls, more dark carpet, an expensive Persian rug on the floor, an antique desk that must have cost hundreds of thousands. A man sat behind the desk. A man Gabriel didn't recognize.

"Mr. Woolf, sir," the security guard said.

"Wait outside," Gabriel ordered before the man behind the desk could speak. May as well show his hand now so everyone in this room knew exactly where they stood.

The guard turned his head sharply to the guy seated behind the desk, who scowled. "Who the hell do you think you—"

"I have a full chapter of the Angels club sitting in the streets outside this casino," Gabriel interrupted him coldly. "Waiting for a signal from me to come in here and start causing trouble. All you have to do is give me reason and I'll call down hell." He gave the man a smile that had nothing to do with amusement. "I'm sure your boss won't be too happy with that."

The man's gaze flickered. "*I* am the boss, you insolent bastard."

"No, you're not. I know a fucking flunky when I see one." He turned to the guard who was still standing there, his hand already reaching for his weapon. "Relax. I'm not going to kill anyone. I just want some information. So how about you wait outside." He paused. "Unless you want to be responsible for the destruction of this casino?"

The guard hesitated for only a minute before he turned and left the room.

The man behind the desk had risen to his feet. He was outwardly impassive but Gabriel had learned to spot fear years ago and he could see it in this guy's face. Excellent. Time to use it.

Slowly, he stalked over to the desk, put his hands on the edge, and leaned forward. "I own this neighborhood, motherfucker. It's mine. And this fucking place has been a thorn in my side for years. I can have it destroyed very easily. Would you like me to do that?"

The man had gone pale. "You can't do shit," he said, still obviously trying for bluster.

"You do know who I am, don't you?"

"You'll be no one soon. I can get security to—"

"You're assuming I'm alone. I'm not. Neither am I bluffing. Also, I don't think your superiors will be happy if a well-known construction magnate ends up dead in an underground fucking casino notorious for drugs and prostitution."

The man paled even further. "I've got nothing to tell you."

"But you don't know what I want yet." He leaned forward. "Tell me everything you know about Guy Tremain."

There was incomprehension on the man's face. "Who?"

Gabriel pushed himself away from the desk and stalked around the outside of it. "What about Daniel St. James?"

The man began backing away. "I don't know who you're talking about."

The guy was obviously even less than a flunky if he ran at the first sign of trouble. What the fuck were the bosses thinking of to employ an idiot like this?

Gabriel reached forward and grabbed the man's collar, hauling him close. "Why is Guy Tremain laundering money for this casino? Who's paying him? Who's paying you?"

The man finally found his balls from somewhere, taking a swing at him, while struggling out of Gabriel's hold. The blow was wild and Gabriel ducked it easily enough, but the man managed to slip from his grip, escaping around the desk and out through the door.

Fuck. He only had moments before security would be on him. Not that he cared since they couldn't touch him.

Not with the Angels waiting. The club's current president was more than happy to come and help out a fellow club member. Especially him.

Gabriel pulled out a couple of drawers of the desk, riffling through the papers and files, not that he expected to find anything. Most of the really incriminating stuff wouldn't be held here. And sure enough, it wasn't.

Double fuck.

The door burst open, the casino security pouring through it, weapons at the ready.

Gabriel straightened and folded his arms. They were no threat. He was too big a deal for them to rough up, especially in this neighborhood. No doubt they wanted to do more than rough him up, but they wouldn't get that either.

The flunky had come back, stepping into the office. "You need to leave."

Fuck that. He hadn't gotten what he was looking for yet.

*"Don't do anything you'd regret . . ."*

From out of nowhere Honor's voice suddenly resounded in his head. Irritated, he tried to ignore it. Because he wouldn't regret dealing out a bit of violence to this shithead, that was for sure. He was part of the machine that had done something to Alex, that had been the cause of more grief in this neighborhood than even the drugs had.

He'd tried to get rid of the casino when he'd been the Angels' president. But he had realized it was impossible. The casino's money was embedded too deeply into the lives of the people here and its withdrawal would have destroyed the neighborhood's economy.

So he'd left it alone. Yeah, leaving it was already a decision he was regretting. It would be better all around if he called down the Angels and destroyed the place.

*A warm hand on his chest, smoothing. "I care about you."*

He shouldn't listen to that voice. He shouldn't feel that warmth seeping through him. He shouldn't want it . . .

*Her arms around him. Not saying anything this time, just holding him. No one had ever held him like that . . .*

Gabriel shoved himself away from the desk, moving before he'd even fully processed it. The guns followed him but he ignored them as he paused by the door, staring at the flunky. "Tell your bosses I want this place shut down. By next week." Hopefully that would leave them exposed and with any luck he could take them down, too.

"But you can't—"

He met the man's gaze, let him see the darkness. "You have no idea what I can and can't do. Are you really willing to find out?"

The man said nothing, his gaze dropping. But Gabriel knew his message had been received, loud and clear.

He went out into the corridor to find a side door being held open by one of the security staff. Clearly they wanted him gone as quickly as possible.

The door led to an alleyway outside and he stepped into the dimly lit street. Neon reflected off the wet pavement, the thump of music in the distance. Behind him the door slammed shut.

A low, black car waited by the curb.

Gabriel paused, all his senses going on high alert.

The car door opened and a man got out. "Fitz?" the man said, his accent upper-class and familiar. "Is that you?"

Tremain.

Gabriel stilled as Tremain came around the car, coming closer to where he stood. The streetlight behind him would hide his features, at least that far away. But who the fuck was Fitz?

"Why won't you answer my messages?" Guy was saying as he came closer. "I've been trying to get in touch—" He stopped dead. "Woolf."

A rush of adrenaline flooded through Gabriel's veins like a drug. Here he was, at last.

His rapist father.

He hadn't meant to confront him now. Not yet. But what the hell? Fate moved in mysterious ways sometimes.

"Tremain. Fancy seeing you here." He walked slowly forward to where the other man stood, staring into the guy's blue eyes, searching his face. He'd done that over the past few weeks, searching for some likeness in the press pictures he'd seen. He had Tremain's blond hair, that was a start. Though he was taller. But then again, children were always taller than their parents, weren't they?

The other man blinked. "What are you doing here?"

"I came to play a bit of roulette. What about you? Poker? Blackjack maybe?"

Tremain's jaw tightened. "I don't know what you're talking about."

"Bullshit you don't." Gabriel met the other man's gaze. "You know exactly what I'm talking about. The casino in this building right next to me. The one you've been laundering money for. The one your friend St. James owned, running up debts so big he took his own life. That you then paid off to hide from the authorities. And married his widow to make sure it stayed secret."

Tremain said nothing, standing quite still. There was no expression at all on his bland, handsome face. But there was fear in his eyes. Oh yes, there was fear.

"Tell me," Gabriel continued on, conversationally. "Did you decide to destroy your own company or was it on orders from someone else? And don't try to deny it this time." He paused, to give the guy a chance to sweat. "I have proof."

"You can't have proof," Tremain said, his voice hoarse. "There's no record—"

"Oh, there are plenty of records if you know where to find them. And luckily enough I do. Though not so lucky for you. Not so very fucking lucky at all."

A silence fell, heavy and thick with tension.

"I always knew you were scum," Tremain said, low and harsh. "I warned Honor. I told her she shouldn't have anything to do with you."

"Bit late for that now. Since she's been sleeping with me."

Something flashed over the other man's face and savage satisfaction turned over inside Gabriel's gut. Fuck, yes. Let him find that painful. Let him hurt.

"You bastard. If you do anything to her, I'll—"

"You'll what? Seems a bit rich to call me names when you're the one making it big in white-collar crime."

The other man shoved his hands into the pockets of the outrageously expensive designer overcoat he wore. "What do you want?"

Excellent. No protests, no denials. At least the man knew when he was beaten.

"Ah, but that's the problem," Gabriel said casually. "I don't want anything. Or no, that's not exactly true. What I want is to see you go down. Preferably blazing, but shit, I'll take anything."

"What do you mean?"

"What I mean is that I have enough proof to see you in jail for years to come."

Tremain's blue eyes didn't flinch from his. "I have friends, Woolf. Powerful friends. There's no jury on earth that would convict me."

"Maybe not. But I think your friends aren't quite as powerful as the media can be. A couple of leaked files is all it'll take. And not just here in the States. I can have them on servers all over the fucking world."

A muscle ticked in the other man's jaw. "I have money. You don't have to—"

"I don't want your money." Slowly, Gabriel came forward, getting closer. Until he could look into Tremain's eyes. His father's eyes. "Like I said. All I want is to see you go down, you raping prick." He smiled. "Or should I say, Dad?"

It was the car she recognized first. Guy's BMW. And then the two figures standing in the alleyway. Both blond. Both tall.

Zac's car, a featureless, black, four-wheel drive was parked opposite, and gave Honor a clear view of the alley itself. And whatever was about to go down in it.

"God," she whispered, reaching for the door handle.

"Hey, where are you going?" Eva called.

But Honor ignored her, slipping from the car and dashing across the street. She couldn't allow whatever was going to happen, not when the lives of two men she cared about were at stake.

As she approached, she saw Gabriel take a sudden step back into the glow of the streetlight, the light striking gold from his hair. But the expression on his face was one of fury.

"No," she heard him say. "That's a fucking lie!"

Guy was standing with his back to her. "I'm not lying," he said forcefully. "You can take a paternity test if you want. Here," he stuck out his hand. "Take some blood. Some skin. Some hair. Whatever you like. Get it tested. The rest of what I did, yes, it's true, but I'm not your father. I never hurt your mother."

She could see the shock on Gabriel's face. See the pain and the incandescent rage.

"Gabriel, stop!" she yelled as he took his hands out of his pockets, his fingers curled into fists.

Instantly, both men froze. Then Guy whirled around, meeting Honor's gaze, his eyes widening in shock. "Honor. What the hell are you doing here?"

Her heart was racing, the words he'd just said echoing in her ears.

*"I'm not your father . . ."*

She took a breath. "I'm here with him."

Guy flashed Gabriel look. "You brought her here? To the casino?" There was rage in his voice. "How could you—"

"I asked to come." Honor cut him off. "I know, Guy. I know everything. You paying Daniel's debts. You purposefully destroying Tremain Hotels. You laundering money . . ."

"Get back in the car, Honor," Gabriel said in the coldest voice she'd ever heard him use.

"No."

"I said, get back in the fucking car!"

She met his dark gaze, saw the fury in his eyes. Rage pushing past his usual icy detachment. And she didn't know what was more frightening, the man of ice or this one, the volcanic rage she'd seen once in his parking garage surging to life.

But he'd never hurt her before. He wouldn't now.

"I said no. I said I wasn't leaving you. I promised."

"Honor," Guy said, taking a few steps toward her. "You need to listen to him. You have to go."

Behind him Gabriel moved, so fast Honor had no time to shout out a warning. His hand gripped Guy's shoulder and he spun the other man around, his fist gripping a handful of cotton and pulling tight.

"Who the fuck is it?" Gabriel demanded. "Who the fuck hurt my mother, prick? And why the hell did you write her that check?"

"It was supposed to be for an abortion," Guy said, panting. He didn't struggle, hanging in Gabriel's grip. "And to shut her up. I had to take the fall if anyone asked. And I had to write the check. No one could know."

"Gabriel," Honor said softly, coming closer. "Let him go, please."

He ignored her. "Yeah, well, she was Catholic, you bastard. She didn't get an abortion. She had me instead."

"God," Guy whispered. "You have no idea what you're doing."

Gabriel tightened his grip, the cotton pulling taut around Guy's throat. "Tell me, motherfucker," he hissed. "Tell me who he is."

He was going to hurt Guy. Honor knew it as surely as she knew her own name. Gabriel was going to do him damage and she was the only person who could stop him.

Guy deserved a good many things, but being harmed by this man wasn't one of them. And neither did Gabriel deserve another mark on his soul. Because he'd regret it later. He'd take the responsibility for it as he did with everything else and the more he took, the more he was crushed by the weight. Until the good man she suspected was underneath all that ice, all that blackness, would be crushed utterly.

She could not let that happen.

"Gabriel," she murmured, coming around the two men, standing at his elbow. "Stop." She put a hand on his back, felt the tension like a live wire electrocuting him. His whole body was tight. Every muscle taut. "Please."

His face was twisted with rage and contempt. He was breathing fast, hard.

His whole life had just been shattered by Guy's revelation and God, she knew what that felt like.

She spread her fingers out on his back, pressing hard, letting him know she was there for him.

For a second no one moved or said anything.

Then abruptly Gabriel let go, shoving Guy away from him, and Honor let out a breath she didn't even realize she'd been holding.

Guy stumbled back a few steps, his hand going to his throat, breathing hoarse. "I could have you up on assault charges!"

"No, you won't," Gabriel spat. "You're going to tell me who my father is, otherwise everything you've done will be all over the media by tomorrow, I don't care who you are."

The older man heaved in a breath, looking at Honor. "I'm sorry," he said. "I never meant to involve you in any of this."

"That didn't stop you from taking her fucking money." Gabriel's voice vibrated with barely leashed violence.

Honor slid her hand beneath his leather jacket onto the warm cotton of his shirt, keeping the contact steady. His muscles were bunched and tight, a tremor running through him.

She ached for him. For the anguish she could feel radiating from him.

Guy was still looking at her. "I had to get out of this somehow," he went on, "I didn't want to keep laundering that cash. Bankrupting the company was the only way out. Without Tremain Hotels they'll have to find someone else."

Her throat closed. "Why couldn't you have just said no?"

An expression she didn't understand crossed his face. "Oh, dear girl. You don't understand. You can't say no.

No one says no. I thought I could do it. Bankrupt the company, leave the country. Get a new life where they wouldn't find me."

"And Mom?" She couldn't stop herself from asking, even though the truth was going to hurt. "Did they . . . pay you to marry her?"

He didn't look away. "I suppose you know about Daniel?"

"That he used to run this place, yes."

Guy sighed. "You have to understand something. He didn't choose it. He was told."

"What do you mean?"

"I can't explain, not here. But you need to know Daniel wasn't happy with it. And then the casino began losing money. They were . . . furious. Especially when he died and they had all these debts to cover up. They used me. I was given money to pay the debts, then marry his widow when the authorities began looking too closely. But . . . I did love her, Honor. I loved you, too. You have to believe me. I want to take her with me when I go."

A complex knot of emotions gripped her, so tangled she couldn't work out which was which. The hand on Gabriel's back closed into a fist, clutching the cotton of his shirt. "What about my company? My money?"

"It's for us when we find a new life." Her stepfather's shoulders drooped. "I thought . . . I thought you wouldn't mind if it meant your mom was safe."

Anger surged. "She wouldn't be in danger if you hadn't married her in the first place!"

The look on his face was weary. "No, she might have taken her own life instead."

A shudder swept through her, because of course, he was right. If he hadn't come along and picked her up out of the hole of depression she'd fallen into, that might have happened. Then what would have become of her? An eight-year-old by herself. Into the foster system she would have gone . . .

"That doesn't answer the most important question," Gabriel said roughly.

Guy lifted his chin. "I'll tell you. But like I said, not here."

"Yes, you fucker. Right now, right—"

"If anyone finds out, you'll be in danger."

"I don't give a fuck about that."

"No, I know you don't. But do you want to risk her, too?"

Honor stilled. "What do you mean?"

"You were both seen at the casino tonight. Questions will be asked, especially about you, Honor. Considering what happened to your father." He paused, looked at Gabriel. "And as for yours . . . He's connected to this and if you make a move against him, he'll know. And it won't be you he'll come after—not when you're too powerful to hurt. It'll be her."

"The hell he will," Gabriel growled softly. "Over my dead fucking body."

"You might be able to protect her, or you might not. Either way, you pursuing revenge or justice or whatever the hell it is, will mean she will never be safe. Not while he thinks she means something to you."

Her shoes were wet, ruined by the snow, and the adrenaline rush that had brought her out of the car was starting to fade, leaving her shaken and chilled to the bone. Whoever Gabriel's father was, he would use her to get to him . . .

She didn't want to look at him. Didn't want to see what kind of expression was on his face. Her hand was still on his back, fingers clutching his shirt, and now the tension was vibrating through her, too.

*"Not while he thinks she means something to you . . ."*

What did she mean to him? A lover he liked to screw? Another responsibility he had to protect? A friend?

It shouldn't matter. She cared about him, but she'd never expected anything from him in return. She didn't want anything . . .

*Liar. Of course you want something. You want everything.*

"I have to know his name," Gabriel said, hard and cold. "Whether I do something about it or not."

Honor shivered, an icy sense of disappointment creeping through her no matter how desperately she told herself she didn't feel it. He wanted the name. He wanted to know more . . .

*More than he cares about you.*

Guy glanced again at Honor, a single look loaded with things she didn't understand. "I'm sorry, Honor," he said softly. "For everything." Then he looked back at Gabriel. "Tomorrow. I'll let you know where to meet." He didn't wait for a response, turning and walking back to his car, and starting the engine and pulling away.

Gabriel took a step away from her, too, his shirt slipping from her grip. And she felt the separation like a blow. Like he was removing himself from her.

She swallowed against the instinctive pain that tightened the back of her throat. "I'm sorry," she forced out. "I know how—"

"Where's Zac and Eva?" He turned to her all of a sudden, the darkness in his eyes blazing. "You weren't supposed to be here. You were supposed to be back home."

Anger. Of course anger. What else did he have to turn on her after this? Well, she wasn't going to take it. She never had.

Honor lifted her chin. "I didn't want to be delivered home like a package, Gabriel. I wanted to make sure you were okay."

"Go get in the fucking car. You don't want to be around me right now."

The aura of danger, of leashed violence around him had grown, thick and almost tangible. But she could see past that. She could see what was beneath it. Pain.

Ignoring the menace in his voice, she walked straight up to him and lifted her hands, taking his face between them. "I'm not going anywhere. I told you, I'm here for you and I'm not leaving."

He moved. Too fast to avoid or escape. One moment she was standing on the pavement, the next she was hard up against the brick wall behind her, his body pinning her there, his eyes burning into hers. "You shouldn't have stayed. You should have left while you had the chance."

Honor's heartbeat accelerated, but she wasn't afraid. Not of him. She only felt an aching kind of sadness, the pressure of the vast, heavy emotion pressing down on her. She touched his face, let her fingers trace the outline of his mouth. Finding the softness there. The warmth. The man he was beneath the cold and the danger. A man in pain. Whose life had been hard in the extreme and who was still carrying the cost of it on his soul.

"I'm not leaving, I told you. And I know what it's like when what you thought was the truth isn't. It's hard, Gabriel. Believe me, I know."

He stared at her and she could feel the shake of his body against hers. Then he knocked her hand away and kissed her, a hard, desperate kiss that had her body waking into life, hungry for him in a way she'd never felt before. She pushed her fingers into his hair, fisting the short golden strands. Kissing him back, harder, even more desperate.

But he pulled away, a savage look in his eyes, a roaring darkness that hinted at all the passions that ran deep inside him. The passions he kept so carefully hidden.

"This is a lie," he said, his voice hoarse. "You and I? It's a lie. I targeted you. I seduced you. Deliberately. Because of your connection to Tremain."

She didn't understand at first. "What? What do you mean you seduced me?"

"I wanted to take him down. And I needed information about him. Information I could get from you."

Cold began to burrow its way under her skin. Heading straight for her heart. "I don't . . . understand."

The lines of his face were so hard. Like they were carved out of diamonds. The only thing that had any life, any heat were his eyes. Burning. Glittering.

"Getting close to you was easy. Every woman likes a bad boy, don't they? Especially rich, pampered little girls like you."

The cold reached her heart, freezing tendrils wrapping around it. Slowing her breathing. Chilling her blood. "I . . . You didn't want me?"

He looked so cold. As cold as she felt. As cold as the snow at her feet.

"No," he said flatly. "I never did."

It hurt to kill the blue spark in her eyes. To make them darken. To see her face go pale. All her precious, vital warmth fade.

It was a lie but it was a necessary one. Because how else could he make her leave? She'd promised she'd stay with him and she couldn't. Not if he wanted to take down whoever his father turned out to be.

Fuck, he'd been certain of Tremain's guilt. But when the man had denied his involvement, he'd been forced to believe him. He knew a lie when he saw one and Tremain wasn't lying.

He'd been chasing the wrong guy for weeks.

The shock was still echoing through him, the ground he'd been so sure of now broken beneath his feet. And all he could think of was how he'd thought that this was the end, that once he'd confronted Tremain he could finally get some peace, put down the intolerable burden of his anger.

But it wasn't the end. There would be no end until he had the name of his father. Until he had what he craved. Justice.

Yet he couldn't have that and keep Honor safe. He couldn't have both after all. And if she wouldn't leave him, then he'd have to make her. Push her away and ensure she never came back.

The sapphires around her neck glittered in the cold light from the streetlight. "You never wanted me?" she demanded. "Never?"

He steeled himself. "No. Never. You were always a means to an end."

It hurt to say it. Hurt more than he'd ever thought possible. And he didn't really understand why. He'd ended things with lovers before and it hadn't felt this painful.

*She's more than a mere lover and you know it.*

No, he didn't know. He didn't know anything anymore. The only thing he was sure about was that she had to leave and if he had to hurt her to get her to do so, then he would.

Jesus, he'd hurt so many people in his life, she'd be just one more.

And sure enough, pain flared in her eyes, bright and sharp. And he felt it slide into his heart like a piece of glass, cutting him. "I don't believe you."

He didn't want to move, wanted to keep the warmth of her close, and pushing her away felt like the hardest thing he'd ever done. But he made himself do it. "Believe it."

She stood still, leaning back against the wall, her eyes wide with shock. Small and pale and fragile as porcelain. And the sharp, unfamiliar pain wound around his heart like barbed wire.

Then something glowed in her face, something brighter than hurt. Anger. "You fucking liar, Gabriel Woolf," she said in a clear, calm voice.

Before he could move, she launched herself at him, her arms around his neck, pulling his mouth down on hers. Hot and hungry, aggressive in a way she'd never been aggressive before. Demanding a response. A response his body gave her before he'd had a chance to stop it.

He shoved her back against the brick, kissing her back with all the demand she'd shown him. Because the pain wouldn't stop and he was so sick of hurting. Of feeling cold. Of being angry. He wanted heat. Passion. The softness of her, the gentleness of her. The beauty of her. The loyalty and friendship of her.

Wanted just one second when he could be free of the burden of his whole miserable fucking existence. Where she was the only thing that mattered.

He lost himself in her taste. The heat of her mouth beneath his, the softness of her body against him. The only beauty in a life where beauty had been painfully absent.

"You do want me," she murmured against his mouth. "You damn liar."

Of course, she was right. He was a liar. Another sin to add to the rest, staining him black down to his bones.

He didn't speak, crushing her mouth under his, pressing against her heat, feeling her arms around his neck, holding him as tightly as he was holding her. Teeth against his lip, a sharp bite that had him growling in the back of his throat. A punishment. Well, fuck yes, he deserved her punishment.

Her hand moved between their shaking bodies, down

to where he was hard and aching, tracing the outline of his cock. She tore her mouth away from his and murmured in his ear, "You want me, little boy?" Squeezing him. Sending jolts of electricity right through him. "You want me to fuck you up against this wall? Right here? Right now?"

"Yes." He couldn't stop the shudder that went through him as she stroked his raging hard-on, her fingers tantalizing.

"Beg me, Gabriel." Her voice held an edge he'd never heard before. "Tell me how much you want me to fuck you and I just might."

*You fucking idiot. You've let her get to you.*

But Gabriel shoved the voice from his head. He wanted this moment and he was going to have it. Because after tonight it would never happen again.

"Please," he said hoarsely. "Please, Honor."

"Tell me you lied. Tell me you want me."

He lifted his head, stared into her eyes so she'd see the truth. "I want you. From the moment you got into my limo, I wanted you. And I told myself it was because of Tremain but it wasn't. You were beautiful, sexy, and challenging. And all I could think about was what it would feel like to be inside you."

There was blue fire in her eyes, burning bright. "Then get out your condom. Now."

He reached into his back pocket, pulled out his wallet. There was a condom in there and it he took it out. But she was the one who ripped it open, who unzipped his fly and freed him from his boxers. She was the one who protected him.

She didn't seem to care they were in an alleyway, that the public street was right there. But he did. He moved them deeper into the shadows then closed the space between them. For all her hard demand, she was trembling and when he ran a hand up her thigh, under her dress, and slipped it between her legs, he felt her wetness. Her heat. He stroked her, looking down into her eyes. They were black in the shadows. Full of secrets.

He wanted to know what those secrets were. Wanted to spend weeks, months, years finding out. But he would never get the chance.

"I always wanted you," she whispered, her voice ragged as he eased a finger into her, testing her, her flesh slick and hot. "Even though you irritated me. Even though you were so damn arrogant I wanted to spit. But I loved your strength. I loved that you didn't care what people thought of you. And . . ." She stopped. "I loved your honesty."

"Don't." He leaned forward, kissing her mouth. "There's nothing honest about me. You were right. I'm a liar."

She gasped as he circled his thumb over her clit. "No . . . you've only ever told me one lie. That you didn't want me."

She didn't know. She didn't truly understand. All he was, all he'd ever done, was lie. To his mother when he'd promised he wouldn't come after his father. To his friends that he wouldn't hurt Honor. To himself that this was all for his mother. For justice.

Because it wasn't.

It was for himself. For the shitty life he'd led. The responsibility his mother had dumped on him when she'd told him he was the child of rape. The responsibility for fixing what had been done to her, because that's what he did. He fixed things.

Because he was so fucking angry at all the world and didn't know how else to get rid of it all.

He lifted her leg around his waist, pulled aside her panties, and pinned her to the wall. Then he thrust deep into the molten heat of her. She gasped, her eyes going wide, never taking her gaze from his. "Yes . . . oh, God . . . yes."

He framed his hands around her face. Her precise features flushed with heat and passion. He was shaking and he couldn't seem to stop.

"Gabriel . . ." She arched against him, rocking her hips, wanting him to move.

But he didn't want to. If he moved, this would end and he didn't want it to end. Because he'd never find this again. She knew everything there was to know about him and despite the fact that he was tainted, that he was full of violence and rage, she still put her arms around him. Held him close. Made him feel like he was worth something.

He closed his eyes. Bent his head and turned his face into Honor's throat. Inhaling sweetness and musk. Letting the warmth of her chase away everything he was. Then he moved because it was physically impossible not to.

She was so hot, her body giving and soft and yet so tight around him, pleasure unfurling inside him, bright and so fucking sharp it hurt.

He moved and kept on moving, deaf and blind to anything but the woman in his arms. Yes, it was painful but this was the kind of pain that he wanted, that he craved. So sweet. Purer than the cold anger, the detachment.

*Better than the justice . . .*

But he couldn't think of that now. He couldn't think of anything as the world began to narrow to an exquisite aching point of tension.

"Honor," he whispered, thrusting deep one last time, feeling her shudder and gasp, her body convulsing around him as the climax roared through him, too.

Afterward he had to stand still for a long time, his

heartbeat struggling to normalize. Once it had, he couldn't bear to move. Only wanted to stay there, holding her trembling body against him.

But this was a cold, dark alley and there were people around, and if he didn't let her go now, he never would.

Gabriel lifted his head, looked down into her face. There was a tear in the corner of one eye, sparkling like the jewels around her neck.

His heartbeat faltered.

"You know I love you, don't you?" she said.

His heart stopped.

Everything stopped.

He shoved himself away from her, breathing fast. Something inside him shifted, a need he'd been trying to ignore for a long time, that had been growing larger and larger, a constant, desperate ache. It made him feel like he couldn't get enough air and he couldn't understand why.

"No," he said flatly. "No. You can't."

Pain darkened her eyes. "But I do. I think I've been in love with you for a while now."

"Stop fucking saying that." He turned away from her, his hands shaking as he got rid of the condom and did his jeans up. His chest was so tight and he couldn't breathe.

"Why?" Her voice was quiet. "What's wrong with it?"

"Everything's wrong with it!" Anger pulsed hot in his veins and he embraced it because it was familiar. Simple. Far simpler than the ache that leaned against his heart, that squeezed it until he felt he might break apart. "I told you what I am. All the things I've done. Didn't you hear a single fucking word?"

"I heard." The tear began to slide down her pale cheek, glittering. "And I don't care what you've done. What you think you are. I know who you are already."

The thing inside him squeezed so tight he wanted to

claw it right out of his chest. "Don't," he said harshly. "Don't say—"

"You're a good man, Gabriel Woolf. Yes, you're hard, but you're also strong and protective. Complicated. Fascinating."

His heartbeat thundered inside his head and he took a helpless step toward her, wanting her to shut up. To stop her saying the things he knew weren't true. "Be quiet."

She ignored him. "But I don't want to watch you destroy yourself. I don't want to see anger eat you up inside the way it's doing right now."

He bared his teeth in a savage kind of smile. "Did you ever think that maybe I want to destroy myself? That I might like being angry? I mean, Christ, what the fuck else do I have?"

Her gaze met his. "You have me."

Something shattered inside him. Something he didn't think he'd ever be able to rebuild. But he ignored the feeling. He *had* to ignore it. "Sorry, sweetheart." He made himself say the words. "You're not enough."

Her mouth tightened, more pain glittering in her eyes. Yet still she didn't look away. "Whether you believe it or not, there's an amazing man inside you. But if you keep going down the path you've chosen, he's not going to exist for too much longer."

"I was never that man, Honor. He never fucking existed."

The tear had left a long, silvery trail down her cheek. But her jaw was firm. Even now, when he was being a prick to her, she had so much strength. "Nothing I say is going to make any difference, is it?"

He met her gaze. Held it. "No."

"And if I asked you to stop. If I asked you to let this go. For me. Would you?"

He didn't say anything. There was nothing to say. They both knew the answer already.

Honor looked abruptly away, the jewels on the necklace he'd given her sparkling as she swallowed. Her lashes fluttered then she stepped away from the wall, smoothing down her dress, wiping away the tear. As if it had never been. "Well, at least I know where I stand then."

Anger coursed through him, heavy and hot and he let it burn. Because that was easier, simpler than the pain he knew was waiting for him once she had gone. "I never promised you anything different," he said harshly. "I never wanted it."

The look she gave him was so full of sadness, so full of grief, he had to look away from her, unable to stand it.

"I know you didn't want it," she said quietly. "But God help me, you needed it and I wanted to give it to you."

A pause. The silence choking.

"Good-bye, Gabriel. I hope you find the peace you're looking for. Wherever that is."

Peace? He didn't want fucking peace. That had never been in his future.

Justice. That's what he wanted. That's *all* he wanted.

He made himself watch as Honor walked away.

And tried to tell himself he hadn't just lost everything.

"We didn't see anything," Eva said as Honor pulled open the car door.

Which of course meant they'd seen everything, not that it mattered now.

Nothing mattered now.

She'd laid herself out for him, opened herself completely, hoping the fact that she loved him would be enough to stop him from continuing down the path he'd set himself on. But, of course, it wasn't.

She hadn't been enough to stop her father from taking his own life or to pull her mother out of her depression. Hadn't been enough to make Alex stay. Why on earth had she expected she'd be enough to save Gabriel?

"Would you like me to kill him for you?" Zac said, his smooth English voice perfectly pleasant, as if asking if she'd like a cup of tea. "Because I can. It would be no trouble."

"No, thank you," Honor said, sliding into the backseat, pulling the door closed behind her. "He's doing a good enough job on his own."

In the rearview mirror she saw Eva's gray eyes watching her.

She had no idea what the other woman saw in her face, but it must have been bad because Eva's concern was obvious.

Honor folded her hands in her lap, quelled the trembling in her legs. Ignored the empty, hollow space where her heart should have been, now full of jagged shards of broken glass.

It had hurt more than she'd thought possible to walk away from him, yet the moment he'd refused to give up his quest for vengeance she'd known she had to. Because she knew an addict when she saw one. Gabriel was addicted to his quest and he wasn't going to let anyone get in his way.

Perhaps another woman would have stayed, would have stuck by him no matter what choices he made. But she wasn't that woman. She'd seen too many people she cared about destroy themselves to stand by and watch, and she certainly wasn't going to feed his addiction by encouraging him.

She'd had no idea where the strength to leave him had come from, but she hoped it would stick around in the

# CHAPTER NINETEEN

Gabriel leaned his elbows on the parapet of Central Park's Bow Bridge, staring down at the ice-covered lake beneath it. Snow was still falling and for the first time in years, he actually felt cold.

Yet the creeping chill had nothing to do with the snow settling on his arms, stark white against the leather of his jacket.

The color of Honor's face before she walked away. Before she left him.

He took a breath. Why the fuck was he thinking about her? She was gone. He'd sent her away. The only thing he should be thinking about now was meeting Tremain. Finally finding out the name of this father.

Christ, what the hell was wrong with him?

A wave of restless energy went through him and he pushed himself away from the parapet, pacing down the bridge.

He hadn't slept since he'd gotten home the night before and arrived at his apartment to find it empty, Honor gone. He'd expected it and yet, he hadn't been able to bear the thought of going into his empty bedroom. So he'd paced through his apartment all night, going over and over what Tremain had told him. That he wasn't his father. That it was some other man.

And Honor walking away from him.

Getting Tremain's text with a meeting time and a place had been a blessed relief.

Soon he'd know. Soon he'd know everything and once he did, he'd be able to start putting more plans into place.

*And then what? When it's all over? What are you going to do then?*

A strange gaping emptiness yawned wide inside him at the thought, a black hole full of nothing.

*Of course you've got nothing. You let the one person in your life who'd started to make you think there was something more, walk away.*

No, fuck, he'd *had* to let her walk away. He'd had no other choice.

*Bullshit. There's always a choice.*

Gabriel pushed the thought away. Hard. He'd think about this later. Once his father was ruined beyond any hope of fixing, once he'd taken everything from him, then he'd decide what to do.

Good Christ, it was cold. Why the hell was he feeling it now? And where was Tremain? He should have been here five minutes ago. If that fucker didn't turn up there would be hell to pay.

Footsteps crunched in the snow down one end of the bridge.

Gabriel turned.

Tremain was coming toward him, his expensive overcoat wrapped tightly around him, his scarf tied around his neck just so. There was no one else around. It was too early in the morning and it was far too cold for many people to be out and about.

His heartbeat began to speed up, anticipation coiling tight. God, what was it with all this emotional shit? For years he'd been cold, like ice, and now it was like all that ice had melted away, leaving him exposed, open to all these damn feelings.

He made himself stay still, folding his arms as the man strode toward him. "You're late," he said curtly as Tremain approached.

"I had . . . things to do."

"Who is it?" Gabriel snapped, impatient and unable to temper it. "Tell me now."

Tremain's hands were shoved in the pockets of his overcoat. He looked pale, drawn. As if he'd had one too many hard nights. "Before I tell you, I meant what I said about Honor last night. She must be safe. I can protect her mother but her . . ."

Gabriel curled his lip. "Like you give a fuck about her."

Anger crossed the other man's face. "I brought that girl up, so don't you dare tell me I don't care about her."

"Not enough to stop the ruin of her company."

A muscle ticked in Tremain's jaw. "I had to get out. This is the only way I can still protect her mother. Honor will survive."

Of course Honor would survive. Because she was strong. She was a fucking warrior. But it was hard fighting all the time. Sometimes you just wanted to sit down and rest.

"She deserves more than survival, you prick," he said harshly.

"And what would you know about what she deserves? You don't know a thing about her."

Lies. He knew she liked pretty things, and being held down while he made love to her. Knew that she was unfailingly loyal and generous and fought hard for those she cared about. That her touch made him breathless. Made his heart ache.

*Stop thinking about her.*

A sharp, burning need filled him and he had to turn away and take a breath, staring out over the bare, icy trees. At the looming spikes of the skyscrapers, spearing up into the cold, gray sky. Stalagmites reaching for heaven.

"Enough of this shit," he said hoarsely. "Tell me what I want to know."

"Not until you can guarantee Honor will be safe."

He fought down the burning, hot feeling in his chest. Taking his hands out of his pockets, he strode over to the parapet and put them down on the icy stone. The cold burned his bare skin. But it didn't do anything to ease the burning feeling inside him. "She and I are no longer seeing each other," he said. "Which makes her importance as a way to get to me negligible."

"That won't be enough."

"I'll protect her." He turned, meeting the other man's gaze. This was one thing he didn't have to lie about. "No one will ever hurt her again."

Not even himself.

A certain tension seemed to leave the other man, his shoulders relaxing. "All right, so you wanted—" The rest of the sentence was cut off as he inhaled then suddenly dropped like a stone onto the snowy ground.

Gabriel froze, staring at the man on the ground in shock. "No," he said into the icy air. "No. Fuck no."

Tremain let out a low moan, blood beginning to pool in the white snow around his head.

Adrenaline surged, breaking Gabriel's paralysis, and he was moving, running over to the fallen man, dropping onto his knees in the snow. Tremain was struggling to get up. Blood covered his face, dripping down the side of his head, the left side a bloody mess from a gunshot wound.

Gabriel looked around at the empty bridge and the trees beyond it but nothing moved. Whoever had fired the shot was gone.

Fuck. And double fuck.

So close. So close and now this.

He bent over the other man, taking some of the overcoat to wipe away the blood. "The name," he said, unable to help himself. "Tell me who the fuck it is."

Tremain was staring at him, the intensity of the stare almost unnerving. He tried to say something but the sound bubbled in his throat, the words unintelligible.

Gabriel swore, furious and desperate and ready to kill someone. "You can't die on me now, prick. You've got shit to tell me."

The man on the ground coughed. With a labored, jerky motion, he took his hand out of the pocket of his overcoat and shoved his fist against Gabriel's chest.

"What—" The words broke off as he realized that Tremain was holding something.

Gabriel took his hand and turned it over. With an almost palpable effort of will, Tremain opened his fingers and something dropped out into the snow.

Two silver dice.

Gabriel picked them up. They were heavy, the numbers mere silvery depressions. All except the one spot, which was inset with a flawless diamond.

He looked at Tremain. "What? What the hell is this?"

The other man just stared at him, his jaw rigid. Then his eyelids fluttered and fell, his body going limp.

"No." Gabriel put his hand on the older man's shoulder, shook him. "No, you can't do this now. Wake the fuck up."

But the man didn't move.

Oh, Christ. Quickly he checked Tremain's pulse. It was weak, thready.

Gabriel sat back on his heels, trying to calm the frustration that sank its claws into him. The man was deeply unconscious—hell, he was lucky he was still even alive given he'd been shot in the head.

But one thing was for certain, he wasn't getting that name out of Tremain today.

He swore again, harsh and raw. The stupid dice were still in his hand so he shoved them into his pocket, grabbing his phone. Then he called an ambulance and the police.

He didn't leave his name. There would be too many complications, too many questions asked if they knew he was here.

Placing Tremain in the recovery position, making him as comfortable as he could, he waited until the sirens drew near then he turned and strode away, over the bridge and into the trees, moving fast.

It wasn't over. It still wasn't over.

He had nothing, the only clue as to the identity of his father the silver dice in his pocket. Clearly someone had discovered Tremain would be meeting him and had decided to silence the guy and his secrets along with him.

Which meant there was something bigger going on here. Something far more dangerous than he or Zac or Eva had thought. Something that was perhaps bigger than one illegal casino.

God. It would never be over, would it?

Weariness swept through him. The same exhaustion that had gripped him the night before. He was no nearer, no closer to the truth than he had been weeks ago, and now, if Tremain didn't survive that shot, there would be murder to add to the list.

And it would be his fault. All his fault.

*If Tremain dies, Honor will be devastated.*

He stopped dead.

Oh, fuck, Honor. If they were prepared to take out Tremain to stop him from talking, then anyone connected with him was going to be in potential danger. And that was his fault, too.

Someone approached him from behind, a flash of black the only hint he got, and adrenaline rushed through him, even though he already knew who it was. There was only one man he knew of who could move that silently through snow.

"What the fuck are you doing here?" Gabriel demanded, temper fraying.

"I was interested in your little meeting," Zac said.

Gabriel turned sharply. "How did you know? I told no one—"

"You don't need to tell anyone. I would have thought you'd know that by now."

Frustration and anger hissed and spat inside him like oil on a hot stove. "This is none of your fucking business."

"You involved us, Gabriel. So now it has become our fucking business."

He couldn't seem to stand still, shifting on his feet. "Then uninvolve yourself."

Zac's unnerving amber gaze searched his face. "Tremain looked like he got shot. I saw him go down but I didn't hear anything or see a shooter."

"I don't have time to stand here discussing this with you." Honor was in potential danger. Unprotected. He turned away.

"You were meeting Tremain for a reason, Gabriel," Zac said, all of his smooth British charm stripped away to reveal the iron beneath. "And now he's been shot. We're a part of this, and if that means Eva is in danger also then I need to know about it."

There was pain in his chest now and he hated it. Wanted the cold, the detachment. But that was long gone, melted away, and now there was only hurt. And he was tired, so fucking tired of the pain. So fucking tired of the anger.

So fucking tired of being alone.

"Honor didn't tell you last night?" he said finally.

"No. She didn't say a thing."

Even though she hated secrets, she'd kept his.

"Don't ask, don't tell" had always been the club's first rule. And they all had secrets. Too many secrets. But perhaps they needed one less.

"Thirty-five years ago my mother was raped in a hotel room. I thought Tremain was the man who raped her. He wasn't but he was meeting me here today to give me the name of the prick who did it. The prick who happens to be my father."

Silence fell, deep and thick as the snow around them.

"You wanted revenge," Zac said at last.

"No, I wanted justice."

*And because you wanted justice, she is now in danger. If you hadn't involved her, she would be safe.*

Fear gathered inside him, so sharp he couldn't breathe. He'd hurt her so many times. First he'd played stupid head games with her, seduced her, shattered her world twice with more truths than one person should have to bear, been the reason the man who'd brought her up had been shot. And now, the final nail in the coffin, her life could be in danger.

All because he wanted justice. For a dead woman.

All the air went out of him in a white freezing cloud.

Zac was right. It was revenge. His mother was dead, she didn't care anymore. She was beyond pain. Which meant this quest for justice was for himself.

But how else could he stop this anguish? How else could he stop being so angry all the fucking time?

"Did he give you the name before he was shot?" Zac asked him.

"No." Reaching into his pocket, Gabriel took out the dice. All his plans, all his investigations, all for two lumps of silver. "But he gave me these. I have no idea what they mean."

*You don't care what they mean . . .*

His hands were shaking. Jesus, he was falling apart.

"Looks like they're another invitation," Zac said. "Like the black dice I gave you and Honor yesterday." His forehead creased, staring at the dice in Gabriel's palm. "What's wrong? Your hands are shaking."

Everything. Everything was wrong.

Tremain getting shot. The mystery behind his father's identity deepening. Honor threatened. Violence begetting more violence. There was no end to it.

*There is an end.*

Yeah, there was. He could choose not to follow this lead. Just let it go. And then . . . what? What would be left for him? What else was there? What would he do with this anger that sat inside him? That poisoned him?

No one could forgive him. No one could take it away. Because the person he was most angry at was himself. For the fact he existed at all.

Which meant following this further was pointless.

Gabriel closed his fingers around the dice, the only link he had to whoever his father was. Then he shoved them abruptly at his friend.

Zac looked at him, eyes widening in surprise. "But don't you—"

"Take them," he said hoarsely. "I have somewhere to be."

The other man's amber gaze searched his. "Where are you going?"

"To protect Honor. After that? Probably to hell."

The city streets were full of snow and heavy afternoon traffic but Gabriel barely noticed, weaving the Norton through the lanes, uncaring.

Handing the dice to Zac should have felt like a weight

lifting from him but it didn't. Instead, it felt like he was walking into the pitch-black darkness, unsure of his footing and with no idea of where he was going. Directionless and blind.

Except no, there was one light in the dark. One compass point.

Honor.

He would protect her. That's what he would do from now on. That would be the whole of his existence. Without his anger, without his justice, he had nothing else. She was his whole reason for being.

Pulling up outside her building, he parked the bike and strode through the front doors. The doorman gave him a suspicious look but Gabriel wasn't in any mood to fuck around. "Honor St. James's apartment. Now."

Five seconds later he was traveling up in the elevator, pacing restlessly back and forward. Christ, if something had happened to her that would be the last straw. The final sin that would break him.

The elevator stopped and he got out, striding down the hallway and reaching her door. Hammering on it.

Eventually it jerked open but it wasn't Honor. A woman with blond dreadlocks and lots of silver jewelry stood in the doorway, a belligerent expression on her pretty face. She looked him up and down, frowning. "Gabriel Woolf I presume?" she said, a spark of anger in her clear, turquoise eyes. "I've been wondering when you'd show up."

This wasn't what he wanted. Or rather, who he wanted. "Who the hell are you?" he demanded. "Where's Honor?"

"I'm her friend. Violet Fitzgerald. And she's not here. She's in the hospital looking after a family member."

Fuck, he was too late.

He leaned against the door frame, cold swallowing him whole, more weary than he'd ever been in his entire life. Jesus, he couldn't go to the hospital himself. It would only draw attention and God knew he didn't want any more attention drawn to the St. James family.

Cursing, he turned away, taking out his phone and calling Zac. A minute later, discreet protection organized for Honor, he turned back to the woman still standing in the doorway.

And he realized he had nowhere to go but back to his empty apartment. To the office he hardly worked in. Back to the life that wasn't really much of a fucking life at all. It had no one and nothing in it but anger and destruction. Violence and death.

*"You have me."*

He was stained, tainted, twisted by anger. By the things he'd done. By the mere fact of his existence. An arid existence, empty of anything of any value.

Except for her.

The world spun, the ground moving under his feet as realization broke over him like a plunge headfirst into an icy lake.

He didn't want to go back to that existence. Where the only thing that mattered was his anger. Where there was no love or passion. No loyalty or understanding. No warm arms around him, holding him tight. Making him feel like he meant something. Like he mattered.

Where there was no future, only the past.

He wanted Honor. She was his future. She was his whole fucking existence.

"I'm not leaving," he said hoarsely.

Violet gave him a long, measuring look. "I think you'd better come in then," she said.

Honor didn't get home until late and as she put her key in the lock, she couldn't remember the last time she'd felt so exhausted.

She'd been at the private hospital they'd taken Guy to

for hours, holding her sobbing mother in the waiting room, still in shock from the news he'd been found in Central Park with a gunshot wound to the head. A miracle he was even still alive.

He'd gone into surgery straight away and it hadn't been till after noon that the doctors had come out, giving them a "wait and see" prognosis. Not good but it could have been worse. He could be dead.

"Why?" her mother had whispered. "What was he doing in Central Park so early? Who did this to him? Why would anyone want to hurt him? I don't understand. It's like . . . Daniel all over again."

She'd said those same things over and over, going around and around, the same questions. Questions that had no answers.

Except Honor knew. Guy had gone to Central Park to meet Gabriel, she was sure of it. And he'd been silenced.

But she hadn't told anyone that, not the doctors who asked or the police who'd questioned her. Because they weren't her secrets to tell. They were Gabriel's.

She turned the key in the apartment door, pushed it open. Violet had arrived at the hospital a couple of hours earlier and told her she'd stay with her mother, that Honor was to go home and get some rest. Even so, it had still taken her a while to get home, the traffic lousy.

The apartment was in darkness and she fumbled for the light, switching it on and closing the door behind her.

Her brain wouldn't stop going over what had happened to Guy. Had Gabriel hurt him? Or had it been someone else?

No, it couldn't be Gabriel. Hurting Guy would be unnecessary and Gabriel wasn't a man who did things that were unnecessary. Which meant it had to be someone else. Someone who hadn't wanted Guy to talk.

Still thinking, she put her purse down beside the table in the hallway and walked slowly down to the darkened lounge area. Finding the switch to the floor lamp in the corner, she turned it on, flooding the little room with light.

And only just stopped herself from gasping aloud.

There was a man lying on her couch, heavy black boots resting incongruously on her precious silk-and-velvet cushions, one of her antique French quilts thrown over the top of him.

Gabriel.

Her heart stopped, the world around her slowing in shock.

He was asleep, the brutally handsome lines on his face relaxed, the hard line of his mouth soft. Dark lashes lying thick and still on his cheekbones. He looked younger and unexpectedly vulnerable.

Emotion swelled in the back of her throat, hot tears threatening and it was only by sheer force of will that she managed to swallow them back. She didn't know what the hell he was doing here but one thing was for sure, she wasn't going to fall apart in front of him, whether he was asleep or not.

Slowly, she took a couple of steps into the room, debating whether to wake him up and find out what on earth he was doing lying on her couch, or to let him sleep.

The light must have bothered him because his forehead creased and he turned over onto his back, his feet scattering cushions, the quilt sliding off him.

He was wearing the clothes he'd worn the night before, black shirt and jeans. Leather jacket. Had he been up all night? Had he even gone home? God, what was he doing here and how did he get in?

Violet probably. Except her friend hadn't said a word when she'd gotten to the hospital.

Honor was just on the point of deciding to wake him up when abruptly, his lashes lifted and he turned his head sharply. Night-dark eyes stared into hers.

Nothing moved in the quiet of the room.

Then he shifted, the blanket coming off as he threw it aside. In a fluid movement, he came off the couch and was halfway toward her before she could move.

She opened her mouth to tell him not to come any closer but before she could get the words out, he stopped dead in the middle of the room, his gaze roving over her as if checking she was all in one piece. "Are you okay?" he demanded roughly, his voice hoarse with sleep. "Are you hurt?"

She swallowed, her heartbeat stupidly accelerating the way it always did whenever he was around. "Of course I'm okay. But . . . what are you doing here?"

His broad chest moved, the black cotton of his shirt pulling tight. "You know about Guy?"

"Yes, I was just in the hospital—"

"It's my fault," he cut her off flatly. "I met him this morning in Central Park. He was going to give me a name. And they shot him."

Grief lay heavy and thick in her throat. For Guy. For the man standing in front of her right now. But she didn't want him to see it, didn't want him knowing how much she still cared. It had taken everything in her to walk away from him the night before and she didn't want to have to do it again.

She had to be strong and resist.

"I see," Honor said carefully. " 'They'?"

"I don't know who it was. I didn't see." Gabriel didn't move. "He didn't tell me, Honor. They shot him before he could say a word. And that means you're in potential danger. Someone was willing to kill him to silence him and it could be that anyone associated with him is also at risk."

"So that's why you're here? To protect me?" More tears prickled but she blinked them back, determined to keep her composure.

He took a step forward toward her then stopped, his hands clenching into fists. "You're already protected. Zac has his people watching you and your mother at the hospital. No one will harm you."

She looked down at her hands folded loosely together in front of her. Blinked hard to force back the stupid traitorous tears. She knew she was weak when it came to him, but she wasn't going to fall apart. Not again.

"Thank you," she said after a moment, pleased with how level her voice sounded. "First you all put me in danger and now you're protecting me from it. With friends like you, who needs enemies?"

He didn't say anything.

"Did you want something, Gabriel, or . . ." The words died in her throat as she looked at him. At the expression on his face. There was nothing hard there now, nothing cold, nothing hidden. Desperation, longing, and grief were starkly written all over his features, his eyes glittering with a raw kind of anguish she'd never seen in him before.

"Help me," he said in a ragged voice. "Honor . . . please . . . I don't know . . . what to do."

Her heart seized up in her chest, all the emotion she'd been trying to hide clogging in her throat. She'd already taken a step toward him before she knew what was happening.

But then she stopped herself.

Last night in the alley she'd told him she loved him. Opened herself totally to him. Even cried for him. And he'd turned her away. Told her that she didn't make a difference. That she wasn't enough. That he'd head on down the path of destruction no matter what she said.

Well, she couldn't open herself like that again. It hurt too damn much.

She swallowed. "What do you mean you don't know what to do?"

"You told me you loved me." He sounded unsteady, hoarse with an emotion she didn't quite understand. "Was that the truth?"

Her jaw tightened. "I don't know—"

"Was it true?" There was a ferocity in his eyes, tension in every line of his body.

*You can't lie to him. Not about this.*

She wanted to. Especially when all her instincts were telling her she had to in order to protect herself.

But then, she'd always hated lies.

"Yes," she said softly. "It was true."

"And is it still?"

"Yes," she repeated, swallowing back the pain. Because there would never be anyone else for her. She'd known it then and it was true now. "It's still true."

Silence fell.

Then abruptly Gabriel dropped to his knees. "I would ask your forgiveness, but I know it's not possible. Not for the things I've done to you. For the position I placed you in. For the hurt I've caused you. But . . . I want you to know that I am going to spend the rest of my life protecting you and your mother. Keeping you both safe. It won't make up for what happened to Tremain, but it's all I have left to offer."

Shock held her silent, staring at him on his knees in front of her, dark eyes holding hers.

"Before he was shot," Gabriel went on hoarsely, "Guy gave me something. Something that would probably have led to my father. But . . . I didn't take it. I realized I didn't want it. Because it's not justice I'm after. I just want to stop being so . . . fucking angry all the time." He lifted a hand, punched his fist against his heart. "It's twisted me. Anger that I am who I am. That I was born from violence and all I ever seem to be able to give back to people is more violence." He took a breath, his chest heaving. "I'm so tired of carrying it. I'm so tired of feeling it. And I just wanted . . . to be free of it."

"You thought hurting your father, would . . . what? Make you less angry?"

"I wanted it to stop," he whispered "I wanted the pain to end."

A large hand squeezed tight around her heart, crushing it. "Oh, Gabriel . . ."

"But it won't, I know that now. Violence will only beget violence, and I've hurt far too many people already. I hurt you. And that's something I will never forgive myself for."

His figure blurred as the tears she'd been holding back filled her eyes. She couldn't stop them this time. "Why are you here?" she asked thickly. "If you've only come to tell me—"

"I'm here because I have nothing. I have nothing and no one in my empty fucking life. And I don't want nothing. Honor, I want . . . you." His voice cracked on the last word and she felt something inside herself crack, too.

"I thought you wanted your justice more," she said, her voice hoarse. "That's what you told me."

"I know. I was wrong. I don't care who my fucking father is. All I care about is you."

Tears slid down her cheeks. Because she didn't know if she could do this again. She didn't think she was strong enough.

*Of course you are. You were strong enough to walk away. You're strong enough to walk back.*

Honor swallowed, her throat thick. Where had that strength come from though?

But that was a question she knew the answer to already. An answer that had been there all along. Love. Her love for him.

It didn't make her weak and it wasn't an addiction that would destroy her. It had made her strong the night before, and it would make her even stronger now.

Honor walked forward to where he knelt. She had to wipe her eyes a couple of times so she could see, looking down into his face, the expression there so naked, so vulnerable she could hardly bear it.

"You have me," she said. "I'm not going anywhere."

He didn't touch her, only bent his head, the light from the lamp touching the gold highlights in his hair. His massive, dark figure kneeling at her feet, with his head bent made her think of an angel. A fallen angel begging for absolution.

"I don't understand," he whispered. "Why would you be there for me? Still? After last night? After . . . Christ, there's so much fucking violence on my soul."

She lifted her hands, sinking her fingers into the soft, golden strands of his hair, the ache in her chest so acute it was difficult to breathe. "Stop defining yourself so narrowly. You're more than that. You're protective and strong. Responsible. You'd lay down your life for those you care about. And more than anything else, you gave me the freedom to be myself, challenged me to step out of the box I shut myself up in. How could I not be there for you?" She paused. "How could I not love you?"

He shuddered, his big body leaning into her hands. "Why? You know what I am."

"I love you because of who you are, Gabriel. Not because of what you've done or how you were conceived. Why is that so hard to accept?"

His hair felt like silk against her fingers, the warmth of his body so close, like a fire. He leaned against her thigh, turned his face into her skirt. "Because no one has ever loved me, Honor. No one has ever forgiven me enough."

Her heart ached for him. For the lonely boy he'd been. For the hard, lonely man he'd become. "You don't need forgiveness from other people, Gabriel. The only person you need forgiveness from is yourself."

He lifted his head, so much pain in his eyes her throat seized. "I don't know that I can."

She didn't want to stand over him anymore because the absolution he sought couldn't be given by her. So she knelt right in front of him, staring into his eyes. "You can. I don't care how rotten you think you are. How irredeemable. I see a man whose whole life has been about protecting other people. Caring for other people. Taking so much responsibility he's almost been crushed by the weight of it. And you did it the only way you knew how."

"Fuck, don't say those things, I don't—"

She put a finger across his mouth. "You think you don't deserve it? You do. Forgive yourself. And let your anger go."

The understanding in her blue eyes nearly broke him apart. It couldn't be that simple. Surely it couldn't. How could he forgive himself for his entire existence?

"It's not your fault," Honor said quietly. "It's not your fault your mother got hurt. The choices she made, the life she lived, is not your fault."

But he knew that, didn't he? Of course he did.

*Do you? Do you really?*

He couldn't breathe all of a sudden.

For the last thirty-five years of his life, he'd taken responsibility. For himself. For his mother's rape. For the whole reason he was even born in the first place. Because her crappy life was his fault. Because he'd been born.

"How could it not be my fault?" His voice didn't sound like his own. "All of it is my fault."

"No." Honor cupped his face in her hands, the warmth of her touch searing him. Melting away the ice around his heart. "You were a child, Gabriel. You weren't responsible for anything. Your mother made her own choices. You can't take them on yourself, too."

No. He couldn't. Just like he didn't have to take on the anger either.

And it turned out it was that simple. To let it all go and let something else take its place. A strange, desperate emotion he'd been trying not to feel for a long time. An emotion he thought he wasn't capable of. An emotion he thought he never deserved.

Until now.

Gabriel gripped her wrists, her skin smooth against his fingers. "I love you," he said helplessly, unable to keep it inside any longer. He'd hadn't said those words to another soul in years, not since the last time he'd said them to his mother, when he was seven years old. "I love you, Honor St. James."

There were tears in her blue eyes and he couldn't stop himself from bending to kiss them away. She trembled and then suddenly buried her face in his chest, her arms coming around him the way they had in his apartment, after he'd told her everything. A way he'd never stopped dreaming of, hoping for again.

"Does this mean you're going to stay?" she murmured, her voice muffled against his leather jacket.

He wrapped his arms around her in return, holding her close. "I told you, I'm going to spend the rest of my life protecting you."

"That doesn't mean . . ." She broke off.

Gently he gripped her chin, tipped her head back so he could see her face, his heart beating strangely fast. "What do you want it to mean?"

Her blue eyes glowed in her pale face. "I don't want

you protecting me, Gabriel. I want you loving me. And I want it forever."

That was his Honor. Strong. Demanding. Challenging. His chest ached but this time he welcomed the pain. "Then that's what you'll have. Because I'm not going anywhere."

Honor reached up, slid her fingers into his hair, and brought his head down for another kiss that was sweeter than any others he'd ever had. "Oh, and I want a vest with 'Property of Church' written on it," she murmured against his mouth.

He smiled, his arms tightening around her. "I'll get one made especially for you."

"What about you? What do you want?"

Her body was warm and soft and everything he'd ever wanted. "Right now? You, naked, on the floor."

Her mouth curved. "Yes, of course. But after that."

"What do you think? I want you to love me. That's all I want."

Honor's eyes glittered as they met his. "Ah, well, that I can do."

And she did,

# EPILOGUE

Alex's blond bodyguard wasn't waiting outside his door this time so Gabriel walked right in. Alex was sprawled on the couch, a console game controller in his hands, his attention on the massive flat-screen TV on the wall opposite him.

Standing near the couch, also holding a controller, was his bodyguard.

"Fuck," Alex muttered as his character on the screen was dealt a flying roundhouse kick. "I can't believe this is the first time you've played this."

"Your reflexes are too slow," the Russian woman said, administering the death blow to Alex's character on screen. "You need more sleep, sir."

"Katya mine, sleep is for the very young and very old. As I am neither, I'll sleep when I'm dead."

"Which appears to be now." She put down the controller as Alex's character expired on the screen, and turned. "I shall give you some privacy?"

Alex threw the controller negligently back on the couch. "Yeah, you'd better. Go check the perimeter or something."

The woman moved past Gabriel, her strong features absolutely impassive.

"What are you doing here?" Alex demanded as the

door shut behind the bodyguard. He didn't look at him, his attention still firmly on the TV screen. "I thought the 'fuck off' text I sent you was clear enough."

Gabriel folded his arms, mainly to stop himself from going over to where his friend lay and dealing him a punch to the face. Because the guy's fucking attitude could use some readjustment.

Honor had told him she'd texted Alex to say she was ready to talk to him if he wanted and the prick still hadn't replied to her.

"I want to talk to you about the casino," he said shortly.

Instantly the scowl on Alex's face vanished, his features an expressionless mask. But Gabriel could see the tension in the other man's body. Taut as a coiled spring.

"Lucky you," Alex said still in the same tone, but this time with a slightly bitter edge to it. "So is that why you're here? You're going to tell me all about it? Because if you are, you can fuck off right now."

Gabriel didn't say anything. Instead he walked over to the table and dropped something on it.

Two silver dice, the diamond sparkling in the center of the one.

"What the hell is that?" Alex demanded.

"Guy Tremain gave them to me before he was shot. It's an invitation."

"An invitation to what?"

"To find out what's behind the casino. Or rather, who."

Alex's blue gaze was sharp. "You don't want it?"

"I'm not in the justice game anymore. I have other, more important things to worry about." Like taking Honor out of the city for a while. Up to his lodge, in the snow. Where he could keep her safe and they could be together, forget about all of this mess for a while.

"So? Why are you giving it to me?"

"Because I thought you might want to do some investigating of your own."

His friend came to his feet in a sudden blur of movement, his blue eyes glowing with what looked like anger. "Why the hell would you think that?"

But Gabriel was already turning around, walking toward the door. "If you don't want it, give it to Zac or Eva. They're more than happy to continue searching. But your sister is more important to me than all that shit. I'll be around to help if you need it but that's it."

Alex didn't say a word but as Gabriel strode through the door, his gaze dropped to the dice.

He stared at them for a long moment.

Then he picked them up.

She didn't respond, her shoulders stiff with tension. Her gaze shifted so she was looking out of the window behind him. "What do you want from me?"

Alex drained the shot glass and put it back on the coffee table then settled back against the couch cushions.

Looking at her, so tall and straight and immovable, the idea that had occurred to him in the limo now seemed ridiculous. He'd decided that if he was going to fucking Monte Carlo, he wasn't going alone. But he also didn't want his back-up/protection to be obvious because that was a weakness he wasn't ready to reveal to anyone, let alone Conrad South.

Katya hanging around in her black suit and shades, looking her usual lethal best would betray the fact that he was afraid.

Katya hanging around in a gown and high heels, with his arm around her waist, now that was different. She could be a stand-in for his latest lover and no one would question it. People might recognize her as his bodyguard, it was true, but once she was wearing a gown and some flashy jewelry no one would care. They'd probably even think the whole bodyguard thing was a fake, especially if they were observed in public being physical with one another.

Of course he didn't have to take a bodyguard at all, but Zac had been insistent on him keeping some backup. That whoever had targeted Tremain was still out there and Alex could very well be in the firing line. Well, he was fine with that—as long as said backup was done his way.

He tilted his head, surveying her. With her height she'd be able to carry any kind of gown off beautifully and he was sure there were curves under that severe black suit of hers. She was fair too which meant her skin would be pale, no perma-tan for his Russian ice-princess, that was for sure. With her green eyes and blonde hair she'd look amazing in a green gown. Or blue. Or white . . .

His gaze settled on her throat. Her shirt was buttoned all the way to the top, the jacket she wore over the top obscuring her shape. Not even an inch of skin beneath that collar was visible.

Abruptly he got up off the couch and prowled over to where she stood. She blinked as he came closer, a crease forming between her brows. "You haven't answered my question, sir."

"No, I know I haven't. I want to see something first." He stopped right in front of her.

"See what?"

His heart was beating rather faster than normal, which was strange. And he was aware of her scent all of a sudden. Not perfume because she never wore perfume, but the fresh scent of apples, her shampoo maybe or soap. He liked it.

He lifted a hand and before she could move, undid the buttons that held her suit jacket closed.

"Sir, I—"

"Keep still. I need to see something."

Her frown deepened as her jacket fell open but she did as she was told, the perfect soldier.

He leaned back, running his gaze over her, and yes, he

was right, there were definite curves there. The white cotton of her shirt pulled tight over full breasts, the hem tucked into her black pants revealing narrow hips. Long legs too, which made her very definitely his type. At least enough to fool the press and anyone else who happened to see them together.

"What are you doing, sir?"

"One second."

Alex quickly flicked open the first couple of buttons at her throat.

She took a startled breath, the sound sharp in the silence of the room. He glanced up at her face and for the first time since he'd met her, he read shock clear in her eyes. Shock that quickly gave way to confusion. But she didn't say anything so he didn't stop, undoing one more button, the fabric parting to reveal smooth, white skin.

Beautiful. Perhaps this would work after all.

His heartbeat sounded even louder in his head and though there was no reason at all to touch her, he couldn't help himself, gently laying a finger on the pulse at the base of her throat. Her skin felt warm and that pulse was beating fast. As fast as his.

She'd gone very, very still but he felt her swallow, felt her pulse beat even faster.

The air around them had thickened, becoming dense with tension.

"Sir . . . ." Her voice was soft but he could hear a faint, husky edge in it. The kind of edge a woman's voice always held when she was aroused.

Interesting. No, scratch interesting. This was downright fucking intriguing.

"Keep still a moment. I'm testing something." He moved his finger, unable to resist the temptation, stroking her and watching as goose-bumps rippled over her skin in response.

Ah, yes, so there was chemistry between them, and pretty damn strong chemistry. Excellent. Sexual chemistry would make everything much more convincing.

Katya moved, taking a quick step back, leaving him standing there stroking empty air. She didn't adjust her clothing but a faint strip of color stained her high cheekbones. "I think you're mistaking me for someone else, sir," she said, her voice not quite level. "If you wanted a companion, I'm quite sure you could find another woman more suited to the job than I am."

He lowered his hand, the warmth of her still glowing on his fingertip. "There are no other women more suited to the job than you are, Katya."

"I'm not going to—"

"Let me tell you which job I mean first, before you jump to any wild conclusions."

Her mouth snapped shut, her shoulders straightening.

His own heartbeat continued to beat like a drum. Christ, he was almost on the point of getting hard, which was weird because these days it took a lot more than the brush of a woman's skin to get him there. It must be the vodka, surely.

Alex ignored the feeling, turning away and strolling back to the couch, sprawling down on it again. "Like I said, I am going to need you at this Monte Carlo game. But this time the job will be a little different to what you're used to."

"How different?"

He met her green gaze. Held it. "I don't want people thinking you're my bodyguard, Katya mine. I want people thinking you're my lover."

At first she couldn't quite understand what he meant because she was still finding it difficult to breathe let alone listen to what he was saying. Her throat burned where he'd touched her, in fact she could have sworn she'd felt the outline of his fingerprint on her skin. Each whorl and each ridge. Like a fingerprint lock keyed to a particular person.

*He's unlocking you . . .*

Katya blinked, trying to orient herself. She was breathing fast, like after a very hard workout and her heart rate was up. Way up. There was also a curious tightness to her skin and an adrenaline spike that had raced through her system the moment he touched her then settled right down low in her abdomen, a pulsing ache that her body knew even if her brain refused to process it.

*Sexual desire.*

She'd never had sex before but she knew intellectually what it was all about. And even if she hadn't, three months shadowing Alex St. James had certainly taught her more about sex and seduction than she'd ever wanted to know.

Except . . . she'd never felt desire before, at least not for a particular person. Not even Mikhail.

Her mouth was dry. She swallowed, trying to recall what it had been that they were talking about. Something along the lines of not being a bodyguard. Being his lover instead.

He was sprawled out on the couch in front of her with the kind of muscular, indolent grace reserved for lions or panthers. His shirt was open at the throat, his black hair hanging over one eye. He looked like he always did, as if he'd had one too many late nights with one too many women.

She'd always despised his utter lack of self-control and yet found it secretly fascinating at the same time. He didn't seem to care what anyone thought of him and that held a certain curiosity to her, especially since she cared rather a lot about pleasing people.

Now, as he sat there on the couch, surely half-drunk from the vodka he'd had, something smoky and dark in his blue eyes, it wasn't contempt or derision she felt.

*He's sexy.*

She shut the thought down.

"And why do you want people thinking I'm your lover?" Her voice sounded like nothing was wrong and that was good. That was very good. Her training was good for something then.

He smiled, his mouth curving in that practiced, seductive way. "It's very simple. I don't want to look as though I need a bodyguard. It's a weakness. And I can't afford to show any kind of weakness at the gaming table. Especially not at this particular gaming table."

Her jacket wasn't buttoned the way she liked it and she was very conscious of how her own shirt was open at the throat. And of how his gaze seemed to keep dropping to that patch of skin left bare by the fabric. It was strange to be so aware of her body when she wasn't anywhere near naked and for some reason it made her angry. "Why do you need me then?" she asked bluntly, forcing away the anger. "Do you need any protection?"

"It's not as if the threat to my life has gone away just like that, darling. And I have reason to believe that this game could be somewhat . . . hazardous."

"And what exactly does pretending to be your lover entail?"

His smile deepened. "You've seen my lovers. You know what to expect."

Oh yes, she had seen them. Hanging off his arm, leaning in to receive kisses. Touches. Caresses. He was a physical man and didn't seem to care who knew it.

She lifted her chin, struggling to compose herself. The thought shouldn't affect her. At all. "Forgive me for saying, sir, but I'm not your type."

"And what, exactly, have you observed about my type?"

"You like smaller women. More . . . feminine. Pretty socialites, actresses. I am not any of those things."

"No, you're not small, I'll give you that." His gaze dropped once more down her body and she was aware of a certain kind of heat flashing through her. One she hadn't felt before because men generally didn't look at her the way he was looking at her. "But you're beautiful, Katya, never doubt it. Which makes you very much my type indeed."

That heat had begun to move through her, warming her skin. Her jaw tightened. No, men didn't look at her like that and she'd always been glad of it. Some of the girls at the military school she'd gone to had been pretty, the jewels in the crown of the Russian army, there for the recruitment posters and for the officers to gaze at. To be put in army beauty pageants and looked down on.

But she wasn't one of those women. She still remembered the day after her mother's funeral, when her father had caught her weeping in her bedroom. He'd told her that she wasn't to cry because her mother had been weak, her suicide an act of supreme selfishness. And that from now on he would protect her from such things. He would make her strong. Then he'd collected up all the pretty dresses in her closet and put them in the trash, along with the dolls her mother had given her.

Femininity was a sign of weakness, of selfishness and therefore not permitted in the Ivanov house. Katya had been okay with that. Strength and purpose was infinitely preferable to the constant ache of grief and betrayal.

"Thank you, sir," she said tonelessly. "But I'm not an actor. I'm not sure I could—"

"All you'd have to do is wear a few pretty dresses, a couple of gowns. Look like you're madly in love with me and sit near me at the poker table. That's it." He shifted in another restless movement. "Oh and naturally keeping an eye out for threats to my life."

"People are aware of who I am already. They know I'm your bodyguard."

"Not outside of the States they don't. And even if they read all the crap the media spouts about me and have seen pictures of you, once they get a glimpse of you in a gown they won't be thinking bodyguard, I can guarantee you that right now. They'll probably even think the whole bodyguard thing was only a gimmick."

Despite her best intentions, a shard of anger spiked through her. Since coming to the States, she'd had to deal with this sort of thing a lot from men. Undervaluing her skills, underrating her.

"I'm not a gimmick," she said.

"No, of course you're not. But that could work to our advantage don't you think?"

"I suppose it could," she allowed. "And then what? After this game has ended?"

"Then I'll give you whatever help you need to find your guy."

Katya didn't say anything for a long moment. It was true she would need help when it came to getting Mikhail out of wherever he was. She did have a few contacts in the army but Alex had been uncannily correct; they probably wouldn't want to help her and risk potential discovery by the government. The General held a lot of influence and no one would willingly put themselves in his path. Even to help his daughter.

And as for the General himself, no matter that he'd been a mentor to Mikhail, his loyalty was to his government first and foremost. To his political aspirations. He'd been clear that as far as he was concerned, as far as the government was concerned, Mikhail Vasin had died on an unrelated visit to Chechnya. And that was the end to the matter.

She'd known the risks and so had Mikhail. Both of them had understood that the government couldn't afford to acknowledge the presence of a black ops unit or else risk escalating the conflict with the state. But the chance of taking out one of the major terrorist leaders had been worth taking those risks.

Except she hadn't realized how she'd feel when the worst happened. When Mikhail disappeared and the government denied all knowledge of him. When even her own father backed them instead of her.

She should have accepted the government stance as part of the job. But she hadn't.

She'd lost her faith in it and her own father instead.

"It's not brain surgery, darling," Alex said lazily. "I would have thought the decision was pretty easy. You come with me to Monte Carlo and I'll help you get your friend."

Of course it was easy. It would mean another couple of weeks before she could start putting into motion any rescue plans but without money or contacts, both of which Alex had told her he could get, it would take her much, much longer anyway.

So why did the thought of going with him feel . . . threatening? Because in the end it was only a job. She could wear a gown. She could hang on his arm and pretend to be his lover. It wasn't a big deal. And in return she'd take all his help and go and get Mikhail.

Why was she even hesitating?

Katya straightened her shoulders, ignored the trepidation that sat low in her gut. "Of course, sir. I'd be happy to come to Monte Carlo with you."